MONSTERS

from

MEMPHIS

EDITED BY BEECHER SMITH

FEATURING STORIES BY

**BRENT MONAHAN
TOM PICCIRILLI
DON WEBB**

**AND TWENTY-THREE OTHER
EXCITING LITERARY VOICES**

Zapizdat Publications
Palo Alto, California

687/1000

SPECIAL LIMITED FIRST EDITION

ISBN 1-880964-21-X

Library of Congress
Catalog Card Number 97-62027

Published by

ZAPIZDAT PUBLICATIONS
P. O. BOX 326
PALO ALTO, CA 94302

in cooperation with

HOT BISCUIT PRODUCTIONS, INC.
44 N. SECOND ST., #1000
MEMPHIS, TN 38103

Printed by

DARK REGIONS PRESS
ORINDA, CA 94563

Cover by Judith Wagner Hanson

NOTICE

COPYRIGHT NOTICES AND ACKNOWLEDGMENTS

COPYRIGHT NOTICES AND ACKNOWLEDGMENTS

CONTENTS

CONTENTS

Introduction

WHY MONSTERS? WHY MEMPHIS? WHY NOT? This anthology serves a dual purpose: to introduce some wonderful new literary talent and to provide readers with more from some of the hottest, most promising contemporary writers in the horror, fantasy, and science fiction genres, all writing about Memphis. As a native Memphian, I can say with authority that this city is every bit as alluring and intriguing as H. P. Lovecraft's Providence, Rhode Island. But I and my fellow authors have the temerity not to fictionalize Memphis the way Lovecraft did Providence, as "Arkham, Massachusetts." Hopefully, this prophet and this product will both be with honor in our own town.

For we have found Memphis as mysterious, sometimes as disappointing, and every bit as fascinating as James Joyce's Dublin or L. Frank Baum's Oz. Here are twenty-seven authors who share this vision of a dark and mythical place renowned throughout the world as the site of two dead kings: Elvis and Dr. Martin Luther King, Jr. It is the home of commercial visionaries such as the late: Clarence Saunders, founder of Piggly Wiggly, and the very much alive Frederick Smith, founder of Federal Express. It is home to St. Jude Children's Research Hospital, founded by Danny Thomas, whose work continues in part through the heroic efforts of Marguerite Piazza.

Out of the turmoil of the civil rights era, this city has taken almost thirty years to reshape itself from a racially and economically polarized community into the center of commerce, industry, education, medicine, and transportation that it rightfully deserves to be. But whether it can keep that promise remains to be seen.

Memphis has a rich, but at times tragic history, one which often touches upon the "Three Great Sins" William Faulkner accused America of committing and not being able to become "whole" as a nation until it accepts the consequences. These are the exploitation of the native American, the exploitation of the African American, and the exploitation of the defeated South under Radical Reconstruction after the War Between the States (often improperly referred to as "The Civil War").

Memphis was founded by Andrew Jackson in one of the most infamous land grabs of all time. He subsequently moved the Native

Americans west of the Mississippi River, along the "Trail of Tears," so they could never reclaim their property. During the "War of Northern Aggression," Memphis fell early to the North and soon became a black market distribution center to both sides. Then, starting in the 1870's, Yellow Fever decimated the population, driving survivors—including many of the brightest and best of Memphis' population—away to St. Louis and points west. By the 1890's Memphis was considered a sinkhole of filth and corruption, with open and notorious brothels, saloons, and gaming houses, That changed with the advent of Edward Hull "Boss" Crump, an insurance magnate who cleaned up the city's negative image by creating a political machine that transformed Memphis into what was nationally recognized as the nation's cleanest, quietest, and safest city for over four decades.

But there was a price for that progress. Long treated as second-class citizens, the black population of Memphis marched in step with their brothers and sisters around the country when the protests began in the 1960's. Perhaps it took the tragic death of Dr. Martin Luther King, Jr. here to make the nation aware that Truth had to go marching on. Today Memphis has a mayor of African-American extraction who represents all Memphians. However, we are faced with some serious problems. Once more Memphis vies for the title of murder capital of the nation. It has a rate of auto thefts near the top, too. Despite what the politicians say, the city school system is a shambles, and no taxpayer who can afford private school would send children to any but a few select public schools.

And you ask, "Where are the monsters?" The monsters are always with us. Not necessarily ghosts, vampires, or werewolves. We have some new monsters for you, such as Brent Monahan's "Shadow," a supernatural predator that literally becomes what it eats; Torn Piccirilli's "Cotton," a Native American spirit that returns to doom Memphis with a new plague; and Don Webb's Mary Hawkes, a bewitching seductress kept alive by the 500-year-old mechanical heart of a warlock. Giving professional football a horror slant, Scott Sigler brings us the number one draft pick for the Oilers, so talented he must be out of this world, and *is*. Steve Climer takes the insurance claims investigation business to a new low with a detective for the paranormal, who seeks loopholes that will prevent having to pay off paranormal, who seeks loopholes that will prevent having to pay off on a policy insuring against demonic possession.

Bill Eakin takes us to his fictitious hamlet just outside Memphis—a community called Redgunk—about which he has written a series of stories. Here he introduces us to the Lizard Queen. Richard Parks takes us fifty years into the future, where people on our Mars colony still believe Elvis is alive and come back to Graceland to prove it. Corey Mesler recounts the original legend of the Cooper-Young Neighborhood, Swift Peter, a monster that is half weasel, half codfish. Was it real, or just a hoax to keep "those people" out of the neighborhood? My twin brother Vassar and I both have genie stories, warning to be careful what you wish for. Allan Gilbreath and Stanley T. Evans perpetuate a couple of radical "urban myths." These are only a few of the treasure trove awaiting within. Here are some wonderful stories with new monsters and new slants on old ones. Every story (and likewise every storyteller) included is truly unique, We believe you'll not only like to read, but want to reread each one many times.

Welcome to Memphis. The monsters are waiting!

Beecher Smith
Memphis, Tennessee

The Shadow Knows
By Brent Monahan

Mahoney is my name. I run a detective agency. Don't expect Mike Hammer or Sam Spade. I'm an unspectacular guy and, despite what the literary liars feed you, I'm in an unspectacular line of work. Most of the time. Lots of married folk cheating but resenting it if their spouses do the same; people getting themselves intentionally lost; embezzlers; some arsonists and insurance frauds; vanished college loan cheats; once in a blue moon a blackmailing or kidnapping. I'm paid to pull back the blankets, shine the light on the darkness, find the path through the maze. My ancestors built this nation's canals with picks and shovels; when I dig, my hands only get figuratively dirty.

The other half of the business is my wife, Siobhan. We came from the Aulde Sod eleven years ago. Settled in Memphis because of the sizable Irish population. Some of our long-departed relatives arrived shortly after the War of Northern Aggression. The gene pool was adventurous enough to cross the Atlantic Ocean, you see, but lazy enough to call the westward advance quits when they had to get themselves across the formidable Mississippi River. That pretty much sums me up, too: motivated enough to get off my butt but ready to sit back down if it gets too formidable. When that happens, it usually takes Siobhan to give me a swift verbal kick in the arse to convince me to finish the job. She holds down the office, pays the bills, but most importantly does seventy per cent of the "legwork" with the modern tools of the trade: computers, the internet, the phone, the fax machine, the databanks, the directories.

You're wondering why I'm here spilling my guts to you instead of at work in Memphis. No, I'm not on vacation. It has to do with a case. A case I already solved.

It began with a call from Irene Scully. You might remember her as Irene Warne. Miss Memphis 1981. Should have been Miss Tennessee except that her only talent was her looks. Her flaming baton twirling act was a disaster. Irene was the wife of Justice Owen Meriweather Scully III, former senior partner of Scully & Burke, Attorneys at Law, and considerably senior partner in his marriage. Owen and Irene had separated, but both refused to move out of the mansion, possession being nine-tenths of the law. Shortly after the agreement of irreconcilable differences, the fifty-two-year-old Owen had taken up jogging and was out for hours at a time. Irene might have bought the sudden health kick except that Owen wasn't losing any weight. And the Nike joggers still had all their tread after three weeks. There's not a woman alive, Irene included, dumb enough to miss what that meant. She contacted me about following him. What we in the profession call shadowing. I was already on a case, but I promised to start the next night. One night too late, as it turned out. Owen Scully left the house at 8:25 p.m. and never returned.

Irene hired me anyway. She was afraid the police and the insurance company would think she had figured out a way not to have to divide the community property. One conversation with Irene, and the police and the policy investigator would drop any suspicions that she could mastermind a clean killing. But I was not above cashing in on some of that community property.

My first visit was to the police station. I hunted down my pal, Detective Francis DePiano. If anybody in Memphis leads a cinema noir life, it's Frank. And yet he, who should know better than anyone else in town, has sold himself on the romance of the private eye. It's not in my self interest to disabuse him. I occasionally leave a case of Ruffino Chianti in his back seat as thanks for the inside information he feeds me.

I officially informed Frank on Irene's behalf of Justice Scully's disappearance.

"Not everyone on the force knows His Honor," Frank said, checking the blotter. "Nope. No John Does last night. But we have had a rash of disappearances lately, each time follow by a body."

I asked him what number constituted a rash.

"Three."

I asked in how much time.

"Three weeks. Every Sunday, like clockwork, somebody disappears. Every Wednesday night they die."

He had my undivided attention. I wondered aloud why I hadn't heard about it.

"Well, several reasons," Frank answered. "They were all black. One from the Riverview Park area, one from near Bellevue Park, one from just east of Glenview Park. Poorest parts of town. None could afford to be your client. Not even important enough to rate the front of the newspaper."

I guessed the police were after a serial killer.

"Nah. Much weirder than that. Sunday night the disappearance. Monday, Tuesday, or early Wednesday night they're seen. But never in their usual haunts. In fact, in haunts they wouldn't be caught dead in. We learn about them after the fact. Some time on Thursday the corpse is found. But it died on Wednesday night."

And why couldn't it be the work of a serial killer I wanted to know.

"Because the 'killer' is some kind of disease. The pathology boys say if it *is* infectious the person transmitting it would have to do more than kiss somebody to give it to them. As far as we can tell, none of the victims knew the others existed. The doctors haven't figured it out, but it seems more like cancer than anything else. It eats away part of their brains and part of their hearts. That's the other reason you haven't heard anything. We don't want to start a panic over some disease that only one person a week contracts. Nobody in the media has noticed the pattern, so we're happy to sit on it. At least for the time being."

I pumped DePiano for specifics on the 'haunts they wouldn't be caught dead in' angle.

"Okay. The first one was named Sammy Morris. Owned an auto junkyard down by the river. Nickname was Tank. Big, macho guy. Five kids by three different women. But on the Tuesday night after his disappearance, he's dressed like a transvestite and parading his stuff in The Pink Lady.

"The second was a woman. LaTrina Miles. Ran a custodial business. Her people cleaned a dozen business firms downtown. She musta bid too low, 'cause she lived on Greenwood. Disappears three Sundays ago. Who knows where-the-hell she hides herself all of Monday and Tuesday day. But Tuesday night, she's at her bank just as they're closing, looking hale and hearty and demanding to get into her deposit box. The employee points to the clock, tells her the vault is locked until morning, and suggests she come back then. Ms. Miles starts screaming, puts the woman into a hammer lock, and demands she open the vault. Two other employees had to come to her rescue. Ms. Miles flees on foot. She does not return the next morning. Or afternoon. So, maybe I'm stretching the point by saying she wouldn't be caught dead there, but once she went berserk she didn't come back. And then she literally was caught dead.

"The third one's Eddie Pendleton. He managed that apartment house on South Parkway with the concrete Greek statues out front.

You know, the one we call the Venus de Milo Arms. A true Homey. Always drove his LaBaron convertible with gangsta rap blasting. But when he's found on Thursday morning, he's dressed in a rented tuxedo with a stub for the previous night's Memphis Symphony in one pocket. We checked with the holders of the seats on either side. He was definitely at the concert and apparently loving every minute of it. Elgar, Delius, and Vaughn-Williams, ferchrissake! Not exactly his haunt or what?

"I'd say Justice Scully's safe," Frank concluded. "He's the wrong color and living in the right part of town."

I didn't feel as optimistic. He had disappeared on a Sunday night.

"Strange shit," DePiano said. "We've got plainclothesmen patrolling the 'poor people's' parks, but I'll be damned if I know what we're looking for."

I thanked Frank for the background and headed for the Venus de Milo Arms, equally damned if I knew what I was looking for. Irene Scully had agreed to pick up expenses regardless, so I bribed the temporary manager to let me into Eddie Pendleton's digs. Fortunately, Eddie had no relatives living in Memphis, or the vultures would definitely have picked the apartment clean.

I was frankly flabbergasted. The putative lover of gangsta rap had a living room filled with classical records and CDs. And the stuff he played it on didn't come out of Circuit City. The amplifier, tuner, turntable, CD player, and other assorted electronic toys were the kind of quality advertised in *Audiophile*. If they were mountains, they'd have been Everest/K2 class. Had to be an easy ten thousand bucks worth of equipment. But no speakers. Studio pro headphones only. Nobody in the Venus de Milo Arms was hearing this music except Eddie. And another ten thousand worth of wax and disk. All concealed behind cabinet doors. Out of view of guests. Other than the bizarre dichotomy between public and private listening tastes, Eddie's pad revealed nothing to shed light on his 'disease' or disappearance. I spoke with three of the tenants. Eddie was well liked. Did his best to see that the apartment house was neat and respectable, himself being the living example.

I waited until nightfall and tried to gain entrance to Sammy Morris's junkyard, but the place was very well lit, the chain-link fence was topped by concertina razor wire, and a pair of famished-looking Dobermans patrolled on the inside. Like I said:

I'm ready to set back down if it gets too formidable. Instead, I uncovered two of Sammy's girlfriends. One corroborated the other: Sammy lived simply inside the junkyard, but he took excellent care of his women and his kids. When I asked if he had any effeminate tendencies, one laughed in my face. The other one slapped my face. They had never heard of Eddie Pendleton or LaTrina Miles.

When I couldn't convince the two nieces who lived with LaTrina to talk with me or let me into her duplex, I waited until they were out and made a keyless entry through her back door. Again nothing. The place was tastefully done. The furniture was better than WalMart quality. Yet not the level I expected for a woman who had six people in her employ.

I have a friend at the state Department of Revenue. She works in the Alcoholic Beverage Commission, but nobody in Revenue would deny access if they thought it was official business. So I asked her to see if Inheritance Tax had any info yet on LaTrina Miles' estate. They did. The bank had reported on the inventory of the contents of the safe deposit box. It contained a passport that had stamps from a dozen countries. It also had thirty-seven thousand dollars in neatly banded hundred dollar bills. Suddenly, instead of thinking Ms. Miles had seriously undercharged for her custodial services, I was thinking she had seriously overcharged. When I called one of her nieces posing as her travel agent, the woman had no idea her aunt went anywhere except "to some religious retreat every year for two weeks."

Siobhan worked her armchair wizardry in getting LaTrina's custodial rates. The woman charged about ten per cent below average. Enough to win just about any client she wanted to. Her people's work was rated high. No complaints.

LaTrina had lots of secret money for travel. Eddie blew thousands he shouldn't have had on music. Sammy was generous to at least three women and five kids via a third-rate junkyard. Wealth was a hell of a common denominator for three supposedly poor people who had died of an exotic disease. It didn't figure at all.

I was working my weary way home on Tuesday night, having vainly interrogated Irene as to any secret money deals her husband may have had cooking, when I heard on the police scanner that Martin "The Thumb" O'Malley had just been blown away getting into his car. O'Malley was a Memphis racketeer who had beaten two indictments for murder. The next morning, Frank DePiano calls me and says that Solly Bosco has also met his maker later that same night. Solly was a hood who had survived numerous raps for narcotics trafficking and who was also suspected of liquidating local competitors. The weapon that ventilated both wise guys was a .45. Maybe the same one that took out O'Malley, but Forensics would let Frank know by closing time. That was a Wednesday.

Now, if I was a totally honest guy I would have shared what I knew with Detective DePiano. But I wanted that reward for pulling in Judge Scully real bad. I figured I'd get square with Frank if I could bring him one of the Sunday Night Missing alive. The thing I knew was that Martin O'Malley and Solly Bosco had both come up in front of Judge Scully's bench and gotten away, literally, with murder. Scully was a hanging judge. He had done what he could within the limits of the law to help the prosecution, but shoddy police work and idiot juries had confounded him.

One other major piece of scum had evaded Owen Scully's legal wrath. This bottom feeder had tried his hand at every illegal act there was, including "wet jobs." His name was Lenzy Rust. Lenzy lived in the Orange Mound district, in one of its grandest houses (which is not saying all that much). Word was he kept his BMW locked up inside a windowless garage and used a remote control ignition to start the car. He had not stayed alive by luck.

I waited until dusk on Wednesday to drive into Orange Mound. In daylight, I'd have looked like a marshmallow in a licorice factory. Besides, from the little I had learned, I knew that nothing would happen until the sun sank beyond the Mississippi. I spotted a cozy nook across the street from Rust's place to stand guard. A shoulder harness was strapped under my jacket, cradling my Smith & Wesson New Century. I used the damn gun so seldom, I had cleaned it and practiced with it out at the local target range that afternoon.

Lenzy was a creature of the night. Like a cockroach. The garage door didn't clank up until after eleven p.m. Lenzy emerged from the house's side exit, dressed in "What A Target" white. He had one hand stuck in his pocket. Before he reached the garage, the BMW's engine purred to life. The blur of white was in the driver's seat before you could say "Ashes to ashes, dust to dust/where there's a 'scratch' you'll find Rust." I'm no poet, but I had plenty of time to kill, so I had dreamed up a few bad epitaphs for Lenzy's headstone. I was that certain he was about to meet the same fate as Martin O'Malley and Solly Bosco. I could have prevented his passing, I suppose, but I'm a better citizen than that.

So I watched Owen Scully materialize from out of the shadows of Lenzy Rust's property, put a bullet into each of the BMW's driver's side tires, then aim a third into the driver's window. I was surprised to see the glass craze but not shatter. But Judge Scully was not. As Lenzy reversed the transmission to mash his attacker into the side of his house, Scully calmly sidestepped and, with his left hand, smashed a brick into the bulletproof window. It crunched in enough to make a silver-dollar-sized hole. A moment after the BMW's fender took out three courses of aluminum siding, Scully was pressing the muzzle of his automatic to the hole, pumping the remaining four shots in his clip into his victim.

The car horn started blowing. I stepped out of my own shadows and yelled out over the noise for Judge Scully to put up his hands. My right hand was already up, pointing my .44 at him. He blinked but clearly was not so astonished that he was about to meekly obey me. Instead, he turned and ran down the driveway. I could have nailed him in the back, but I was not about to commit murder for what Irene Scully was paying. I was especially not eager to murder somebody who, if he was indeed like the three before him, would be dead by dawn anyway. And then there's the fact that live men generally give explanations better than dead ones. The Memphis police would no doubt be very grateful to me if I could shed some light on the phenomenon of the Sunday Night Missing.

I gave chase. My purpose was to keep Owen Scully in sight, not to apprehend him myself. I didn't think it would be too difficult. He was, after all, almost twenty years older than me and fifty pounds heavier. With my free hand, I used my cell phone and pressed 911 while I ran. The Memphis cops are generally not bad when it comes to response time. I figured within five minutes it would all be over. While I was talking with the dispatcher, Scully jogged across a major thoroughfare and turned at the far sidewalk. I was between two parked cars on the opposite side of the street when something told me to duck. A moment later, three hunks of hot lead remodeled the car to my right. Scully had at least one spare clip on him.

I finished the call in a tight squat. By the time I risked a peek, the Judge had vanished. In spite of the danger, I couldn't let him get away. He hadn't recrossed the street, so he had gone east or west with the sidewalk or north into a nearby alley. I took the alley. Slowly. Smith & Wesson out in front. The corridor made a sharp left turn. I hugged the dark wall and inched forward. When I looked around the turn, I saw Judge Scully lying face up under a utility pole lamp. Gliding away from the body on the far wall was the full-size shadow of a man. I dared the light and, with my weapon cocked and raised, called out for whoever was retreating to halt. The shadow continued along the wall and disappeared into inky blackness. I strained to see the person who had created it, but to me the other end of the alley looked totally empty. Like some giant monster's maw yawning open.

I glanced down at Owen Scully. His maw was definitely yawning open. Fresh blood coated his teeth and lips. His eyes were wide open and bulging, as though his last seconds had been extremely painful. Just beyond his right hand lay a Colt automatic.

Traffic whizzed by out on the thoroughfare, but the alley lay as silent as Scully. It invited me forward. Against my better judgment, I rushed into the blackness. I wanted at least a glimpse of the owner of the shadow. I jinked and darted down the long, narrow space, like a pinball in a frenzied game. Once within the darkness, I saw that the alley ended not far beyond. Dead ended. Only one door and two heavy barred windows back there. The door was sheathed in metal and locked. I figured if it had been opened within the past minute, I would have heard some creaking. I had heard nothing. I looked up and down. No fire escape. A sewer grate along the alley curb but no sewer cover in the asphalt. As I stood in the darkness doing a slow 360, I heard the approaching wail of a police siren. I jogged back along the alley and out into the street to flag them down. Fortunately, I knew one of the cops, so the tedious crap of identifying and exonerating myself was dispensed with.

By five o'clock on Thursday I had two bits of information. The first was the ironic fact that the Colt that had blown away O'Malley, Bosco, and Rust had ostensibly been used by Lenzy Rust in committing a murder three years earlier. It had vanished from the evidence cage on the day Rust had been acquitted. The other news was the official report on Judge Owen Scully's demise. Same cause of death as the previous three Sunday Night Missing. Part of the brain and heart eaten away. Tears in the tissue of the lungs and esophagus. Massive bleeding that would have been a lot more messy except that death came within seconds. When I told Frank DePiano about the shadow figure, he dismissed it as temporary hysteria. Probably my own shadow from another light behind me. I went back to the alley to check it out. There was no other light.

Irene Scully paid me my out-of-pocket and per diem, but she held to our deal of no big pay-off unless Owen came back to her alive. Fair enough. That wasn't bothering me half as much as the whole incident in the alley. Someone other than me had made that shadow and then vanished. Houdini couldn't have done better. I had stood on a New York City corner for half an hour when I first got to the U.S., until I figured out how Three Card Monte was done; I wasn't going to walk away from this either until I understood it.

. I had the chance for a week-long dockside surveillance right after Judge Scully died, but I turned it down. It was across the river and would have made chasing the next Sunday Night Missing impossible. Sunday found me and my Smith & Wesson strolling through the sylvan shadows of Tobey Park. It's located between Christian Brothers College and the very tony Chickasaw Gardens bedroom community. Judge Scully had lived in Chickasaw Gardens. But his wallet had been found in the grass at the edge of a parking lot for the Mid-South Fairgrounds. Not in a park. Which told me two things. The first was that whatever had overtaken the four victims had not chosen parks because they were parks but rather because they were dimly lit and sparsely peopled at night. The fairgrounds were not in use and quite dark and deserted that time of year. That was probably the reason Owen Scully had picked that particular area. He had walked the safe distance from home and was picked up by his girlfriend and driven to their love nest. The second thing was that if you had a map of Memphis you could draw a ruler-straight line through Riverview, Bellevue, and Glenview Parks and right on up to the Fairgrounds. Whatever it was that had infected the four victims had done so along a precisely southwest to northeast course and was now halfway across the city, in its very heart. The next isolated spot on the extended line was Tobey Park.

The one thing I did not want was to be the next victim. As I walked, I turned often and watched over both shoulders. I had practiced enough times to know that my revolver could be in my hand in two seconds flat. I had visions of a mad scientist skulking through Memphis's dimly-lit and isolated areas on his night off, hypodermic in hand, seeking out guinea pigs for his latest formula. My vision did not put him in a white lab coat, easy to spot.

There were even fewer people out that night than I expected. One was a majestically white-haired priest, dressed in a black cassock and sitting on one of the park benches, no doubt on a constitutional from Christian Brothers, a block away. I dipped my head in deference to him, but he did not see me, seemingly lost in thought, his eyes focused at infinity. I made a perambulation of the park's outer path, spotting nothing out of the ordinary. Then I was back at the priest's bench. The priest was no longer there. But his cassock was. It lay on the grass behind the bench, trailed out toward the bushes.

I had brought with me a flashlight. It wasn't the ordinary variety but rather the krypton type. If our Revolutionary War patriots had used one in Boston's North Church, they could have signaled minutemen in Providence. I plunged into the vegetation, swinging the powerful beam back and forth. Far ahead of me was the priest, lurching through the undergrowth. He turned when the light hit him. He lifted his arms to ward off the blinding beam and gave forth an inhuman roar. Since I was within fifty feet of him, I chanced balancing the flashlight in the crotch of a tree and circled swiftly and silently to his right. Just as I was nearly upon him, he rushed in my direction. I sidestepped and caught him behind the left ear with the muzzle of my revolver. He fell hard. This one was not slipping away from me.

I sat on the old man's back. As quickly as I could, I took off my belt and secured his hands behind him. Then I removed his belt and hog-tied his legs, pulling his feet up close to his hands. By the time I returned with the flashlight, he was regaining consciousness. He rolled over and stared up at me. With eyebrows raised in a look of surprise.

"You again!" he exclaimed. "I should have killed you last week."

I am sure my look of surprise greatly outdid his.

"You're the shadow I saw in the alley," I said.

He struggled vainly against the belts. "That's right."

I leaned against a tree for much-needed support. "It was a dead end. How did you get out?"

"I went down into the sewer."

"But how could you fit?"

"I can fit through a keyhole if I choose," the priest answered. "Turn that light away! It has wavelengths that hurt me."

Despite the strangeness of his words, I obeyed. Then he laughed. "I thought you understood. I've given you too much credit."

Suddenly, I did know. "You *are* the shadow in the alley. Nothing more."

The priest rolled over, so that his face was away from the light. "I'm sure I'm more than that. But I must look so to humans. Close enough so that I can glide up to your mouths and noses and crawl in without your becoming suspicious. I truthfully don't know what I look like."

"What are you?" I asked, once I had recovered my voice.

"I have very little idea. I don't know how I began or where. My guess is not long ago and somewhere near the Mississippi River."

"You're damned articulate for something that began not long ago. Do you understand the word 'articulate'?"

"Of course. I understand whatever Tank Morris, LaTrina Miles, Eddie Pendleton, and Owen Scully understood. I have all their memories inside me."

I kept my revolver raised and walked around to look at the priest's face. "You understand that you eventually kill those you invade, don't you?"

"Yes."

"Why do you do it?"

"Because the nearest thing I can compare myself to is a computer diskette. I'm filled with memories, but I can't use them unless I get myself inside a human mind. The mind acts like a microprocessor for me. Outside on my own, I operate on simple instinct. I crave completion. I can only be without it for four days. Then I have to get inside someone."

"Unfortunately, you kill them after three days," I said. "Eat away parts of their brains and heart."

"Yes. I can feel it happening. When the heart starts to go wild, I force my way out again, and seek dark water."

Then I understood the pattern of its victim taking. The Memphis sewer and storm drain systems empty to the north into the Wolf River and to the south into Nonconnah Creek. One large drain runs southwest, under the Fairgrounds, Glenview, Bellevue, and Riverview Parks. One runs northeast, under Robert Howze Park, the Chickasaw Country Club, and Gaisman Park. Both begin by draining Tobey Park. It was a creature of water and of darkness. Even when inside a human body, it couldn't abide sunlight. That was why the victims had never been seen during the day. They probably holed up in the storm drains until dusk.

"If you have only a simple nervous system yourself," I said, "how do you choose your victims?"

"By smell," it answered, without reflection.

"Smell," I repeated. "Do humans give off a particular smell to you?"

"Yes. But not all humans. Only a certain kind."

I knew it couldn't mean blacks, because Owen Scully and the priest were white. I knew it couldn't mean old, because Sammy Morris and LaTrina were not even thirty.

"Can you define the kind?" I asked.

"Hypocrites," it answered. "Again you look surprised. Perhaps you can't smell them, but I can. Not when I'm inside a human body, you see. But outside, it's like beer to a slug. Do you want me to prove it?"

I admitted I did.

"Tank Morris claimed he owned a completely legitimate junkyard. But a lot of his inventory came from a chop shop he ran, four blocks away. If he was just selling stolen hubcaps, he might have lived. LaTrina Miles had her employees go through wastebaskets, drawers, file cabinets--locked and unlocked—even into computers, digging for stuff she could sell to the competition. She was very clever about it. Never once arrested. She cleaned up all right. Eddie Pendleton was so publicly proud of the good reputation of his apartment house. Around the corner he was running a whorehouse, stocked with a couple of runaway teenage girls. Very low-key and exclusive. The other pimps didn't know about it, much less the cops. The righteously indignant Owen Scully took bribes."

"Let me guess the priest's hypocrisy," I said. "He's a pedophile."

"Trite but not true. No, this old phony lost his faith twenty years ago but was too afraid of having to earn his living in the outside world. He's a complete atheist." The priest smiled. It was a beatific expression reminiscent of Barry Fitzgerald movies.

I felt like a fishwife gathering facts about a particularly grisly accident. I could not stop asking questions. I wanted to know why each of its victims had behaved so bizarrely on the nights just preceding their deaths.

"I suppose I should be satisfied just reveling in their memories, in the sheer joy of human intellect. But once I'm wrapped around their brains, I can't resist the rush of chemicals that flow through me when I suppress these people's inhibitions and let them do exactly what they long to do. Tank wanted to feel just once what it would be like to be a woman. LaTrina hadn't acted the grand lady outside the country in almost a year. Eddie was tired of hearing good music second-hand. Owen Scully had always wanted to kill. This coot wants to piss in the sacramental wine and let the other priests drink it. So, am I the monster or are they? Am I doing good or bad in killing them?"

"That's not for me to judge," I said. "You can tell this all to the authorities and let them decide."

"There may be nothing left to question if you don't let the priest's legs down," it answered, in a laboring tone. "He's not a young man, and his feet and hands have gone dead already. Now he's having trouble breathing. You may be killing him."

Warily, I rolled the priest over onto his stomach. Then I loosened the belt that held his feet up against his buttocks. The instant I did, he kicked back, catching me squarely in the groin. For a moment, my eyes were filled with a red as bright as Japan's Rising Sun. Then I collapsed to the ground, all my neural circuits overloaded with pain. I watched helplessly as the krypton light showed the priest bucking and shimmying like a wind-up toy whose spring had popped. A shrill scream of agony erupted from his mouth.

I regained enough control to roll away from the writhing man. In another few seconds I was finally able to gasp in a ragged breath. While I filled my lungs, I watched a projectile hemorrhage of blood explode from the priest's nose and mouth. Suddenly, he lay still. Out of his mouth, like a stream of nothingness, flowed the thing that had invaded him.

The adrenaline of fear brought me to my fear. I watched in horror as the being became a long shadow, roughly mimicking the shape of the dead man. It was so thin that it conformed to the blades of grass over which it flowed. Yet in the powerful light, I could just make out a network of hair-thin nerves running beneath its surface.

It glided in my direction. I fired the revolver at it until all the chambers were empty. It seemed totally unfazed. The holes closed up within seconds. I snatched the flashlight from the ground and thrust it forward. This, at least, bothered it. It shrunk back. I focused on its center. It retreated, picking up speed. I was amazed at its noiseless quickness. I realized that it was trying to flank me and attack from behind. I pivoted the light around, driving it back. With much effort and movement I herded it toward the edge of the park.

The only thing I could think of was to force it into a busy street, where heavy vehicle tires could mash it flat. Unfortunately, I did not see the storm drain soon enough. By the time I realized it was there, the thing had half vanished down it. And then it was completely gone.

My father—may he rot in hell--fancied himself a great wit. One of his favorite jokes was about Queen Elizabeth II and Philip, Duke of Edinburgh. On their wedding night the Queen said, "Sir, I offer you my honor." To which the Duke replied, "Madam, I honor your offer." And the rest of the night it was honor and offer, on her and off her.

Not content to leave this a disembodied play on words, when I and my fraternal twin sister were born, dear old "Da" insisted that we be named Siobhan and Siobhough. The joke was on him. We've been literally inseparable since age fifteen. No fools, we knew that sooner or later we'd be caught at our great crime. Caught and permanently separated. The only way to stay together was to flee to another country and take up new identities, as husband and wife.

I telephoned what I had learned in Tobey Park to an expectedly incredulous Detective DePiano. I made the call from Nashville. There was no way we were hanging around in Memphis. Siobhan and I live close to where the storm drain empties into the Wolf River. I doubt that the smell of hypocrisy would be stronger on any other residents of Memphis. We won't be back there again until we know for sure that it's been destroyed. Never mind Friday morning confession. If your heart's not as pure as the driven snow at the North Pole, I suggest you stay out of that fair city as well.

Bridge of Brothers
By Tom Piccirilli

Another war begins between separate hells—brothers, of course—as all wars arise. They sit on the bridge with their thorny shoulders slicing and pumping venom into each other's flesh, ten thousand millennia of wrath caught between them. Black blood and ichor pool beneath them, slowly easing into a spear-point that runs off the bridge and into the Mississippi River, where the djinn grow in the steam of the weeds, feeding on fish murdered by the murky clouds of contagion.

The Chickasaw settled around the two seraphim long before any bridge had been built, neither praising, damning, nor even fearful of the raging twins, for archangels acted too much like petty men. Their own gods remained holier and more terrifying—more satisfying—than these, who sat in silence bleeding together as churlish children harbor their pain.

On occasion, to prove one's manhood, or perhaps merely out of pride or sympathy, the bravest warriors would approach and fill the brothers' wounds with poultices, clearing the sweat from their fiery eyes. For centuries before they were forcibly relocated to Oklahoma, the Chickasaw passed down the legend that during the worst year of fever, in the sanguine glow of a hunter's moon, a maiden offered herself to the twins if they would only save her family. The brothers took the maiden—mutely, together, and with ferocious vengeance upon the other--but let her family die regardless. Alone and dying herself, it took only minutes for her to give birth to a child who soon perished following the hideous, marrow-soaked end to his mother.

They say the ghost of this offspring still wanders Memphis.

I am he, who knows my fathers, and I am the substance of their hate. It has no drama or worth, their fury, only an endless darkness of impossible redemption. Since the war in heaven they've found no part of God that wants them, no home beyond their seat, no comrades in hell.

I have no name, but Laurel, my love, calls me Cotton. I am soft to her touching, but still have barbs and briars upon which she hooks herself. She sings more beautifully than anyone ever has, in a city known for its lineage of music. I've listened to them all since even before W.C. Handy, and my lovely Laurel crumples against the microphone with her soul full of blues, voice more potent and earnest than paradise. I close my eyes in the club on Beale Street, and there is momentary relief from the fetid knowledge of my fathers.

She swaggers forward pressing her lips into the mike, swaying with a timeless realization of anguish and delight. Her hair cascades in a dark arc, covering half her face, and one naked, sweaty shoulder glints with somber light. Languorous movements stir the smoke-filled shadows. Her words are soft, heady moans that make the audience tilt back in their seats.

She spent her childhood on Wolf River, and teen years in Crittenden County, where she learned the lessons and depth of what would become her blues. She's passed my fathers on the bridge when going back and forth between Shelby and West Memphis. She sings of dog races and the logging camp of Bragg's Spur, of Martin Luther King and the riverboats. Of her grandmother in the fields, and her grandfather emasculated and hanged from the bridge.

My Laurel. I weep in the back of the club and a drunken woman turns to face the dark corner where I hide. "Did you hear that?" she asks too loudly, slurring, her breasts nearly fallen free from her tight dress. Her date shushes her with a kiss, and helps to steady her hand so she can lift her glass to take another drink. His leer is like the grin of the djinn.

In the night, Laurel sleeps above her mother's blankets, and I rest beside her smelling the perfume of her soul. Such sweet breath, her songs continuing on toward dawn, as I press myself to the angles of her face and greedily gulp her beauty and purity. Come morning, she calls her friend and manager, Jill, and tells her, "I dreamed of Cotton again."

Jill has a dry laugh that heaves itself over the receiver. "Laurel honey, your father didn't get his doctorate from Southern College of Optometry just so you could suffer a guilt complex."

"No, listen, I'm not talking about baling and picking, simply lying beside it."

"That's the third time this week. What is this, some new fetish? What the hell are you dreaming about Cotton for?" Jill hasn't come to see the show in almost two weeks; she is busy with her husband and two lovers, and has stopped listening to Laurel's songs since they began to make money. "You're working too hard. Beale Street might have to do without you while you get away for a vacation. You were always talking about Hawaii. Don't you think it's time?"

"No," Laurel says. She'll never leave the South. She is as tied to the land as I am.

Her empathy carries great power, those perfectly formed veins flowing with the effrontery, history, and victories of her people. When her racial memories falter I share my thoughts on all I have witnessed. She cries for her grandfather because I can so clearly recall his face: the way he slowly twirled in the wind, soft creaking of the rope underscored by the whoosh and crackle of his burning church, and the ugly chuckles and whispers of his killers.

In her dreams, she calls to me, "Cotton, Cotton," and I reveal my nature to her spirit. We can dance here in her thoughts if nowhere else, holding my Laurel in my feathery arms. She murmurs and hums against my chest, composing passionate songs even now. "You're an angel," she says.

I grunt in the same fashion as my dying mother. "Please, no," I beg.

"Why?"

She can't understand this is the greatest curse upon me. "Sing for me." Smiling and laughing, she begins a sultry song I've helped to compose. Leaning forward, as I hug her closer, her chest expands with panting lyrics from the past. She grimaces, occasionally pricked by my thorns, but eventually she comes to a comfortable position. Her blues are significant, and I purr along with her. We can share all things in a secret comprehension of rhythm and purpose.

"I love you, Cotton."

My breath comes in bites as large and intoxicating as the universe. "And I love you, Laurel."

In the morning the humidity is intolerable and full of malevolence. The televisions and radios bark horror. Details are sketchy at first, but there is no mistaking the fact that this is a summer of war. She awakens with her eyes stuffed with panic as she reaches for the phone. Jill answers sounding ill, complaining of a backache, chills, and fever.

Laurel whimpers, "Oh, God."

I've shared much, and she understands.

Hovering in the air behind my love, about to land on her neck, writhes a mosquito with the face of my fathers. I lash out and crush it in my fist, listening to its inherent curses. I race from Laurel's bedroom and pass neighbors already staggering in the streets, the disease spreading so quickly. Their gums are bleeding as they topple against one another, turning their jaundiced faces to the sky. In the gutters runs the crimson vomitus as it did in years past.

The city is dying again—-they've loosed another plague, serving no purpose except to kill and torment what they do not hate, but wish they could hate. I stand at the bridge and grab my fathers by their scrawny necks and shake them until their tongues unfurl between their fangs. From their mouths crawl the newly-mutated *ædes ægypti*—a million mosquitoes loose with the yellow fever, bringing on the murder of Memphis.

"Stop it," I say. "Not again, please, not again. For me, I'm your son, please, do it for me. I'm your son. Don't take my Laurel."

My entire life my fathers have never said a word or acknowledged my presence in any way. "I'm your son! For me, do it for me!" I slap them again and again to no effect, the mosquitoes boiling over their lips and from their nostrils, so much venom gushing. "Not my Laurel."

I fling them down and witness the death of my home. It takes no time at all for the bodies to flood the streets and drop into the rivers. I scream and draw children from the corpses of their parents, the djinn feasting on the bloated bodies that lay tumbling end over end, stuck in the weeds. The dying pour into the hospitals and the usual medicines do little. Blood is coughed onto walls. Mosquitoes crawl on the eyelids of newborns. Yellow fever runs wild, accelerated beyond mortal belief. Jill, her husband, and both her lovers lie dying in the same ward. In her delirium she somehow recognizes me and gasps,

"Oh, you are Laurel's Cotton... Why is this happening? Stop it, help us . . . "

She reaches for her latest lover and dies before their hands can clasp.

Laurel's apartment is empty.

I find her where I know she must be: at the base of the bridge, having bequeathed herself to them in an effort to save our city, and my Laurel is already giving birth. She lies there dying, sweating. Her smashed torso pumps her life against my face, and she gasps my name. "Cotton... "

"I'm here, my love."

She growls a last song against my neck, her legs spreading. As my brother falls from her womb, born laughing with his poisons already leaking and killing the land, my beautiful Laurel dies in my arms.

He is of my fathers, and the substance of their hate. He knows them, and so knows me.

Another war begins between separate hells—brothers, of course—as all wars arise. We sit on the bridge with our backs to our fathers, our thorny shoulders slicing and pumping venom into each other's flesh, ten minutes of wrath caught between us.

I sing my blues, and soon, in a voice similar to my own, he joins me.

The Heart of the Matter
By Don Webb

It was shortly after the American Civil War that a dark and alien past intruded into the life of Dr. Alfred Pointers. It came in a beautiful and charming package and was to teach Dr. Pointers many things about this world and the next.

The twilight sky glowed with orange and salmon and lemon clouds—a beautiful display cheering to everyone in Shelby County save for Dr. Pointers, who had hoped for a stormy night. Dr. Pointers was a Romantic, and the world could not have enough stormy nights, maidens in distress, or dragons to slay. He was about to re-enter the smartly painted yellow cottage that served both for his residence and practice, when he did hear (to his delight) a maiden weeping.

She was a pretty little thing, half hiding herself in the shadow of the great cedar just beyond his picket fence. Flaxen hair and fair skin, her eyes and nose reddened with tears. Dr. Pointers could easily put both his hands around her slight waist, which seemed to Dr. Pointers an excellent idea. With what he hoped to be manly strides, he crossed from his porch to as near the weeping maiden as his fence would permit.

"May I help you, my dear?"

"Are you Dr. Alfred Pointers, founder of the Memphis chapter of the Society for Psychical Research?" she asked. Clearly she had been rehearsing the question.

"Yes, ma'am. I am the co-founder of the Society. Mr. Vincent J. Harris and I founded the society. Mr. Harris has relocated to Boston."

"Dr. Pointers. I am obsessed by a spirit whom I believe wants to do me harm."

"I can recommend several mediums who have experience dealing with such entities."

"I am not interested in such. I, like my mother before me, have tried many. I am interested in your theories of using electricity to kill a spirit."

"The murder of a soul is a serious matter."

"Yes," she said. "The regents at Botanico Medical College certainly thought so when you presented your talk there last year. But once you've heard my story, I'll let you be the judge of what method should be used."

The Tale of Mary Hawkes

"My name is Mary Hawkes. I never knew my father. From my earliest childhood I was told that he had been 'lost at sea.' My mother, Rebecca Hawkes, was a beautiful but frightened woman, who filled her house with crucifixes and holy water. Mother was determined that I should become a nun, and insisted that the only man I could love was Jesus. I went to a girls' school run by the Dominican Order. Mother walked me to and from school, telling me to avert my eyes whenever I saw a man or boy. Indeed I came to view such creatures as being akin to Satan himself. Mother served as a seamstress for the wealthy women of Boston, and went to great pains to insure that no men ever even visited our home.

"Never could I leave my home to visit my friends. I could have—on rare occasions—a girl from school visit me. This continued until one of my friends and I had gone to my tiny attic room and engaged in an earnest and giggling conversation about the male sex. My friend was shocked that I didn't have a boy that I was 'sweet' on, and I listened with both horror and fascination of her description of a butcher's son, with whom she had done certain things, the very existence of which I had no idea. While my friend was in the midst of describing his embraces, my mother, who had been safely altering dresses to fit expanding matrons, paused to eavesdrop, and then broke into my room like Jesus into the Temple to drive forth the moneychangers. The story of my mother's wrath became a legend at my school. Mother needn't have worried about my friendships, for after that incident I had none.

"But the seeds of temptation had been planted. I would spend my evenings hugging myself while I watched the sunsets glow upon the ancient gambrel-roofed houses of my native Boston. I would imagine suitors with hair as red as the sunset's glow and arms as luminous as the falling sun. But my life was so carefully hedged that I would never meet such.

"During my last year at St. Martin's School, the year before I was to take the veil, I was given the charge of a class of the youngest students. This required me to interact with Billy McNeil, an eighteen-year-old Irishman who supplied the classroom furnaces with coal. His hair was the red of the window-reflected sunset, and his arms were muscled like steel. His smile was the light of the sun at noontide, and like the young and not-so-young women in the school,

I was in love with him, even before he first spoke to me with his beautiful brogue.

"I began to do little things to keep him in my presence longer. I would have him fetch this or that, or run some errand I could do myself. Soon I saw yet another light—the dawning of love in his eyes. Mother took ill and stopped walking me to and from the school. Perhaps she thought I was safe or in some sense believed that my nearing Vocation would protect me from wandering fancies. Billy began walking me home. It was a great secret of course. I would have cost him his employment and me my hopes of the veil.

"One day a thunderstorm took us unawares, or more frankly our growing ardor distracted us from the heavy skies. We took refuge in a livery, and Billy warmed me with more attention than necessary.

"I told my mother that evening that I had become responsible for the school library and that would keep me an additional hour or two on some days.

"My trysts with Billy became frequent and abandoned. My only fear was to explain to mother my intention of becoming a bride of McNeil rather than one of Christ. Yet I felt in my heart that she would surely see my happiness and in the face of great joy, what could she do but submit?

"One winter afternoon my sport with Billy lasted too long and I had to make my way home in the dark. It was cold and blustery and the streets were dark and for the most part deserted. I spied a tallish man half-concealing himself at a corner ahead of me. I was sufficiently worldly to know that men sometimes lurk for young women. I increased my pace and crossed to the other side of the street, but, when I looked to that corner, the tall man returned. Clearly I would have to confront him.

"I walked resolutely forward. I smelled rotting flesh, and then I saw two things at once. The man was wearing an antique costume and a huge hole was in the center of his chest where his heart should've been. His eyes were filled with rage. He began floating toward me, and I could see from the little light available that he was translucent. I thought it was God come to judge me for my sins. The figure spoke, 'I will have my revenge.'

"Then it vanished. I ran home as fast as I could.

"I didn't tell Momma. Her health was shaky, and I feared that what had been a near-mortal shock for me would've done her in.

"The next day Billy was not at school. The day after that all of Boston knew of the terrible murder. He had been found in the livery stable, our livery stable, with his heart cut out.

"I figured the spirit must have meant to have revenge on Billy, since surely I had done it no harm. But I lived in fear of its remanifestation. Perhaps the world was as horrid as Mother had always portrayed. In any event, I would never know happiness now that Billy was dead. I resigned myself to taking the veil.

"My mother continued to decline in health. She often spoke of 'wondering whether or not to tell me' but whatever great secret she had went with her to the grave some two months before my projected date for entry into the convent.

"I found myself in need of legal services in dealing with a small investment my mother had left to me—a very small interest in a shipping firm, the only contact I had ever had with my father. My lawyer, Mr. Elias Blackwell, served the papers for me, as well as giving me some advice on selling Mother's things.

"Mr. Blackwell, a Harvard-educated widower, proved to be the most interesting and cultured person I had ever met. He had traveled in Europe as a young man, he seemed to have read everything experienced everything and above all to be a terribly lonely man. Once again I began to fall in love. We began to dream of the happiness that we could have. My horizons expanded. I began to dream of going everywhere in the world, giving something of myself to each person I met. I told the sisters that I wasn't going to take the veil.

"One afternoon Elias told me that he had found a letter addressed to me among my mother's papers. He did not know how he had overlooked it. He dropped it by my tiny home. We kissed and courted and made plans for announcing our wedding. He left and before I could open the letter, the room was filled with the smell of rotting meat. The phantom with the wounded chest appeared before me. This time he wore a look of grim satisfaction. He pointed to the letter. Then he vanished before my eyes.

"I found the next day that Elias had met the same fate as Billy: heart ripped out and missing. The police, who had connected me with Billy, believed that I had done the deed. There was talk of putting me in an asylum, but the alienist convinced the authorities that I was both sane and incapable of such a horrid deed. I did not tell him of the contents of the letter, but I knew they were true. Read it for yourself and you will understand."

My dearest Mary,

It is my supreme hope that I will be able to cast this letter into the fire and that you will never know of the horrible curse that has struck the women of our family for generations. But if you are reading it, it means my plan of locking you away from the world has failed, and instead of being behind convent walls you are mourning the outré death of a lover.

My mother Sarah Jermyn had learned it from her mother Briget Dudley who had learned it from her mother Margaret Haekel. Sometime in the past we'd had an unbearably wicked ancestor Juliette Roumond. Juliette had allowed herself to be beguiled by a Dutch sorcerer named Hendrik DeJung. His devil-cult was based in Rotterdam and he offered her great wealth and power in exchange for love and beauty. Juliette was greatly taken with the sorcerer's tales, particularly so when she learned that DeJung possessed the secret of eternal life. He had lived for centuries beyond the span of normal men.

Juliette found his embraces cold, and although she enjoyed her newfound status as High Priestess, she began to long for other men. The authorities got word of DeJung's cult, and one night Hendrik and Juliette fled to New Amsterdam. There she found her true love, Fenix Meyer. At first the lovers were cautious, meeting only while DeJung pursued his alchemical experiments in certain caverns beneath New Amsterdam.

One day however as Fenix presented roses to Juliette, one of the roses began to speak and by the time it had finished its song, Fenix lay upon the ground his flesh shredded from bone, torn by invisible demons brought from the rose's spell. Juliette ran to the cavern to beg DeJung to finish her as well. But the immortal merely laughed and told her that she was his forever, as he had already immortalized her.

Juliette discovered in the Livre de Eibon, *one of the evil tomes which had come with them to New Amsterdam, that the undying part of alchemists was their* heart. *It would be difficult to pull out her own heart, but perhaps she could pull out*

DeJung's.

The sorcerer did not sleep as did other men. Only once a month, and then on the night of the new moon did he slumber, but that slumber was a profound one. She risked purchasing a sleeping draught from an apothecary and mixed it with the o l d brandy DeJung favored. Hopefully he was like enough to other men as to be stupefied by drugs.

While he slept Juliette carved. She removed the heart and threw it into the Hudson River. Then she buried the carcass. The alchemist had a large store of gold and Juliette lived very well.

Eventually she fell in love with the English governor of what was renamed New York. A short time after their wedding, the ghostly figure of Hendrik DeJung appeared to her and reminded her that she belonged to him. He tore out her husband's heart, a familiar horror to our family.

Juliette sought a physician to kill her with surgery for she feared that somehow the phantom would find a way to materialize permanently or to take her back to whatever quasi-material realm he dwelt in. He did after all possess the power to take the hearts of his victims back with him. The physician, persuaded by gold more than our ancestor's story, agreed to cut out her heart.

But he found that Juliette was with child. She decided to have the baby, and she would leave the physician all of her gold if he would agree to raise the child as his own. After the birth of her daughter, the doctor made his first attempt. He had not really believed the tale and merely plunged a scalpel in our grandmother's chest. The shock knocked her out, and he tossed her body in the river.

Our ancestor came to, swam through the freezing currents and in her bloodstained dress hunted him down. He saw her beating heart through the wound he had made and finished the job.

For many years he kept the beating heart of Juliette, but as the young woman he now thought of as his daughter was approaching young adulthood, he decided to have the heart buried. He had told his daughter nothing of her mother's tragic fate—saying simply that she had been one of his patients.

The daughter Elizabeth Sudyam became enamored of the son of the apothecary, ironically the apothecary who had unknowingly aided in the slaying of her sire. After a decorous courtship, they wed.

Early on she was with child—fecundity seems to be part of our curse. One night the ghost appeared to her and her husband—and with its terrible strength, tore his heart from his chest.

She went screaming to her 'father,' who then told her of her mother's history. Since that day, any woman born of the family has never known a man save that the ghost has murdered him.

We all resolve not to love, but something in our nature draws us to men. I had studied the occult for many years, and have come to believe that Hendrik DeJung did not love Juliette, but that he needed her and her offspring to provide hearts for him as a terrible sacrifice.

My first love Manfred West met his fate in my sixteenth year. I resolved to kill myself after my mother had revealed the terrible secret. I booked passage on a ship to Britain intending to throw myself overboard in the middle of the Atlantic. I did so, but lacked the resolve to make myself drown. I swam or treaded water for two terrible days. A sailor on a ship coming from Britain saw me, and saved me. It was your father. He risked his life for me, and I took it from him by loving him.

I am sorry to have brought you into this world of tears, and hope and pray that you are spared by the curse. Perhaps time and a merciful God will weaken the will of the evil alchemist.

> *Tearfully,*
> *Rebecca Hawkes*

Dr. Pointers put the letter aside. It had grown late into the night, and the warm lamp light and recitation had convinced him that this was the Quest he had waited his whole life for.

He asked Mary, "After the first two deaths, were there any more?"

She looked long and hard at his floor before answering. "Yes. I tried very hard to avoid men completely. Perhaps the curse drives me to meet men. I had managed to hide away in upstate New York living almost as a wild beast. I spotted a farm boy in the valley beneath the hill where I hid. I merely looked on him, surely there was no harm in looking. And yet my fond gaze was powerful enough to draw the spirit. I heard the men hunting in the woods for the wild animal that had torn out his heart."

"And you knew then you had to destroy this spirit."

"Yes. I thought of destroying myself, but I could not be sure that I was the only descendent. Perhaps a race of sons somewhere exists, and when a daughter is born to one of them—there won't be anybody to tell her of the curse."

"My work is only theory," said Dr. Pointers. "If I had my research assistant still here, I would feel better. Then we could do studies, make experiments."

"No, I don't have time for more studies, I don't have time for more experiments. Life is short and should not be spent in unhappiness."

"But there is the question of other methods that might be used, such as exorcism."

"That is not the question," said Mary. "The question is whether or not you would take the risk."

"What risk?"

"Well in order to bait the ghost I would have to fall in love with someone. I would have to fall in love with you, Dr. Alfred Pointers."

* * *

Much to the scandal of his maid and then of the general Memphis community, Mary Hawkes took up residence in Dr. Pointers's house. Most of his practice immediately found new doctors, but this allowed Dr. Pointers time to construct his ghost-catching device. He had set aside a good deal of money having intended to retire from the practice of medicine early and devote his life to psychical research (if he had indeed not been fortunate enough to find love). He did not know quite how to act with a woman living in the house. Well, his maid was a woman, but not a pretty little thing whose hope was focused entirely upon him. Indeed, if men tarry too long in life without marrying, they will never learn the art, and will find themselves at loose ends in the presence of beauty—always reaching for their pipes or some small object to play with.

He did not know when Mary would fall in love with him. It seemed a matter beyond will and rational decision. It should not be so, he reasoned, one should be able to fall in love on schedule with the proper stimulants.   Perhaps in addition to making his ghost-catching device, he should in some manner seek to woo her.

Now this proved an entirely different problem. He picked her roses from his garden, tried singing to her in the early twilight; he even made a laborious and unsuccessful attempt at composing a sonnet for her. She smiled at these attempts, and bravely told him that she was trying quite hard to fall in love with him, and inquired after the construction of the ghost catcher.

The ghost catcher represented what Dr. Pointers called the "best of the scientific method applied to the lore of ghosts." The original design had been drawn up three years ago by Vincent Harris and himself. The "little problem" he had with the regents at Botanico Medical College had dissuaded them from completing the device. Harris had left for Boston where he felt he could pursue his experiments more freely, while Dr. Pointers decided to keep his studies of ghosts at a merely folkloric level.

He had made a meticulous study of every ghost tale he could find. He had collected hundreds of reports of seances, dozens of files of apparitions during the Civil War. It was his theory that ghosts were some sort of electromagnetic phenomenon. They drew from the bodies of mediums at sittings, from the sexual energy of young girls in poltergeist manifestations. They could be stopped by various grounding devices notably cold iron and running water.

To catch a ghost all one need do is to suddenly surround it with a cage of iron.

It was the sudden part which was giving Dr. Pointers troubles. What if the figure of the dead alchemist came too early—or didn't manifest in the right place for the trap to work?

While working through these fears and desires, a letter came to him from Boston. It contained a personal letter from Vincent Harris, a note from a Mr. Calone, and a blueprint for a ghost catcher. The letter from Harris was almost as disturbing as the note.

The Letter of Vincent Harris:

May 17

Dear Alfred,
        After three years of speculation I have found an opportunity to test the ghost catcher. As we thought might be the case, it

will be used not only as a ghost catcher, but a ghost killer — in this case my target is a very nasty alchemist of Dutch origin named Hendrik DeJung. He was an associate of Ludwig Prinn, author of De Mysteriis Vermis, an occult tome of various methods of prolonging and restoring life. This unsavory fellow — I am speaking here of DeJung — has attached himself to all the daughters of a certain bloodline in the most foul fashion. I propose to kill Hendrik with a strong magnetic field that will be unleashed moments after he materializes. The mechanism for doing this is outlined in my drawings. I am, however, worried that the field might dampen the effect of the ghost catcher causing the spirit to be released before the magnetized iron can draw off sufficient ectoplasmic charge to kill the ghost.

My design for releasing the twenty-four lodestones simultaneously I think will solve the problem. I am hoping to put off the experiment as long as possible, but the young woman I am doing the work for is quite insistent, and may talk me into the experiment before I have a chance to consult with you on matters of design.

She is really quite something, I am totally smitten with her blonde hair, her fair skin, her deep soulful eyes that seemed to have glimpsed the secrets of heaven and hell. I have told her all about you, and as soon as the problems of her spirit obsession is over, she and I are to be wed. I hope that you will do us the honor of being our best man.

Please write back as soon as you can with your opinion of my design. I hope that I may prove your best student by doing that thing that society warned us against. Seeking your advice and wisdom I am

S/ Vincent J. Harris

The Note of Mr. Jeremy Calone:

Dear Dr. Pointers,

The enclosed letter and mechanical drawings were found among the effects of Mr. Vincent J. Harris, 2 Poplar Street, Boston, Mass.

Mr. Harris had been murdered by person or persons unknown in a very brutal fashion. He was found next to a large

> *mechanical contrivance of unknown purpose. The Boston police are looking for a woman who was seen fleeing the house the night before the body was discovered for questioning. Any help that you can supply us would be greatly appreciated.*
>
> *S/Jeremy Calone*

Dr. Pointers called Mary and handed her the notes.

"Why didn't you tell me?" he asked.

"I couldn't, you don't know how much Vincent idolized you. He spoke of you every day. You were his best friend. Would you have worked for me, if you knew that I was responsible for your best friend's death?" Mary said.

"Of course I would have worked for you. I—" Dr. Pointers paused, "I love you."

"You love me now, because you have worked to do so. Our love will weather this knowledge. True love always does."

"Did you love Vincent?"

"Yes. I loved him with all my heart. Just as I love you now. Please help me—can you fix what Vincent did wrong?"

"I must study the diagrams, very carefully."

Dr. Pointers did study the diagrams very carefully. But even more he studied on the image of his prize pupil with his heart torn from his body. Facing the specter had not been a truly daunting idea until he could see so clearly (with his mind's eye) what such a death would be like. He began wearing vests all the time—he felt protected by having something over his very vulnerable heart.

He began seeing the image of Vincent all the time. Being a doctor he had a very good idea of the look of such a body, the blood pouring backward through the aorta, the pinkish lungs, the top to the abdominal wall—the exposed muscle, fat, skin and bone.

Doctors are much better at scaring themselves than the rest of us: they have so much more to go on. It would be worse, worse than anything he saw in the war.

He studied over the idea of Vincent. Of course she had sought him out. He was younger; better looking; easier to fall in love with than Dr. Pointers. Dr. Pointers had been the second choice. There was no denying that.

He studied on Mary's silence too. Could he believe such a woman? Oh why did he trust her so when she would flash a smile at him? All of his adult life he had been very reasonable, he was perhaps the incarnation of the idea of progress. He wanted to be romantic, to be ruled by his passions—and now that he was, he hated it.

There seemed to be a basic flaw in Harris' design, which Dr. Pointers grimly noted he never would have found out had it not been for Harris' letter. Harris placed the lodestones inside the Faraday cage. Whereas this would drain the ghost, if the ghost chose to stay around—the ghost could simply ride on the magnetic forces as they radiated outside the cage.

Now if—and this was a very big "if" indeed—the magnetic forces were placed all around the outside of the cage at the same time—and IF the forces were all of the same magnitude—the ghost could not move free and would remain to be drained.

At last the device was ready. He explained the intricacies of the machine to her. He admitted that he was unsure how to lure the ghost to the trap.

"Why, Alfred," she said, "you must make love to me. That will surely cause Hendrik to show up."

* * *

He had initially protested that this should not be done without the sanction of clergy, but Mary had refused. The clergy had been no help to her in trying to rid herself of the curse, she had abandoned religion for science. He did get her to agree to the rewriting of his will in her favor. After all if he was slain, she would at least have a small fortune to help her carry on.

Alfred Pointers was not a virgin, but it had been so many years since he had engaged in lovemaking that he was greatly afraid he had lost the technique. He almost dreaded that aspect of the coming experiment as much as the appearance of the heartrending ghost.

The night came and she had scented herself with jasmine. She was like fire burning wild in a snow-covered forest. Such pleasure she awoke in him as he could never have dreamed of. Every touch, every smell rising from her yellow hair, every look was a thousand times sweeter than he could believe the saints enjoyed in paradise.

Each new moment was so cuttingly fine that had Satan himself told him that eternal hellfire was the price for another minute, he would have gladly accepted his damnation. As their passion rose, he began to notice a ticking sound such as a small clock would make.

He did not remember having such a clock in his bedroom, but the intensity of the moment was so great that he certainly wasn't going to give further thought to the matter.

Suddenly the sweet smell of jasmine left and the overpowering stench of rotting flesh filled the room. The fire of love chilled in the presence of a great cosmic cold. Mary cried out, "Hendrik!" —and he pulled the bell cord which sprang the trap. The cage unfolded from the ceiling, snapping around the specter like an unwary rabbit. The forty-eight lodestones clicked into place, outside the cage. As he pulled himself free from both Mary and bedclothes, she threw herself from the bed and ran from the room. He made it to the kerosene lantern which had given a tiny light to the scene and quickly turned its wick. As light flooded the room he saw that he had captured the ghost of Hendrik DeJung.

The figure stood a bare five feet tall. He could see the bars of the cage behind it, but this was the least compelling aspect of this mystery. First, the gray eyes, whose intensity told Dr. Pointers that this man had not only looked upon forbidden world, but had stared down some of the dwellers of those worlds. Secondly, the great hole in its chest—a terrible blackened wound that caused Dr. Pointers pain just to look upon it. The figure grew slightly less distinct as he watched; soon it would be dispersed into the earth by his clever cage. Everything would be good by dawn. Dr. Pointers began to dress. He would go find Mary and comfort her, tell her that the battle was won.

"No."

The word had ripped into his mind like a whip.

"No! No, little man you will hear my tale. She has caught you with hers. Now mine. Now the truth. I suffer an eternal damnation because of my love for her."

The Tale of Hendrik DeJung

The words and images poured so swiftly into Dr. Pointers's mind that he lost his sense of self. It seemed that he was living through the experience.

"The great project in 1345 was the digging of a canal to the Schie. My father's father had helped create the land by damming the Rotte. We Dutch are not dependent on God for the creation of the world; God created the world, but we created Holland. My family had money, but I created vast moneys. I finished the building of the triangular walls of what would one day be called the "old" city. I even donated a small amount—some of the burghers said far too small an amount—to building the cathedral. After all perhaps God had some small part in our Dutch success. My money waxed, and I gave with a free hand to all manner of learning and celebration. There was not a scholar in the low countries that knew not of my largess. My wife I loved not, nor she me—but our children were loved by us both. Our marriage was a good alliance, and Mammon blessed all we looked upon.

"When I was forty the pains began. The doctors said that too much rich food had spoiled my life. The priests openly claimed my suffering as the scourge of God. Well perhaps God had turned against me, but my business has always been based on looking for those who would trade for me. I sent for a man known to be in League with the Powers of Darkness. Ludwig Prinn. He came.

"He sold me a heart to replace my ailing flesh. It was a pretty little thing of gears and glass. He caused me to fall into a magical sleep and when I awakened the new heart lived in my chest. Ludwig told me two things about the heart. He said that it would always be linked to me. He said that I could never destroy it since it drew its power from a fundamental core of myself, an inner soul unknown to each of us. Second, immortality was not a simple matter—it wasn't just living forever. Most fools who happen upon eternal life do not perform the mental exercises and arcane rites necessary to insure that their will, their sense of self, survives. They become mad in only a few centuries.

"For many years I lived and prospered in Rotterdam, but Dame Gossip began to point out that perhaps my advanced years might speak an alliance with the Dark One. So at the age of 91 I faked my own death and began to travel Europe and Asia—returning periodically to my beloved Rotterdam where I had to perform certain rites to insure that the force of my will should not fail during the wearing centuries. It was there I met Juliette Roumond, a French serving girl. In my many years of wandering I had grown away from human affections and feelings. I thought that I had died to such, but her sweetness of smile, the fire in her eyes, all and everything caused love to return to my chest like a phoenix to its burning nest of myrrh. I would share with her my immortality, vast wealth, wisdom and knowledge, my strange powers gained during my long maturity.

She seemed to return my love, to share my love of the mysterious, to long for the long life of adventure I promised her.

All went well until she developed the same sort of chest pains that had led to my change three hundred years before. I had not learned enough arcana to construct for Juliette a heart such as mine. I tried to contact Ludwig Prinn, but it seemed that he had in fact fled the very earth to a place which at that time I could not fathom, but now know too well.

There was a rumor that he dwelt in New Amsterdam, so we sailed. Juliette grew worse and worse. Perhaps another heart attack would end her life. We reached the New World, but Prinn could not be found. What was I to do? Could I lose the woman who was life itself to me?

I found a surgeon who would perform the needful task. He would cut from me my magical heart and place it in Juliette's chest. I was willing to die because I loved her so. I died that she might live. I had enjoyed three lifetimes by that point, and maybe I was longing for the peace that I thought death would bring.

But my death was not an end of my consciousness. I had strengthened my will over the years so that I could face the pains and pleasures of immortality.

I went to another... place. I cannot describe it to living men, but from that dimension I could look into the world of men.

But I was not wholly free from the world of men. When the heart, my precious heart, beats too quickly—it pulls me to the world again. I ache wildly with pain, and I go mad. I cannot kill Juliette, no matter what she calls herself: Mary, Sarah, Constance, Amanda. I cannot touch the body with the heart. But her use of my unknown soul drives me to an unbelievable pain. I long to destroy her and the heart, but I cannot. So in my madness and rage I rip out the hearts of her lovers. I have brought painful death to hundreds of men. You have at least freed me from my torment. But like all who love Juliette, yours is just beginning."

* * *

When Dr. Pointers regained his sense of self, the cage was empty. He had thought that he would find Mary, and discover if the ghost's tale was true.

She was not in the house.

In fact, she was not in the city.

Someone had seen her taking a carriage with John Hardy, the banker's son. In fact she had often been seen with Mr. Hardy before she came to live at the doctor's home.

He hired men to find her. New York, they said. So he went to New York, to the hotel where Mr. and Mrs. Hardy were said to be.

He had to find out, to know.

So he went one night, intending to force a meeting. He stood before their hotel room ready to call forth with angry knocks his lost love.

But he heard from within the sounds of love, and above all a great ticking—louder and faster than he had heard. He marveled for a moment at the heart fashioned by Ludwig Prinn still faithful to its task after five hundred years.

The ticking was a hundred times louder than when he had made love to her, as were all the other sounds. He had probably never impressed her at all after her hundreds of years and hundreds of lovers.

He turned and left. The next year yellow fever began burning Memphis as the Yankees had burned Atlanta; he returned to his practice, and forsook spiritualism entirely. He died a community hero, with only one well-known eccentricity: he could not tolerate the sound of a clock.

He was sometimes tormented by young boys in this fashion when they wished to see him cry.

MS. ADAMS
By Beecher Smith

1

Blake Stuart slumped at the hopelessly antiquated classroom desk he would occupy three nights a week his final semester at Rhodes College. He silently cursed both the Dean and his scholastic advisor for not telling him until registration that he needed this course in ancient history to graduate. Who cared about people and events that happened centuries ago?

He already anticipated graduation and a posh job awaiting him at his father's bank. Money and women were the two things he loved most. After graduating he could make money and meet more women. Campus co-eds were starting to shun him because of his well-deserved reputation for dating a girl until she gave in, then dumping her. His last conquest had been a naive AOΠ. Her sorority sisters were spreading the word across campus that he was a *devil*.

He didn't mean to hurt anybody; he just wasn't ready to settle down. Campus gossip made it difficult for him to find new flesh. All he wanted was a little healthy excitement. Why couldn't the co-eds be better sports?

His only consolation about this course would be having Dr. Bill Watkins for the instructor. Like most of his fellow students, Blake deeply admired the semi-retired Episcopal priest, who, despite his Ph.D. in history, could make even the dullest subject seem interesting. So far Blake had only known Bill through church and Sunday school—the few and irregular times Blake went.

As he waited for Bill to arrive, Blake noticed an attractive older woman of Armenian or Lebanese extraction—obviously in the adult degree program—take the seat to his right. She was probably in her mid-fifties, but still gorgeous.

She wore her gray-streaked hair pulled neatly back. Her scant makeup softened the few wrinkles on her face. Her lips appeared full and red without lipstick.

But it was her eyes that captured Blake's attention—large and green, like those of a jungle cat, hypnotically wild and exotic, hinting of forbidden knowledge and the lure of far-away lands. As they made contact with Blake's, she smiled, as though saying, "I'd like to get to know you better—under the right circumstances."

She dressed like a co-ed, amply filling out her navy cashmere pullover sweater and designer jeans. He marveled at the slender shapeliness of her hips and thighs.

Blake's assessment was interrupted by Bill Watkins' arrival. True to form, Bill immediately introduced himself and called roll. When he spoke the name of Lily Adams, the lady raised her hand.

When Bill came to Blake's name, he paused. "Ladies and gentlemen," the professor announced, his droll tone signaling the coming joke, "we are honored to have in our midst a young man who almost slipped through his *entire college education* without being exposed to a single one of the liberal arts! Mr. Stuart, a business major, must suffer through this *history course* in order to graduate."

Mild laughter emanated from the class. Blake felt a blush come into his cheeks. Glancing to his right, he caught Lily's smile.

Dr. Watkins proceeded so smoothly with his lecture that the forty-five minutes allotted seemed more like five. Blake's mind had not wandered once throughout the entire time. He and the rest of the class had sat spellbound listening to their professor speak about the pantheon of Assyrian deities, their account of Creation, and of Prince Gilgamesh and his adventures with the wild man Enkidu.

Afterward, so many of the students asked Bill questions that he ran out of time. When Blake sought his professor friend in the hall, he found Bill involved in an intense discussion with Lily. He felt odd that neither acknowledged his presence.

When he overheard Bill invite her for coffee, without him, he felt snubbed. And what about Bill's wife? How would she feel if she heard any gossip about him having coffee with Lily? Enid Watkins wasn't known to be jealous or shrewish, but if Bill were to have an affair, that would certainly put their marriage to the test.

Blake had other assignments and needed to study. He would have to follow up on these matters Wednesday night.

2

To Blake's surprise, when Lily entered the classroom for the next evening of the course, she seemed much younger. She appeared taller, slimmer and more full-busted. Her face showed no wrinkles. Her hair was now a raven black, without the least hint of dye. However, her haunting, hypnotic smile was unmistakably the same.

When Bill entered, an audible gasp arose from the students. Generally considered robust and youthful for a man in his early sixties, the professor now bore the demeanor of an octogenarian. He walked with a shambling gate, using a cane. His shoulders, militarily erect two nights ago, were now stooped. Even with glasses he was having difficulty seeing. When he spoke, his formerly resonant voice cracked and quavered.

What had happened in 48 hours? What had caused Bill to age and Lily to grow younger? Oddly, no one but Blake seemed to notice Lily's change, but Bill's metamorphosis was obvious to all.

In his diminished state Bill attempted to give his lecture. Every so often he would pause and struggle for breath. When he finished he announced, "I must... leave early... this evening. We'll start the next session with any questions about tonight."

His eyes scrupulously avoided Lily, but when they met Blake's, for an instant Blake felt he saw in them something frightened and fleeing—a feeling reinforced as he watched the elderly professor shuffle hurriedly from the room, ahead of his students.

In the hall Blake felt a tap on his shoulder. He turned around. Lily was smiling radiantly at him. "Have you got a moment? I had trouble hearing Dr. Watkins. He's such a silly *old* thing."

Normally her derogatory remark about Bill would have offended Blake, but for some reason it didn't register.

"Would you mind reviewing your notes with me?" Lily asked. "We could do it over coffee, or something stronger, if you don't mind being with an 'old lady'?"

Blake laughed. To his surprise, he suddenly found her exceptionally beautiful and entertaining. How could he have previously questioned the motives of such an attractive person? Besides she couldn't be *that* much older. Maybe ten or twelve years? Monday night he had thought her at least thirty years his senior, but he must have been wrong.

"My notes are at your disposal," he said, bowing gallantly to her, as he'd seen Errol Flynn do to Olivia de Haviland on the late-late show, and asked, "Where should we go?"

"Let's try the Student Center."

Blake enjoyed reviewing with her the scribbled entries about the reign of Sargon of Assyria. He wasn't sure if he had suddenly developed an interest in history or in Lily.

When they were almost finished, she announced, "I'm hungry,how about you?"

His stomach answered with a growl. She glanced briefly toward his midsection, then giggled like a high school girl, "That answers my question. Where should we go?"

He drove them in his Tercel to Alex's Pub on Jackson Avenue, one of the most popular neighborhood spots for a cold mug of beer and a quick, tasty burger. He ordered cheeseburgers and drafts for them both.

While he ate and drank, she told him how she had returned to complete her degree. A career nurse who had seen much of the world, her doctor husband had recently died, leaving her a wealthy, bored, childless widow.

Something about the lilting quality of her voice mesmerized him. Her life story was probably no different from those of many other widows, but to him it took on epic dimensions. He found himself wanting to redeem her from monotony and boredom, to be her knight-errant, her Sir Lancelot. Blake wondered if he could coax her into the sack. Obviously not unless she *wanted* to. She seemed so totally in control.

At Lily's commands, the bartender kept refilling Blake's mug. He noticed that she was barely halfway through her first beer, while he was on his fourth. His watch said it was eleven-fifteen.

He blurted out, "I didn't realize it was so late."

With a canny smile she responded, "Time means nothing to me." She opened her purse and retrieved a twenty from her billfold. Laying the bill on the table, she rose and asked, "Are you all right to drive?"

"Piece of cake," he responded, but noticed himself speaking with a slight slur.

When he drove into the college parking lot, she pointed to a top-of-the-line model Mercedes. "That's mine," she told him. As he stopped, he hoped she would at least allow him to steal a kiss. Instead, she bolted for her car.

His hopes rose, however, when she turned around before getting in, and asked, "Do you live nearby?"

"Yes."

"Why don't I follow, to make sure you get home safely?"

He didn't like being mothered, but agreed to let her trail him to his duplex apartment. Maybe she would come in, but not likely.

He parked in the driveway, stepped from his Tercel, and waved to her, expecting her to drive off. Instead, she pulled into the driveway and got out of her car.

In the dark she could have passed for a co-ed. She moved close to him. "Why don't you show me around?"

Was this a come-on or what? Now *she* was hitting on him. The four beers had released all his inhibitions. As good as she looked, she could hit away.

"It's pretty messy. I haven't had time to clean up since summer vacation." He unlocked the solid oak door and ushered her in, hoping the place wouldn't gross her out.

She must have sensed his thoughts. With a laugh she exclaimed, "This *looks* like a student's apartment!" Her voice dropped to a throaty and sensuous tone. "Show me your room." It was more a command than a suggestion.

Meekly, like a grade school student obeying his teacher, he led her down the tiny hall to his small bedroom. Had he been sober, his unmade bed with the wrinkled, week-old sheets would have been an embarrassment.

But Lily did not allow him to think about it. Instead she pressed close to him. Her green eyes shimmered and held him fixed. She moved closer, inches from his face. He suddenly wanted desperately to kiss her. He brushed her lips, before she gracefully backed away.

"We'd better not," she protested, turning her gaze modestly toward the floor. "You don't know how vulnerable I am."

Blake struggled from his repertoire of cliches for the right one. He let his face become serious. "We're all vulnerable. It all depends on where we put our *trust*." He'd found the right buzz word.

"I—I'd like to trust you, Blake." She had taken the bait. Now he had to reel her in.

He stood with arms outstretched for her. "That's why I'm here—for you, Lily!"

She came to him and kissed him hard, passionately. Her arms closed around him, then slowly, like kitten's paws, her hands traced down his spine. Her lips parted and he darted his tongue into her mouth.

Lily broke away, panting, "You devil!"

With a tantalizing smile she drew close and gave him another smoldering kiss. She cupped his buttocks the way he had done to so many women.

He responded by grinding his lust-inflamed groin against her. Yes, he desired her, but what was the nagging sensation he also felt—something sinister, lurking beneath the guise of the demure widow?

He withdrew one arm and flicked off the overhead light. Spinning her around, they tumbled onto the bed. In an instant she was struggling out of her clothing and undergarments, as he fumbled free from his own.

It was pure, raw animal sex, but as engulfing and consuming as the vortex of a tornado. Blake was caught in her physical sensuousness and never wanted their coupling to end. Her kisses seemed to suck the very life out of him, and, at the moment he didn't care if he died, so long as it happened while fulfilling his lust with her.

Within moments he experienced the most powerful orgasm of his life. Once it subsided, he collapsed into deep sleep.

3

At first there was only oblivion. Then a floating sensation. No—he wasn't floating—he was flying! Was he having an out of body experience or merely dreaming? Ahead was a circle of glorious light. He headed toward it. Now he was in the sky, like Superman, soaring over a barren desert with the Sun over his shoulder. The ground became verdant and lined with streams and rivers. In the distance he saw an ancient Mesopotamian city. As he came closer he beheld a tremendous procession of people, all elaborately dressed and sad-faced, thronging into the metropolis. Many were weeping.

In the center of the city stood a great ziggurat on which lay the body of a dead king atop a funeral pyre, waiting to be lighted. The dead king had Bill Watkins' face! Startled, Blake screamed. The scene vanished.

Darkness again overtook him as his "dreams" continued.

Earthbound, he found himself standing naked, amid lush semitropical vegetation, unbothered by insects. All about him stood trees bearing every type of fruit imaginable—pears, peaches, oranges, grapefruit, pomegranates, and cherries—all ripe and ready to be picked. But no apples. Because he especially liked them he noticed their absence. He was hungry and began an impromptu feast.

A rustling sound distracted him. He turned to see Lily, naked and beautiful, walking toward him, smiling, arms outstretched as if to embrace him. In one hand she held an apple.

"Take it," she commanded. "Eat!"

But upon seeing her, his desire shifted.

"No," he replied. "Make love to me first."

She pushed him back. "Not till you eat."

He did not know why he refused, or why he protested in such silly, stilted language, "I cannot. You know it is *forbidden*."

With a haughty laugh she said, "Fool!" and turned from him.

At that moment another naked man appeared from the bushes and stood behind her. He was black-skinned, but with otherwise Caucasian features, like a Moor. The pupils of his yellow eyes were convex, reptilian. Tiny spiked horns protruded above his temples and, from behind, he flicked a scaly tale, like a lizard that walked upright.

The Dark Man embraced Lily, who eagerly responded by sticking her tongue into his mouth. He withdrew from her smoldering kiss, threw back his head and, with a hollow, mocking laugh at Blake, declared, "Did you not know she is and always has been *mine* alone? Why do you think the hated Almighty made the *second* woman from your rib?"

At that point Blake felt embarrassment and shame at his own nudity. A chill coursed through his body, causing him to tremble violently. He was still shaking when he awakened, alone on his bed with the covers thrown on the floor. The first gray light of dawn came filtering through the blinds.

4

He rose and ran throughout his apartment to see if Lily might still be there. Her absence confirmed, his almost-bursting bladder drove him to the bathroom for relief. As he stood over the toilet bowl, his reflection in the mirror caught his attention. What he saw sent shock waves throughout his body. It was his face all right, with its blue eyes and coppery blond hair, but—lined and gray at the temples—he looked like a fifty-year-old! What had Lily done to him?

Pulling on his clothes, he tried to run the three short blocks to the Rhodes campus infirmary, until his wind left him. That had never happened before. Usually he was good for at least two miles.

He found the door locked. It was early. But he needed help, so he rang the bell and pounded on the door until a fat nurse opened it. His Angel of Mercy stared disdainfully at him with piggish, watery blue eyes. "What do you want?"

"I need a doctor."

She rolled her eyes and exhaled loudly. "So does everyone else. He'll be in at ten. You can wait or come back. Either way you'll need to fill out a form." Opening the door wider, she motioned toward a stack on the receptionist's desk. "Take one and complete it so the doctor can see you. Also, you need to sign the book."

A patients' registry on the desk caught his attention. The last name on it was "Bill Watkins." Beside it another hand had entered the notation, "Ambulance."

"What happened to Dr. Watkins?" Blake asked.

She waddled to the desk and examined the entry. "Dunno. I wasn't here last night. Looks like he had to be taken to the emergency room."

"Where?"

She gave him the name of the new east Memphis hospital.

Blake handed her back the blank patient card. "Forget it. I'm going there."

The drive took thirty minutes, the wait for a doctor another forty-five. Finally he was referred to a Dr. Steele, an internist in his mid-thirties. As soon as the exam was over, the doctor said, "Please come to my office."

Steele scratched his high forehead and smoothed back his thinning black hair as he looked over Blake's chart. "I'm a *gerontologist*, Mr. Stuart. That's a fancy term for a doctor who looks after older patients."

"I understand. Why are you seeing me? I'm only twenty-one."

Steele's brown eyes blazed in deadly earnestness. "Chronologically. Physiologically you're almost fifty, as you suspected when you came to us."

Hearing the chilling confirmation, Blake shuddered. "What can you do to help me?"

Steele shook his head. "Not much. You appear to be suffering from a rare disease called *pernicious progeria*—an abnormally rapid aging process which causes a person to age by hours instead of years. It brings premature death. I'm sorry. There's no known cure. We can treat you with vitamin injections, liver extracts, and iron supplements, all of which might slow down or even arrest the process temporarily."

"But," Blake responded, "no matter what you do, I'm going to die soon, right, Doc?"

Steele coughed and cleared his throat. "Right."

"Please," Blake protested, "I don't want your *sympathy*."

Steele straightened and drew in a deep breath. "Mr. Stuart, I *do sympathize*. What's really weird is that, whereas most gerontologists would never see a case like yours in their whole career, you are my *third*... I saw the *second* last night!"

Blake felt his legs turning to jelly and hastily sat down. In a weak voice he whispered, "Bill Watkins?"

Steele's eyes widened. "You know?"

Blake stated wryly, "Maybe it wasn't a coincidence. Can Bill have visitors?"

5

With a pass from Dr. Steele, Blake entered Bill's room in the intensive care ward. The nurse at the reception desk told him that Bill was awake and alert, Mrs. Watkins having just left.

Upon seeing Blake, Bill's rheumy eyes brightened. Weakly, almost inaudibly, he said, "Glad you came."

"What happened, Bill?"

Watkins pointed toward the gray on Blake's temple and rasped, "I think you already know—Lily!"

With a macabre laugh Blake replied, "Yes. Who is she? *What* is she? How could she do this to us? Why?"

Bill pointed at the oxygen tank, from which two small green plastic hoses extended to his nostrils. He motioned for Blake to turn up the flow.

Breathing better, Bill answered, "Someone... something... as *old* as mankind... and more *evil* than sin. Too bad she got you, too. Too weak... to explain.

"You'll figure it out. Go... my home. Old encyclopedia. Under 'L.'—'Lily.' Look it up. Read... carefully. *All... of... it.*

"Ask my wife for the 'wedding pennies.' She'll know.... Use them. Hurry." His voice grew progressively weaker. When he finished, he closed his eyes and fell into an exhausted sleep.

In the hall Blake asked Steele, "You spoke about another case? Tell me."

Steele shook his head. "It wouldn't be ethical."

"Please. You must. My life... and Bill's depend on it."

Steele shepherded Blake into his office. "All right, if it'll help, here goes. That first case was a doctor on our staff—Richard Adams."

Blake asked, "You said 'was.' What happened?"

An expression of hopelessness and frustration spread over Steele's face. "Richard was my friend. He'd been through a nasty divorce and needed to get away. Traveled to the Middle East—one of those half-assed tax deductible conferences. Anyway, he met Lily, this nurse about his age—mid-forties—and married her. He came home looking tired. We thought it was from travel.

"Lily started working in the maternity ward. Within a couple of weeks there was a rash of S.I.D.S. cases—Sudden Infant Death Syndrome—four baby deaths at the hospital. One minute they're normal and healthy, next minute they're dead. No explanation.

"Two deaths occurred during Lily's first week at the ward. There was no evidence of wrongdoing. However, after the second death people became suspicious. When a third infant died, nobody believed it was coincidental. After the fourth occurred, Lily Adams resigned from the hospital.

"After that, Richard's health steadily deteriorated. He aged abnormally. Lily stayed at home and cared for him, but he died in six weeks, his body completely worn out—a fifty-seven-year-old man with the physiology of a ninety-year-old."

Blake thanked Steele and left. Perhaps the information at Bill's home would help.

6

Patient, plodding, sweet Enid Watkins ushered Blake into Bill's study, where he found the ancient encyclopedia and looked under "L." There was nothing about a Lily, but there was an entry for "Lilis"—more commonly known as Lilith. In wonder, Blake read the account from ancient Hebrew and Babylonian mythology about the first woman. The reason Eve had been created from Adam's rib was that God had made her predecessor from dust, like Adam.

Lilith had been a failure. She refused to serve both God and her husband. She had tempted and teased Adam without ever submitting to him, choosing instead, to serve Satan and become his concubine, the mother of all demons—a murderous phantasm who sucks the breath of life from the newborn as well as older victims to preserve her youth. And Blake now knew she was *no myth*, but only too terribly real.

Although the article made him shudder, Blake smiled when he came to the part that explained how superstitious Hebrews and Christians dealt with Lilith. Closing the volume and tucking it beneath his arm, Blake asked Enid, "Bill wondered if you could find the 'wedding pennies' for me. Do you mind?"

Enid hurried upstairs and returned a few minutes later, carrying a small white cardboard box. She handed it to Blake and said, "I think these are what he wants—our wedding present from some Mennonite friends."

Lifting the lid, Blake found six old copper English pennies and a tiny parchment scroll. Each penny had etched upon both sides the letters "A-T-L." Unrolling the scroll, Blake read, "...For onlie bye banishing her forevere can ye recouver what the dæmonness hath stolyn."

Hope filled his heart and made him smile. "Thanks, Enid."

At the door, she gave him a concerned look. "What's happened to Bill? He won't talk. I'm quite worried."

"I can't explain, but something tells me Bill's going to get much better, and *soon*." He kissed her affectionately on the cheek and left. He now had his plan.

7

A teaching assistant filled in for Bill at the next class. Blake noticed the empty desk where Lily usually sat. Would she come tonight? Two minutes after the lecture began, she entered. As she seated herself, she glanced at him, barely acknowledging his presence. She looked no older than twenty.

Upon the end of the lecture, she left the classroom, oblivious to him, as though their intimacy 48 hours ago had not happened. He chased after her with middle-aged awkwardness.

Panting, he overtook her. "Can you spare a few minutes? Tonight I'm the one who had trouble taking notes. Can we go over yours?

At first she looked disdainfully at him. Then her face softened. "Oh, all right."

He moved close to her and whispered, "Is my place okay?"

Hesitantly she replied, "I suppose so. But you look tired. I'd better not stay long."

She followed him home in her Mercedes.

Once inside, suppressing his fear and revulsion, he struggled to maintain his role as a Lothario. He moved close and kissed her.

She broke away. "I thought we came here to review my notes?"

He kissed her again. This time she yielded. Easily. Too easily. He felt his strength being sapped by her—in such a way that he *wanted* her to take it.

Summoning his utmost will power, he broke from her embrace. "Let's go to my room. It's more comfortable."

Without a word, she followed. Her face bore the smug expression of a cat who has just thrust its head inside the canary's cage and knows nobody is around to stop it.

Once in his bedroom, she peeled off her clothing, shimmying exotically, enticing him with the removal of each article, until she was completely naked. Then she slipped between the covers. With a smile she said, "Come on. I'll make it even *better* than last time."

"How about some music?" Blake asked.

A puzzled expression passed momentarily across her face. Then the alluring smile returned. "Whatever."

He pressed a button on the jam box and reached toward his jeans, as if to unfasten them. Instead he pulled the last of the six old English pennies from his pocket and flipped it on top of her abdomen, at the exact moment "Brahms' Lullaby" began playing.

The dulcet musical strains invoked demonic shrieks from Lily. She writhed beneath the penny, which pinned her down as though it were a two-ton boulder.

In a horrible, rasping voice, she screamed, "Stop that infernal music. Release me—or you'll never see the end of the suffering that I and *my Master* will inflict on you!"

Blake laughed. Thank God his plan was working. "Shut up, bitch. You're the one who's gonna suffer!" He turned up the volume as loud as it would go.

Her shrieks almost drowned out the music.

Thank God, the instructions on the scroll had worked!

Five of the six pennies—one placed in each corner of the room and one outside in the hall, opposite the bedroom door—formed a pentagram, which, coupled with the sixth on Lily's stomach at the center, effectively imprisoned her. All bore the inscription "A.T.L."—"Avaunt Thee, Lilith!" At the same time she was being tormented by Brahms' Lullaby—set on continuous play—the most famous of all lullabies—songs originally composed to make "Lilith begone!"

Her once beautiful face withered into that of a hideous crone. The rest of her body shriveled almost into a skeleton.

"All right," she conceded, "what do you want to release me?"

Blake thought carefully, while Lily continued to scream and thrash. He hoped the neighbors wouldn't call the police. "Can you give me back my youth and health?"

"Yes."

"How about Bill? Can you restore him, too?"

"It is *done*. Now LET ME GO."

"Not so fast." The song replayed for the third time, sending her into further convulsions.

Weeping demonic tears, she asked, "What *more* do you want?"

Jackpot time. "Okay. I'm not gonna be greedy. You've put Bill and me through a lot of grief. We deserve to be properly compensated. How about giving us both ten years more of life than we would have had, all in excellent health?"

"Yes. You have them. Now free me."

"Not yet. Suppose I wanted the passbooks to all Swiss bank accounts of a certain Middle Eastern dictator who recently got his butt kicked by the U.S.A. over in the Persian Gulf. Could you do that?"

A purple vapor appeared over the dresser. When it dissipated, Blake noticed six small numbered plastic folios. He examined one and found it represented several hundred million Swiss francs.

"Release me," she demanded. "Now!"

"Two final stipulations—first, that you must leave the United States and never return."

"Agreed. And?"

"There must be no repercussions against me, Bill, or any of our loved ones. Ever. Understood?"

With hate in her reddened eyes she answered, "Yes. Of all the vain, arrogant mortals I have ever dealt with, you drive the hardest bargain. You really are a *devil!* Now do your part."

Cautiously, he lifted the penny from her abdomen and prayed she would keep her word. Immediately she transformed herself into a cloud of violet mist. His bedroom window suddenly shattered. The vapor filtered out through the blinds, into the night.

Then Blake was alone, with six Swiss bank passbooks.

He rushed outside. Lily's Mercedes was gone. Frantically, he jumped into his Tercel and drove to the hospital.

8

Racing to Bill's room, he found his friend once more the picture of health—robust for a man in his early sixties—except unable to recall why he had been admitted to the hospital and complaining mightily that he should be released right away.

Blake would share both the knowledge and the money in due time with his older friend, but first he had to check himself.

In the private restroom he studied his face in the mirror. To his great relief it was again that of a twenty-one-year-old—except for the unnaturally light, almost white streaks in his otherwise copper hair at the temples, turning up stubbornly in tufts on each side of his head, resembling horns.

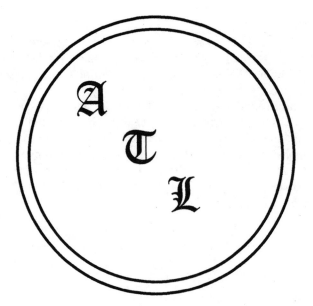

"Avaunt Thee, Lilith!"

"They shall name the place
No Kingdom There, and all
its princes shall be
nothing... There too
Lilith shall repose
and find a place to rest."

— Isaiah 34: 12-14

Number One With a Bullet
By Scott Sigler

Cutter peeked around the overflowing dumpster, blinking stinging sweat from his eyes. The buildings blocked glaring streetlights, draping shadows across the empty alley. Empty. But not for long. Patterson was out there. Waiting. Hunting.

Cutter ducked his head back behind the dumpster's dark cover. He popped the last clip out of his Beretta; three bullets left. He slammed the clip back and wiped at the sweat on his face. His jacket sleeve—already soaked through—did little more than spread the moisture around. Even at 3:00 a.m. sweat drained from his every pore. He should have known better than to bring a wool suit to Memphis. He kept the jacket on because it was dark; it covered his blood-drenched white dress shirt.

The garbage reeked and he smelled like piss. His lungs burned with needle-like poking pains and his stomach threatened to heave up dinner. He had to start running again, try and get to the car and get the fuck out of there. If he didn't, he'd go mad or die or likely both.

All because of football.

* * *

Lawrence Cutter eagerly stepped off the plane. He hadn't been to Tennessee in years and never to Memphis. Hopefully he could take care of this Patterson business quickly and get on with enjoying the city.

He worked for NFL Security, a secretive collection of 30-odd ex-CIA and FBI agents who "researched" NFL players and prospective rookies. Cutter's main job was Draft Candidate Risk Analysis. He rarely dealt with established players. Tracking the comings and goings of world-famous people like Steve Young or a Deion Sanders was a cakewalk. The media mostly took care of that.

Keeping track of the kids was the tough job; kids who were nobodies before football-field fame endeared them to NFL owners and coaches—and who kept tabs on nobodies? These kids came from all walks of life, from Iowa farm boy to East St. Louis gang-banger. Every kid had some off-field dirt clinging to the ol' spikes. That was Cutter's job; find the dirt for the edification of NFL franchises.

At the height of his FBI career, he'd investigated dangerous people. People with guns. People willing to kill. He'd been shot at three times (never hit) and stabbed once in the arm. That took 27 stitches. Made a helluva scar, which he loved to show off after the fifth or sixth Jim Beam & Coke.

Those dangerous days were behind him. These were just kids, after all—snot-nosed brats born with the gift of football. It never occurred to these kids that 30 ex-FBI agents were researching their collective pasts, examining police reports, team disciplinary actions, wrist-slaps by the college. Compared to terrorists, drug-ring enforcers and nutcase assassins, the kids didn't pose much of a threat. The kids were *safe*—and that was just the way Cutter liked it.

Luke Moore waited for him in the terminal. Luke looked closer to fat than skinny, although he was neither. Luke had paid his dues in the CIA's snoop shop. He could find out anything about anybody. He was normally a warm, jovial man, but that day a severe look dominated Luke's face.

"Hello, Luke!" Cutter beamed extending his hand. "You look about as happy as a dickless dog."

"Wish I could be that happy," Luke responded coolly, shaking Cutter's hand. "Let's go. We can talk in the car."

Cutter didn't bother with further small talk—they collected his luggage and headed to Luke's Acura. The new leather seats had cooked in the afternoon sun, filling the car with a rich, hot smell.

"I've found more, Cutter," Luke said as they drove away from the airport. "It's bad. If his ex-girlfriend is telling the truth, Eugene Patterson is the biggest nightmare the NFL has ever seen."

Cutter sighed, looking out the window at the beautiful Tennessee weather. Such news made the day hard to enjoy. This wasn't what the league wanted to hear. Not about Eugene Patterson.

Every year NFL Security found rather compelling dirt on several players. Drugs, violence, alcoholism, steroids; many things defined a candidate as a "risk"—a multimillion dollar risk. Sometimes franchises took a chance and drafted these players anyway. Sometimes the players worked out, but more often than not they proved to be financial and public-relations burdens. Those players were simply a waste, and in the NFL a wasted draft pick was considered far worse than original sin.

Every couple of years such a questionable player turned out to be a projected high first-round pick, an electrifying young talent who could jump-start any franchise. Eugene Patterson was that and more. Most analysts figured Nashville would take him with the first pick of the draft. It was, as they say, a no-brainer. Cutter could hear the

Commissioner's voice on draft day— *the Nashville Oilers select, with the first pick of the first round, Eugene Patterson from the University of Memphis.* Patterson would mug for the cameras with his perfect smile, his #1 jersey and a Nashville Oilers' cap.

Patterson was a beast of a man, 6-4, 265 pounds, yet impossibly quick with great acceleration and speed. He was a brutal, savage player; his bone-crushing hits often ended careers. On ESPN's Sports Center, Chris Burman showcased Patterson's vicious hits with the now-ubiquitous phrase "and here comes the Pitter-Patterson of little feet! BOOM!" Patterson's skills led the Tigers to a second-place finish in Conference USA and a Top-20 placing in the final AP poll. He was a once-in-a-generation talent. Some coaches even said he was better than Butkus.

In addition to a surplus of talent, Patterson had poster-boy good looks and graduated U-of-M with a 3.81 average in Criminal Law. He was a member of the Baptist church, a community volunteer, and in general a very classy young man. Madison Avenue was already slobbering over his appeal. Rumors abounded about deals with McDonald's, Sprite, Ford and a dozen shoe companies. Patterson had yet to play a down in the pros, and he was already a star.

In short, Eugene Patterson was the NFL's prize of the decade.

That was, of course, until the call from Coletta Williams, Patterson's ex-girlfriend. She'd read a *Sports Illustrated* article on NFL Security and knew what the group could do to a draft prospect's chances. Via the phone, Williams worked her way through the myriad of NFL's corporate offices until she reached Cutter. She had dirt on Patterson. Big dirt. No, she couldn't mention it over the phone. Someone had to come see her. In Memphis. Where Patterson was. Where the dirt was.

It was probably bullshit, some spurned woman out to hurt Patterson any way she could. That or a golddigger, a private in the army of women who try to leach a buck off famous athletes. But as a first-overall draft choice, Patterson would command around 60 million for a five-year contract. With that kind of investment, the owners wanted to be sure. Sure with a capital S. Cutter sent Luke to check it out.

Less than 48 hours after Luke landed in Memphis, he called Cutter.

"So what is it," Cutter had asked. "Did he assault that girl? She pregnant? Drugs? What?"

"It's worse than that," Luke said. "This is some ugly shit. The owners aren't going to like it."

"Luke, what is it?"

"Devil worship," Luke said quietly. "Our boy Patterson is some kind of a Satanist."

Luke related Coletta's wild story. Sounded like bullshit. Crazy-person bullshit. Even so, Cutter booked the next flight to Memphis. If only half her story was true, it was a bad situation for the NFL. Bad with a capital B.

* * *

The NFL would take a chance on players with drug problems, possibly a few convictions, assault charges... hell, just about anything. But a devil-worshiper?

As they drove, Cutter read through Luke's case file on Patterson. The kid's record was spotless, both in high school and at college. What Luke focused on, however, was Patterson's two high school buddies who also attended U-of-M. Darius Klein and Andy Jacoby. The pair's alleged acts included hanging a cat from a dormitory stairwell, scrawling occult symbols on dorm walls in cow's blood, sacrificing German Shepherds and digging up graves to do God-knows-what with the corpses. Jacoby was convicted of the latter. The university quietly expelled him, but he didn't go home to—he still lived in an off-campus apartment with Klein.

Cutter poured over the file. The surveillance pictures of Jacoby and Klein spoke volumes for their character, unless the shots were from October 31st. Klein was a small fellow, wiry, with thick black hair tied up in a long, snaggly pony tail. Jacoby was tall and a bit chubby. He sported a spiral tattoo on each side of his stubbly head. They both dressed all in black, wore a ton of jewelry, and were pierced all over their bodies enough to date a porcupine.

"I bet you wish your daughter would bring home a nice young man like that," Cutter deadpanned.

Luke ignored the remark. "I looked up that tattoo," he said. "It's a symbol of Buranti, a sixth-century Asian demon."

Cutter stared at the ugly black tattoo. It looked like a lumpy snake with a bull's head. "Any significance between this tattoo and the devil-worship thing?"

"Probably," Luke said "Klein's got the same tattoo on his arm."

"What ever happened to '*I love Mom?*'" Cutter mumbled. "Eugene Patterson's childhood buddies, eh?" he spat. "The Oilers will love this. Have you seen him with these upstanding young men?"

"Only once," Luke replied. "Patterson seems to know they're bad news. He isn't seen in public with them, but Coletta said he's with them every Thursday evening, so we might catch them tonight."

"Is she still in Memphis?"

"She is and she's scared shitless," Luke replied in a monotone. "We're going to see her right now. She lives on Poplar Avenue in some student apartments. She waited until graduation and now she's getting the hell out of Dodge."

"I think she's nuts, but I want to hear that bullshit story of hers with my own ears, "Cutter said. "Take me to her place."

* * *

Stacks of boxes littered the small apartment, each one sealed tightly with packing tape and clearly labeled in neat, black marker on the top and all four sides. The stereo appeared to be the last thing to go; Whitney Houston crooned from the CD player.

Coletta was tall and graceful, with light-brown skin and long, curly hair tied back in a no-frills ponytail. Her eyes looked bleary and red from lack of sleep.

"We talked on the phone," Cutter said to Coletta after Luke introduced them. "I'm here to listen to your story."

"You're here to see if I'm nuts or full of shit," Coletta said. "I'm neither."

Cutter smiled patiently.

"I'll make this quick," Coletta said. "I haven't talked to the cops about this, and I'm not going to. You subpoena me or tell the press and I'll make you look like a fool. Get the picture?"

"Yes ma'am," Cutter said, still smiling.

"Good," Coletta said. "Now listen. I'm telling you this because Patterson is a freak. If this screws up his draft chances, that will hurt him, and that's good enough for me."

She lifted her hair and turned her head. "See this scar?" she asked. Cutter couldn't miss it. He counted at least 20 stitches running from her right temple down below her ear.

"Twenty-five stitches," Coletta said. "That's what the bastard did to me."

"Why didn't you go to the police?" Cutter asked.

"If I went to the police ... he'd kill me."

Cutter saw she fully believed that. "Can you tell me the part about the devil worship?" he said.

"It's not devil worship," Coletta said. "We'd dated for six months when he told me he was this spiritual leader. He wanted me to join this—"church." I was shocked, but I loved him at the time. I went with him to a ceremony. I thought I could get him out of whatever it was. Power of love and all that, you know?

"I thought it might be some college kids and a Ouija board or some candlemass thing. I didn't know what to expect. He went out with Andy and Darius every Thursday night. Just the boys, you know? No girlfriends allowed."

Coletta's eyes showed fear, but also fury. She was almost shaking with anger, a proud woman who wasn't about to submit helplessly to some man slapping her around.

"We went to Andy's house on Watuga Street, just west of the main campus. The house has a huge basement, really dark, a lot of little rooms—it's like a dungeon. There's this fire-pit thing in the back of the basement. They had a dog. People chanted some shit I didn't recognize. I thought it was all a big joke on me, but... they... they killed the dog with a knife. They used the blood to smear these weird symbols all over the basement. Eugene wasn't just a part of it. He was in *charge*. He called the shots. There was blood everywhere, but none on him."

"I was scared shitless. When we got back here I told him I never wanted to see him again. That's when he did this— *"thing"* —to his hands and cut me."

"'Thing' to his hands?" Cutter asked. Luke had told him the story over the phone, but he still wanted to hear it from the horse's mouth. Even crazy people sometimes base their fiction on an ounce of truth.

"Yeah," Coletta said in a whisper. "His hands changed, like that morphing thing they do in the movies, you know? His hand turned into this gray *thing* with claws on the end. Used it to cut me. Said if I went to the police he'd kill me. I know that sounds crazy but I don't care, it happened. Just go to the house. It's Thursday and they'll have their weekly little dog-killing party."

She glared at Cutter defiantly, almost daring him to call her crazy. Cutter showed no emotion.

"Ms. Williams," Cutter said. "One final question and then we'll leave you alone. I have to ask you flat out, just to make sure I didn't misunderstand. Do Eugene Patterson, Darius Klein and Andy Jacoby worship the devil together?"

Her face wrinkled slightly with confusion, only for a second, and then her eyes widened with understanding. "No, you don't get it," she said softly. "This has nothing to do with devil worship. Andy and Darius and the others at the ceremony don't worship the devil.

"They worship Eugene."

* * *

"I see why you brought me in, Luke, you did the right thing," Cutter said, staring out the window at the explosion of spring greenery.

"Crazy fucking story, eh?" Luke said.

"Yeah," Cutter said. "Crazy. She talk to anyone else about this?"

"No one I can find," Luke said. "No cops, no press, no lawyers; as far as I know we're the only ones."

Cutter mulled over the situation. If she was a golddigger why would she throw in that crazy part about Patterson sprouting claws like some movie monster? People would listen to her tales of devil worship and assault; that was guaranteed to get her on talk shows, net movie-of-the-week deals and draw the attention of ambulance-chasing lawyers like flies to shit. But add that claw part and she went from victim to nutcase on 0.02 seconds. No one listens to a nutcase.

"Her story is too fucked up," Cutter mumbled to no one.

"The claw shit, yes," Luke said. "But she may be telling the truth about that dog. Jacoby and Klein have done this shit before."

Cutter nodded. They had to check it out. You couldn't give the NFL hearsay about a payer like Patterson. They needed to know.

"We always treat vindictive ex-girlfriend stories with kid gloves," Cutter said. "Especially *loony* ex-girlfriend stories. Right now Patterson is clean as far as the league is concerned, but we have to know for sure if he's a Satan worshiper. That kind of shit can destroy a whole franchise."

"But she said they don't worship Satan," Luke said quietly. "They worship Patterson."

Cutter said nothing in reply. That comment bothered him as well. Even if she were out for revenge, why would she say something goofy like that? Goofy with a capital G. She could have implicated him as a devil worshiper and been done with it. Odd. Bullshit, sure, but odd.

* * *

It was a delightful part of town. Large old houses lined both sides of the street amid sprawling elm trees that looked heavy and dark in the night. The smell of fresh-cut grass lingered in the heavy air despite the late hour. They drove by Jacoby's house once, then parked four blocks away, well out of sight.

Jacoby's place was a huge three-story affair with ugly fire-escape ladders crossing past almost every window. Some entrepreneur had divided the once-beautiful old house into niche apartments and packed it with college kids. A steady, thin tendril of smoke drifted out of a narrow pipe on the roof.

Cutter and Luke checked their pistols, then quietly moved to the house. Gnarled shrubs grew near the fire escape, enough to cover an entrance into the second floor hallway. Inside the place was a shithole with sagging floors, scratched doors and peeling plaster. Graffiti and posters covered the walls. Some of the graffiti looked ominously obscure. Cutter didn't want to think about what medium the artist used.

They carefully walked through the silent house. Naked bulbs illuminated hand-me-down furniture. Unmade mattresses graced the floor of every room. The place smelled of stale beer, cigarettes and pot.

Just as Coletta predicted, the house was empty. Strange sounds faintly filtered up from the basement. The two NFL Security agents walked softly down creaking stairs to the first floor. The closed basement door was under the stairs, only a few feet from the house's front entrance.

Luke cracked the basement door and peeked in. "I don't see anything down there," he whispered. "If we get into any shit, we come up the stairs and go right out the front. The basement runs the length of the house, so it's big. Coletta said they're in the back. We should be able to go down without being seen."

"Let's go then," Cutter said. "I'll follow you."

Luke descended. Cutter peered through the faint light, watching for potential cover spots every step of the way.

The cinderblock walls were crumbly and faintly damp to the touch. Sand gritted on the concrete floor under their shoes. Cobwebs, invisible in the dark, tickled at their face and hair. Frames without doors gaped at them every few feet, showing the thick blackness of many small rooms. Old, rotting furniture and wet cardboard boxes seemed to cover every inch of the basement. In some places clutter stacked all the way to the ceiling.

They quietly turned a corner, keeping close to the walls. The strange noise solidified into a distant bastard cousin of some Gregorian chant. Cutter didn't recognize a single word. The sound sent a primal chill up his back, made him instinctively uneasy. They moved toward it.

* * *

A fire burned in the center of the floor. Smoke rose up to a wide metal funnel, then up a pipe and out of the basement. The flickering flames fucked with Cutter's night vision.

The number of cultists surprised him. He'd expected maybe three or four, but at least 10 sat in a circle around the fire. The dancing flames cast moving shadows on the chanters' faces. They were all so *young*. College kids with college-kid clothes.

He stopped a good thirty feet from the chanters, crouching behind a sagging Lay-Z-Boy covered with rips and duct tape. He glanced at Luke, who stood about ten feet to his right behind a stack of old Chiquita Banana boxes.

As if on cue, Patterson walked out of the shadows and into the firelight. He stood opposite Cutter's position. *Got you now, you sick little puppy,* Cutter thought. If they were killing a dog tonight, Patterson was finished.

He looked much bigger in person than he had on TV, even without football pads. Perhaps it was because he stood tall while all the chanters sat cross-legged on the floor. Perhaps it was simply because he was monstrous; 6-foot-4, 265 pounds of walking muscle. Dressed in a tight-knit shirt, his rock-solid body took on superhero proportions. Cutter hoped feverishly he wouldn't have to confront this kid tonight. He'd seen the "Pitter-Patterson" of little feet on TV—the kid could hit like a freight train.

Patterson's black eyes were wide and flaring, glistening and flickering in the firelight. His mouth opened in a sick grin of pride as he surveyed the chanters. For the first time in his life, Cutter knew he was looking at something completely evil.

"My children," Patterson's voice boomed across the basement. "The start of our expansion is near."

Cutter recognized Patterson's cultured voice; that and his million-dollar smile made him a media favorite for post-game interviews. Only now the voice didn't talk eagerly of blitzes and team and confidence and all that football rhetoric. Now the tone was dark and much deeper than Cutter remembered.

"Praise Buranti," the chanters said in unison.

Patterson raised his arms and all sound stopped suddenly as if a guillotine had severed the chanters' necks. The fire crackled in the silence.

"Every church needs money, and we are no exception," Patterson said. Cutter thought Patterson sounded like a televangelist, full of passion and over-emphasis.

"Draft day is almost here, and I'm a lock for the first pick. My agent is talking a $10 million signing bonus, and we've got tentative deals with both McDonald's and Nike."

Great. Cutter mused. *Air Evil. I'll run right out and buy a pair.*

Patterson's sermon continued. "In a matter of weeks we'll have $20 million at our disposal. The media will make me an instant celebrity—my influence over young minds will grow stronger. You will all help me spread our church as we travel from city to city."

Cutter stared at the surreal scene. Coletta Williams wasn't a gold-digger; these people *did* worship Patterson. You could see it in their eyes as they looked up adoringly from the floor. He towered above them, arms outstretched in some crucifixion parody.

"Andy, Darius," Patterson called into the other end of the dark basement. "It's time."

Showtime, Cutter thought. They'd kill the dog, then he and Luke could slink way from this fucked-up Vincent Price flick. As a prospect, Eugene Patterson was finished. Finished with a capital F. Stick a fork in him, he's done. When they cut the dog's throat, they'd also be cutting Patterson's.

Dressed all in black, Jacoby and Klein came from the far end of the musty basement. The chanting started up again, louder and more intense, bouncing off the cinder-block walls with a lethal energy. The chanters' circle broke to give them room and suddenly Cutter got a full view of Jacoby, Klein, and the dog.

Only it wasn't a dog. It was a girl.

* * *

Cutter's jaw dropped. Jacoby and Klein dragged the girl inside the chanters' circle. She looked about seventeen or eighteen. She wore jeans and an orange Memphis University Tigers sweatshirt. Tears streaked her face, their trails glistening in the firelight. A bandanna gag masked her sobs. Her wide eyes and shuddering body betrayed her terror. She couldn't have weighed more than 100 pounds soaking wet.

Cutter's mind whirred like a buzz saw. This was way beyond NFL Security matters—the girl's life was in danger. His hand immediately went for his gun, but he stopped himself; Cutter never acted on first impulse, never acted without thinking. He glanced over at Luke, who crouched in the shadows, his weapon already drawn.

"It's time, my children," Patterson shouted over the chanting din. He smiled from ear to ear like a predator closing in on wounded and exhausted prey. "As I promised, you get to see my true form."

He ripped off his shirt, exposing his chiseled frame. His muscled body started to shudder, convulse, as if he were caught in a standing epileptic seizure. Cutter felt the room's ambient energy spike to a new level. The chanting increased in intensity and volume; the excitement felt tangible.

And then Lawrence Cutter discovered that Coletta Williams was far from crazy.

* * *

No wonder he's so fucking good, Cutter mused, and it was the last rational thought of his life. Cutter's eyes gathered information that his brain simply refused to deal with, as if his intellect hung an "out to lunch" sign in the window and quietly slipped out the back door. But he couldn't look away, and his eyes sucked in all the madness before them.

Acid flashback, his vacationing mind decided. *Jerry Garcia has the last laugh.*

Patterson's jaw seemed to wither into his head, wrinkling like a raisin as it shrunk backwards. Only the thin lower lip remained, looking like the blade of a shovel jutting out from Patterson's neck. His eye sockets extended forward like bull horns, ending with bright green eyes instead of points.

Oh, I am not seeing this, Cutter thought.

"Buranti!" The chanter screamed passionately. "Buranti!"

Patterson's thick neck stretched and thinned. His head reached away from his body with a nasty grinding sound. Bony thorns poked through his skin in twin lines running up each side of the elongated neck.

Nope, Cutter thought. *No fucking way.*

The wave of transformations reached Patterson's shoulders. Each arm grew thinner and longer, becoming more graceful, almost as if the bone inside dissolved leaving only coiled muscle. The hands stretched into long, claw-tipped talons. Patterson's pectoral muscles each sprouted another tentacle, identical to those that danced from his shoulders like spasmodic anacondas. His skin quickly turned grayish and took on a pebbly texture. Patterson, or what used to be Patterson, towered over everyone; at least eight feet tall, thin and solid like a scratched piece of lead pipe.

The chants of "Buranti!" and Patterson's transformation noises stopped as if on cue, leaving only the crackling fire and the girl's sobs. His mind blank except for well-honed instincts, Cutter silently pulled his gun and clicked off the safety.

"My children," Patterson called in an inhuman voice. "Let's get this party started! Carve her up and tap the keg!"

Someone hit play on an unseen boom box and heavy, techno dance music filled the basement. The chanters bounced to the heavy synthetic drum beat, but remained seated, watching the girl. Klein held her sagging body by the shoulders. Jacoby produced a huge, ornate knife with a jagged foot-long blade.

The room roared with gunfire, shocking Cutter so badly he pissed himself.

* * *

Luke's two gunshots blasted the still basement like close-range cannons. Jacoby grunted as the bullets slammed into his chest and drove his body backwards. The knife dropped from his hands and clattered to the concrete floor.

The scene instantly shifted from pause to fast-forward. Impossibly quick, Patterson dove for the far shadows. The chanters sprang from their cross-legged positions and scattered like cockroaches.

Luke's gun roared out three more rounds. One bullet caught Klein high up on the right shoulder, spinning him around and dropping him on the dirty concrete like a toy top that's just run out of steam. The bound-and-gagged girl stood alone, frozen in place.

"Cutter, get the girl!" Luke screamed. On auto-pilot, Cutter leapt over the pitted Lay-Z-Boy and sprinted forward. He threw the girl roughly over his shoulder and lumbered toward the stairs.

"Get those motherfuckers!" Patterson hissed, his dark, raspy voice audible over the thumping industrial music. "Don't let them get out!"

Cutter worked his way through the maze of dead furniture and musty boxes. He stumbled forward, encumbered by the wiggling, panicking girl. He heard three more shots off to his left, just before something popped out of the debris to his right. Cutter turned and snapped off four quick shots. He heard a cry of pain and felt a splatter of something hot and wet on his face.

The muzzle flash toasted his slowly adjusting night vision. If he could get to the wall, he could find the stairs and get out. Two more shots rang out from Luke's gun.

"Luke, let's get out of here!" Cutter screamed, working his way through the floor's musty clutter.

Something moved in front of him. He didn't bother checking his target, he just fired twice. Whatever it was flew back and hit the wall, falling in a still lump on the floor.

He reached the wall and slid along its rough, damp surface, keeping a careful hold on the squirming girl. The stairs finally appeared. He turned at the landing and crouched as Luke sprinted around a ratty old dresser, heading for Cutter.

Later he could blame Luke for taking so long, the dim light for not seeing, himself for not paying attention, the girl over his shoulder for blocking his view. Whatever the reason, he didn't see the knife-wielding college boy just off to his right. The kid jumped at Cutter, bringing the Bowie knife down in a vicious arc. It plunged into the girl's back, culling a stifled scream through her bandanna-gag. The boy's weight knocked the three of them over in a pile. He landed face-down on Cutter, whose back hit hard against the concrete floor.

The boy—quick, young and agile—rose to his knees with the knife clutched in his hands, an evil snarl covering his face as he grinned down at Cutter.

Cutter fired at least five times point-blank, ripping the kid's chest to hamburger. Blood showered down in fine droplets and great gouts, covering Cutter's face and chest. He rolled to the girl and felt for a pulse; faint and fading fast. The blade had pierced her heart. Cutter's mind slipped a few more notches.

Luke ran up, his flat-soled shoes clattering loudly against the dirt-strewn concrete.

"She dead?" Luke asked, eyes flickering through the darkness.

"With a capital D," Cutter said, his voice full of panic and bordering on insanity. They both heard movement and fired randomly into the black basement. Cutter led the way as the two bounded up the stairs, heading for safety.

* * *

Cutter reached the top of the stairs and sprinted for the front door, popping a fresh clip into his gun as he exited. Streetlights dimly flickered, illuminating the weed-filled lawn with a surreal, moon-like glow. He'd escaped that madness and was only a short jog from the car, from safety.

Luke exited the door a second later, only he didn't make it all the way out.

Cutter turned to see several tentacles, one clinging tightly to each side of the door frame, one on top of the door itself, and the other wrapped around Luke's chest, lifting him off the ground. Surprised terror etched lines on Luke's face. Patterson's eye-horns peeked out from the door, followed by the rest of his horrific head perched on the long, snakelike neck. His pebbly, gray skin glistened softly under the streetlights, his thin mouth twisted into a grin of evil victory. A blast of fear erupted in Cutter's soul like a mushrooming hollow-point bullet. Luke squirmed in panic, shooting behind himself trying to hit Patterson. The hammer clicked on empty after only two shots.

Cutter's gun came up lightning quick, both hand's firmly on the handle, but Patterson was faster. He effortlessly lifted Luke, blocking the shot.

"Jesus, Cutter!" Luke screamed. "Shoot this fucking thing!"

Patterson's horn-eyes never left Cutter, even for a second, as a free tentacle snaked toward Luke's stomach. The tentacle moved quickly, punching it's way through Luke's shirt and stomach like a huge gray snake sliding into a fleshy burrow. Luke's scream of agony ripped through the street, echoing off the brick walls and fading into the sweltering night.

Nope, Cutter's brain droned. *There's no WAY I'm seeing that!*

Luke's screams stopped as the tentacle suddenly pulled free of the ravaged gut with a squelch and a splatter. Luke's mouth opened, frozen in mid-gasp, eyes staring wide as the blood-slimed tentacle rose up before him—holding his still-beating heart. Cutter didn't know if he could hear its last beats or he just imagined it. The organ's final contractions squirted blood onto the dark, dirt-covered sidewalk.

Time stopped. Luke staring at his own beating heart. Cutter staring at Luke's expression of death. The faint sound of blood splattering on the ground.

The heart hit Cutter in the face with a slapping sound like raw hamburger. It fell to the ground, hot, wet and twitching. Cutter blinked and fell to one knee, automatic instincts his only link to sanity as he brought the gun up once again.

Patterson dropped Luke to the ground and quickly slipped back into the house's shadows, slamming the door shut behind him. Cutter's gun erupted. Bullets splintered through the door.

He stopped firing and looked at his friend. Luke's eyes remained wide, mouth clutching as if trying to find the words to plead for his life. His blood-soaked shirt appeared wet-black under the streetlights. He'd be dead in seconds. Cutter didn't wait that long. Hating himself, he reached into Luke's jacket pocket and grabbed Luke's keys.

He sprinted down the street toward the car. It was like a ghost town—nothing disturbed the night's hot, damp stillness. The sound of far-off traffic faintly faded in like background Muzak. Cutter heard his own footsteps clatter loudly on the street.

It was time to call in the cavalry; cops, FBI, the motherfucking army. Raze this whole area to the ground, whatever it took to take out that thing. All he had to do was reach the carphone.

He saw movement up ahead in the street, possibly human, possibly not. Cutter dashed for the narrow, paved space between a four-unit apartment building and another fire-escape bedecked house. He had to hide. Catch his breath. Re-group and get ready for a dash to the car. An overflowing dumpster filled half the alley. He dove behind it, landing on bags both full and open, sliding into the stinking garbage and the welcome shadows.

* * *

Approaching police sirens scratched at the night. Cops would be here in seconds. Maybe Patterson would hide, maybe he wouldn't. Cutter wasn't taking that chance. Let Memphis' Finest deal with Patterson (*who was NOT, his brain reminded him firmly, some fucking Asian demon*). Cutter was getting to the car and not stopping till he hit Manhattan.

Cutter gripped the gun and stood, madness clutching furtively at his brain. He peeked into the alley: nothing. He took a tentative step forward, pressing his back to the dumpster, sliding along its length. He sucked in a deep breath and cautiously moved out of the alley. Up the street he saw the first flicker of red and blue flashers dance off the trees and houses.

Gotta run, gotta run. Patterson's coming. Coming to get me.
The cop cars screeched to a halt in front of Jacoby's house less than a block away.

Cutter stepped out of the alley and took off at a dead sprint.

He heard fast footsteps accompanied by a snarl a millisecond before something thick and solid and strong slammed into him like a super-sonic wrecking ball. Thickly-muscled arms—human arms—wrapped around Cutter as 265 pounds of pissed-off All-American linebacker drove him into the ground. Cutter's weapon fired once, the bulled harmlessly tore up a divot of grass.

Police flashlights swung toward him, probing the darkness for the shooter. Patterson lithely rolled off Cutter and slipped unseen into the shadows.

Nope, I didn't see that either, Cutter's mind mused just before sliding into darkness, *but I heard it coming, I sure as fuck did.*

* * *

"That's your story, Mr. Cutter?" Memphis Assistant DA Kelly Fife asked incredulously. "You're saying that you and your partner shot and killed six college kids, stabbed another, and wounded two more because Eugene Patterson is a shape-shifting Asian demon named Buranti?"

"Didn't stab nobody," Cutter said, rocking back and forth in his chair. He knew it made him look crazy, but his ass itched and the straightjacket just wouldn't let him scratch. "Patterson's getting into the NFL to make money to gain power and influence so he can bring more kids into his church. He killed Luke."

"Uh-huh," Fife said. "Even though we can't find Luke Moore—or his body, for that matter—and the surviving students say Patterson was nowhere near the place?"

What was that? Cutter thought, turning suddenly to look to his right. He'd heard a noise, same fucking noise he'd been hearing since he woke up.

"Are you OK, Mr. Cutter?" Fife asked.

"Thought I heard something," Cutter snapped. Sweat beaded on his forehead and upper lip. His breath came in ragged gasps, and the damn jacked *itched* so bad!

What was that? Cutter turned hard to his left, so violently he fell off his chair. He lay on the floor, staring at the wall.

Fife stood up and looked at the cop who watched over Cutter's cell. "He always like this?"

"Yes ma'am," the cop said.

"This guy is goners-ville," Fife said. "There's no way we'll get this murdering nutcase to stand trial." She walked out of the cell. The cop grabbed the two chairs and hauled them out, then shut the cell door, leaving Cutter alone.

He looked furiously left, right, and behind himself.

He heard it.

He knew he did.

The Pitter-Patterson of little feet.

The Ghost of East Shelby Gales
By J. Richard Hancock, Jr.

The gold of morning spread from the East across the emerald dew diamond East Shelby Gales Country Club. Guy Warren Haggard watched the long shadows of big oaks shorten.

His wicker chair behind the bush creaked like distant crickets. Guy reached to get the covered beer stein full of coffee centered on the little oak tray table. "They'll be out there soon", Guy muttered to his coffee "cup". He leaned back maneuvering the stein past the gun barrel balanced between his legs.

Soon, through the branches of the bush that concealed him, he would see them coming. He would hear the whine of the golf carts, the distant voices calling to each other, hooting and bragging about God knows what. No longer would Guy have peace or silence.

There had been a time when Guy rose early and sat on the porch of his home. He relaxed there on weekends in the cool breezeway of the long porch, in the silence thinking deeply about life. The porch had been his refuge, his cloister, his Eldorado. There had been a woods with birds, rabbits, and squirrels. At night the owls hooted, and whip-poor-wills lullabied him to sleep. His only alarm clock had been a lark's call. But now, his seclusion was gone. The developers took it. Their bulldozers groaned and clanked the woods away. Trees went down everywhere; houses went up. Until, only the thick woods next to Guy's property remained.

But, the developers soon returned to build East Shelby Gales Country Club and golf green. Their bulldozers gouged away the last green leaf of Guy's garden of peace. It could not have hurt more if the bulldozers had gouged out his own heart.

Guy let his bushes and hedges go after that and only moved the smallest portion of the yard next to his house. The rest he let grow wild. Guy wanted seclusion and concealment from the destroyers of worlds. He needed a buffer between him and the earth-stripping builders. He wanted a shield between him and the crying children, the blowing auto horns, the throbbing stereos, and the dogs that barked incessantly at night.

Wild bushes and trees, surrounding his house on the half acre lot, were all Guy had left in the world for a defense. He did not have the money to move and rebuild, out where he would never be crowded again. He had bought the land with his G. I. Bill and erected the house in 1970, two years after his discharge from the Army. His wife Ruby's operation, his disability, and a failed business had depleted all cash reserves.

The crowding started years ago, or so it had seemed to Guy. In reality, it was only five years after he and Ruby moved into their new house. But to Guy, it felt more long ago than when Buffalo herds, numbering in the thousands, covered the Western Plains, or when New York State was a thick forest inhabited only by Native Americans.

"They were the true Americans who knew the proper use of the land", he often preached to Ruby. That's what she heard every time Guy saw a woods being bulldozed to make another shopping center, filling station, fast food restaurant, bank building, or housing development.

"Too bad the Indians lost. They never would have allowed this. They were the true Americans, who knew the proper use of the land. I wish to God they'd come back and haunt these people."

"You can't change the world G. W.," Ruby would remind him. Grasping the car's passenger door handle, she would try not to scream at Guy, "Well, why don't you just do something about it instead of preaching to me. I can't help what these people do to your precious earth."

She always used those exact words to short circuit Guy's Indians and trees tirade, when she lost her grip. But Ruby had grown up in the city. How could she know how Guy felt.

She would look out the window on her side of the car for awhile, as they drove in silence for a few moments. Then, to change the subject she would ask, "What do you want for supper tonight? Salad?"

She knew he liked salad. Something about supper and the mention of salads would cause Guy to speak almost poetically about the color of fresh tomato against the deep green of lettuce and the orange of carrots, the correct balancing of pepper cuttings mixed just so with special herbs to bring out a delicate something to tease the palate. Next, he would run on about the nutritional value of fresh foods grown in his personal garden, without the aid of modern fertilizers. Finally, he would end up pointing out the comparative ease of digesting vegetables and bread compared with the strain to digest meat.

Ruby could recite this speech from memory, as well as the Indians and trees speech. But she wouldn't interrupt Guy. Because he always relaxed and smiled during his "salad sermon". That was her objective now. Guy needed to relax.

At times, Ruby feared Guy might actually have a stroke and die at the wheel of the car, while raving about the destruction of the ecology by thoughtless people. She imagined him there, hands locked onto the steering wheel, eyes set in rage, mouth still wide open exhaling his last tirade, as the car crashed into something and finally killed her, too.

Ruby could never have imagined what actions her words, "why don't you just do something about it instead of preaching to me", would one day cause Guy to take.

One morning he rose before sunrise. He moved his wicker chair, the tray table, and his "coffee" stein to the thickest bush near the 18th golf hole. He went back to the house to get, one more item, his pneumatic BB rifle with the scope on it.

He sat in the cool of the morning flanked by bushes, like a big game hunter. The bushes, he no longer bothered to trim, concealed and shaded him. The BB rifle rested between his legs, pumped to the perfect pressure for the job in mind. Its butt rested in the damp grass. He sat, "coffee" stein in hand. His brown eyes scanned the 18th hole green. He sat as motionless as a snake poised to strike.

A breeze was kicking up now. In the distance, through his field glasses, he could see golfers gathering near the club house. They loaded their golf clubs and mounted their carts. Some golfers touched their clothes and smiled, as if they had been complimented on their attire. Their mouths, soundless to him because of the distance, were opening and closing. It reminded Guy of a silent movie.

"Why, of all sports, does golfing require such ridiculous hats and plaid slacks?" he questioned.

He brushed back a long lock of gray hair from his forehead to clear his view through the field glasses. A lady bug dropped from a tree. It landed on the shoulder of his olive drab army shirt. The worn battle shirt was a leftover from his tour in Vietnam. It presented a strange contrast to his burgundy pajama bottoms and the old leather sandals on his feet, worn without socks.

He salvaged the sandals one day from a trunk of high school clothes his mother almost threw away while house cleaning. He was thankful he saved the archival treasure.

The golfers played toward him, gradually coming closer. The silent movie became a "talky. He could hear them babbling and bantering above the whining of the golf carts.

"Here they come in with their little carts hauling their fat 'duffs' up one slope and down the next. Soon they'll be in range." All this he whispered out loud. Guy had talked to himself, when alone, since childhood. He didn't know why.

Two fully loaded golf carts whined to a stop. Golf shoes pointed toes away from the cart and down toward the damp grass. The golfers jumped out to tee off on the 18th hole. Hands searched pockets for tees. Golf bags were dragged lazily to the edge of the cart beds, for easy choosing of correct clubs. They were just fifteen yards from Guy's "golfer's blind".

As soon a the golf shoes sank heavily onto the grass, the inevitable shorts tugging and slacks smoothing began. It seemed to Guy, that it always did. At least one Bermuda shorts cuff was curled outwards, showing the threads and the back side of the cloth. One golfer was having trouble pulling a "wedgie" from his fat butt. The discussions, or arguments, started about which club to use. Someone wanted to light his cigar, but realized he had lost his lighter en route. Another sports addict had a radio tuned to a ball game, so nobody could miss it. The radio blared raucously.

Guy had watched this identical thing happen a hundred times before, while he wondered what to do about the loss of his peace and seclusion. This time he did not wonder. Today, old Corporal G. W. Haggard had a plan. Today when the "plaid barbarians", as he called them, broke down the "walls" of his tranquillity, they would be attacked by bees. More exactly, a BB that whistled through the air at 600 feet per second and straight to the fat plaid "buns" of a golfer.

One golfer bent over to pierce Guy's defenseless Earth with a tee. His shorts rode up tightly against his buttocks. Guy aimed, as he was taught in sniper school, carefully but quickly. The scope's cross hairs were on butt. He squeezed the trigger. Air rushed from the BB rifle's muzzle, with a snapping hiss. The BB hit the golfer's expansive rump solidly.

"Oooh shiittt", the anonymous sportsman loudly brayed. He dropped his club, straightened up stiffly and grabbed his bottom in a single motion. Guy speculated the golfer accomplished the maneuver, perhaps, in one hundredth of a second or less.

"What the hell is wrong, Bill", someone yelled. "Bill is having another heart attack", another golfer yelled.

Everyone rushed to Bill's aid. Bill grasped the golf cart with one hand, to steady himself, and grimaced in pain. His colorless face dripped with cold sweat. His other hand continued to rub his stinging bottom.

In a moment Bill's plaid shorts were pulled down. Bill's encircling fellow golfers inspected his wound.

"God Bill, looks like you been shot", one golfer said. Another surveyed the area for trajectory of pellet to target. He saw the bush where Guy now hid. Two and two makes four. Guy's convulsive snickering factored in. Mystery solved. Somebody shot Bill in the butt with a BB rifle from behind a bush.

The golfers quickly moved to the leeward side of their carts. They crouched for safety. With a cell phone, one golfer "911'd" for police.

Guy, still seated in the wicker chair, continued to laugh loudly. Tears streamed down his beard shadowed face.

When the police heard there was a "nut" with a BB gun at East Shelby Gales Country Club shooting golfers in the butt, they went into full alert. The golfers clearly said BB gun, but policy don't always hear things like most people. The rookie officer heard " nut with a rifle shooting people at East Shelby Gales."

In twenty minutes, two squad cars and four uniformed officers skidded up in front of Guy's "golfers blind." They jumped out of the squad cars, newly issued nickel-plated .40 caliber automatic pistols drawn. They immediately crouched behind squad car doors for cover.

One officer, with a pasty mouth and a megaphone, commanded Guy to, "throw the piece out and come forward with both hands up. Both hands up."

Guy tried to explain he only had a BB gun. What was the fuss anyway. He had snipped a silly golfer in the ass on Sunday morning, not killed somebody in the bush country of Vietnam. Guy stood up from the wicker chair and stepped from behind the bush still holding to the BB rifle.

Several .40 caliber hollow points made ugly holes in Guy's old army shirt. Guy crumpled like a dish towel dropped on a kitchen floor. Golfers and police rushed forward, as dogs do to sniff a freshly killed comrade hit by a speeding car. They stood staring down at Guy. The front of his army shirt was red. Guy rolled on his back, and from his pale face and through glazing eyes, smiled up at them.

Rookie policemen and golfers looked down in astonishment. For just before he stopped breathing, Guy, the BB rifle, the wicker chair, the tray table behind the bush and the "coffee" stein faded away. As if it were a snap-shot left exposed to the sun, it all faded away. Golfers and police were left looking down into the grass, as if searching for lost keys.

They looked up at the source of a man's gleeful laughter. As the sound faded away, they realized the well kept little house with the wide porch and minuscule front yard was, instead, an old, dilapidated building with weeds and hedges grown nearly above its painted, chipped, broken out windows.

At last, all they could hear was the whisper of the breeze. The golfers and young police officers had become the latest victims of the East Shelby Gales Country Club ghost. Guy had been shot on a fourth of July under these same circumstances, but it had been 22 years ago.

After his death, Ruby moved back to San Francisco to live with her spinster sister in California. She and Guy first met there while Guy was off duty from his Special Forces advisers job in South Vietnam. To this day, every time Ruby makes a salad for herself and her sister Marie, she thinks of Guy.

Guy's ghost still appears now and again. But, it does so only on the Fourth of July—celebrating Guy's own Independence Day—and only when the local police department has left its greenest rookies on duty, covering for the holiday. And then only when some four golfers, new to that particular suburban community, come to play the 18th hole at East Shelby Gales for the first time.

Floods
By James S. Dorr

The trouble was, no one ever believed him.

Not even his wife.

He remembered one dream: A line of children in some kind of hospital. Joking, laughing—it couldn't be too bad—but some crying also. His and his wife's best friends had schoolage children.

He mentioned it to her. "I think they were getting shots, some kind of sickness." But his wife's answer was, "Kids that age are always getting sick. You know that, Charlie."

Then two nights later, the first dream having repeated itself the night before in increased detail, Charlie Bishop dreamed of strawberries. Some kind of fruit anyway, in individual-sized portions like schools might serve for children's lunches.

Again Janice laughed, not mockingly—not at him—but still in a way that made it clear she did not believe he was seeing the future. Not even when a few days later they were watching the news together and there was a story about tainted fruit, and school kids who ate it having to get shots for hepatitis.

"At least it's not our city, Charlie," she said. "Just some place up north—in Michigan somewhere. But like I say, kids are always catching something. And last year, too, wasn't there something on the TV about frozen raspberries making people sick? From Guatemala or some place like that had picked up some kind of weird bacteria? That's the trouble with dreams and stuff. Your mind just stores things, things from the news maybe years ago. Even from movies. Except when you dream it, it seems so real you think it's something new."

Charlie nodded. He listened to the rain beating outside, then shrugged and nodded. Most of the dreams he had seemed ordinary or, if they were really views of the future, it was of events so distant or else so trivial that they didn't even get in the news. Or else so commonplace that, when they did—like floods in the springtime in a city like theirs on the river—they were so expected that anyone might have had dreams about them.

Anyway his wife was a psychologist—it was her job to know about dreams. Even ones like his that, from his childhood, had seemed to him to be more than just dreams—to be signs or something—except, as she said, the mind stored so much junk that how would you know if a dream did come true that it still wasn't anything more than coincidence.

And so he nodded and smiled back at her and gave her a kiss as the news on TV turned to local events, about how some inmates from the state penitentiary had been drafted into helping with sandbags to build up the levee upriver from them.

"I had another dream," he said finally.

"Oh?" she answered.

"Yes," he said. "But this one was nicer. It had to do with us making love tonight."

Janice kissed him back.

"You know," his wife whispered, "maybe some dreams do foretell the future."

* * *

Afterward, with his wife sleeping at his side, he had a dream about shadowy figures moving hundredweight bags in an ancient, stone-arched basement. He didn't know where yet—perhaps that would come later, on another night. That was the problem with his dreams really, that he always remembered so much of them, in such detail, that they seemed so real when he woke. More so than most people's. And, on nights afterward, he still remembered so, if a new dream came that added new details to one he had before, he was able to recognize it as an unfolding story.

He woke up feeling apprehensive. He thought about the convicts upriver and then of his dream. Were the figures he'd seen wearing some kind of uniforms? But there were real enough worries as well—the rain continued to come down in torrents and, as he drove to the university where he worked, he could see without his car radio having to tell him that the river below was still rising.

He drove through downtown, detouring once to avoid a torn-up street behind the old Covenant Church—Memphis sewer repairs stopped for nothing, not even spring flooding, he thought as he realized he'd probably be late now—then tried to make up time after he'd turned east, to climb the bluff away from the river. But even here where the ground was higher, the driving was slow through the blinding rain.

He parked in the lot, finally, finding a space near his usual spot by the Chemistry Building, then pulling his hat down, he dashed inside to be met in the hall by a graduate student.

"Mister Bishop," the student shouted. "We need you downstairs. They've canceled classes because of the river, but we've got to move some stuff out of the basement."

He nodded. He kept his coat and galoshes on as he followed the student down, then joined his fellow faculty members moving carboys of chemicals upstairs. "Won't get 'em all," his chairman told him. "Especially stuff that's already open in some of the labs. But we got a load of new reagents just yesterday morning, still packaged up like this, that we can bring up just in case all this rain starts to get inside. What with the EPA regs and all, it won't do to have any of this stuff break and wash into the river."

Environmental regulations, yeah. Charlie shrugged, then got back to work with the others, students, full professors, assistant professors like him, everyone in between. Two years before, the department basement had flooded and afterward, when there had been fish kills downriver, they'd been involved in the investigation. Not that other things didn't get into the river as well with a city like theirs, a major river port even before the Civil War, and now, with the New South, with all kinds of factories and ships and even the military and who knew what else to add into the mixture.

Afterward, when the day finally was ended, he took the higher road back home, still feeling apprehensive. According to the news after supper, the river crest was still miles upstream from them, not due till the next night. He thought of his dream and the work he'd done that day, but the basement he'd dreamed about was not his school's basement. But then the thought came to him—maybe he'd know for sure if he dreamed that night—that it might well still be some place not far from them.

"Charlie, look at this," his wife suddenly said from where she sat on the couch next to him.

"What?" he said. He'd nearly dozed off.

"Up in Tiptonville. Up the river. Would you look at that."

He blinked his eyes and watched, on the TV, a developing story. How floodwaters there had gotten so high they'd inundated the town's cemetery, washing out some of the newer graves and floating the caskets up to the surface.

"Ugh!" his wife whispered. Her arms were around him.

He hugged her back to reassure her. "I wouldn't worry about that here," he said. "Most of our graveyards are on higher ground. But I'll admit I'm just as glad I'm not one of the people who has to clean that up."

He went on later and told her about the day he'd had, moving possibly toxic reagents upstairs from his department's basement, and later, exhausted, when they got to bed, he went right to sleep. Once again he dreamed of the basement, not his school's basement, but the one with the ancient stone arches. He saw a sign this time, dirt-smeared and faded but under a light where he could just make it out: General Organics.

He'd heard that name somewhere.

And now he got a closer look at some of the men, moving sacks and also some drums now, but not upstairs. Rather stacking them up on pallets within the basement, lining its corridors. And what they wore were not convicts' uniforms—he could see that now.

They looked more like soldiers.

* * *

The sewer repair had spread the next morning when he drove to work, almost surrounding the old church and churchyard. He cursed as he had to detour even farther, threading his way with the other motorists up the bluff road to the higher ground above, then on through the cold, gray Tennessee rain where, even where he was now, the road in places was starting to be covered with standing water.

At noon his department closed down altogether, letting people like him who lived nearer the river get home early. He was thankful. He didn't think his home was in danger—it wasn't that low—but still he went down into his own cellar, checking things out, moving some books he had stored onto higher shelves, just in case they did take in some water.

And then he remembered—the name from his dream. He was sure it was local. He went out again and got in his car, noticing the rain seemed to be slacking although, of course, the river crest was still coming down toward them, carrying with it whatever witches' brew might have washed in it from cities upstream. He headed downtown, glad the streets sloped here so there was less worry about standing water, and stopped in at the city library. He thought he might look through lists of businesses, just to see if the name he'd dreamed matched one, then, maybe, meet his wife at her clinic. Then maybe go out to dinner together.

He found what he wanted without much trouble. General Organics—it used to make plant food. Fertilizer. Except it had closed down a decade or more before. And there was no record to indicate who, if anyone, had bought it.

He wondered. The men in uniforms. Soldiers? The Cold War was over, but it was no secret that not that long ago the Army had bought up old buildings to use as warehouses. To disperse whatever it was they might want to store, just in case there might be some need later.

Perhaps to disguise some, in sacks perhaps to make it look like it was fertilizer in case spies should get wind of what they were doing.

He almost laughed out loud. Spies, sure, he thought. And now maybe they were storing some new stuff, powdered nerve agents, perhaps, or even worse chemical weapons. Or maybe these were just teenage workers in military surplus fatigues—the latest fashion statement among the kids at his college in any event—moving sacks of real plant food, to clean the place out, left over from who knows when, getting ready to fix it up. Maybe to make it, like so many old buildings were these days, into some kind of Yuppified downtown condo.

Real estate, yeah, he thought, after he'd picked Janice up at five and taken her to a restaurant they'd used to go to when they first began dating. His father had been a real estate broker and he knew the secrecy that surrounded that. Property values—if people caught on to what you were doing, land would get too expensive too quickly. Even the sewer work could figure into that, maybe with the city itself planning a major renovation.

"What are you thinking so hard about, Charlie?" his wife finally asked him after they'd finished and gotten back home, and switched on the TV to check out the late news.

He smiled, kind of sheepishly. "I had another dream the last few nights. That was the reason I was downtown, to look up some things. Maybe this might be a good time to think about investing there, maybe buying a little piece of land...."

"Oh, Charlie," his wife said, cutting him off before he could go on. "You and those dreams of yours." Just from the way she was looking at him he knew that, no matter how much he tried to explain his theory, she wouldn't believe it.

And the problem was, he thought, after he'd made sure the windows and doors were locked, just in case with those convicts upriver—the TV had hinted that, with the flood surge expected to peak sometime before morning, a few might already be being sent down to help there at Memphis too—that, for some nagging reason he couldn't quite put his finger on yet, he didn't really believe it either.

* * *

Connecting the clues was the problem, he thought later. Like kids getting shots, and strawberry lunches. No one dream, or set of dreams, told the whole story—you had to take all the hints you had together. Including things you got from the news, or from movies, from places outside of dreams you might have noticed.

Like cleaning out his own department's basement. Or detours around churches that had been there from before the Secession. But also throwing out the false clues, the ones, like his wife said, that might be just coincidence. No more than red herrings masking the true ones.

But right now he wasn't thinking about churches, herrings or old fertilizer companies, or anything else except the second look Janice had given him as they went upstairs. That clue he didn't need dreams to respond to.

They made love furiously in the darkness, the rain outside having tapered down to a romantic patter. The river below might rise as it might, but he was rising too, and Janice with him, going at it as athletically as they had when they had first been married. Finally, slippery with sweat, his wife pushed away.

"I love you, Janice," he whispered, reaching out to take her back into his arms.

"I love you too, Charlie, but, look, I've got to pee. I mean really pee. And while I'm at it, I think I'd better take a shower. You just go to sleep, okay. I mean, I know you've had a hard day the last two days, moving that stuff at work. And then us being up late like this and—well, you know. I know you're tired."

"You watch yourself, though, okay?" he said. He was tired, he realized, almost falling asleep even now as he tried to push up to kiss her again. "In case, you don't know—I'm worried about those convicts."

"Charlie!" she said. She was almost laughing. "They said on the TV the crest wasn't going to be that high after all. That they'd been thinking about having them help down here, but then they'd sent them back. Anyway, you've got the place locked up tight, and we are upstairs. Like no one could even peep in through the windows...."

"I guess so," he said. He was practically groggy. "I guess I've just got too much imagination."

This time she did laugh. "Look I'll just be gone fifteen minutes. Maybe a half hour —I may fill the tub up and have a nice, warm soak. So you just go on to sleep, like I say, Charlie. And none of those dreams, you hear?"

He nodded. "Uh-huh." He heard her pad down the hall as he rolled over. He wanted to wait up, but he couldn't help himself. He thought about dreams as he realized he was dreaming, of water rushing down basement hallways. He didn't know if it was General Organics or his own school's basement—or maybe both basements—or maybe a mixture of stuff that washed out there, and other basements all over the city.

Even the water that rose in the river.

He dreamed about sewers and cemeteries, the one at Tiptonville with its new coffins that popped up above the ground, but then of older ones. He dreamed of graves dug beneath the Covenant Churchyard, that had been there since the time of the War Between the States. Some of them longer. Coffins there long since disintegrated.

And liquid from sewers, cracked and disintegrated as well, washing through corpses with gelatin-like bones, flexible—like snakes' bones—from the sheer time they'd lain in the earth's dampness. Writhing now, twitching through some kind of chemical rejuvenation. Or maybe a kind of a fertilizing. Or both. Or maybe it didn't matter.

What mattered was this: That the corpses began to crawl, flesh-rot still clinging like glue to their twisting bones, into the ancient pipe. To claw their way up to the surface above through encrusted tunnels, through water that rushed down in torrents from drains. From sinks. From bathtubs.

From. . . .

* * *

He woke, the bed cold and empty beside him. He sat bolt upright, shivering in the dark. Hearing the rain continue to fall outside through the window.

How long had he been asleep?

Dreams were funny. Funny about time. It might have been hours—or only moments. He fumbled to find the clock.

"Janice!" he called out.

He heard, down the hall, from the bathroom at its far end, the sudden sound of a toilet flushing.

Then he heard his wife's screams. . .

Inner Enemies
By H. David Blalock

The yellow glow of the bridge lights is a parody of a sunrise I will never see again. The thing inside my head is aware something is amiss, but it has yet to grasp the danger. It will all end here. My car slows as I glance in the rear view mirror. At this time of the morning the Interstate 40 bridge across the Mississippi River is quiet. The odd eighteen-wheeler roars by me, and those cars that do approach change lanes quickly to continue on with their business, oblivious to what I carry.

I pull over to the emergency lane, what there is of it, on the south side of the bridge, pop the hazard blinkers switch and sit for a second, listening to the click-click-click of the blinker relay. Fat raindrops begin to splatter against the windshield while the last strains of something by Led Zeppelin choke out of the radio. I kill the engine and open the door.

It is a brisk October night. There is a breeze here, throwing the gasoline and diesel fumes off the span and into the river. I follow the flow of the wind until I am at the south rail and look to the east, toward the Memphis skyline. I catch the lights from the hotels on Union and note the orange canopy of light over the city, a false dawn that never wanes once the true sun disappears.

Over the side of the rail I see nothing. The water of the Mississippi is a very long way down, too far to pick out. The raindrops fall away from me and into the dark. It is in that darkness that I hope to find peace; peace from something that began years ago.

Larry Calligri was my closest friend. We frequently spent long nights haunting the bars and underbelly of the city, secure in the immortality of youth that nothing could touch us. We shared alcohol, lies, grass, and women. We were kindred spirits, interested in the same things, given to the same vices. We spent hours in spirited discussion over drinks at bars on Beale before staggering home well after midnight.

It was the early '70s, and we were med students at UT Medical. Larry was headed for top of his class and had his eye on neurosurgery. I was a year behind him, set to take *summa cum laude* and go on to greatness as the Mid-South's foremost cardiac specialist. For kicks we latched on to the occult, the latest designer drug for the intellectual appetite. We were convinced that there was scientific truth behind everything, including the occult, and determined to find it. We dabbled in the arts, played with the rituals, laughing at its pretensions while inwardly quivering just a bit at its possibilities. We even drove all the way to Oklahoma City and then to Kansas City to buy books at occult bookstores, building an impressive library of quasi-esoterica. We convinced ourselves we knew what we were doing.

We were children playing with a loaded weapon.

The night of the seance I served as the medium, with Larry on my left and the other eleven arrayed in a circle on the floor of the apartment. A single candle provided the only light in the room, casting flickering shadows across the walls and on the ceiling. The seven men and five women sat quietly listening to the occasional crackle from the incense imbedded in the candle wax as it combusted.

Our group had grown from just Larry and me to this size over the space of three years. Each person had been chosen from among several candidates, retained because of their intelligence and insight. Those who didn't measure up were slowly excluded from the circle. We never forced them out of our society, just became more cool toward them until they left of their own accord. How could we know that we were leaching out those qualities we would need: compassion, care, empathy? They seemed to interfere with what we wanted to do, bring ourselves to a higher understanding of some "greater level of being."

Pompous bullshit.

We sat there and I performed as I had dozens of times before, mouthing the words. We were one in the circle, thirteen hard intellects with hardly a real soul between us. There was fear, true, but it was subdued and chained under scientific detachment, just another thing to be analyzed. We all expected to review this session afterward as we had the others, taking it and our feelings apart, reducing it to terms and formulae without blood or bone.

I mumbled the incantation, repeatedly conjuring the entity to appear to us in graceful and comely form, abjuring it by the power of the Names of God to come in peace and without malice. The words I had said dozens of times. The answer I would experience once. The consequences I would live with for the rest of my life.

I choked as something squeezed my throat shut. I tried to open my eyes, but found them just as tightly sealed. I could hear the others, hear their murmurs turn to alarm, then terrible screams that faded away as my hearing shut down.

I strained against the force that held me fast with inescapable strength, trying to move just the slightest part of myself, to convince myself I was hallucinating, by simply opening my eyes so that I could reconnect with reality. But no part of me would listen to my commands. I was detached from my body, yet contained within it.

In the darkness that was all I could see, I began to perceive tiny lights, infinitesimal but distinct against the homogenous blackness. I was afloat in a night sky that extended as my heaven and earth, without reference of up or down. And, for a moment, I was alone in that darkness, the only living thing in that universe.

Then I sensed something else there, sensed it in that its very existence announced it in a universe where only I should have existed. I felt its approach with a dread that cannot be expressed, a certainty of lingering death. It was a disease, a filth, a horror that was given life by a call from the power of thirteen intellects and manifested in an essence that could only exist by feeding on that quality that made up its fabric. It was aware, conscious, in the way any predator is aware.

And it hungered.

Then, somehow, Larry was there, within the universe. He seemed unaware of the thing's existence, more concerned with me and my condition. He called to me and reached out to touch me. I wanted to shout, to warn him of the threat, but it was too late. I saw it melt into him and become a part of what he was as easily as I might pull on a coat. He showed no discomfort and I soon doubted my feelings as the sense of dread I had experienced vanished in a moment.

I gasped and found my eyes open, staring into Larry's. He asked me if I were all right, then turned to tend to one of the women who had fainted. There was a large burnt area on the ceiling, twelve feet above the floor, and the carpet around the candle was scorched well beyond where we were seated.

We dispersed that night by unspoken agreement to our homes, never to discuss that session again. It marked the end of our meetings, and we eventually grew more distant from each other until only Larry and I kept in touch.

For years, I have awakened from a nightmare in which I watch the thing that clambered out of the darkness and fed on our combined power take on psychic form and depend like some horrendous tick from Larry's back, its misshapen head buried in his neck, gorging itself.

Then, two weeks ago, I received the call from Larry.

"I'm in New Orleans," he said. He sounded tired and upset, his voice slightly slurred. "I'll be coming in on the 8:30 train. Can you meet me at the station?"

"Why not fly, if it's that urgent?" I suggested.

"No, no, I can't. It's too dangerous."

"Flying isn't all that dangerous..."

"That's not what I mean, Mark," he interrupted. "I can't talk about it over the phone."

"All right, Larry. Eight-thirty?"

"Right. And thanks."

And he was gone.

I met the train, but Larry wasn't on it. The police got my name from a note on his body. They told me that he had died peacefully in his sleep during the trip. They asked if I could come in to identify the body. What I saw turned my soul to ice.

It had been seven years since we had last seen each other, but I knew him. Barely. The hair had gone completely gray, the face slack in more than death. His clothes were stained badly, old stains, and the body, even though the coroner had done his best to clean it, showed signs of bad hygiene and abuse. I did the necessary and quickly excused myself. On my way out, a policeman handed me an audio tape they found on Larry. It was in a large manila envelope and the policeman gave me an odd look as he handed it to me.

"Was he a drug user?" the policeman asked.

I shook my head. "Not that I knew of. Haven't really been close enough to him to know, though. Why?"

The officer nodded at the envelope. "Don't listen to that in a dark room," he said cryptically.

Back at my apartment, I dropped the tape into my player and sank into the sofa with a drink to calm my nerves. I lifted the remote from the coffee table and pushed play.

"Mark," Larry's voice came out of the stereo speakers. I could hear a television playing in the background and every once in a while a siren or passing car. He must have made this before leaving New Orleans. "If you are listening to this, then I am dead. At least, I hope so. God may yet have mercy on me and let it happen. I have tried so many times, but it won't let me. One way or the other, please pray for me." He paused and gasped as if in pain. His voice was haunted, hollow. I could hear despair and desperation in that voice. I sometimes heard that same quality of confusion and resignation from patients just before surgery when I had to warn them of the possible complications.

"I have to be quick. The alcohol only slows it down. Hear me out, Mark. Please.

"Eight years ago we brought something into being. During the seance, something came through. You couldn't see it because it was all around you, holding you down and paralyzing you, but we could see it. Several of us tried to get to you, but it struck at us until we had to give up. We had to watch while it coiled around you, through you. I thought I could explain it away later, Mark. A mass hypnotic hallucination. A figment of the light. But, whatever it was, it was *real*. I know now, it was real.

"When you woke, you seemed fine, and it all seemed to melt away so quickly that it was easy to rationalize. We should have talked about it. We shouldn't have let ourselves be separated. We let ourselves be used, Mark. We became carriers."

There was a choking noise and I leaned forward to listen more closely. Larry sounded as if he were asphyxiating, but suddenly his distress disappeared and his speech became more hurried.

"Why I can sense mine, I don't know. Maybe one person in a million can, and they call them insane, I don't know. What I do know is that it's in me and it's feeding on me. I believe it gets its sustenance from intelligence and memory. I have learned to sense them in others, Mark. In Alzheimer patients they are very strong.

"I'm fairly sure they incubate in the midbrain. Trauma brings them to the surface, and they get diagnosed as schizophrenia, manic depression, nervous exhaustion, anything to deny their true nature. They live and feed, Mark, live and feed on their favorite prey: mankind.

"I had to get to you before yours became too active. Mine has recently increased its feeding, and I think it's about to breed. I shudder to think what happens to the host—to me... when it—they— do. I hoped that I could stop it by suicide, but I can't find the strength to do it. Or maybe it won't let me.

"If you get this, you must believe me... Your parasite is ten times larger than the one I carry. It was the original that tore through the opening and held you in place. Once it gets ready to breed, it will pick a time when you are near people and make its move. I think they propagate and travel through physical contact.

"I read that you will be speaking at the Cardiac Surgeons Compendium at the Convention Center this weekend. It is absolutely vital that you at least postpone this, Mark. Stay away from large crowds. For your own sake and the sake of others."

The tape fell silent. A twinge of pain brought me back to the apartment.

I looked at the glass that lay shattered on the rug by the sofa. I did not remember picking it up, dropping it, or cutting myself on the shards. Blood coursed across my palm as I walked into the kitchen and turned on the tap. I picked bits of glass from the cut and ran warm water over the gash.

It was too fantastic. What kind of insanity had taken hold of Larry? I wasn't qualified to diagnose this kind of disorder, that was the purview of a psychologist. Still, as I listened to the echoes of his voice in my head, I imagined I felt something stir within, as if awakening from a long sleep.

The rest of the night is a blur. I dressed to go to the Convention Center, even got as far as Riverside Drive before realizing where I was. If not for the car that darted out of Union against the light, I might have pulled up into the Center garage and finished the night with all the awareness of an automaton. The adrenalin surge of the near miss wrenched me back into consciousness. I leaned over the wheel and sat staring at the light as it turned yellow, red. The situation was unacceptable. I was a man of science, a man of reason, and this thing that Larry described was impossible. Nothing like that could exist on earth. Yet, here I was, listening to a replay of Larry's words in my mind, and, incredibly, I could sense a movement within my mind.

I guess I had always known it was there. I just had never considered it a threat before. It was a part of me, and as I thought that, I remembered the vision the night of the seance, how the thing had become a part of Larry. It had put him on like a coat, I recalled, to protect it from the cold of the outside. It had used him... me. And, in a few hours I knew it would become more powerful. It was ready to breed, and it was manipulating me to find its young new hosts.

In a flood I recalled the arrangements I had pushed and sponsored, the markers I had called in, to get this Compendium together. More than anyone else, I was the motive force behind it. I had bullied, begged, cajoled, promised, and threatened peers and subordinates to break schedules, alter timetables, and change itineraries so that only the finest minds would attend. It had already been billed by the local news media as an historic meeting, something that happened once in a lifetime.

The depth of my guilt pounded into me, strength pouring into my mind, and I felt something inside recede, puzzled, almost alarmed.

I downshifted, swung right on Union to Third, left and up on to Interstate 40. I know what has to be done.

I look down again at the blackness under the bridge. Somewhere there is a faint sound of a boat's horn, and I can sense the coolness of the evening deepen. The water will be cold. Very cold.

* * *

The rain drummed steadily down now, and the security guard at the Convention Center garage yawned. The sound of the rain and the early hour worked to lull him to a nod. His head snapped up at the sound of an approaching car.

The guard recognized the Beamer sliding quietly down the ramp as Dr. Mark Anson's. The doctor's silhouette behind the wheel was a familiar pattern. The guard accepted it without question. He waved the vehicle through.

As the guard turned and reached for his coffee mug to fend off the damp chill, he missed the face turned briefly toward him, a face slack with more than fatigue. The car rolled into Dr. Anson's parking spot and the door opened. If he had been watching, the guard might have noticed the doctor was soaked to the skin. He might have noticed the dull, haunted look in the man's eyes. He might even have noticed the state of the man's clothes, as if he'd been swimming in the muddy waters of the Mississippi.

Dr. Anson stepped on to the escalator leading to the Convention Center.

By Any Name a Devil
By Steven Lee Climer

Pausing, Ed tapped the ashes from his unfiltered Camel into an ashtray shaped like a female breast. He stared at it often, recalling what it was supposed to mean when he was fired from Mutual Life Insurance Company. It was a gift from Mr. Prescott, Mr. "Mutual" himself. You were a big boob, Ed, that's what it meant. You can't sleep with the boss' daughter—and wife— and still be employed. The ashtray was overflowing with spent butts, chewed gum, and crumpled Post-It notes: it was a big boob for a big boob.

That was five years ago. He had to gather his thoughts, fish them out of the perpetual hang-over that was his mental environment. Sometimes he wished he would just get hit by a car out on Elvis Presley Boulevard and die happy in the shadow of Graceland.

But Ed Cooper's life always fell short of being blessed. As a kid, he was the one caught stealing when everyone else got away with it. In college, he was the one who missed out on the scholarship because he was second-best. And as an adult, he was the adulterer caught with the boss' wife when a dozen men had done the same thing. Ed couldn't stand life, it wasn't fair. He was sure of one thing, however; everyone wins the lottery once in their lifetime. His turn was coming, he was convinced.

Ed took a drag on his cigarette. In front of him, a small pile of paperwork beckoned. But his most pressing matter, outside of smoking his cigarette, was the file in his hands. Mrs. Althea Waymouth, 51, Memphis, Tennessee: the only person who tried to make a claim against her policy in the five years he'd been with the shady outfit calling itself an insurance company.

Mostly, his day consisted of a pot of coffee before lunch, a few sports magazines, a pack of Camels and a pint of Scotch, lunch at some barbecue shack (extra onions, please), followed by an afternoon nap. Staring at the boob, he couldn't believe this was his lot in life after 37 years. His eyes wandered out of his office window, resting momentarily in the distance. Just beyond the high-rises and riverside warehouses, he could see glimpses of the Mighty Mississippi cutting a path toward New Orleans. God, how he wished he was on a barge going downstream.

MONSTERS FROM MEMPHIS 91

The beeping phone brought him back from the fantasy. Ed quickly poured over the adjustment claim form before picking up the holding Mrs. Waymouth. The actual policy was not taken out on Althea, but on her daughter Vera. Vera Waymouth, 33, unemployed, unmarried, possessed. He hated adjusting cases of possession. Usually it consisted of bad acting, theatrical makeup, and if he was lucky, some entertaining home wiring.

Reluctantly, Ed picked up the phone. "Mrs. Waymouth, this is Ed Cooper. Yeah, I'm the adjuster."

He paused, trying to answer her rapid-fire questions. There was no way Mystical Insurance Corporation was going to pay this claim. They never paid any claims. If people were stupid enough buy paranormal insurance, they deserved to be ripped off. It didn't matter if Big Foot smashed their Winnebago or if a UFO made off with their case of beer, no one was going to get paid. Except him, of course. That was Ed's philosophy.

And the more claims he could deny, the bigger the bonus. It was hard enough finding a job after being blackballed by Mutual. He was lucky Mystical needed a liar and shyster at the time he was at the peak of his craft.

"Look, I can't..." he listened. "I'll have to come for a visit." Again, he paused to listen.

She rambled on. Ed put the phone on the desk and poured some Scotch into his coffee cup. In between sips, he offered nondescript responses in the direction of the phone ...really...wow....that's unbelievable...huh?

"Are you listenin'?" Mrs. Waymouth suddenly blurted.

Ed scrambled for the phone, nearly spilling his beloved Glenlivet. "Mrs. Waymouth, I can't process your claim unless you've had clerical diagnosis by a recognized clergy member."

"What?"

"You need to have a priest come and diagnose your daughter as possessed."

"Our minister was here already, says it's possession."

"Your policy states that any non-Catholic clergy that makes a diagnosis of possession must have it verified by a Catholic priest."

"We're not Catholic."

Ed suddenly saw the possibility of closing this case right over the phone. "I'm sorry, the Catholics are experts on possession and we rely on their word to process a claim."

"Really, well I'll get one over here, directly. My sister-in-law's Catholic."

"Oh," Ed sucked on his cigarette, knowing in his heart he'd have to see Mrs. Waymouth eventually. "Okay, I'll come to your house this afternoon. I have to ask a few questions before I can deny....I mean ....process your claim. See you later, Mrs. Waymouth."

Ed hung up the phone, tapped his ashes into the ashtray and thought about what to do next. He reached into his drawer and pulled out a copy of the Mystical Insurance Paranormal Adjustment Manual, then turned to the page concerning Satan.

* * *

He liked to arrive unannounced to investigate a claim. Mrs. Waymouth lived on a small cul-de-sac in one of the historic districts of Memphis. Historic? What bullshit, Ed thought. That was a fancy way of her saying her house was a piece of shit you couldn't tear down because some slave or soldier got laid in the upstairs bedroom. The quiet little neighborhood was a study in dichotomy: home to a major university and surrounded by working class neighborhoods. If the devil was going to visit, Memphis would be the armpit in which to nestle.

The southern heat had started early this year. Ed parked nearly a block away from the Waymouth house — and around the corner. As he passed by, he noticed the bright sunshine failed to illuminate their front yard even though glorious late-spring beams bathed the neighbors on either side.

"I hate the heat." Ed grunted as he walked the broken concrete to the lot directly behind the Waymouth house.

Through the back yard of a neighbor's house, Ed could see into the lot of Mrs. Waymouth. The two-story house was indeed shrouded in darkness. Leaf-bare trees rose like dead fingers around white clapboard siding, reaching up to pull the house hell-bound; and a dog whined in an unseen backyard pen. The trees in all the surrounding lots were bursting with new growth, and buttercups could be seen in nearly every garden except hers.

Skeptical to the last, Ed pulled out his binoculars and focused on the upstairs room. The curtains of one room stood out with sheers bathed in red light. Ed lowered his binoculars, reached into a pocket on his briefcase and took out the Mystical Insurance Paranormal Adjustment Manual. He thumbed through the pages until he came to the information he sought.

Ed read aloud from the book: "'Absence of sunlight onto subject property on a cloudless, sunny day...' Okay, I'll give her that one." He flipped again, "'Hounds of Hell howling...'" Ed looked and saw a tiny white poodle in the pen. "No Hell hound." He closed the book and held it tightly. "Well, let's get a look inside."

Ed heard a gentle roll of thunder as he turned and walked around the block toward the house. The winds grew chilly and brisk, catching him in the face like a fist. He walked past the neighbors on the left, a "FOR RENT" sign hung in the window. "Damn," he thought, "no neighbors to talk to." His mind again wandered to the meandering river just west of this stinking neighborhood. He dreamed of floating downstream to New Orleans, a hurricane in his hand. That would be his big lottery win, it was just around the corner.

As he stood at the gate leading up to the house, icy rain began to fall. Suddenly, something slippery hit him hard on top of the head. Looking down, Ed saw a frog squirming on the ground. Others began to splat, squish and squash on the sidewalk. Three more hit him in the head. Then, a downpour of frogs and toads rained. They croaked and their bodies crunched under Ed's feet as he walked.

"'Shower of frogs,' hmm." Ed thumbed through the book. "Damn, I'll have to give her this one, too."

Climbing onto the front porch, Ed tossed a couple of writhing amphibians back into the yard. He didn't even have to knock on the door, for Mrs. Waymouth was there—fear blazing in her eyes and her apron covered with some foul-smelling yellow gelatin.

"I saw you comin' up the walk and knew you'd get a shower." She said through a mouthful of discolored teeth. "Better get in before the lizards start to fall."

"Lizards?" Ed made a mental note to check for them in the book. "You're Mrs. Waymouth, right?"

"Yeah, that's me." She shut the door behind them.

"Hopefully, this won't take too long," he said aloud while finishing the sentence in his mind, "...and I can get the hell outta here and get a drink."

"Believe me, I just want it to end." She said while leading him into a small, grim parlor in the front of the house. "I want to get my money so I can get some help for my poor baby upstairs."

There was an uneasy silence as Ed followed her trailing eyes to the commotion coming from the upper level. Something was bumping and grinding, and a low growl penetrated the walls.

"The priest will be here in about ten minutes," she said.

"Good, that'll give us a little time to go over your case. I'll need to ask you and your daughter about ten questions. That will give me a good idea on where your claim stands. Can we go upstairs now?"

Gripping her silver cross necklace tightly, Mrs. Waymouth hesitated. "If you're sure you want to. We can just settle it down here."

Ed's skeptical core and unflinching stomach lit again. He was sure they were faking it, no one in all his years had ever been possessed or kidnapped by UFOs. Surely, one glance at Vera, possibly bathed in animal blood for effect, Ed would see through their charade.

"No, let's go upstairs," he said while offering her the lead. "You first, Mrs. Waymouth."

Without further words, she led him back through the front room, past the front door and to the dramatic stairway going up. The wallpaper, a hideous stripe of pink, yellow and umber, seemed to bar their passage. Ed looked at the paper, it had to be the work of the Devil. He also noticed a collection of velvet unicorns and Elvis paintings displayed with overhead lighting.

"These are Vera's," Mrs. Waymouth glanced backward. "She's so proud of these, Elvis was her favorite. When she was just one year old, he picked her up and kissed her. That was it, Vera was his for life."

"When did all of this start?"

They made it to the top of the stairs and paused. At the far end of the hall, red light slobbered from beneath a scarred, paint-chipped door. The foul stench of bananas stung Ed's nose. Mrs. Waymouth whispered a quiet prayer to herself before answering Ed.

"When did what start?"

"When did your daughter show signs of alleged possession?"

"Four months ago, why?"

"I need to know for the claim. When did you buy the policy?"

"Seven years ago when her daddy got possessed?"

"So, possession is a family condition?" Ed tried to remember if there was a clause about pre-existing demon possession in the contract.

"No, he just got it and killed himself." She reached into a pocket of her apron. "I've got a copy of my policy right here. I'm pretty smart about these kinds of things."

"Hmm," Ed sighed. He hated an informed consumer. "Well, let's go in and see her."

Mrs. Waymouth went to the door and turned the shiny, cut-glass knob. It was icy, dripping with condensation. Ed followed her across the threshold; the smell of rotting bananas was now accompanied by body odor and peanuts. For him, though, years of smoking Camels had damaged his sense of smell so significantly the nausea barely registered. Mrs. Waymouth looked like she was going to throw up, however.

After entering the small bedroom, Ed turned to a figure resting in an ornate rocking chair. Slowly, Vera glided back and forth, letting her considerable girth provide the momentum. She was a filthy, disgusting mess. Her brown hair hung like tired strings soaked with grime and sweat.

"How long since she's had a bath?" Ed said frankly.

But it was Vera who answered in a decidedly German accent: "Four weeks. I saw you coming up the walk."

"Who are you?" Ed asked.

"Who should I be?" She replied, the skin of her face pock-marked and ripe with open sores.

"I need to know for my paperwork. I'm the insurance adjuster."

"I'm Lily Marlene," Vera replied.

"Lily Marlene, huh? Isn't that a song by Marlene Dietrich?"

Vera laughed, only this time the voice was that of an old gentleman. "You got me, I knew you were a smart one. Anyone who could do insurance has to be my kinda guy."

"Look, sir, can I speak to Vera." Ed wanted to get this over with as soon as possible.

It wasn't as if he believed in possession. The bottom line was money. If he could legally deny the claim he'd get his bonus. So, the best thing for him to do was ignore the Devil if that was in fact who Vera was.

"This is Vera." Her eyes changed; they softened and tears began to flow.

"I need to ask you a few questions before I can settle your claim of possession. Now, I have some information about spectral events: the shower of frogs, icy winds in Spring, and so forth."

"I am the Devil," A frightfully different voice erupted from the woman's mouth. "Dare you doubt me?"

"It's not that I doubt you personally, my life's been nothing but hell, but I got to prove it for insurance purposes."

"Here is your proof."

The last word hadn't even dripped from her lip when it was followed by an issuance of putrid yellow slime. Ducking aside just in time, Ed avoided the majority of the vomit. The bulk of it smashed against the dresser, knocking over a mirror and tiny music box, before oozing down the veneer. The stench was of bananas and peanuts. Mrs. Waymouth couldn't contain her disgust any longer and bent over to wretch herself. Ed simply removed his coat, laid it on the bed, and continued.

"Have you ever seen the movie The Exorcist?" Ed commented.

Whatever was inside Vera ignored the question, "I am Satan, I'll eat you alive."

Ed remained calm although his insides quivered just a little. Vera Waymouth spooked him in a way like never before. Perhaps, this was the Devil. Still, that was no reason to honor the policy and give up his bonus. He'd be scared later.

"Mrs. Waymouth?" Ed asked. "Is the priest coming soon?"

"He should be here any minute, why?"

"I need him to verify the identity of the Devil for me. Your policy is for possession by the Devil."

Before she could answer, the front door chimes echoed through the house.

"Must be the priest," the deep, scowling voice inside Vera said.

Mrs. Waymouth opened the bedroom door, "I'll go get him."

"Thanks, that will give Vera and I a little time alone."

Mrs. Waymouth shut the door and Ed turned to the repellent hag in the rocking chair. "Mind if I smoke?" Ed took out a Camel.

"Not at all," The smile was sinister.

Ed lit the cigarette, inhaled the pungent smoke that delighted him so, and exhaled while talking: "So, what's that shitty smell?"

"Peanut butter-and-'nana sandwiches, fried," Vera spoke with yet another male dialect. She sounded like a bad Elvis imitator playing a second-rate Vegas dive. "Muh, little girl married that freak. That's why I'm back."

"Are you saying you're Elvis Presley?"

"Mind if I have a puff on your cigarette?"

Ed thought about those sickening lips on his butt and declined. "I'll give you one, how about that?"

"Don't need to."

Suddenly, Ed felt his lips lock around the cigarette. He was unable to control his mouth and tongue; Vera grinned with slyness as she watched. Slowly, an unseen force caused Ed's diaphragm to distend, pulling air through the cigarette and into his lungs. Smoke rushed in, quickly filling him to capacity.

Vera then exhaled, spewing cigarette smoke from between her teeth, "Ah, Camels."

The vise-like grip on Ed's body released and he exhaled also. But his air was free of smoke, only clear breath poured from his nose and mouth. Whatever his doubt was before, Ed was convinced he finally came upon someone with a valid claim against Mystical Insurance. Fear that he'd never known before inched up his spine like a crab. Before now, the Devil and Satan was just talk. Evil was a thing that nested in the hearts of men, that's what he believed no matter how much he saw as an insurance adjuster and categorical non-believer. Now, though, he felt the grip of evil on him.

Above all else, Ed had to keep calm and in control. In the face of true terror for the first time in his life, Ed knew it would be a contest of wills. Calmness and brilliance was the only thing to keep the devil from getting inside him, too. Vera grinned, knowing Ed now believed.

The bedroom door opened and Mrs. Waymouth entered with a diminutive white-haired man. "This is Father James."

Father James immediately crossed himself, "What evil has come to this child?"

Vera recoiled like a vampire in the rays of dawn, "Get him out of here!"

"She fears me," the priest whispered to Mrs. Waymouth. "Fear me, Devil!"

"I'm Ed Cooper from Mystical Insurance Corporation." The priest only gave him courteous acknowledgment. "Can you verify that this is possession by the Devil?"

"This isn't a game or a joke. This poor child is indeed possessed."

"Yes, but by what?"

"By what? By what?" Vera laughed mockingly.

Her face began to twist and contort. Vulgar amounts of slick black hair sprouted, forming a perfect DA. Thick mats of hair punched out of her face as sideburns filled in, and her jowls filled with fat.

"I'm the King." She said as the wounds on her face split open from the tension squeezing her face.

"You know, that's going to leave an ugly scar." Ed said sarcastically. "I really don't think you know who you are."

"Damn you, non-believer." The distorted imitation of Elvis snapped. "Come here, priest."

"In God's name, I command you Devil begone!" Father James shouted as an unseen hand drew him closer to the bed. "By all that is holy, I command you to leave this child."

He fumbled with a small bottle of Holy water and splashed it towards Vera in the chair. A few drops hit her skin, causing painful blisters to appear on contact. Then, Vera's invisible hand shook the feeble old man until he dropped the bottle, spilling half. Carefully masked by the commotion, Ed swiftly retrieved the bottle that rolled near his feet.

"Keep your filthy water off of me!" Vera screamed. "This is what we do to your kind in Hell!"

The mildly whimsical image of Elvis melted into a darkly sinister facade. Vera's skin, nearly at the breaking point, buckled and wrinkled as her mouth distended until it nearly rested upon her chest. From within her mouth, a pair of spindly arms reached forth. A mouth, complete with writhing barbed tongue squirmed in the palm of each hand. The hands punctured the priest's abdomen with surgical precision, and dug in deep until they were buried past the elbows.

Father James' body suffered great, soundless seizures as the hands moved deeper. The man couldn't speak nor get away, but the anguish was far beyond suffering. Gruesomely, Ed could see an outline of the hands moving beneath the old man's skin. Knuckles pressed up against the flesh of his neck from the inside, and a swirl of one of the tongues trailed below an ear. In the corner of the room, Mrs. Waymouth shrieked at the spectacle. The priest was being eaten from the inside out.

Then, as suddenly as the attack began, Father James' body slumped lifelessly in the unseen grip. Whatever had a hold of him, let go. The empty shell of the priest fell to the floor. The hands still protruded from Vera's foul, cavernous mouth. Both tongues twirled, cleaning the hands before they disappeared back down inside her gullet.

He didn't know what to think or how to act in the wake of the carnage. Ed felt urine soaking his pants as Vera's face returned to the pre-Elvis state. He took the bottle of holy water and drank it down quickly.

"Oh, now you've gone and ruined yourself. I can't eat you now."

Ed stared at the priest's body, the tongues had removed every organ, every vein, and every ounce of juice.

"Do you still doubt who I am?"

Somewhere beyond his panic and fear, the insurance adjuster that shared his mind spoke out: "You still haven't said who you are." He took out the Mystical Insurance Paranormal Adjustment Manual, "Do you answer to any of these names: Satan..."

"Yes."

"Lucifer."

"Yes."

"Mephistopheles."

"Ditto."

"Beelzebub."

"Affirmative."

"Old Scratch."

"Scratch me a winner."

"Old Nick."

"That's me."

"The Archfiend."

"Ooh, haven't heard that in awhile."

"Monarch of Hell."

"Like Prince Charles."

Ed Cooper exhaustedly lowered the book, "You said you were all of these."

"That's because I am evil incarnate."

"Mrs. Waymouth," Ed turned to address the woman, but she was splayed out on the floor. "Mrs. Waymouth!"

"She's not dead, she fainted." Vera said.

Ed turned back to the twisted creature in the chair, his sly brain working among raging emotions of fear and shock. "Look, I need for you to say your name so I can finish my paperwork. I don't give a shit if you keep Vera Waymouth or Althea Waymouth. I'm not here to save them—only my job. Just give me your name and I'll get out of here."

Ed looked at Vera as she laughed. Taking out the checklist from his shirt pocket, Ed quickly went through the claim form. Each clause had been satisfied on the form, only one more to go.

"My name," Vera began, "is Nergal."

"Nergal?" Ed repeated. "That wasn't on any of the lists."

Ed noticed Mrs. Waymouth was waking up, "What's happening?"

Flipping swiftly through the handbook, Ed victoriously found the name Nergal. "Mrs. Waymouth, your daughter is possessed by the Sumerian god of war, destruction and pestilence known as Nergal. Section 4, paragraph 23 of your policy states the possessee must be inhabited by a Christian demon or devil. Vera is possessed by a non-Christian devil. You purchased the Christian-only policy instead of the Universal Damnation Comprehensive Policy. Therefore, Mystical Insurance will have to deny your claim."

"Deny my claim!" Althea screeched.

"I'm sorry, there's nothing I can do."

"Nothing you can do!" She picked up a baseball bat that was resting in the corner and took a wild swing. "Damn you to Hell!"

Ducking just in time as the Louisville Slugger obliterated a table top full of family photos, he dodged another blow while making his way to the door. All the while, Vera laughed, shouting Sumerian words.

She chased Ed to the stairway, "You're just as bad as that thing in that room!"

Ed stopped and turned, hoping to quell the woman's fury. "Now, Mrs. Waymouth..."

She wasn't interested in any more of his insurance bullshit, and she hit him squarely in the forehead with the bat. Tumbling backward, Ed fell down the flight of stairs and crashed into the far wall. Bones broke and skin ripped on his way to the bottom. As Ed came to a headfirst halt, he lapsed into unconsciousness.

* * *

Lounging in the warm sunshine of New Orleans, Ed wiped condensation from his hurricane with a starched cloth napkin. His neck was the only thing that still bothered him, and in one more week he wouldn't have to wear the brace anymore. He watched all the beautiful girls lounging poolside at the luxurious resort where he went to recuperate, and in the distance he could hear the horns of ships heading from the Mississippi out into the gulf.

Mrs. Waymouth was in jail, and Vera in some institution still babbling ancient Sumerian. He didn't care, though, he didn't have to. The sunshine felt too good against his face. His memory was still vague about that spring day in Memphis when he went to see Mrs. Althea Waymouth and her daughter Vera. The doctors said he might never regain total memory of it all. That was fine with him, because there was one thing he did remember. Never again would he question the existence of the Devil. He'd seen it for himself, and in a strange way, Satan made him a rich, rich man. Mystical had a worker's compensation policy, and Mrs. Waymouth had homeowner's insurance and plenty in savings. Ed had a really, really good lawyer.

Everyone wins the lottery once in their lives. Some meet the perfect mate, others have a great job, and some win lawsuits. Ed just knew his turn was coming, and he was so happy he was right. He took a sip of his hurricane and lit a Camel.

Dance in Crimson
By Trey R. Barker

Gentlemen, fight as hard as you always do and we shall have Memphis."

"Whooee, we all ready to ride, General. Ride and fight."

* * *

The banisters stretched out like loving family arms. Descending the stairs, she swept her hand along the banister, ignoring the splinters that dug into her palm. Through the tattered stairway curtain, moonlight bathed the stairs in a pale light.

Once upon a time, the dress had been a bright, laughing red, with a white hem. Now the dress had faded to dirty pink, forgotten in a moldy trunk alongside a handful of ancient pictures. But a stitch here, a patch there, and she had repaired most of the tears.

At the bottom of the stairs, she sneezed. Dust. Mold. The mustiness of a too-long closed house. She wiped her nose and waited expectantly, as though for a gentleman to call. But no gentlemen would call, there were none left.

Never lose hope, Charlotte.

Throughout the room, shadows danced to the music coming from her small tape deck. She danced with them, glass from the broken window crunching beneath her worn boots, and listened to their whispers in the abandoned rooms. Their voices were soft and gentle, comforting...

"Charlotte, dammit! Are you up there again?"

Gritting her teeth, she looked through the window. Erich stood on their porch. How many times had she wished their house—the servants' old quarters—were much further away than a scant hundred yards?

"If it were further," she whispered, "he would be, too."

"Charlotte, come on."

He tramped through the riot of weeds and tangled vines between their house and the main house. Altogether, the land was more than 100 acres, slowly dying under the harsh Tennessee sun. She had never seen the land farmed. To her, it had always been a scar in the middle of the flesh of dusty roads and broken fences. The farm was dead and the house was dead and her marriage was dead and what else was there?

"Charlotte, I'm getting tired of this."

It was a horror to let this beautiful, rambling house waste away. Her gaze swept back through the receiving hall, up the wounded wood of the stairs, along the second floor banister, past the man, to the...

She froze. Her eyes swept back along the pitted walls. To the man.

He stood quietly, half of his face bathed in moonlight.

"Oh, God," Charlotte whispered. She ran for the door.

"No, wait..." His voice was lost in the fear banging in her ears.

She dashed through the door and outside. Her bootheels clacked on the wooden porch. Where was he? How long would it take him to drag her back into the house?

"Charlotte?" Erich called.

No hand clamped her shoulder. No cool gun pressed against her. Behind her, the house stood quietly, the moon showing half a face from behind the chimney.

She swallowed. The man had been there.

"Dammit, Charlotte," Erich said, his washed-out green eyes blazing in the moonlight. He had his shirt off and the jagged scar on his belly shined in the moonlight. "How many times...? You had t' get that damn dress out again?"

It was lost on him; the glory and splendor. It was a delicious subtlety in a romantic novel, but he only saw the torn dress on the cover. "So what?" She softened her tone. "I'm sorry. Let's have some tea. I put up a jug this afternoon."

"Again with the tea? I don't want any tea or juleps or any of that crap. I just want some dinner and maybe a few beers."

Yeah? And I want to be loved. And I want you to clean this house up and get this land working again. But we don't get every damn thing we want, do we?

"Charlotte, you ain't no southern belle, you're just a two-bit housewife."

She stomped back to their house, sat heavily on their bed, hands clenched. It would be so much easier if he would just kill her. Kill her and be done with it. No more occasional beatings, no more nights spent in town with some bimbo, none of that.

She glanced through her window. Dark shrouded the main house, but she knew what was there: broken glass, warped beams, rotted walls, overgrown weeds, choking vines. And maybe a man clever enough to stay hidden? Her stomach tightened. She raised a shaking hand to her throat. If he'd been there, he'd seen her while she pretended.

After a while, she lay down, wrapped herself in the bed's single sheet and fell into a disturbed sleep.

* * *

"Colonel Soloman, your company will patrol this section of Memphis."

"Yes, sir, General. You a Memphis boy, ain't you Burke?"

"Yes, sir."

"Then we'll stop at your place for lunch. God help any nigger contraband we find."

"Uh...yes, sir, Colonel Soloman."

* * *

In dreams, Charlotte recognized the man. His picture had been in the trunk. "Hello, ma'am," he said, smiling and bowing. In his free hand, a pistol. "A beautiful evening, ain't—isn't it?"

In dreams, she smiled at him, unafraid.

* * *

"Look there, Burke: niggers in Yankee blue."

"Yes, sir, Colonel."

"If they was just prisoners-of-war, we'd send 'em to Andersonville, but they're niggers. Only one thing to do."

"Colonel, wait. You ain't gonna burn 'em like you did them freedslaves?"

"Questioning a command decision, Burke? I ain't got time to burn 'em. I'm just going to shoot 'em. You get rid of their bodies."

* * *

In the morning, the taste of the dream-man was heavy in Charlotte's mouth. Under an oak tree, she stared at the house. It was just over the low rise in the land, beyond a cluster of pines. A few steps...and a world away.

And somewhere in the house: him. Maybe watching her as she watched for him.

Charlotte swallowed. What in hell was she doing? Watching for a man who didn't exist or who did and was a psycho armed to the teeth, waiting to go out in a blaze of glory?

Her heart pounded. "He's no killer and he's real, I saw the pictures."

He stood for a moment in the main window, then slipped out the front door. Coming toward her, he dusted his shirt and pants.

Charlotte waited breathlessly for him. "I know you."

Caution rode high in his steely gray eyes. "Then you got—have—the advantage, ma'am."

She grinned at his soft drawl. "I don't know you, but I've seen you."

"That right?"

"In the...in the picture."

He sat on a nearby stump. "Only took one picture in my life. Left it with Molly. I guess she showed it to you?"

Shaken, Charlotte turned away. She should be scared, and somewhere inside she was, but not for her life. She was scared because this was new, unexplored territory. "I don't know Molly."

"My sister."

He was beautiful. She could picture him coming down the main staircase, or working into a fine sweat chopping wood. Tremor in her voice, Charlotte said, "I don't know her, and I still don't know your name."

He stood stiffly. "Jesse Hunt Burke, only son of Hiram T. Burke." He stared at the land. "Goddamn, they—excuse me—tore the land up, didn't they?"

Charlotte frowned. "They who?"

He shrugged. "The Yanks. Molly was hiding me from them." He hesitated. "Well, from my colonel, too." His eyes clouded. "This was my home. Molly hid me in the sub-basement and told me to wait." Jesse Hunt Burke sighed. "I've been waiting a long time, ma'am."

* * *

"Ain't you shot enough of 'em, Colonel?"

"You gettin' some big bollocks, Burke. Get that nigger bitch out of the way. Her man's a nigger, probably in the army, too."

"He ain't wearing blue."

"Don't matter, he's contraband and he'll die. Bitch! Move!"

"Ain't no call to go hittin' a woman, Colonel."

"That's insubordination, Burke. Do it again and I'll have your ass. Now get those bodies out of here."

* * *

Swathed in brittle afternoon heat, Charlotte sat on the porch. Her wicker chair sagged beneath her while she stared at her husband's land. It was a few miles outside Memphis, beyond the cheap cafes and tittie bars. She tried to imagine the area a century earlier, when

Confederate General Nathan Bedford Forrest had ridden in with a whoop and two-thousand cavalrymen.

The Memphis librarian had been intrigued with the bit of 1864 history. She found it mentioned in a single book and had read it to Charlotte over the phone. General Forrest and his men had taken part of Memphis for a single day.

Charlotte looked at the main house. A dangerous game, she realized. Playing along with this man's illusions. Dangerous but delicious.

...been waiting a long time....

"The flower grows how it's watered," Charlotte's aunt used to say. Charlotte believed it to her very bones. They had both been waiting, hadn't they? Each watering their own flowers, waiting and hoping for a blossom.

Except... she was real and he was imagined.

Oh, the man was real enough—a drifter, a fugitive—but Jesse was not. Jesse was who Charlotte wanted to see. He was as unreal as her idealized dreams of marriage.

"Hello?"

Charlotte froze.

"Ma'am? You here?"

Jesse stepped from behind some trees, face anxious, cap tilted on his head. He held an arm behind his back. Charlotte backed away, her breath scared. "Stay away from me," she whispered.

Jesse's face flamed. "I didn't mean to put a fright in you."

"My husband didn't go to work today," she lied. Where in hell had Erich left his fish-scaling knife? Was this the only time he had actually put the damn thing away?

"Husband?"

Was that disappointment flashing across Jesse's face? "Well... could I give you these?"

A handful of lush yellow flowers. The petals seemed so delicate in Jesse's huge hands. He held them gently. "I don't know what they are. Molly would know."

Charlotte took the flowers. "They're lovely." They smelled of springtime. *Oh, God. What is happening here?* She shook the thought away. "Molly the gardener of the family?"

"Yeah. There were four of us. Mother and Father, Molly, and me." He nodded toward the main house. "I didn't hear them so I came out. I don't remember what they sounded like."

Charlotte swallowed. They aren't here anymore, she almost said.
Jesse stepped back. "Sorry I intruded, ma'am, I..."

"I'm Charlotte and you're not intruding." She paused, then said
in a rush, "Stay for a while." Was she as crazy as he?

Maybe, and that scared her to death. Because she had already
fallen in love with him; with his soft accent and his uncomfortable
politeness.

"Mostly I been lonely. But I had some company sometimes."

Charlotte frowned. "Company?"

"The General . . . every so often."

"The General?"

"General Forrest. We took Memphis, got my home back,
but..." Jesse hesitated, then raised a hand to Charlotte. A scar danced
across his palm. "The General gimme this when I was in the
basement."

"But what...?"

"Cowardice." Jesse lowered his eyes. "General thought I was a
coward. He don't like no cowards." Jesse's face became hard as
granite, but Charlotte thought she saw pain chiseled in his eyes.
"He's come to see me a few times since then. Yells and shouts,
carries on like any red-blooded soldier. Waves his sword. Only hit
me a couple of times. Shot at me once, though."

Charlotte stared at the scar, and at another one running the length
of Jesse's arm. From the General's sword? "Christ," she whispered,
closing her eyes. A madman soldier, a madman general. It was all
madness, but it whispered gently to her.

And she wanted to listen.

* * *

*"Shit. How many nigger soldiers they got in this town? Line
those two up against that wall."*

"Sir, I think—"

"Damn you , Burke, line 'em up and shoot 'em."

"Sir, I can't do that, it's—"

"You refusing to obey an order, Burke?"

"No, sir, I—."

"Shoot 'em and do it now."

* * *

`In the afternoon, the sun bearing down on them, he asked for
her red dress. When she put it on, they danced to a tape of waltzes.
They twirled until they fell to the grass, laughing. Delicately, Jesse

swept his lips across her cheeks and neck, her arms and legs. Delicately, gently, he undressed her. Gently, tenderly, his hands roamed her breasts and thighs. She held his head tightly, moving him down her body, then lifting his face and kissing him deeply. When he entered her, everything was perfect and clear.

* * *

"On the charge of refusing an order, I find you guilty. And bein' that this is wartime, the punishment is death."

"Colonel, please, I wasn't disob— "

"Yeah, you was, Burke and now I got to— "

"Colonel, no!"

"Goddamn you, get off a me. Give me back my gun."

"Colonel, don't— "

"Aaahhhh, Christ. I'm shot . . . oh, Mamma, I'm shot...."

* * *

Erich came home late. Sitting in his Barcalounger, he stared at her. Did he see it? Could he smell the sex? "We're moving," he said.

Her mouth fell open. "What?"

"I'm no farmer, and there's a guy in town wants to build some self-storage units. He'll pay enough to buy a house in town and open my own garage."

She stared at him coldly. "But this is your home, Erich. Your family has lived here for generations."

"So what? They ain't me. They ain't gotta pay taxes on it."

Charlotte's head swam. Images of full, fertile fields filled her head. Images of Jesse, working those fields, making love to her, keeping her alive and vital. "Are you trying to kill me, Erich? I feel like I'm dying here."

"Dying? I'm the one workin' to the bone. If anybody's dying, it's me; with you running around in that house pretending you're somebody."

"But..."

"You wanna wear that dress and carry around some old picture, fucking knock yourself out, but do it without me."

Moments later, Charlotte stood on the porch, fighting back tears.

"So good to wake next to a pretty lady."

Jesse's words, when they had awakened after love. His face had been pleased, his eyes satisfied. He had said "Stay with me." Erich had said "...do it without me."

"Fine, then," Charlotte whispered. She headed for the main house.

She had never wanted to be pulled in two directions. She had wanted a sweet, happy life. Children. Friends. But somehow, on the way to that place, she had taken a wrong turn.

"Charlotte," Jesse said softly. "I was hoping you'd come see me tonight."

Charlotte stepped into him, pressed her chest against his. After a delicious moment, she asked. "What were you waiting for, Jesse?"

"My family... and..."

"They're gone."

"I think I knew that after a while. I didn't hear nothing in there." He sighed deeply. "It's good to hear the crickets and birds again, Charlotte. And the air smells so clear."

"And what else?"

He hesitated, his face flushed, heated with shame. "To explain it to the General. When he came the first time, I wanted to tell him, but he don't listen sometimes."

"I'll listen," she said.

Softly into her ear, he whispered, "I love you." He pulled back. "You hear that?"

She kissed him.

* * *

"Jesse! I knew you boys would liberate Memphis."

"They're leaving, Molly. Cain't hold the position. The General be outta here by tonight. Molly, you gotta help me."

"What's the matter? What happened?"

"The colonel brought me up on charges. Wanted to shoot me. We got in a tussle and his gun went off."

"Oh, Jesse, what charges?"

"Molly, I shot him. He ain't dead but he's close to it. Molly, I'm scared."

"Sshhhh. Don't you worry, your family will take care of you."

"Molly, they're all lookin' for me. The General thinks I shot the colonel on purpose."

"Mother and I dug a place beneath the basement. You'll hide there. Let me get you some food."

"Molly, they ain't ever gonna stop looking for me."

* * *

Days later, as the sun released the day, they had a quiet dinner. Jesse had cleaned out the dining room while she prepared sandwiches.

"It isn't much," she said apologetically. She wore the red dress.

"Better than what I had in the basement."

She stared into his sparkling eyes, dinner forgotten, cleaning the house forgotten, Erich forgotten. She was in love. Real love this time, not convenient love. She was in love with a man who asked after her and who talked to her without watching TV and who laughed with her.

She had found her love and yet tomorrow would leave him. Erich had packed everything in less than a day.

"I don't want you to go."

"I don't want to go, either."

Teary-eyed, Charlotte glanced at the banister. Jesse had cleaned it until the wood was smooth and shiny. The curtains were still torn, she hadn't yet gotten to them. She squeezed her legs together. The curtain had been forgotten in steamy afternoons.

"Charlotte, I…"

"COWARD!"

A horse bore down on them, crashing through the dining room. Atop it sat a gray-clad soldier.

"General . . . " Jesse whispered.

"Damn you, boy," the man shouted, waving his sword. "You shot the Colonel."

The horse ran through their dinner table, knocked it over, sent the sandwiches flying. With a yelp, Charlotte fell back.

"Not like you think," Jesse shouted.

"Coward!" the General screamed. His sword sliced the air, nicking Jesse's shoulder. Jesse screeched and fell backward.

"Hey!" Charlotte shouted. "Leave him alone!"

"Coward!" the General shouted again. From the horse, he kicked Jesse twice, then turned and galloped up the stairs. Halfway up, the General and the horse faded into the dirty walls. A moment later, animal and man disappeared completely.

Charlotte ran to Jesse's side. "Are you okay?"

"It's just a cut."

"Who the hell does he think he is?"

"He's the General," Jesse said.

"Bullshit. You didn't do anything wrong." She cradled Jesse against her chest.

"But I did, I shot the Colonel."

"Charlotte, dammit, get out here."

Charlotte felt Jesse stiffen next to her. "He shouldn't talk to you like that."

"No, shouldn't."

"Charlotte, come on," Erich called again.

"No gentleman would talk like that to a lady. A man who would talk like that to a lady is a man who would as soon beat her."

"He has," she whispered.

"What?" Jesse demanded. "I'll knock him into a cocked hat."

Charlotte grabbed his arms, her mind whirling with images and thoughts, random and chaotic. "No, no. Just a slap sometimes, nothing bad."

"A single slap is bad, Charlotte," Jesse said.

She kissed him. "I had better go."

"Stay."

"Not tonight. Don't worry, I'll figure this out." Her kiss lingered for a moment between them, then she pulled away and left.

Erich was coming up the porch. "There you are. Playing old South again."

"I like it, so sue me."

"I wasn't saying nothing about it."

"Colonel?"

Surprised, terrified, Charlotte glanced behind her. Was that Jesse's voice? Quiet and surprised?

"I want to go through the big house before we leave," Erich said. "Get anything I can use."

A cold finger of panic slipped up her spine, she didn't want Erich in there. But at the same time, the panic dissolved and the random images came together. And what was that Jesse had said? Colonel?

* * *

The next morning, she stood on the stairs, staring through the tattered curtains at the early morning sun. Erich rummaged through the house, checking each room. "All right," he called. "Let's... Had to put that dress on, didn't you? Shit, whatever, let's go."

Charlotte swallowed. "No."

"What?"

"Which part didn't you understand? I'm not going. This is my land, too. We're married and that means I own half of everything. I'm not selling my half."

"Your half? This is my family land." Erich's hands clenched into fists. "You got no half to sell, all you brought to this marriage was a decent piece of ass."

Charlotte leaned into Erich's face. "I'm not going anywhere, fuckface. And you can kiss this piece of ass goodbye."

He grabbed her, slapped her cheek. "Goddamnit, let's go."

She shoved at him, felt the dress tear, and shouted, "Rapist!" As she pulled away from him, she tripped and fell to the ground.

"Charlotte?" Erich reached toward her. "What the hell is this? You don't mean rape?"

"STAY AWAY FROM ME!" She scrabbled backward, kicking at him. "Get away! Somebody help me!"

"Charlotte, shut up." Erich came after her, his eyes on fire. "You goofy bitch." He hauled her to her feet. She punched him twice in the chest, and landed a solid blow to his face. He dropped her, swearing and staggering.

"Don't hit me anymore! Don't beat me again!" As she fell away from him, she glanced around. Nothing. Except for them, the house was quiet and empty. "Help," she called again. "Please, somebody help me, he'll kill me."

Erich stood in front of her, rubbing his cheek. He snorted. "You're a fuckin' lunatic, you know that?" Shaking his head, he left.

She stayed behind, staring up at where she had first seen Jesse. She had expected—counted on—him to rescue her. Sighing, tears at the edges of her eyes, she wandered out of the house.

And saw Erich.

Also Jesse.

Her heart leapt.

Jesse had Erich pinned against the truck, a pistol in his face, the hammer pulled back.

"You're fucking crazy," Erich said as she ran up. "Charlotte, call the cops. Goddamn fucker's going to kill me."

"Shut up, Colonel. I heard you in there…"

"Colonel? What in hell are you talking about?"

Charlotte's eyes went wide. That had been Jesse last night in the house, whispering when he had seen Erich.

Jesse brought a lightning-quick knee into Erich's groin. Erich slumped to the ground.

"I shoulda killed you, Colonel. Burnin' and shootin' blacks, beatin' their women. There wasn't no call for any of that." He

paused, glanced up into the sky. "Is this what I been waiting on?"
He turned to Charlotte.

"What are you talking about, Jesse?"

He nodded toward Erich. "Colonel Soloman."

"No, it's Erich."

"Same man," Jesse said.

"Jesse, that can't be."

"Yes, it can," he shouted. "I'm here, ain't I? And the General.
He's here."

"Charlotte, please," Erich begged. "If you ever loved me, call
the cops."

She turned on him. "Like you loved me? Like that? Like when
you ignored me? And hit me? Like that?"

Jesse stared at her, his face suffused with anger. Charlotte
swallowed. He wanted a nod from her; a nod to end all the pain and
torment.

Wasn't this what she had been waiting for? The flower grows
how it's watered. Hadn't she watered enough? Hadn't she waited
enough? It was time for the flower—for her—to blossom.

Erich had no family and only a handful of drunken friends. No
one would raise any questions. The police would chalk it up to a
drifter.

Charlotte nodded.

His jaw set, Jesse turned to Erich. Two quick shots and then
silence.

* * *

She glanced out at her husband. He worked the land, clearing it,
resurrecting it. She cleaned the house, and every so often, Jesse
would come in and tell her how he remembered the house when he
was growing up. Charlotte planned to make it exactly that way.

Standing on the stairway, the tattered curtain tangled around her
feet, a new one in her hands, she watched him. Jesse stood in the
middle of the field on a small rise, stamping the dirt down. Jesse had
wanted to put him near the river with a small cross. Charlotte had
argued against it. She did not want to advertise their secret.

After another moment of stamping down the dirt, Jesse raised his
hand over his eyes to shield the sun. Charlotte followed his gaze to
the edge of the property. The General. He crossed the field and
stopped next to Jesse.

Charlotte's stomach knotted as the two men spoke. They seemed to argue, the movements becoming more animated. Finally, the General pulled his sidearm, fired two quick shots, then rode his horse into the trees.

"JESSE!" Charlotte shouted, running for the door and her fallen lover.

* * *

The banisters stretched out like loving family arms, opening wide to comfort her in her grief. She leaned against the banister, staring out the window at the soft mound of new earth near the river. She wore the red dress, newly repaired, and clutched Jesse's picture to her chest.

Near the door lay Jesse's pistol. She had cleaned, oiled, and loaded it. If the General ever came back, she wouldn't bother trying to explain what happened with Jesse and the colonel, she would simply kill him.

With a satisfied nod, she punched the `Play' button on her small tape deck. Soft, comforting music floated through the house's stale air. She danced until the tape ran out.

The Lizard Queen
By William R. Eakin

The opossum of Blake County had disappeared, and in these times on lonely nights when the paved part of County Road 63 shone with the moon, nothing crossed the road except with trepidation, because even the littlest mammals sensed in their blood the movements of the crawling thing. They felt it creep through the brambles and the muddy river bottoms like a giant spider on four misshapen legs; they watched it push through the silver-tinged kudzu and across the road; and for the evening after that no animals dared come up the animal trail, because it waited there for them, waited with a bloodthirst that was almost palpable. The sickly smell of the beast confused the other animals; they could not understand its strange, awkward shape and gangly movements; its hunger; its intelligent eye. And it was only after it caught something in its mouth—a rat, a snake, a muskrat—that the animals again made their way out of the thickest underbrush and walked down the ancient animal trail to old Miz Haskins' cow pond.

* * *

Mary Contrary was really Mary MacCartney, and she'd once killed a man. Strange how an evening's walk could change a woman's life. She was majoring in design at the University of Memphis and had a local catalog company already waiting for her to come aboard. Then there was the night walk back to her apartment, down the quiet street, and the man leaping in slow motion from the bushes, the gleam of the knife in the shadows.

The whole event was a blur and she often would quiver and fight to force away the memory only to make it more acute: she could feel her clothes ripping, and then that surge of adrenaline that gave her strength enough to turn the rapist's knife around and slip it back into him. And she remembered with lucidity and a knotting of her stomach that when she stood, she did not let him lie there with his eyes fluttering. He watched her with shocked eyes, and he suddenly seemed an innocent little boy, but she did not let the vision cause her hesitation: she ripped him with the blade from below his navel to the sternum, and let his guts fall out onto the pavement.

And instead of going to class the next day she went to buy a gun and met Jack for the first time at the gun shop, where he was buying yet another automatic for his collection, and they got to talking and ended up somehow with a bottle of Jack Daniels and some crack, and life changed; those early days were blurred with a drunkenness and a hollow ambiance of desolation and excitement, but she was glad for the company of Jack's sweaty thin body and for the dream he had, which was to deal enough crack to retire to some farm. And that was her dream too, now, mostly because of that guy lying in his own entrails on the pavement of her old life.

* * *

They bought the Haskins' property and set their camper at the edge of a blackberry field, just some short walk away from the cliff and near the woods on the side that has the old cow pond. From the cliff top she could see the river valley even in the night, and the shaking leaves of the river bottoms, and a tiny highway far in the distance. And from the big picture window in the dining area, she could look down into the woods.   Pretty place, there off County Road 63.

Their first morning, Jack went into town to buy a dog.

"What the hell you want with a dog?" she asked him. He told her it was to guard against snakes, but she knew he was just being paranoid. Jack had killed three men that she knew about, three pedestrians gunned down while he danced wild dances of decadence up and down Mississippi Boulevard, in his Fairlane, and he'd come out one of the chief drug lords, too, on his six blocks of territory in West Memphis, Arkansas; and he'd once robbed some asshole preppie kid in Germantown, in his front yard, in broad daylight. But now out here, why be so damned paranoid? It didn't make sense to her.

When he left, she did what she'd long said she would do. She went outside stark raving naked, and felt the warm southern sun surround her with its sheer freedom. She stood on the metal steps of the camper and felt the sun on her face and thanked God—even though she did not believe in God's existence—for the sudden possibility of being truly alone with sky and birds and trees. Alone meant being in control.

She threw her arms out and felt the open air, and then walked down the steps to the ground; it was grassy and the few rocks and pine cones magically did not hurt her feet. She walked to the edge of the woods, smelling the red cedar. In the brush and kudzu at the edge of the woods, she saw the animal trail; it wound up from the woods and then back out into the field where they'd put the camper, then past into the farmlands beyond. Jack had seen "eyes" out here the night before: must have been deer on this path last night.

Deer: Now that was a nice thought. Who would have thought over the past few years that she and Jack really would end up someplace with deer instead of dead in the alleys behind the shining glass Pyramid or off the tourist-beaten paths around the Peabody Hotel, where drugs were exchanged for cash and guns? She smiled—and she walked, and instead of following the clearing to the cliff, she followed the animal trail, and it seemed to her that she walked in the path of gentle forest folk. The trail wound down through the woods into the wild and woolly overgrowth of the river bottoms and stopped at an old cow pond. She stood in the weeds at its bank. So this was where they came to water. She stepped back and felt something crunch, scraping against the tender inner part of her instep.

"Damn!" she said as she stepped again and felt something sharp break the surface of the skin. She picked up her foot, the blood starting to well up in a diagonal cut. "Damn!"

She put the foot down next to the little animal skeleton she'd stepped on, the offending rib still protruding like a knife out of the ground. "You didn't make it to water, did you? Got your revenge on my foot I suppose."

She stepped away and felt another crunch: another skeleton. Perhaps a rabbit's. "Jeez! Animal burial ground."

She looked up back into the trees and felt a cold shiver. That rapist: she could imagine him standing there in the shadows, green and decayed from his years in the ground, looking over her naked body. She shook away the dread. Imagination could get the better of you alone in the woods.

Now she felt alone, and in a single vision saw she was surrounded by little twisted animal skeletons. It really was some sort of animal boneyard.

"Damn!" she said, and she started walking back up the trail. There was probably nothing unnatural about the bones—just someplace the wolves brought their prey or something—were there wolves in Mississippi woods?—but she did not like the way this place made her feel. Besides, her foot was bleeding.

She had not heard the battered yellow pick up roll into the clearing and creak to a stop at the camper site and so was as surprised as Albert Danielou when she came limping naked into the clearing. She stopped like a deer caught in the headlights of a car, and he stopped what he was doing, likewise, which was getting out of his truck, and he said, "I've never seen a pretty girl comin' outta the woods like..."

She nodded at him and did not mind that he looked at her, because he was at least ninety and didn't leer at her. He just—appreciated.

"I'll get my robe," she said, and she did. When she came out to sit and bandage her foot he said, "Excuse me, miss, I didn't expect, you know, someone to..."

"That's all right," she said, and she introduced herself as Mary MacCartney.

He shook her hand with an arthritic but still powerful farmer's grip and said, "I guess I'm your nearest neighbor, 'cept for Uncle Joe; 'bout two miles down the road... yellow farm house on the left. You give a holler if y'all need anything."

"Thank you," she said, smiling into his country eyes.

And he said, "I wouldn't hang around that animal trail too much if I was you."

"Oh, but it's beautiful in these woods!" Despite the bones at the watering hole.

"Lot of reasons not to, though."

"Like what?"

"Just a feeling... but when that little Aversham girl disappeared..."

"Little girl?"

"Three years old, disappeared from the First Mount Zion Christian Church of Redgunk annual picnic, just last year. They found her bones right here." He toed the ground right at the edge of the animal trail. "Pretty much licked clean."

* * *

"I'm glad you got that dog," said Mary to Jack as he tied the end of the rope to a large oak limb jutting into the field.

"Shepherd. Make a good watchdog." His kind of pet, of course, not hers.

"I believe you should tie him closer to the camper."

"Rope's long enough he can run around in the field."

"But where you've got him is an animal trail, right in the middle of it."

Jack looked at her with his typical impatience.

"It's just that..." She wasn't sure how or what to explain. "It's just that the deer won't come up with him there."

"We'll put a deer lick out in the field sometime if you're wantin' to watch the deer." Of course she wanted to watch the deer—that was something she'd said time and time again as they made plans and dreamed dreams.

"When, Jack?" she said. No answer. Somehow being in the country wasn't going to change things, was it?

He did not like her tone and besides, he was pissed at her. He said, "Someone's been here, haven't they?" He'd seen the tracks of Albert Danielou's pick up. "Haven't they?"

She shrugged at him like she did not know what he was talking about.

"Who?" Was he jealous? She smiled inwardly: jealous of Albert Danielou?

"I believe someone must have been here and you're just not telling me. Now why wouldn't you just tell me if someone was here or not?"

She looked at him blankly.

"Why not?" he snapped at her and when she still did not reply he grabbed her arm so that his fingers felt like daggers and left little blue marks on her skin. "What the hell would you be hiding from me?"

"You're being paranoid, Jack."

He sneered, released her arm and stormed off to the trailer.

She looked down at the mean-looking dog he'd bought, the dog standing rigid but quietly, sizing her up, and she let her eyes wander past him right into that dark earth where the little Aversham girl had been, where they'd found nothing but her bones.

It rained in the afternoon, and they played cards and did not talk, and she did not tell him about the bones at the watering hole or about the Aversham girl. She simply resented him, looking over her straight. He just grumbled at her as he put some pennies in the center of the table and called.

The rain came harder and it depressed her, that and the realization that she and Jack were no different here than they were in Memphis, that he was still aloof, cranky, violent; that she could feel nothing stronger for him than she'd ever felt; that the amorphous fear she carried with her was not for the police squad car going by nor for someone shooting both of them in cold blood, but it was for what they felt for each other: nothingness, disdain. He was still the man who'd killed Simon Legree—accidentally, he'd claimed—Simon Legree, her iguana, the damned iguana that she'd wanted all her damned life and that Daddy would never, never let her have, the thing she'd wanted all her life with a need that was very nearly—sexual.

The day the AK-47 "accidentally" went off and chopped Simon into bits, Jack simply said, "Someday, Mary Contrary, I won't be dealing but we'll have a hundred thousand dollars and I'll buy us some land to build a house and raise a family, and we'll have a sweetness together which we could never have here in the city, where things turn violent so quick, a sweetness you couldn't find with some damned lizard. Someday, you and I will be happy, Mary Contrary. I'll make you happy."

But it wasn't sweetness she wanted. And all that was bull, anyway, because here they were in the camper in the middle of that acreage and there wasn't a single tender feeling between them. No doubt she could be happy in this land, but not with him.

The rain intensified again. And there was a howl.

"What was that?" whispered Mary Contrary.

"Damned dog," he said, getting up and walking to the picture window. The rain was splattering against the screen, making it impossible to see outside.

"You ought've bought a dog house."

"He's a damned animal, he can take the rain."

Another howl, louder, then loud continuous barking and a quick, sudden yelp of pain. And silence. Jack cupped his hand to the window to look through.

"What is it?"

"I believe that damned dog has escaped."

"Escaped?" She was flashing on an image of bones.

"I'm going after him. I spent good money on him."

"Wait until it stops rain—" The image of the bones weighed more heavily into her imagination. The idea did not lack its appeal.

"I'll be back." He opened the door to the wind and the pelting rain.

"You'll get soaked!" He was already outside. She watched from the open door as he went and stood where the animal had been, where—surely enough—the rope had broken and now dangled from the oak limb.

Jack knelt down, the rain already soaking his clothing and his long black hair. He looked up from paw prints in the mud and pointed that the dog had gone down the animal trail.

"I'm going," he shouted. And she could have stopped him. What about those bones at the end of the trail? What about the Aversham girl's bones licked clean? Were there wolves out there? A warning: it would take little effort to warn him, to caution him there might be something out there. But she could also let him go without warning, let him go into the darkening rainstorm, let him go to stumble into the muddy animal boneyard, let him fall bleeding to the ground while the wolves circled. That she could do! *Kill my Simon, will you? Kill my control?* He turned onto the trail and she shut the trailer door and went back to the kitchen table and did not look out, and played solitaire.

No, it was two men she'd killed, not just one. It was hard to keep track of such things, but she remembered him now while she was staring at the Jack of Spades and trying to determine if he should be played on the Queen of Hearts or the Queen of Diamonds. She chose the latter: cold, hard. Funny how it was hard to forget killing one man, and hard to remember doing so to another.

"So maybe everyone has killed someone once, only to forget it, to remember it only in some disturbing dream," she thought to herself. "Maybe you always forget the first one, like the first of everything, bury it in your gray brain matter until something digs it up; and maybe I am not alone in who I am, but everyone is like me, really like me, and would chose to do everything I have done if they were in my place, and maybe I am just more conscious than most folks. More ready to decide. More real than they are. For who would not murder if given the necessity, and who would not rip her soul and body apart for something—adventurous and new and powerful?"

It was on the night of her senior class party when she killed the first man. The old fart had made a pass at her: old; probably in his late twenties, fresh out of college, teaching her Advanced Placement English class and Chaucer. She should have known he would make a pass at her that day when they discussed the Wife of Bath's Tale and he asked, "So what does the knight discover all women want?" and she said very, very methodically, "Sovereignty. Over men."

And he nodded and looked into her eyes meaningfully and surely everyone in the class knew what crossed between them like a spark across the synapses of a single mind. Late in the night, deep into the wildness of the senior party, teacher Jonathan Williams drove his star pupil around in his little MGB and ended up again at the Peabody high above the city. Somehow he'd got the key and all the locking codes for the service elevator and they went to the roof. High in the fortress tower, with the lights of the city glittering and sparkling with a drunken neon movement, he started munching on her neck—he the one in control, the teacher always in control—he started licking and slurping, and suddenly she knew she'd had enough, because she'd had far too much of this same thing from her father, who took control of her very body and who would never, never let her have her own way, and belligerently refused to let her have that pet-lizard in the window of Ally Devonshire's Exotic Pets of Redgunk, and she said again, "Sovereignty, Mr. Williams," and she pushed him off the ledge and he landed with a great squashy, empty melon sound on the pavement below. Two men, not one. Two men and her parents.

* * *

Jack shook. He was full of anger and fear and hurt. He was wet, and the water kept coming like a monsoon, and the woods seemed unfriendly. And that hurt him most. He'd spent all of his adult life saving up for this, for a little chunk of land where he could escape all that city life had done to him. It was a desire to return to something lovely and beautiful and gentle that had propelled him through everything he'd done, every drug deal, every fight, even the killings. All he wanted was comfort now, to be happy with Mary Contrary, to love her like normal people loved each other, to have tenderness and health. Already it was not turning out that way. Already he sensed in Mary a strange reticence to live in that dream. What the hell was wrong with her? She had a cold-bloodedness worse than his own. And why—he should not have started shooting up. He never shot up when he was dealing; strictly business. Now: he had the shakes and he was in the middle of a rainstorm looking for that stupid dog, and he felt he was being watched, pursued, hunted.

He slipped on the wet leaves of the animal trail and tumbled. "Damn!" picked himself up and went on, calling out for the dog. Nothing but the sound of rain and wind in the treetops, a rushing violent wind.

"Dog!" he called out again, and the trail went downward into the woods, through waving brambles and poison ivies and big-leafed snaky kudzu.

"Dog!" and he emerged into a partial clearing at Old Miss Haskins' pond and stepped into something, something smushy and wet and simultaneously brittle.

* * *

Uncle Joe Howdy wheelchaired himself to the battered screen door of the makeshift plywood zoo and looked out into the increasingly violent storm. A mist from the rain spattered his warty age-misshapen face and he called out for his son. His "son."

There was no response and Uncle Joe cursed, "Friggin' boy ain't got enough sense to come in outta the friggin' storm. And us with a Tornado Watch out."

A snake flipped down from a two-by-four he'd nailed at the ceiling: a boa. It slithered down and came to a sluggish rest at his feet. The chameleon sitting in the wire cage close to the door simply blinked. Uncle Joe closed his eyes: tired, tired of doing all this by himself, trying to control that boy. He was tired.

When Joe Howdy was a young man he'd returned with a lot more energy than he had now, though without a leg, from the Battle of Guam, and he'd carried with him a shrunken head stolen from a Philippine soldier. All his life he'd had a dream to make Redgunk, Mississippi, more than just a fleck on a map and the shrunken head proved a start: he set up Uncle Joe's Corner Liquor Store and Gas, which included his now-famous "Museum of Science and Egyptology," with its giant frogs and baby sharks in cloudy jars of formaldehyde and that shrunken head. When he couldn't stuff anything else in the Museum of Science and Egyptology, to which of course the public can still be admitted for the price of two-bits, he started a private collection of things that the public was not allowed to see, and he built a bunch of cages and pens and secretive strange structures right up next to his mobile home out on County Road 63. And some say he had alligators out there and that he once had chimpanzees he had to dispose of because they caught a virus, and folks let it be rumored that he was planning to open a Lizard Zoo. And that was where he sat now, in that Lizard Zoo, calling for Frank.

"Don't know what to do about that boy," muttered Uncle Joe to his other "children." "I believe it ain't worth spending 40 pesos Cuban on a new life form if it's gonna catch itself pneumonia or get sucked up in a twister. I'll have to go after the boy. And me in a wheelchair."

The snake responded with a cool silence.

* * *

Mary's hand started twitching and she had to throw the rest of the cards onto the table. "Damn!" she hissed at them. She couldn't get the ghosts out of her head: the two men; Mom and Dad, too, even though they'd deserved to die for not letting her go with Bobby Barnhart to the high school damned prom, and for never, never getting her that damned lizard, though she'd wanted it more than sex. And she hadn't really killed them at all, not directly, it was the gas she'd turned on that did it; besides they were so miserable in their mundanity that what she'd done amounted to euthanasia. They should have given her a little more leash, a little control. That was all she ever really wanted.

Jack appeared at the door, wet and distraught and strung out: she was glad she'd tossed his needles and the rest of the horse. He had a wildness in his eyes: "All I ever wanted was peace, peace and gentleness for you and me and a normal life—"

"What's got into you Jack?"

He showed her what was in his hand: the dog, the dog's head, ripped from its body. Arterial blood still ran from its jagged neck.

"God, what the hell did you do, Jack?" *Like what you did to Simon?*

"I—" He was shaking. He needed his fix. Too bad he wasn't going to get any. "Found it... this way... at the pond. Its body..."

"Throw it out there, Jack, I don't want to see it." The beady little dog eyes looked at her vacantly. *Like Simon LeGree's!* "Throw it out or I will not tell you what I did with your drugs."

The wildness flared in his eyes: fear, panic, desperation. He tossed the head behind him to the tree line, to the animal path. Mary saw something else there, something living, something watching them. She ignored it. She said, "Good boy, Jack."

"Where—"

"I trashed it all while you were gone. Broke up the needles and flushed the junk into the john."

"You—" A darkness came over him.

"Sorry, Jack. Time to straighten up."

He shook. Why the hell was she doing this to him? Why? He was too weak to beat her, to kill her, though he would have done so. He felt nauseous, drunken, woozy, like he was dying. "I gotta lie down."

"You go lie down," she told him, and he did, shaking, nearly convulsing, doing his best to still his own bodily madness.

A little control is all. She watched him from the dining area as he tried to keep from shivering. To hell with him: all she wanted was a little control.

Something moved again at the animal trail. She looked out and saw the thing again, and this time it stepped from beneath the shadows of the tree and she could really see it. It was something like a small man, crouching naked on all fours, only that was not skin that covered his body: partly flesh, partly reptilian scales or loose mucous. The scales and mucous covered his face, much longer than a human's, much more like something part-lizard, part-rat.

"Good God, what are you?" she whispered at the thing with a strange, physical curiosity. Its powerful arms and legs brought it forward; it had talons that could have easily ripped through the little Aversham girl, or Jack's dog.

"Are you hungry?" whispered Mary, looking at the thing, looking into its eyes that seemed so strangely like a human child's. And Simon Legree's. "You didn't eat the dog, did you? Just tore him up, huh?"

It cocked its head and looked at her quizzically.

She said: "You followed Jack here, didn't you?"

Jack: suppose Jack just disappeared. Who would care?

Mary was not afraid. She opened the screen door of the camper and heard the creature's hissing breath and saw that it had come to sit at the bottom of the steps. She nodded at it and it again cocked its head to the side, and she opened the door wider, and the thing tentatively crawled up a step, then another, then another and suddenly it was in the trailer with her.

Jack was unconscious. The beast moved its reptilian head from side to side, saw Jack in the other room, looked back at Mary as if questioning her, then leapt into the bedroom.

There was a commotion: Jack squirmed half-consciously against the beast. Suddenly he was being dragged across the floor with a loud thumping by the lizard-boy who now yanked him to the door. Which Mary held open.

The thing leapt to the ground, and Jack fell out like a lifeless sack. Some limb—a leg or an arm—broke; there was a cry; and the lizard creature had dragged Jack to the animal trail and beyond into the darkness of the trees, and they were both gone.

* * *

There was a knock at the door and she went to find an old man sitting in a wheelchair at the bottom of the steps.

"Howdy, Ma'am," he said in a gruff, sleazy, friendly tone. "I'm sorry I ain't been out to say hi to my new neighbors—I keep pretty busy. Uncle Joe."

"Hello, Uncle Joe. What can I do for you?"

"Well, I'm…"

"Care to come in outta the storm?" She motioned inward.

He nodded and eased himself up out of the wheel chair and with her help, hobbled in on that one leg. He sat down at the dining table and sniffed the air and knew the lizard-man had been there: he could smell the genetically engineered skin; it was unlike any other smell in nature. He was tired, damned tired of this.

"My boy. I'm lookin' for my boy Frank."

"Is it the monster you're callin' Frank?"

Uncle Joe's black eyes lit up. "So, you seen him! Oh, he ain't a monster, he's just a child—just a pet."

"What the hell is he?"

He looked squarely at her and somehow knew he could confide in her, something in her face; or, no, maybe just the stress of the storm, looking for him in the storm, the stress of looking yet again for that kid, looking again for the umpteenth damned time. He really was so tired of doing this on his own. He said, "You're intrigued by him, ain't you? You like him I can tell."

"How the hell could someone like Frank?"

"He is part human, you know, almost all his body is human—and unique. That's why I wanna find the poor boy before—somethin' happens to him—before he gets ripped up in the storm. He's been here, ain't he?"

"Why do you let him run around loose like that?"

"Boy's gotta eat—too big an appetite for me to keep him locked in the zoo."

"Zoo?"

"You've heard, surely, that I'm making a zoo, tourist attraction big enough to keep people coming here for years—with Frank as my main attraction. He is a unique life form, and I can tell by the look in your eyes, he will intrigue a lot of people. Charge them five bucks to see him."

"Where the hell did he come from?"

Uncle Joe winked: "They're paying biotech engineers just forty pesos a day down in Cuba to do quality genetic engineering work. You think they're gonna work in their hightech barrios for what amounts to ten dollars a day when for just a little more, they can engineer me a major world-class tourist attraction? I'm talking about a world-class lizard zoo. And there ain't no others like Frank; at least, not so far."

"Do you have more on the way?"

"No—some problems with customs. No more in the hopper. But I'd just soon not talk about—"

"I'm interested in hearing about it."

"Why?"

She looked out the window into the woods and tried to envision that thing sitting on Jack's carcass. She said, "The same freak show curiosity that will make people come to see Frank, I suppose, makes me interested, too." But of course it was a hell of a lot more than that; the desire was tickling and urging her insides with something she'd always wanted. Always. "Besides, I have a right to know something about what my neighbors are up to, don't I? Especially if they're killing little girls."

"I—"

"I don't give a damn. Just tell me about this—this boy..."

"I tried mating him..." Joe caught the light in her eyes, the release of pheromones she'd put out into the air. Strange, but perceptible. "He has human genitalia, you know—thought if I could try him on some primates, I'd have a whole family of—"

"Primates?"

"Dead. They wouldn't hold still. They just would not hold still. And not enough intelligence to control the boy, to calm him down when necessary, to guide him—I told everyone they caught some disease and died."

"He is like a boy, then." She remembered the look in his eyes.

"And of course will always be that way. Just enough intelligence to do what he's told. And to hunt. Hunts like a lizard does."

"I see." She looked for movement in the black trees. Someplace in the southern part of the county, a twister was blowing its way down the river valley. But it would bypass her woods, her animal trail, her Jack, her Frank. "So what's left for mating your boy?"

"I believe it would take something just like him, half-lizard, half-human. But no such being is forthcoming. In lieu of that, a woman..."

"A real woman? Who would do such a thing?"

"Some of the older whores at Burly Bob's Bar and Grill down in Newman County, the ones who can't earn enough the usual ways to pay for their various and sordid habits, they'd do just about anything for a hundred dollar bill." He gave her a sly look and added "Maybe two hundred."

She shook her head. "You're talking about getting a woman to have babies with that thing—"

"Could rip her up, too—I mean, the process of doing it..." Uncle Joe's voice trailed away and his eyes got a little glazed as if he were remembering something that was too much even for his twisted comprehension. "That sex act could rip her up. Unless she controlled the boy—unless she could control him."

"And you are talking about getting a woman to give birth to reptile things, Uncle Joe, reptile-monsters, whatever came out of her because of whatever he put into her. You are talking about getting her to become a monster, too, you know, to become part of your zoo. A woman's not going to do that for money, Uncle Joe."

But they both knew a woman, a particular woman, might do it for something.

"I would not make her part of my zoo."

"But you would have to—birthing those beasts and mating with that thing, she would be part of the zoo. No one would do that. Unless you made her queen of the zoo."

"What the hell are you talking about?"

"Unless you gave her the run of the shop, gave her control."

"Over Frank? That's the point—"

"Over their children, too; over the animals, and the whole attraction. Over you."

"You mean, she'd want to be some kind of partner? I'd never thought about—having a partner. This zoo business can be pretty grimy sometimes."

"Pretty grimy, I'm sure," she said.

Uncle Joe eyed her curiously, knowing certainly now that she wasn't just shooting the breeze. He'd told her far more than he would have told anyone else, for any other reason. She was his answer. But it made him uncomfortable. She made him uncomfortable. More uncomfortable than he'd been in his life, in the bloody jungles of the Pacific, in the back rooms of seedy genetics labs; more uncomfortable than he'd been in his whole damned life. He said, "I gotta go get Frank before that boy gets in trouble. The worst of the storm's comin', I can feel it."

"Of course," she said and she offered an arm, which he took as he lowered himself out of the camper and into the wheelchair. "No doubt the worst is coming. But things are—under control. Don't you worry about that, Uncle Joe."

And he tried to balance what he and Frank needed against the revulsion even he felt for her, and he wheeled himself with difficulty back onto the animal path and headed toward the watering hole calling for Frank, with no luck.

She watched him go. It was dark and the storm made the oncoming night even darker. She turned on the dining room lights.

Someplace nearby in the woods, the openings in Jack's body were still bubbling with his fluids and Frank was getting his fill, and wondering in his lizard-brain what kind of creature might have helped him to his feeding like that, and what kind of creature would look him in the eye as Uncle Joe sometimes looked him in the eye: with curiosity and courage and control.

Mary Contrary looked at her reflection in the open window. She smiled. She'd never imagined living in the country could be like this, so free. She let her wispy body sway back and forth a bit; then very slowly, very seductively she removed her shirt and then all the rest of her clothing. She moved and twisted a bit and watched for movement in the woods at the edge of the animal trail.

Eucharist
By Richard Parks

"Elvis is still alive. I know."

Charlie looked up from his fifth bottle. His eyes were red but focused; he wasn't beer drunk or any other kind. Billy knew that for a fact. Charlie's dirty blonde hair always got wilder when he was for sure drunk, as if beer made little cowlicks grow all over his head. But Charlie's hair still looked like it remembered a comb, if in fact it had not seen one lately. Billy shrugged.

"It's been nearly fifty years, Charlie. Even if it wasn't him they found in that bathroom, even if everyone was in on it and all the stories are true.... well, it don't matter—the King's sure dead now."

"No," Charlie said, very calm and serious. "He ain't ."

Billy took another pretzel from the bowl on the bar and looked around the Triangle. It was quiet, even for a Thursday night. The antique-revival jukebox was playing "Love me Tender" off an old CD. He and Charlie were the only two people at the bar. Old Lyle played a listless game of eight ball with Young Lyle in the back. President Danforth Quayle III was giving a speech on the second anniversary of the Mars Colony on the bar's new HD set; Lucy glanced at the set now and then between bringing Charlie beers. No chickies to hit on. Too soon for another beer.

Billy finished the pretzel, reached for another. "How do you know that?"

"I seen him."

That got Lucy's attention, and that was something in itself. Twenty plus years at the Triangle, first as a good-time girl, later as owner when her money was worth more than her looks, Lucy had seen or heard pretty much everything. "When did you see him? Hell, even the *Enquirer* stopped running 'I saw Elvis' stories twenty years ago."

"Last night," Charlie said, "and I was stone sober."

"Where?" Billy asked, getting another pretzel. He didn't know why he was so hungry; he just was. Always, these days. Youth and energy kept his waist trim, but that wouldn't last. Billy had his father's example to prove that.

Charlie got the last pretzel in the bowl, chewed thoughtfully while Lucy opened another bag. "I was at the new hotel across from Graceland—" he stopped to glare at Lucy before she could ask her question. "Never mind why, Lucy; it's private. Anyway, from the thirty-fifth floor you're practically looking down on the Meditation Garden. It wasn't the first time I'd been there; this time I brought my binoculars. And I saw him," he finished, simply.

"You saw somebody," Lucy corrected. "One of the guards, maybe."

Billy shook his head. "No guards at night," he said. "They switched over to an isolation field three years ago."

"How do you know that?" Lucy asked.

"Don't you look at your newsreader? There was an article just last month. No one lives in the house anymore, so they seal it off at night."

"I know what I saw," Charlie repeated to everyone and no one.

* * *

The shuttles were electric now. Billy remembered the old gasoline buses from the first time his mother and father had brought him to Graceland just after the move to Memphis; they bought their tickets across the street at the little bus station by Elvis's jets and Cadillacs, and they trundled across the street and through the wrought iron gates forged with notes of music. The buses were the only way through the gates then as now. Billy's mother was almost bouncing in her seat and his father had that silly grin on his face that Billy didn't understand until very much later.

You'd think we were going to see Jesus.

He looked at his fellow passengers on the shuttle and saw the same silly grins, the same barely-contained excitement. Billy felt neither, these days. He did not envy them. Every day was not like the first time, could never be, and it was far better that way. Billy felt no giddy excitement as the shuttle wound up the long drive, passed under the ancient trees; what he felt was something deeper and older than novelty or the echoes of a living legend.

It felt like being in church.

The outside of the mansion was superb stonework and simplicity. Inside was confusion. The bottom floor was cut into too many rooms; Billy felt the walls closing in a bit by the time the tour was half done. There were windows cut along the far side of the Jungle Room; that helped a little. Billy half-listened to the familiar spiel about the famous recording session held in that room. He paid more attention to the furniture carved into little Hawaiian gods.

Idols.

He remembered the word from a hundred Sunday School lessons. It came back to him again and again as they went from shrine to shrine in the tour: the Grammys for the Gospel music, the Gold Records for everything else, and the Vegas costumes that looked far too small to enrobe a god.

God?

There was that thought again. It always popped up about then when Billy came to Graceland. Silly, maybe blasphemous. Billy wasn't too sure what "blasphemous" meant, but he'd heard a TV preacher use it once and it seemed to fit. Didn't matter; the thought had its own reasons and came in its own time.

Billy came to Graceland the same way. He didn't understand his reasons for coming; never had. He listened to his parent's records, bought his own later when they split up, watched the movies, knew they weren't very good movies but that didn't matter. All the records and movies, everything done and over long before he was born. Only it wasn't done, wasn't over.

Wasn't enough.

Billy felt his stomach grumble. He glanced around, but if anyone heard they were not letting on. The Graceland tour emerged into the sunlight, past the big earthen vase that Elvis or one of his friends had left bullet hole in, and onto the little sidewalk that led to the Meditation Garden. Billy had never known a cemetery called that before Graceland. He liked it. Billy followed the others in the line toward the little wrought-iron gate; to the right were the windows of the Jungle room and above that, the upper story windows where no one was allowed to go. Billy glanced up at them as he always did.

Elvis looked at him from the third window.

* * *

"I know what I saw." Billy thought the words sounded familiar, then he remembered. Charlie didn't say anything, though he had the look of someone who'd think about smiling, if there weren't too many people around. Lucy just looked at him, slowly twisting one strand of her dyed red hair. It was another quiet night at the Triangle.

Old Lyle shook his head; the light from the bar lamp glistened across the bare skin on the top of his head.

"First Charlie, now you. Elvis is dead, Billy. Died before you were born."

Billy nodded. "Don't you think I know that?"

Lucy frowned. "I thought you said you saw him or do you think it was his ghost?"

"It wasn't a ghost. It was solid. But it wasn't Elvis," he said.

"How do you know that?"

"He was young. Like in the movies. Young like Nineteen-fifties Elvis young."

Charlie shrugged. "*National Star* said Elvis had a secret son. Maybe it was him."

"I said *young*, Charlie. Any natural son of the King's would be pushing fifty harder than you are."

Murmurs all around. Charlie subsided, looking thoughtful.

Lucy spoke up. "Suppose he had those... whatcha call... longevity treatments? Suppose he didn't die, and he lived until the treatments were available, and they're keeping him young looking? Then he puts in an appearance now and then to keep the rumors going? It'd explain an awful lot."

"Suppose Jesus didn't die on the Cross?" Billy asked, softly. The inhabitants of the Triangle Bar to a man and woman stared at him. Billy went on, his voice barely above a whisper. "Don't you think there might be more to this than we've ever let on to ourselves? Why do people come from all over the world to visit a dead singer's house?"

"They visit Mozart's and that other one, Beethoven's, I hear," Charlie said.

Billy shrugged. "But do they bring flowers and stand there and cry like they'd lost a son? Do they name their firstborn 'Ludwig?' Do they claim 'Image of Wolfgang healed my arthritis?' If Elvis was Catholic he'd a been a saint thirty years ago. Who did you think about more last week: God or Elvis? And don't tell me; I don't need to know. You do."

There was a very long silence. Old Lyle broke it. "I'd like a beer." Charlie echoed him and there were beers all around. Even Lucy had one as they took turns at the pretzels again.

"Why are we always hungry?" Billy asked. Everyone stopped eating.

"Billy..." Lucy began, but he didn't let her finish.

"I know, Lucy. I'm scared too."

"What do you think it means?" Charlie asked. "Elvis, I mean."

"I don't know," Billy said. "But I need to know. I think we all do."

"I know someone who might can help,"old Lyle said.

* * *

Math Langford lived on the fringes of the city. Almost in the hills, almost in Memphis, his ramshackle house lay on the foot of a high bluff like some debris that had fallen off the edge and collected there. The group from the Triangle stood there at his door: Billy, Charlie, Lucy, Lyles Elder and Younger.

Billy shook his head. "If this guy is who you say, I think he'd live better."

"He lives this way because he likes it," Old Lyle said. "You'll understand when you meet him."

"Understand what, Lyle?"

Math Langford stood in the open doorway. Billy recognized him immediately from Lyle's description: Hair long the way men hadn't worn it in years, tied back and pulled close to his skull. Skinny as a rail and two feet longer, he almost had to duck under his own door.

"Hello, Math. I have some friends who want to meet you," Lyle said.

"Do I want to meet them?" Math asked. There was nothing harsh in the question, though Billy thought he heard Lucy mutter "Well I never!" under breath. Math asked the question like someone who just needed an answer.

"Yes, Math. You do." That was Lyle again.

Math brightened. "Well, then. Come on in."

The inside and the outside of Math Langford's house were two different worlds. If the outside was a mess, the inside was... well, *organized* was the word Billy came up with. Not that it was "company clean," as his mother would have said. There were very few level surfaces in the living room that were not covered with the insides of some electronic device or other; tool rolls were spread out at strategic areas around the room, easy to hand from anywhere you happened to be. Two wall-mounted flat TV's were set to two different satellite news feeds; there was no sound from either of them.

Math led them past the first room and into what seemed to serve as a den, though it was obviously a workroom, too. The only difference was, instead of newsreaders, this one had a framed, autographed picture of Elvis Presley, Vegas Performer Period. Bill's head grew a little light thinking of how much that picture was worth, if real. And Billy had no doubt it was real.

He stood with the others in a tight little group while Math sat down cross-legged in front of an old coffee table that currently held an open black box whose function Billy couldn't begin to guess. A five-inch CRT on the side flashed a set of numbers. Math glanced at them and slowly turned the screw of a potentiometer until the were a different set of numbers. He didn't say anything else, didn't even seem to notice them.

"Mr. Langford..." Billy began, but Math waggled a finger at his general direction without looking up and he subsided.

A bit more twiddling, a few more numbers, then Math grunted with satisfaction and deigned to look at his guests again. "That needed doing," was as close to an apology as he came. Lucy was fuming, but Billy figured it was Math's house, and it wasn't like they were *invited* or anything.

"I told them you knew about Graceland, Math," Lyle said.

That and not much else. Old Lyle had met Math Langford on a construction site the previous year; Old Lyle was hanging drywall and Math was installing a security system. One beer led to another and the story had come out. At least, that's how Lyle told it.

Math nodded. "What do ya'll want to know?"

Silence. No one really expected him to ask the important question right away. Billy tried an answer. "We want to know how the isolation field works."

Math smiled. "No, you don't: Every time someone asks me that, and I tell them, and after a bit their eyes glaze over and they remember somewhere else they need to be. It's great for getting rid of people."

"If you want to get rid of us, Mr. Langford, just say so. I'm not one to overstay a welcome..." Lucy stopped when Math started laughing.

"That'd imply you had a welcome to start with, Ma'am. You and your friends came here because you want something from me. I haven't decided if I'm going to give it to you yet, but for *damn* sure someone's got to ask first." That was Billy.

Lucy and Charlie both glared at him but Billy didn't pay any mind. He felt focused. He felt like a rifle with the cross-hairs on target, and he wasn't about to move now. He said what he knew had to be said.

Now Math was smiling. "Yes, that's what I thought. Now tell me why."

Billy and Charlie pieced together their parts of the story while Math listened to every word. He finally nodded. "Interesting. But you still haven't told me why."

They all stared at him. Billy managed to speak first. "We saw Elvis! Ain't that enough?"

Math shook his head. "Not for me or you either. Elvis was a man. A musician, a singer, but mostly a man. He moved on the earth a long time ago and he died, just like any other man. We all know that. *You* know that, if you still have a foot in the real world. And despite knowing that, you and lots of other people have seen Elvis down through the years."

"Lots of people aren't me," Billy said, then, "I got to know."

"The rest of you got to know, too."

Nods all around. No hesitation.

Math nodded. "All right. What's it worth to you?"

This part they had expected, and answered one and all before the trip to Math's house. Billy led off. "I got three thousand put away in the bank. You can have it all."

The others repeated their offers, one after the other. The amounts varied, but one thing was the same: in each case it was all the money they had in the world. Billy brought his bankbook to prove it.

Math glanced at the balance, seemed to consider. "All right, I'll tell you how to beat the isolation field." And he told them. And it was ridiculously easy.

"What about the money?" Charlie asked, surprised. "Are you gonna trust us for that?"

Math shrugged. "Not a question of trust. I don't want it."

They all stared again. Lucy shook her head like a punch-drunk fighter. "But... you asked what we'd give!"

Math nodded agreeably. "I wanted to know. More important, I wanted to make sure *you* knew. This was a test, people. You passed."

"Test?" Billy asked.

Math sighed. "Doesn't anyone read any more? You people are on a sacred quest, and I'm an obstacle. The dragon at the mouth of the cave, the guardian Naga at the temple," he smiled at them, and finished, "the stone in front of the tomb. And I have just rolled away."

"You're crazy," said Lucy.

Math's smile didn't flicker. "That, too."

"How do we know you won't call the police as soon as we leave?" Billy asked.

"You don't. And it don't make a damn or you wouldn't have gotten this far. But don't let your guard down. I'm the first test; I didn't say I was the only one." He reached under the collar of his shirt, pulled out a key on a little silver chain. He pulled it over his head, paused to untangle it from his ponytail, and handed it to Billy. "You'll need this."

Billy looked at the key. It was just an old-fashioned brass key of a kind that palm-scanners and keycards made obsolete years ago. "What's this?"

"The Key to the Kingdom."

* * *

Billy wore the key around his neck as they made their way on foot down a back street near Graceland. Now and then one of the others would ask to see the key and he would show them. After the third time Charlie asked, Billy started to take it off.

"You wear it a while."

Charlie stopped him. "Math gave it to you."

Billy glanced at the others, a little surprised to see the looks of awe there. Awe and... envy, he thought, in Young Lyle. "It don't matter," Billy said, and didn't want to believe it.

They came to the place Math spoke about, at a place where an ancient magnolia grew by the eastern wall of the estate. Billy peered behind it first, found the metal box bolted to the wall.

"It's here, just like Math said."

"How do we know it's what he said it is?" Young Lyle asked.

"We try it," Old Lyle said.

"I don't think we should," Young Lyle said.

Lucy put a hand on his shoulder. "We've come this far."

"Yes," Young Lyle said, "and no farther. We haven't done anything wrong, yet. We can turn back now."

"Turn back to what?" Billy asked, mildly. "Beer at the Triangle five nights a week?" He glanced at Lucy. "Bad marriages?" He turned to Charlie and Old Lyle. "Working day in and out for next to nothing, every day the same damn thing as the last, only we're a little older and fatter every time?"

Young Lyle shook his head. "Better than prison. And suppose we don't get caught, never mind if the grave's empty or not, what happens then? I'll tell you: We go back to where we were, being what we are, Billy. It don't make no difference."

The others were looking at Billy now. He saw the question there. "Math said there would be other tests. This is one."

"Just common sense," Young Lyle said.

"Just fear and doubt." Billy smiled. "Did you think you were the only one, Lyle? No. I don't understand this any more than the rest of you, but there's a question I've been asking myself all my life and didn't have sense enough to know it. Tonight I may get the answer."

"What question, Billy?" Young Lyle asked.

"'Is this all there is?'" said Billy, softly. "I've looked where you're supposed to look: Church, School, the Army, the Triangle and dozens like it. Nothing. That's why I'm here tonight, whatever we find. I think that's why you're here, too."

Billy put the key in the lock and turned it before anyone could think to stop him. The box opened. There were no flashing sirens, no red lights. The others watched, forgetting to breathe, as Billy pushed the coded buttons in sequence. A crack in the wall suddenly widened, and they were standing by a hidden door.

"I'm going in," Billy said. "The rest of you will have to make up your own minds."

He stepped through the door. One by one, the others followed, all except Young Lyle. "I can't," he said, "I'm sorry."

"It's all right, Son," said Old Lyle. "You wait for us."

Young Lyle shook his head, backing away. "I—I won't tell anyone..."

Billy tried to smile, couldn't. "Yes, you will," he said, as Young Lyle disappeared.

"Judas," said Old Lyle, sadly.

Billy patted him on the shoulder. "There always is, one way or another; it's not your fault."

Charlie looked across the grounds. "It won't take him long to find someone. We better hurry."

* * *

The old man watched the monitors as someone split off from the pack.

Has a hound abandoned the chase?

Perhaps that's all it was. Perhaps there was more. Could he take that chance now that the goal was so close? The old man studied the retreating figure for another few moments. He prided himself on being able to discern intentions, separating what a man might say and what a man would *do*. This man was not walking away from anyone, he walked with purpose, toward a goal.

He's going to turn them in.

It was time for a decision and the old man did not hesitate. He judged the young man's speed, then studied the grid map of the west wall, activated a system, unlocked a safety and took manual control, all within a few seconds. One-eighty degree rotation and the slim tube pointed away from the grounds and toward the road. The young man retreating down the side street walked into an invisible beam and died. In an instant his blood boiled in his veins and super-heated air from his exploding lungs forced open his mouth in a dead imitation of a living scream.

In a moment it was over. The old man notified the clean-up crew and turned his full attention back to the rest of the intruders, the incident already fading from his memory. At his age he only had time for the important things, and it was for him to decide what was important.

* * *

"Did you hear that?" Old Lyle demanded.

They had. Everyone froze in place, waiting for what they didn't know but nothing happened. The mansion remained dark except for the floodlights in front that let you see it from the road. The door in the wall was just beyond the lights; Billy led the others into the deeper shadows out back. Overhead the stars shimmered softly through the haze of the isolation field. "They had to leave a way in just in case the automatic timers failed," Billy said. "I figured Math was telling the truth."

There were no guards; no one challenged them. They filed under the walkway that connected the mansion to the small offices from where the Elvis Empire had been managed. They moved past the shadow of the broken pot. They saw their faint reflections in the windows of the Jungle Room. Billy glanced up, but no face watched them from the second story windows. Billy was a little disappointed.

I still don't know what it means.

Math had asked him the right question, Billy knew. Maybe it was because he *hadn't* been able to answer it that Math had given him the key. He didn't know Math's game, but Billy did know it was more than a whim.

They walked through the gate of the Meditation Garden, past the statue of Jesus with his arms spread wide.

Witness, Billy thought, and then they all stood at the marble slab.

"Name's misspelled," Lucy said.

"Or spelled right, for once," Charlie said. "Depends on who you ask.: Charlie had brought a shovel. He put it down. "We don't have enough time."

"Help me," Billy said. He reached down into the earth by the stone and found a corner easier than he expected. Charlie got in the middle and Old Lyle on the other end. They lifted. It wasn't very heavy. They carefully stood the slab up on its side.

Lucy gasped. "There's no dirt!"

Old Lyle nodded. "They used a capping stone. More like a tomb than a grave."

The new stone was only a foot or two below the surface. It was a little harder to get the grip, but they managed. Another minute and the coffin was in view.

"What does it mean if he is?" Billy asked.

"Open it, Billy."

The coffin lid wasn't even screwed down. Later Billy would wonder about that, a little, but it didn't matter. It really didn't. He opened the lid.

"It's him," Charlie said.

"It's a miracle," Lucy said.

They were both right, as far as Billy could see. It was Elvis. Not the Elvis that died old and sick in some dirty bathroom. Elvis in his twenties, tops. Just out of or just before the Army Elvis. Elvis with firm, healthy flesh. Elvis with no smell of the grave at all. Elvis the way they all saw him, the way everyone who remembered him, remembered. This was Elvis, the real Elvis. The heart and soul of everything that was Elvis. Not what came later, not the tragic ending but the beginning, forever and ever.

"Oh..." It was a collective sigh.

"It's a miracle! We have to tell people..." Lucy said.

"No." That was Billy.

Charlie frowned. "Wasn't that why we came?"

"No," Billy repeated, firmly. "It wasn't. Suppose we tell? It's two minutes on the newsreader and some hired doctor explains about secret cosmetic surgery on the body and the way it was sealed with no air. The world believes them, locks us up for a bit and moves on. That's all. When we die the miracle dies with us."

"Why did we come, then?" Lucy asked.

Billy looked at the body in the coffin. "What do you feel right now, more than anything."

Dead silence was the only answer, for a while. Billy waited as if he had all the time in this world and the next. Old Lyle answered first, though the words seemed to tear at him.

"Hungry,"he said.

Billy nodded. "Yes."

"God help me..." Charlie looked sick. "Young Lyle was right. I'm leaving."

"Your choice," Billy said. "But if you do I guarantee you'll be hungry without relief for the rest of your life."

"We had the music all these years," Old Lyle said. "Wasn't that enough?"

"No. It's past that now," Billy said, and knew he was right.

"Cannibalism," Lucy said.

"Communion," Charlie said, like a man in prison who just found the only unlocked door. "That's all it is. The Eucharist."

Billy went first, hesitantly but reverently. He kissed the hand, and then he ate it. Surprised at the sweetness, understanding it for the divinity it was. The knuckles cracked like sugar candy, the bones dissolved in bliss.

"More..." he said, as the others joined in. More. *All!* Lucy chose her portion and no one questioned or commented. It seemed... right, somehow. Then Charlie, then Old Lyle, and then they were all together in a divine frenzy, reverent ghouls, eating, becoming full for now and forever.

No one left until the service was ended, and at the end there was nothing left. That, too, was part of the miracle. Fifteen minutes later the wall was solid and the box locked, and Graceland as quiet as the slumber of saints.

* * *

A technician nodded at his instruments. "It's almost ready."

The old man standing next to him examined the form in the vat and finally nodded, satisfied. The coffin clone had been a special problem, but now the recipe was right. Matt Langford's information helped keep the internment time to a minimum so no embalming was needed, but that wasn't enough. Using epithelial cells was what had turned the trick; that and a few special treatments left the cloned flesh about as dense as angel food cake and almost as tasty. Tonight was the acid test, so to speak, and it had passed. No matter; to finish the next one properly would take a bit more time.

No more Elvis sightings for a little while, he decided. He'd inform Langford tomorrow.

He left the technician to his work and walked back down the tunnel. There was a warm bed waiting for him in that secret place, and he was a very tired, very old man. He checked the serum level in the autohypo on his arm. It needed replacing, but there was something he needed to do first. A small ritual of his own.

The old man came to the single door at the end of the tunnel, opened it with the key he alone possessed. He pulled aside the velvet curtains, stood alone at a massive gray cylinder set into an alcove shaped like a Gothic arch. He looked down into the view plate at the familiar face. He leaned on the cylinder, the reliquary, the source of Elvises without end. It was cool to the touch, despite the insulation.

"I am large. I contain multitudes." Or close enough.

"I loved you, Son, and I forgave you for what you done to me," he said. "But I still wish I could have made you understand. Proper management, that's the key." He smiled. "The records? The movies? Small time, compared to where we're going next, I promise you. It took me a while, but now we're set and ready. Just watch, is all I ask. Wherever you are, just watch what I'm going to do for you now."

"Mmmm??"

The old man turned, and for a moment he felt as if his heart had turned to ice, though he knew what he saw standing there in the doorway. He knew. EP Mark VI. The face was perfect but the blank, lifeless eyes gave it away, that and the tiny trickle of drool from the corner of its mouth. Not hard to understand in a creature whose brain was not much more than a swelling of the spinal cord.

There was a polite cough from the hallway. "Colonel?"

Another technician, standing at a discrete distance. "What do you want us to do with the walking clone? It keeps bumping into the wall."

The Colonel turned back to the reliquary. "Lock it up," he said, "until it's time for the next miracle."

Swift Peter, The Beast of Cooper-Young
By Corey Mesler

Listen up, children.

This was Cooper-Young, a neighborhood once considered a carbuncle on the side of the great rusting ship of Midtown Memphis, Tennessee, circa 1910 or so. There is a stir in the air, a buzz. Something is happening, we know, because there are people in the streets, people running this way and that, people with serious expressions, people with guns. Colored folk, we used to call them, or "those people."

Let's get a closer look (as we look back) and see if we can discover what was going on this Summer evening, with the syrupy heat and the breeze barely pumping, and so many folk out in the street.

Seems something sinister was afoot. The men with guns are out protecting the neighborhood, protecting their loved ones. This neighborhood, for better or worse, is where they've come to live, where they've decided to settle and raise a family. It's a nice neighborhood, tight little rows of pretty, new houses in the bottom, near the Union Railway train tracks. Sure, the N.C. and St. L. rumbled their walls, shook the rice off their tables, Sure. But this smelled like home to them and home it would be.

They were not to be routed by any iron horse, nor lose their land so recently bought from old man Meachum, because of any monster. For, it turns out, there is a monster on the loose, wending its evil way through the alleys and backyards of Cooper-Young, leaving in its wake a trail of dead dogs.

This monster, as we've heard tell, is called Swift Peter. Swift because he glides through like the night winds, silent and deadly, smooth like a switchblade with eyes that shine like Mr. Death himself. And Peter, because, well, who knows, because it goes with swift, because Peter is the vacillating Apostle, the johndory, the one-eyed trouser snake. Swift Peter because he can steal your dreams, live inside you, eat your children.

Swift Peter was half codfish, half weasel and he could fly over fences. He was six feet long and two feet high. The number of dogs he killed was said by some to be seventeen and others to number in the triple digits. Many saw Swift Peter and no one saw him. He moved like a phantom, like a nightmare, like a yawn. If neighbor

Sam saw him Tuesday, neighbor Willie saw him Wednesday, clearly, up close. Sally Yarborough lost a child to the beast, though few today believe her story, preferring to postulate she killed the baby herself, leaving it squalling to save its soul, one weakly moonlit night, near the slide in Peabody Park.

But today, despite the brave hunters with their elephant guns, and their steely gazes, Swift Peter exists as surely as the grown-up children who remember his terrible run. As surely as the trestle which still stands at Cooper and Central, or the Peabody School with its honorable facade and its playground of death-black tar.

He exists still as surely as Cerberus, the Jabberwocky, the Squonk. For Swift Peter, for all his horrible oppressiveness, was a myth, is a myth, shall always be a myth, amen, children, created out of need, created out of hate. And is as real as myth, for all that.

Anybody Meeks owned the drugstore in Cooper-Young, the only apothecary in a tight radius of about three miles, a small kingdom but one he ruled with a laugh as quick and loud as a horse and a firm handshake and a hearty, though normally uncalled-for, slap on the back. Meeks spent as much time out in front of his store as he did behind the counter selling snakeroot and liniments and potions. He was a fixture in the neighborhood, a guardian, if you will, of the lifestyle he and his other white brethren felt justified in preserving and protecting. He loved his neighborhood, his city and his country. He loved his wife and three pig-eyed children.

Anybody Meeks was looked up to in Cooper-Young. He was trusted and he was loved. He was surrounded by a daily assembly of cohorts and cronies, all with similar likes and dislikes. There was Jud Crenshaw, tile barber, Willoughby Wilkins, Lamont Reichbacher, Cal Harkins who owned Harkins Hardware, Joe Lykins. Good men, solid men, churchgoing men. The kind of fellas you would want on your side, playing softball or fighting overseas. The kind of guys you'd want to live near, neighborly guys, nice guys, white guys.

And these men decided, in their collective wisdom, in the marvelous interworkings of their groupthink, to keep Cooper-Young as pure as possible, as clean as possible. They couldn't abide standing still and watching their little kingdom be spoiled by the introduction of alien Culture.

No, these boys were sure they were right. Right and white, amen. They decided to take a stand, to keep the blacks from further encroachment on the god-loving soil of the Cooper-Young neighborhood.

Now, most folks say, it was Anybody Meeks who came up with Swift Peter. It is said he invented him one droopy night on the sidewalk in front of Meeks Drugs and Sundries with all his cronies in attendance.

And it might be true, for Swift Peter sounds like the workings of the intellect of Anybody Meeks, though as the story got rolling some of the details were surely added by the others gathered there. How Swift Peter was first seen emerging from the darkened woods near Southern Avenue. How his eyes were like a cat's and a snake's. How his movement through the air whistled so that it was often thought he sang as he slaughtered. How he could eat a small dog in one swallow, a medium size dog in two atrocious bites and a large dog in a series of appalling bite-and-gulps.

Swift Peter grew rapidly. And from that night on it was as if a flame had been touched to dry paper. Anybody told the story to January Cobbin, the wood man, whose mule and wagon were used to sell stovewood throughout the greater Midtown area, with all the fellas standing there, nodding their leonine heads.

January stood listening with solemn brow, his hand to his grey-whiskered chin. He would look up occasionally and grin grimly and shake his head. This was the devil's business indeed. And when it was all told, when the story had unwound itself like a tight ball of yarn set a rolling, Anybody sent January on his rounds with an ostentatious slap on the back, as if to say, "Ye out and be fishers of men," and the evil wheel began its decisive and diabolic revolutions.

Within the week word had spread. Swift Peter stories were everywhere. And how the men on the sidewalk laughed and snuffled when the first sightings were reported and when the first guns began to appear. Oh, what sport! Cooper-Young was alive with the energy of legend and terror. Swift Peter was on the prowl! Swift Peter was hunger and rage, apprehension and dread! Swift Peter, Swift Peter! Save the children, lock your doors, haul out the heavy artillery!

Swift Peter, the Beast of Cooper-Young! Saints preserve us!

Charlie Ivory was a good man who loved his family. He was not given to superstition or spook-tales. But, when his neighbors began gathering firearms and forming posses he went along to stay

friendly, he went along to keep an eye on the proceedings, to make
Sure his friends didn't make fools of themselves or worse. He didn't
want any accidental shootings, any more death in the Negro
Community. He worked at Crescent Oil Mill for $1.50 a day and he
wanted nothing but respect and quiet and for everyone to stop this
dangerous folderol.

He went because he had a squirrel rifle and his children begged
him to take it and protect them. He went for the children.

He also went just in case the stories were true.

Charlie spent three straight sleepless nights patrolling the
neighborhood with three other men and all they saw for their troubles
were four wild dogs, numerous cats, one owl (which flew low over
them and scared the hell out of all four men) and a couple of families
of raccoons. Nothing bigger, nothing more frightening.

Charlie was beginning to smell a rat. He approached Anybody
Meeks on the sidewalk one day to question him about his assertions
concerning the Beast of Cooper-Young, but the stony stares of the
five or so white men congregated there and their sudden silence,
which seemed to swallow up all sound around them, intimidated
Charlie and he never approached closer than the sidewalk across the
street.

He also never went out on another hunt.

Eventually it all began to sour, of course. Anybody and the
boys got a lot of cheap laughs at the Negroes' expense and a load of
havoc was wreaked, backyards trampled, fences bent and broken, sleep
ruined by marauding vigilantes and shots fired. When Stan Pott's
Alsatian was accidentally shot and killed and charges brought against
Luther Baker and Luther hauled off to the pokey with his wife and
children boo-hooing and Luther hanging his big head and feeling like
he'd liked to die, even gentlemen like the Drugstore Gang began to
suspect things had progressed past the point of propriety.

Anybody Meeks and the boys didn't give up on the idea of an all-
white Cooper-Young, oh no, of course not. But, when the
Commercial Appeal sent a reporter around to get the scoop on all the
nighttime activity in the neighborhood, Anybody decided to fess up
and expose the hoax for what it was.

"Well, Hank," Anybody began his confession to Hank Kepple,
the city-beat reporter. "I gots to admit that it was my original idea to
put a little of the fear of you-know-who into the local Nigra
population. I admit that was the how-you-say genocide of the plan."

"Whatsa point?" Hank quickly put in, ever the nose for Old Style Southern BS.

"The point, Hank-buddy, was to keep Cooper-Young, my lifetime stomping ground, white as the Pope's ass, dontcha see?"

"Mr. Meeks, you didn't move here but four years ago."

"Four hard-working, law-abiding, God-fearing years, Hank, my boy. And I don't intend to see that work trampled on by the impure pure... "You with me?"

"Go on."

"So's me. and the boys invented a little night creachur to put the scare on the jigs, them so gullible about haints and all, to send them back to wheresoever they come here from."

"Back to Africa, perhaps?"

"If that's what they want, God bless 'em, I say. But Cooper--Young ain't the place for mixing the races, no sir."

"And the hunt for the beast got out of hand, is that what you're telling me now?"

"Well," Anybody blew through his veined honker. "I guess so, yeah. Them colored—" And here he had to stop and guffaw a bit, snorting through his nose.

"Anyway," he continued when he'd collected himself, "They started toting guns and shooting pets and whatall and I guessed it was my time to use my cool head and put an end to this tomfoolery. Yep."

And with that the story ran the next day in the morning paper and most of the fear was dissipated, though a few folks chose not to believe the newspaper and insisted they had indeed seen the fearsome beast in all his toothy, dog-killing glory.

Eventually, as all stories do, the energy of the tale evaporated, leaving a limp and limpid legend to die its own natural death. Cooper-Young went back to the business of bike-riding and lawn-watering and ball-playing and church-going and the only smell in the air after the gunpowder and blood stench died away was the lie-arty, healthy aroma of seared meat on backyard pits.

Everyone began sleeping again.

Everyone except one.

It was a month later, a month after the story ran in the *Commercial Appeal* it is said, when Anybody Meeks was awakened in the middle of the night by the crash of his garbage cans in the dogrun under his bedroom window.

Annette Meeks jerked straight up into a sitting position and her husband eyed her with annoyance.

"What the hell," he said, glibly.

"Any, there's a commotion outside. Get your sorry ass up and see what gives."

Anybody reluctantly found his slippers and bathrobe and shuffled through the kitchen and unlocked the side door. Instinctively, he picked up a small log from the pile outside the door and stood for a minute on the side porch, waiting for his eyes to adjust to the murk.

Something moved to his left, out near the fence. The sound was like a tired kettle on the boil, a sputtering whistle, accompanied by the sibilance of wet on wet. Any squinted toward the back yard, whence the noise came. Something was there, like a shadow of a shadow, dark against the dark fence, but moving.

Anybody raised the piece of wood slowly, his arm moving unawares. Now the shadow was slithering up the fence itself. As it crested the wooden fence the moonlight caught it and Anybody dropped his wooden weapon and his jaw went slack, or slacker.

Swift Peter was easing himself over the Meeks' fence with the stealth of a thief and with a practiced thief's nonchalance. He had just about disappeared, like a snake going into a hole, the last inches of his six foot body sliding over, seemingly unaware of the audience he had garnered, when he lifted his weaselly head and turned it back toward the house. The effect was like being recognized by the night itself.

Anybody went down abruptly onto his knees. Swift Peter, his sleek head reflecting moonlight off his glistening hair, slowly spread his cheeks into a toothy, monstrous grin.

The grin as good as said, "I remember you, Anybody Meeks, and I'll be back."

Just then the oldest Meeks boy, Jasper, pushed open the screen door at his father's back. He beheld his dad down on his knees on the damp porch, awash in his own urine, his head lolling as if he were drunk.

"Dad, you got the dropsy?" the lad spoke.

Anybody Meeks turned to his firstborn with the visage of the broken-spirited and wept an incomprehensible repentance.

Well, this is the way it is told. Anybody Meeks is God's fool enough for readers today to suspect the twist in this tale to be so much more hooey. After all they were primitive times, the early years of the century. Anything could have happened, storywise, anything could have triggered a nervous collapse in poor Mr. Meeks. Guilt, perhaps.

Or perhaps after the limelight of those atrociously enjoyable weeks of the monster hunt Anybody Meeks was hungry for a little more attention. Maybe he was inventing his own fear just to keep the narrative ball rolling, so to speak. Today psychiatry probably has figured this kind of thing out, children. So we suspect.

Anybody Meeks spent the next day and the next in a sleepless panic. His chinless features took on an ashen quality, his face, some said, began to resemble a mink or a possum. Anybody showed up for work all right, but he was not a well man and much comment was made upon it.

"Heckfire, Anybody, " Jud Crenshaw said, stepping over from the barber shop. "You look like you was rode hard and hung up wet. Wha's the matter?"

"Cain't talk, Jud. Devil's got me, sure as hell."

"Aw, Any, you off again.   Let's let this one rest, what say?"

Anybody turned toward Jud a look of Revelation.

"C'ain't rest, damn ye," he said.

Jud Crenshaw trotted off, marking his friend as hexed, or as his wife later so lightly put it, "tiched."

It was two nights later when Swift Peter came back. Anybody was sitting at his kitchen table drinking milk and whittling his nails with his knife. Sleep, for him, had become a foreign concept. Occasionally he heard a cat on Nelson Avenue, squalling its plaintive love, sounding for all the world like the lovechild of Old Scratch himself.

There was the susurrus of a breeze outside and then a faint knock on the door. Anybody was up like a flash and pulled the door open. Darkness greeted him.

From the back of the yard came that sickeningly sweet sound of silk, water, death.

Anybody stepped outside. He was no coward.

He peered out into the blackness, which answered him with a mocking sigh.

" C'mon, you thing from Hell," Any challenged.

"C'mon and show your sorry self. I'll choke ye till your miserable excuse for a soul goes a-runnin' back to the depths from it come."

Anybody stepped out into the grass and the breeze seemed to pick up a bit and surround him, caressing his cheek like the passing by of that cat. He stood there and suddenly he felt foolish for there was nothing there, nothing to be afraid of. He was alone in the middle of night in his own backyard.

He relaxed a bit and felt for the first time the weight of the knife in his hand. He chuckled a bit to himself—it is told—and turned to go back inside.

Swift Peter stood over him like a wraith, that sick grin on his pinched, furry face. Suddenly he was just there, as close as a hug. Anybody swung outward with the knife, an arc designed to create space, or maim if necessary.

Swift Peter was as if born of swamp-gas and cyanide; the swing passed through him. He leaned in close, swift as retribution, and Anybody felt the heat of him near his cheek, and the beast licked Anybody's neck, as if in love, or as if to tenderize him.

Anybody turned and ran like a frightened dog. His spindly legs turned under him, a lopsided wheel. He ran and ran and behind him he could hear short exhalations as if he were pursued by a steam engine, and a faint murmur like faraway singing. He dare not chance a look over his shoulder; his fear was the fear of Lot's wife.

His feet found Cooper Avenue. He headed North, the moon above him chuckling into its cheesy sleeve.

He headed for the train track and he knew not why. Once there he scampered up the cinder-strewn hill and leapt onto the tracks, for the first time since he began running, now turning to face his pursuer.

He leaned over, hands on knees, sucking night air. Swift Peter stood below looking up at him, leering like a mooncalf. His teeth glinted and showed the drool of hunger, an appetite not of this world.

And then the strangest thing of all happened. Peter spoke. Swift Peter spoke and his voice sounded like that cat's and it seemed to vibrate in Anybody's own throat, as if the sound were coming from deep inside him, as if born of his own craven powerlessness.

"Anybody," it purred. "Child is the father to man." Anybody was not sure he had heard it right.

"How's that?" he asked.

"My authority increases as yours diminishes. Your days are as the dandelion, as the mushroom."

"You speak in riddles, sir."

"Do not mock me with your spurious manners. I come from you and hence know whence you come. "

"Swift Peter, if that be your name," Anybody said, trembling afresh. "What do you intend?"

"Like the sea the rains, Anybody Meeks, I intend to swallow you up."

Anybody made as if to turn and run but the beast leapt to his side as swiftly as the fall of a scimitar.

And, it is said, children, that Swift Peter, child of hate and horror, in the biblical moonlight on the trestle over Cooper Avenue, ate Anybody Meeks, with slow and sinister relish. Anybody's blood ran down between the tracks and dripped and pooled onto the thoroughfare beneath; some say you can see the place there today. He swallowed parts of Anybody in stages, saving his blackened heart and empty head until last, so that Anybody's head spoke once before it was devoured, and the words that the head spoke were these:

"I didn't mean to hurt nobody."

Well, that's the tale, believe it or dream about it. It has survived the test of time, the twentieth century keeping it alive despite the numerous horrors since, which threatened to drown it and banish it to the realm of the forgotten folktale.

And how are these details known today, you ask? How do we know what happened on that damned trestle in the middle of that ghastly night? How do we know about the words spoken, about the breeze, about the sounds of a cat in heat?

We know it because we know it, amen.

I was there, children.

Hunt's End
By Tim Waggoner

The Helsing was nearby; Gareth could sense it. He felt his excitement build. After all this time, all this searching... soon, it would be over. And his people would finally be safe. Safe for all time.

Gareth moved through the city streets, keeping to the shadows, passing among the humans, a vision glimpsed out of the corner of the eye, soon forgotten, like a half-remembered dream which vanished upon waking. He was careful to avoid detection by humans, but not because of the Bloodborn desire to remain hidden at all costs. In truth, the seclusion his people valued so much meant little to him for, as far as he was concerned, the warm ones had seen through the Bloodborn's deception long ago—when the Helsing first appeared.

No, he avoided human eyes for fear that the Helsing might see through them and realize it was being hunted. And Gareth couldn't afford that. Not if his people were to survive.

Gareth had tracked his quarry to a city in the American South, one whose name recalled a near-mythical place of glory, a seat of power for ancient Egyptian kings. The streets, buildings, people, the very air all seemed vaguely familiar to him; had he hunted here before? He couldn't remember. After four centuries of life—not so long for one of the Bloodborn, but not so young, really, either—places and names tended to blur. But otherwise, his mind was sharp, his thoughts ordered and clear, and focused on a single goal: the destruction of his enemy.

And while these streets were hardly gilded with Pharaohs' gold, they would make as good a place as any to run his prey to ground. And Gareth was confident he would have a chance to do so tonight, for the Helsing was here, in this city, somewhere close ...

And then Gareth thought he spotted him, walking on the opposite side of the street. Alone. Gareth stopped and stared intently at the man. There was nothing about this particular human to mark him as the Helsing, at least not visually. He was just a man, no more or less remarkable than any other. But there was something about how he carried himself, something about the subtle way other humans moved out of his path, as if subconsciously recognizing the true nature of this special being who walked in their midst.

If Gareth had been human, he might've felt his pulse speed up in anticipation, and, yes, more than a little fear. But he wasn't human, and his body didn't react at all as he stepped into the street and hurriedly crossed to the other side. The hunt, at long last, was on.

He prayed to all the Lords of Darkness for success.

* * *

Gareth first became aware of the force he was to name the Helsing one night in the mid nineteen-thirties. He was in a city. New York, perhaps, or Chicago. It hardly mattered. What mattered instead was that this evening, Gareth had decided to treat himself to his latest indulgence: the cinema.

Most Bloodborn avoided it, wanted nothing to do with the crowds of humans crammed into theatres, felt too uncomfortable, too exposed.

But not Gareth. He was enamored of this new technology, entranced by the flickering images on the screen, drawn to the stories they created. He wasn't worried about detection in the slightest. No one paid any attention to their fellow audience members. Like Gareth, they only had eyes for what occurred on the screen.

This particular evening, after feeding on an unfortunate prostitute whose body he had made sure would never be discovered—at least, not all of it—Gareth decided to sneak into a theatre at random. He didn't care what was playing, didn't care if he'd seen it before. All that mattered was the moment when the lights dimmed and the screen came to life. He slid like a shadow though one of the theatre's exits and remained hidden in a dark alcove, cloaked in blackness, while he waited for the humans to take their seats. When the lights finally began to go down, he slipped into a seat far in the rear, away from anyone else, and settled back and waited to be carried away. He enjoyed the preliminaries, the cartoon and coming attractions, well enough, but they were hardly a film. But when the main feature finally began, he almost burst out laughing. For the film was *Dracula.*

He'd heard rumors that the film had been financed—secretly, of course—with Bloodborn money. Now that the warm ones were growing more numerous, their weapons more powerful (witness their last great war), some among the Bloodborn believed it more important than ever to reinforce the idea that they were nothing more than fable. And what better way to do this than through the cinema, the latest, greatest fable-maker of them all?

But Gareth didn't care about that. Let the rest of the Bloodborn play their games. He merely hoped the film would prove diverting.

And at first it had. The actor portraying the Impaler was delightfully histrionic, and the castle he inhabited little more than a child's spookhouse that no self-respecting member of the Bloodborn would— he smiled to himself in the darkness—be caught dead in.

But then something happened as the film continued unfurling its Grand Guignol tale. Gareth sensed the humans in the theatre coming together somehow, in a way far more intense than the mere bonding that sometimes took place between members of an audience, on a level far deeper than merely the shared experience of an evening's entertainment.

And then came a scene set in a drawing room where Dracula verbally sparred with the human who was to become his nemesis, Professor Van Helsing, the latter portrayed by a bland, stiff human in glasses and short white hair, whose uninspired performance was hardly a match for the deliciously overwrought but still charismatic actor playing the Impaler.

But despite Van Helsing's dullness, Gareth could feel the audience responding as one, as if a primal chord had been touched deep within their collective soul. A chord crystallized by a moment where Dracula and Van Helsing stood face to face, glaring at each other, saying nothing, not needing to, for their very stances declared them to be implacable foes for all time.

And then Gareth realized what was happening. Not just here, but in movie theatres all around the country. This revelation filled him with a cold horror unlike any he—even as one of the Bloodborn—had ever known.

He couldn't help himself; he shrieked, the inhuman sound echoing throughout the theatre, frightening many of the warm ones, who in turned screamed as well.

Those screams seemed to cut into his very essence, and he fled before they were the end of him. He bolted from the theatre and into the street, not bothering to conceal himself, knocking down humans right and left in his mad haste to be away from the theatre, from the audience, from that presence on the screen.

From the Helsing.

He had no idea how long he ran, had no idea if he was even in the same city when he stopped. But eventually he found himself atop a building, prone, looking up at the stars and panting for breath, even though he didn't need to breathe. He didn't want to think about what had happened in the theatre, what he had become aware of. He wanted to push it from his mind and return to his wandering life of feeding and idle pleasures. But he knew he couldn't.

For somehow the Bloodborn's efforts to use Dracula to help reinforce the illusion that they were mere myth had backfired horribly. The film had stirred the warm ones' collective unconscious, had made them aware of the Bloodborn, and the threat they posed. It had galvanized them, brought them together as a race to fight back, to rid their world of the undead vermin which infested its dark corners.

Brought them together to create a champion: the Helsing.

Who better to serve as the humans' defender and avenger? For if the character Dracula was the embodiment of the Bloodborn, then his foe, the Helsing, was the incarnation of humanity. And if the film ended like the novel—and while Gareth knew that moviemakers often took liberties when adapting other material for the cinema, he was sure it did—that meant the Helsing won. Won in every grand theatre, every cramped small-town moviehouse, won in every matinee, every evening performance. Would continue to win day after day, night after night, week after week.

Would always win, forevermore, any time the film was taken off the shelf, dusted off, and screened again. Whether it be in the movie theatre or, as Gareth was to discover in a couple of decades hence, through a medium called television.

Dracula, the Bloodborn, would die, and the Helsing, humanity, would live.

Soon the Helsing would not only be on the screen; soon the Helsing would be real. And it would come for the Bloodborn, just as surely and unrelentingly as the character Van Helsing hunted down and dispatched the dread Dracula in stark black and white.

Gareth knew something had to be done, and fast, or the Bloodborn would be finished.

He sought out the Elders of this particular city, but was able only to speak with an underling who laughed off his revelation and said he was insane. So Gareth tried another city and another group of Elders. And when he received the same response, he tried again. And again. But no matter the city, no matter how strongly he made his case, no one believed him.

Eventually, he realized that if the Helsing was to be stopped, he would have to be the one to do it—alone. He would have to take on the mantle of the Impaler, to become the embodiment of the Bloodborn itself. It was an awesome responsibility, but in the end one he could not walk away from.

And so he set out on the trail of the Helsing, hoping to find and destroy it while it was newborn, still young and weak. But while he often sensed the Helsing over the decades—thought he glimpsed it from a distance a time or two, even dispatched hundreds of humans he suspected were the Helsing, but who, in the end, all turned out to be mere mortals—he was unable to put an end to it. The Helsing was still out there, somewhere, growing stronger by the day.

And so he continued on, from sundown to sunrise, year after year, searching, hunting, waiting, and praying for his chance.

A chance, it seemed, which Destiny had finally seen fit to offer him.

* * *

Gareth tracked the Helsing as it wandered the city streets seemingly without purpose, though Gareth knew this was unlikely. The Helsing was most probably hunting Bloodborn, but without appearing as if it were hunting. But this night, it was the hunted. Eventually, the Helsing came to a night club and paused before the entrance, as if considering whether to go in. Gareth quickly ducked into an alley and concentrated on keeping his thoughts, his very presence, hidden. Even after hunting the Helsing all this time, Gareth was unsure of its capabilities. Better not to take chances.

After several moments, Gareth risked edging cautiously out of the alley and saw that the Helsing was gone. Had it entered the club or instead continued along the sidewalk? Gareth frantically scanned the streets, searching for the Helsing's nondescript mortal form, panic rising. After so many years, had he finally found the Helsing only to lose it?

He stepped onto the sidewalk, nearly running into a young human couple in the process. They gasped when they saw the being who'd nearly collided with them, but Gareth didn't care that he had let his guard down and allowed the warm ones to see him as he truly was. All that mattered was finding the Helsing.

He ran toward the club, weaving gracefully between the humans on the sidewalk, drawing startled looks and exclamations from them. If another of the Bloodborn had been present to witness him revealing his true nature, Gareth would have been marked for execution. But he didn't care. Finding and stopping the Helsing, protecting the

Bloodborn, was far more important.

He decided to take a chance and go into the club. If the Helsing had by some means detected Gareth's pursuit, then it might've gone inside to lose itself among a crowd of fellow humans, counting on the normal Bloodborn desire to conceal their true nature to keep him from following. But it wouldn't work. Gareth would kill everyone in the club if he had to in order to get at the Helsing.

He took no note of the club's name as he moved silently and swiftly around to the back of the building. It was no concern of his what designation the humans had given this place. He found a rear exit, locked, but with a twist and a yank the lock was broken, the door open, and Gareth was inside, moving through a dingy, cramped kitchen, startling an overweight cook dressed in a sweat-stained t-shirt. And then he was through the kitchen and into the club itself.

The place was a swirling miasma of smells—perfume, aftershave, alcohol, cigarettes, and hot human flesh. Music blared from speakers bolted to the walls, so loud that all Gareth could make out was the thump-thump-thump of the bass beat. But it was all the humans needed to fuel their gyrations. Gareth was old enough to have seen many styles of dance come and go among the warm ones, and to his mind, this spastic flailing about was little more than ritualistic sex play. He pushed his feeling of distaste aside. He hadn't come here to play critic; he had come to hunt.

He made a slow circle of the club, keeping near the wall and whatever shadows the place offered. He searched the writhing mass of humans, looking for the Helsing. And when he found it, he would kill it, along with anyone who got in his way.

There! Over by the bar... He started through the crowd, intending to cut directly across the dance floor, when he got a better look at the man ordering a drink. No, that wasn't the Helsing. Similar features, yes, but not the same.

Gareth moved back against the wall and continued searching. Several times he thought he spotted the Helsing, only to find each time that he was mistaken. Frustration and confusion gripped him. Had he guessed wrong? Had the Helsing not sought refuge here? Or had it perhaps slipped out, undetected? No, his instincts told him that he had made the right choice. The Helsing was here. But where?

Frustration became rage and before he could stop himself, he shouted, "Show yourself, damn you!" with the full power of his inhuman voice.

The sound cut through the throbbing beat of the music, and the humans stopped what they were doing—stopped dancing, drinking, smoking and fondling each other—and turned to stare, some startled, some curious.

For the first time since he had become one of Bloodborn, Gareth found himself amid a crowd of humans, the center of their attention, completely exposed. But that didn't bother him as much as what he saw in the humans' eyes. A passing glint in the corner of a small red-head's eye; a knowing twinkle, there only for an instant in the gaze of a shaven-headed black man; a momentary flash of amusement from a tall brunette with a tattoo of a tiny black rose on her shoulder.

Gareth understood then, understood why he hadn't been able to kill the Helsing all these years. The Helsing wasn't a corporeal being. Instead, it moved from human to human as it chose. And it had him here, in this crowded club, among dozens of warm ones, any one of which could become the Helsing at any moment. Worse, what if the Helsing could somehow be all of them, at the same time? He wasn't sure, but he thought he detected the crowd of humans move toward him the merest fraction of an inch.

He had to get out of here. Now.

Gareth let out a shout that was a mix of defiance and fear as he bolted for the kitchen.

* * *

He huddled in an alley on the other side of the city, miles away from the club. And the Helsing.

He drew his knees up to his chest and hugged them and leaned his head back against the cold brick. Not that he noticed the temperature. His own flesh was far colder.

He understood now that all the humans he had killed over the years, the ones he had thought he had mistaken for the Helsing, weren't, in fact, mistakes at all. They had been hosts for the Helsing. Hosts it had abandoned before Gareth could destroy it.

Now he was faced with a realization he didn't want to acknowledge. If the Helsing had no physical being, then perhaps it couldn't be killed. Perhaps the Bloodborn were doomed.

He shook his head violently, grinding his hair against brick. He refused to accept that. There had to be a way, must be a way. He just had to find it.

A soft rustle came from farther down the alley, and Gareth snapped his head around to face it.

A lanky, shadowy form crawled forth from a cardboard box. "What the hell you doing here? This is my alley, dammit!" It stood on wobbly legs, and Gareth could tell by the voice and smell that it was an elderly human male. At one time, Gareth had known his type as bum. Now the warm one would be considered one of the homeless.

"I got me a good box, buildings cut the wind, and there's a restaurant a block and a half away where they give me a free meal now and again." The old man shuffled toward him. "I ain't about to be run outta here, so you just go on and git!"

Gareth's Bloodborn eyes were able to make out the man's features, even though the alley was dark. His eyes were rheumy, his nose swollen and red with broken capillaries. His breath reeked of cheap wine and—Gareth sniffed—cough syrup? The human was obviously an alcoholic, and not a very discriminating one at that.

The old man continued toward Gareth, and the Bloodborn unfolded himself and rose to his feet with an inhuman, liquid grace. He was in no mood for this tonight. He had far more important matters to—

And then he saw it, deep within the old man's eyes. The Helsing.

It had followed him here, intending to catch him off guard by pretending to be nothing more than a grizzled old drunk and finish him once and for all. But Gareth had been too smart.

As the old man came near, Gareth's hands shot out and fastened to his shoulders, clawed fingers digging through his khaki army jacket and into the unwashed flesh beneath. The old human gasped in pain, but Gareth knew it was just an act. The Helsing was surely strong enough to endure such trifling injuries.

At that moment, Gareth was possessed of an overwhelming sense of destiny, or rather, of two destinies colliding. The Bloodborn's and the warm ones', the Impaler's and the Helsing's, his and the old man's. For in this instant, history could go either way: either the Helsing would slay him and, thus unopposed, continue in his campaign to hunt down Bloodborn, eventually eradicating them; or Gareth would finally destroy his hated foe and save his people. If only he could figure out the way.

The human went slack in his grasp and would've fallen to the ground if Gareth hadn't been holding him up.

"Please," he mewled, his sour breath washing over Gareth's face, a thin line of spittle rolling from his mouth. "Please don't hurt me. You can have the alley, have my box, too. Just let me go, huh? Please?"

Gareth peered into the old man's eyes and saw nothing there but terror. And for the first time in over six decades, he wondered if perhaps his fellow Bloodborn hadn't been right, if perhaps there really wasn't a Helsing, if it had all been nothing more than a delusion conjured up by his fevered mind.

Angry, confused, Gareth snarled, baring his fangs.

The old man gasped and breathed a single, soft word.

"D-Dracula."

Gareth's doubts were washed away, for the Helsing had recognized him. And in that moment, Gareth understood what he had to do to destroy the Helsing forever.

He felt the hunger take hold of him, and he gripped the back of the human's head and exposed his neck. He sank his teeth into the sweat-and-dirt-caked flesh and drank deeply.

As the blood gushed hot and sweet down his throat, he could feel the Helsing's essence being drawn along with it. He sucked at the human's ragged neck until the old man was dry, and then he released the empty husk—empty in more ways than one—and let it fall.

He stepped back and wiped his mouth with the back of his hand. He could feel the Helsing within him, and he knew he had succeeded; the Bloodborn were saved.

He turned to leave, but paused as he felt a strange stirring within. A coldness began spreading through his body, a sensation unlike any he had ever experienced before. Cold—and determined. Ruthless.

Gareth opened his mouth to scream but before any sound could come out, he felt his Self being overwhelmed, being absorbed by the irresistible force he had taken into his body.

And as his consciousness began to break down and be subsumed by the invader within, Gareth understood that history had indeed been made this night, but not in the manner he had thought. For tonight, the Helsing had merged with one of Bloodborn, had access to the powers and knowledge of the Bloodborn. The world have never before seen such a hunter as it would become.

Gareth's last thought was for his people. I'm sorry, so sorry...

When it was over, Gareth—or rather Gareth's body—stepped out of the alley, ready to begin the hunt anew.

People Change
By H. R. Williams

Tom Simpson parked his Cadillac opposite the abandoned warehouse and stared at it through the side window. He was reluctant to leave the car's excellent air conditioning because this was August and he was in Memphis and he knew what lay outside. He sighed, picked up his 35M camera, and cracked the door. Heat boiled in and, by the time he stepped to the curb, his face was gleaming with sweat. He pulled his suit coat off, flung it across the front seat, and slammed the door. Damn, it was hot and damn Frank Seeger for sending him out here.

"Tom, I'd appreciate it if you'd handle this one personally," he'd said. They were sitting in Frank's fourteenth story office, windows looking out on the wide Mississippi.

"Handle it? What do you mean, handle it? What you want me to do is go out to this warehouse and take some pictures. Hell, any of our boys can do that."

"Well, that's not quite all. What I mean is, I want you to..."

"What?" asked Tom.

Examine the building," Frank replied.

"I thought you did that yesterday."

Frank got up and walked over to his windows. He stood looking out at the river. A striped seersucker suit hung loosely on the large, soft body and his bald head gleamed in the light. "Actually, I had some other stuff to do and, by the time I got there, the sun had set."

"So you didn't finish." Tom said in reproof.

Frank came back to his desk, sat down, and stared at his partner. "What did I just say, Tom? Nighttime had set in, for chrissake, and it gets a little hard to find your way around an unlighted warehouse after dark. Now, we've both got full schedules, but if you don't want to stop by the goddamn place on your way home, then I'll do it myself."

Tom noted with some surprise that his friend's face had lost some of its color and that his eyes were blinking rapidly, a sure sign of distress.

"Relax Frank," he said gently. "I'll take care of it."

And so, here he stood, in the heat of late afternoon, staring upward at the building Seeger & Simpson, Commercial Realtors, had agreed to handle. Simpson passed this way often and reflected that, in his memory, the building had never been occupied. He seemed to recall someone telling him that it had once been used to store cotton. He hadn't met the seller, a Mr. Helmut Meyer. Frank was handling this deal and, for some reason, had neglected to introduce Meyer. Tom thought this unusual, but chalked it up as another example of Frank's recent odd behavior. He seemed preoccupied and given to periods of silence. On a couple of occasions, Tom had caught his partner staring at him, the gaze vacant and far away.

Seeger & Simpson had grown, over the years, to become one of Memphis' most successful realtors. They dealt exclusively in commercial properties and, along with prosperity, had gained a reputation for integrity and a demonstrated ability to keep a confidence. The latter was imperative to clients with millions to lose or gain, depending on what certain people knew or did not know. Frank said it was this last quality that had brought Mr. Meyer to them.

Tom sighted through the camera and snapped a picture of the warehouse. It rose three stories high, darkened all over by grime and soot. The crenellated roof line brought to mind some ancient fortress. Each floor was highlighted by massive windows, holding a large number of ordinary sized panes. Some were broken or missing and starlings flew through the openings. The building stood somber and still and the birds seemed like bats, flitting in and out of a cave. Viewing this desolate scene brought on a sense of foreboding. Simpson had always been a loner, but at this moment, he wouldn't have minded some company. He felt like the last man on earth. The realtor shook himself impatiently, locked his car, and walked across the street. Course weeds grew around the building's heavy oak door. It stood slightly ajar. Tom gave it a push but couldn't make it budge. Placing his shoulder against it, he shoved mightily and the door creaked and scraped and slowly swung back.

He left it open, walked to the center of the mammoth room, and looked about him. The sun, now low in the west, shed weak rays through the windows. Dust particles drifted about in the light. Thick supporting columns stretched upward, casting long shadows away from the windows. Before him, a rough staircase rose in a straight slant through an opening in the ceiling. He climbed it, arrived at the second floor, and saw that it was roughly the same as the first.

Second verse, same as the first; second floor, same as before. What put that in my head, he thought, a case of the nerves? While he was thinking this, an animal, huge and hairy, ran from behind a cardboard box and headed toward him. "JESUS!" he yelled and leaped sideways. The sewer rat scuttled by and disappeared down the stairway. Tom leaned against one of the center posts and breathed heavily. Damned place has got me spooked. Straightening, he snapped two more pictures, hung the camera around his neck, and headed up the stairs again. At least the air seemed cooler.

Third floor, same as be-... "Cut it out," he murmured aloud, and tried to concentrate. He was here to examine a property, for crissakes. The third floor was the same as before, but now the massive windows were lit a rusty red. Tom walked to where a pane was missing and peered out. Looking across the southern part of downtown Memphis was only to look at more vacant warehouses and deserted buildings. The three or four immediate streets were empty of traffic, no movement anywhere. Tom turned from the window and headed for the stairway. The room had darkened considerably, and utter silence prevailed. Even the fluttering of bird wings had ceased. Simpson glanced about and quickened his steps. His nervousness, apprehension—call it whatever the hell you wanted to—came back in full force, along with an overwhelming desire to get out of this goddamn vacant void of a warehouse. He came to the square hole in the floor and looked down at the steps, sinking into gloom. It was then he heard the entrance door, three floors below, slowly scrape closed.

Simpson did not remember descending the staircase. He remembered hesitating for a very long time before starting. He recalled that it took a great effort to make that first step downward. Now he stood on the ground floor with his head pivoting left and right, trying to take in everything at once. He saw immediately that the door was tightly closed and it came to him that someone might have pulled it to from the outside. This thought calmed him somewhat and he looked around again in a more deliberate manner. Everything was visible except the four shadowy corners. Nothing disturbed the dust laden air. Tom relaxed slightly, but he remained alert, ready for anything; that is, anything but the sound of his partner's soft voice.

"Good evening, Tom," said Frank Seeger from one of the dark corners, "What do you think of the building?"

Simpson watched as Frank came into view and walked toward him. His partner stopped a few feet away and regarded him calmly. "Surprised to see me?"

"Jesus Christ, Frank. You scared the hell out of me. What are you doing here?"

"Oh, I had to be here, Tom. On this particular evening."

Tom squinted at Seeger, while his mind dealt with a couple of facts. First, his partner seemed a different man and it wasn't anything trifling like manner or appearance. This was something fundamental; and inexplicable. The other thing to be dealt with was the obscure shape remaining in the corner. Frank hadn't entered the warehouse alone.

Tom cleared his throat and said, "Do I get to meet your friend?"

'Why, of course," said Seeger. He glanced behind him and a smaller man walked, no glided, out of the corner. The movement was sinuous and silent and graceful. Tom had never, ever, seen anyone move like that before.

"This is the building's owner, Mr. Meyer. He's been anxious to meet you."

"Yes," said Tom, "I wondered why you never introduced us. "

"What? In the office? Oh no," said Frank with a chuckle. "That would have been far too informal. Helmut and I had something more, how shall I say, ceremonious in mind."

How he's enjoying this, Simpson suddenly thought. This is not the man I know. Reserved, diffident, often detached; that was Frank Seeger. The person standing before him was filled with exuberance. He could scarcely contain it. Tom took a closer look at the small, swarthy figure that was Helmut Meyer. He saw a face, etched and set, and out of that face stared round, expressionless eyes. Meyer's coarse hair began in a widow's peak and was combed straight back. Thick eyebrows grew across the forehead in a precise, unbroken line.

Tom's attention switched to his partner and he said what was foremost in his mind. "What is it with you, Frank?"

"What do you mean?" said Seeger.

"What do I mean? What I mean is you're…"

"Different?"

"Yeah, I guess so," said Simpson.

"Oh, I don't know, Tom," said his partner. "What can I say? People change." He and his companion looked at each other and smiled.

Helmut Meyer took a step forward and extended his hand. Simpson took it and was surprised at the heat radiating from the man's palm. "How do you do, Mr. Simpson? It is a pleasure to finally see you." The voice was soft, yet deeply guttural, and the German accent was quite noticeable.

"Nice to meet you," said Tom, stiffly. His eyes widened when Frank actually retreated a couple of steps and stood to the rear of Meyer. He didn't comment but, right then, he decided to have it out with his partner next morning, because all this had become just too damn weird. He realized Meyer was speaking again, the voice unhurried and even, the words precise.

"Mr. Simpson, I am a very direct being and have no inclination to—how do you say it?—beat about the bush. Also, it is quite difficult for me to converse with one of the herd.'

"The what?"

"The Herd, Mr. Simpson. Yes, you are making the correct associations; like cattle. The Herd as opposed to the Pack. Tell me, are you familiar with the term, Vukodolak? Loup Garou? No? Perhaps the word 'Lycanthrope' means something to you?"

"No," said Tom, "and I can tell you right now, Mr. Meyer, that we'd like to have your business but I'm not about to— Wait a minute! Lycanthrope? Is that what you said? Hell, that's another word for... ."

"Yeesss, Mr. Simpson. Now you have it. The popular name has just come to you. Now, you're following me, aren't you?"

As far as Tom was concerned, there was nothing more to be said. He gave a short laugh and headed for the door. He had almost reached it when a chorus of voices rang out.

"TOM!"

He turned around and there they were, all six of them, standing side by side. There was Frank and Helmut, plus three women and another man. Where had the other four come from? Of course, he thought. There'd been more than one dark corner. He stood transfixed as they all came forward. He didn't recognize any of the newcomers and there seemed nothing remarkable about them. They formed a circle around him and Meyer spoke again. "Be still and listen," he commanded. Simpson, held by the German's steady gaze, did exactly that.

"All that you see are Werewolves. Well, that's not quite true. Frank has a little way to go yet. He received the Bite a couple of weeks ago, August 11th to be precise. That was the proper time, the night of no moon. He has enjoyed certain changes in mind and body since then, most not apparent to one of The Herd; but then, so little is apparent to them, anyway." Subdued laughter from the group. "His perceptions are heightened and all his senses have sharpened, especially his sense of smell. Tonight, during the Moonspell, he will know the ultimate change."

Simpson tore his gaze from Helmut and looked at Seeger, Frank Seeger, who'd been his friend and partner for ten years; Frank Seeger, family man, member of the Memphis Country Club and founder of their business.

"I can't believe I'm listening to this, Frank," he said. "And I can't believe you're listening, too."

"Hear the Lupercus' words," his partner intoned. "You will soon know of their truth."

"And so you shall," continued Meyer with a slight, bright smile, "so you shall."

Tom turned in a complete circle and looked at all the faces. He lifted his head toward the German. "What's a Moonspell," he asked.

He didn't know exactly how much time had passed. His wrists were tied behind one of the oak columns, so he couldn't look at his watch. He stood upright with his back against the column and faced an east side window. He'd been carried to the third floor, now swallowed in darkness. The eastern window was huge, like the others, with panes missing here and there. However, the remaining glass seemed to have been washed and, through it, Tom could see an occasional star. He was alone. He remembered Meyer's motionless eyes and his voice answering, "You will behold it soon enough."

Something glistened on the floor, but Simpson couldn't make it out. Then, Helmut and his friends came from behind him and walked in front of the window. Their feet made a sliding, slick sound and Tom realized that someone had laid down a sheet of thick plastic. He craned his neck, but saw no sign of his partner.

The window glimmered faintly, silhouetting the five figures. They stood quietly, for a moment, then removed all their clothing. Tom watched as a female gathered everything up and carried it out of sight. She returned and they all stood naked before him. The center figure, Meyer, walked toward him, a dark shadow growing larger against the window. He stopped and Tom caught the glint of white teeth.

"This is the 18th night in August, the night of the Moonspell."

"You mean there's a full moon?" Simpson spoke in a high, tight voice, edged with contempt and anger. It had filled him all at once, like a hot gall, and he raged inwardly at what had been done to him by these maniacs, by their indignities toward him and the fear they had made him feel. He felt a special fury toward this Meyer and toward a partner who had betrayed him. "Well," he continued, "I guess a full moon does mean a lot to you crazy bastards. When it comes up, I'll bet you really freak out."

The teeth glinted once more. The calm, deep voice replied "You have no idea." A chill entered into Tom Simpson and he was afraid again.

"You scoff," said the shadow, "because you have not seen and without seeing you cannot imagine the wonder of it."

"Wonder!"

"Oh yes," said Meyer and glanced back toward the window and the other four shadows. "That is the word for it. It is wondrous and, when you have seen it, nothing will be as it was. The world will tilt and you will have a new conception of reality."

Tom could barely make out the outlines of his captor's face, but he knew where the eyes were. Within their depths, moved fiery glints of red. He twisted his body and tried to look behind him.

"Frank is still here," said the shadow. He'll join us in a minute."

"Frank's being here is his business," said Tom, "and you people's being here is your business, but why the hell am I here? What is it you want with me?"

Helmut Meyer snapped his fingers and one of the women walked into the darkness. A match flared and she came back carrying a lighted candle. She handed it to Helmut and returned to the group. "An excellent question," his captor responded, "and one which requires an answer."

The candle shed a saffron light about them. Simpson's gaze strayed to the others and lingered longest on the women. All were young with graceful bodies, their nakedness softened by the candle's flickering glow. In spite of the growing fear, he felt a surge of arousal.

"I am one hundred forty-three years old," began Helmut, "and I have been a Loup Garou for one hundred twenty of those years. The Werewolf is not immortal. We age. We die. What we are makes for a long life. As you see, I am in early middle age. I may live past three hundred years and then I will die, as we all will, in my human form. It must also be said that I am, even among my kind, exceptional because I am a Lupercus, a 'wolf priest.'" Here, Meyer paused and studied his captive with flat, onyx eyes. Tom tried to return the stare and then he looked away. "The Luperci are the only ones, who in their human form, carry the classic werewolf traits. Yes, a lot of what you may have heard from the legends is true. I saw you looking at the eyebrows. All Luperci have those. Also, the distinctive middle fingers." Meyer held up his right hand, palm outward, and Simpson saw the middle fingers, both abnormally long and both exactly equal in length. "We are the wanderers," said Meyer, "The others regain their human form and continue to lead their human lives. So do the Luperci, but we retain much more of the wolf: its strength, its speed and its grace." Helmut smiled and the teeth flashed. "And the Luperci are the only ones who can create another Werewolf. We alone have the gift of the Bite and we can give it in either of our forms."

Somewhere, in the far distance, Tom heard a freight train blow its mournful note. He looked into Meyer's immovable eyes and at the motionless figures behind him. Beyond the candlelit circle lay darkness and silence and, Tom, hearing nothing but Helmut's words and seeing nothing but the scene before him, knew that Helmut Meyer spoke the truth. With this awareness, an enlarging fear came; and even more strangely, a need to know more, to know all. In a low and fateful tone, he asked, "Why are you telling me this?"

"It is needful that you know," responded Meyer. "Moreover, there are other things."

"Like what?"

"Oh, like the elemental one. When the rays of the full moon strike us, we change into wolves. Or," he continued, "we take on the appearance of that animal. There has never been a wolf like us; there has never been anything like us when we take that shape. Nothing so elemental, or so omnipotent."

Tom fought to keep his voice steady. "Except when you're shot with a silver bullet."

Helmut Meyer's mouth opened and he tilted his head toward the ceiling. Tom knew the sound coming from his throat was intended as laughter, but it was really something else.

"Ohhhoooooo," his captor howled, "the business of the silver. Oh, I'm afraid not, Mr. Simpson. We can be killed in either of our forms, but silver is just another metal."

"What else can you tell me?" asked Simpson, and there was real curiosity in his voice.

"The hunger," Meyer answered, the wonderful hunger and the rapturous kill and the joy of preying on all those cattle you must associate with between the spells of the moon."

"What else?"

"Yes, there are other things," Meyer responded, "but those cannot be told. They must be experienced. They must be lived."

Tom's voice creaked out the words, "You want to give me the Bite."

"I wish to bestow it, yes," said Helmut, "that is why you are here. With these words he backed away in three measured steps. Melted wax flowed down the candle and over Helmut's hand. He didn't seem to notice it. Kneeling, he stuck the candle on the floor. He rose, gazed vacantly at Simpson, and said, "Tonight, we feed here, but on other nights you must hunt. Kill carefully and kill only in the company of your Pack. The Loup Garou are few in number. If the herd discovered our presence, the weight of their meat could destroy us. What you see before you are all of our kind in Memphis. In other cities, we number no more than a score. Luperci do not give the Bite freely and you, Mr. Simpson, will be one of the few to receive it during Moonspell. All will happen to you in one night. I have never seen this. I must admit to a certain curiosity."

With these words, Meyer resumed the backward steps until he stood with his companions. All were looking toward Simpson. Suddenly, a mewling whimper came from his right and five faces snapped toward it. Tom twisted around but could see nothing beyond the candleglow. Then, his partner stepped out of the darkness, pushing a man and woman before him. The man was elderly and clearly a derelict. His dirty, tattered clothing was topped by a greasy cap. Clumps of gray hair stuck out beneath it. The woman looked to be in her twenties and wore a short sundress. Her clean, blond hair shone in the light. She stared wildly around and gave another low whimper. The man seemed dazed and unaware. Both had tape stretched across their mouths and their hands were secured behind them. Someone had bound their ankles loosely and they advanced with short, mincing steps.

Frank Seeger was naked. He pressed forward to shove the captives and his bulbous belly bumped them obscenely. All three passed in front of Simpson and onto the plastic covering. The man and woman sank to the floor when Seeger pressed down on their shoulders. He looked at them for a moment, then joined the others. The naked figures faced the window and candlelight glowed on their backs and buttocks.

Simpson knew the talking was over. Now came a deep and awful silence, while the planet slowly turned.

He saw the moon first as a small dab of golden light, just above the window sill. The light widened and thickened, its rounded top moving upward. The standing figures did not move. Nothing moved except the moon in its inexorable rise. It seemed to Tom that in no time he could see half the sphere. His teeth began to chatter and he clamped his jaw shut. The moon continued upward and became a globe and seemed to fill the wide window. Its color deepened and a crimson light washed across the warehouse floor. The candle, as if in submission, flickered once and went out. Tom watched and waited. A twinge of pain ran through his shoulder and he pressed it against the column. The moonlit figures remained motionless and, as Tom watched them, a sweet realization crept in.

He'd been watching all this, watching the moon rise, for some time now and nothing had happened. With flooding relief, he knew that nothing would happen. There was danger here because he was dealing with a bunch of pychos; no telling what they might do. But how could he have believed they were what they said they were.

This bare-assed group, gawking at the moon, began to look absurd. Tom Simpson's straightened his back and his lips twitched in a smile. His fat partner looked especially foolish. He thought of Frank and Meyer together, one man biting the other, and his smile widened.

Then the fur began to grow on top of Frank's bald head.

The change occurred almost in an instant. Six humans were standing in the moonlight. Their shapes shimmered briefly, their forms wavered, and they dropped to the floor and were wolves.

No, not wolves, thought Tom. They had that appearance, but this was something else. Meyer was right. There had never been anything like them. The enormous bodies bulged with muscle and their heads, atop thick necks, showed powerful, prominent jaws. The round eyes were set in front; staring unblinking eyes, wide and intelligent. All were covered with short, dusky and rough appearing fur. One of the creatures, darker than the rest, circled his nearest companion and gave him a couple of sniffs; the leader admitting Frank to the Pack. They paid not the slightest attention to Simpson, but trotted immediately to where the couple lay.

The man looked almost comatose, his eyes half closed, the face vacant. The woman's eyes were stretched wide and rolling in terror. Shè squirmed and gave a high pitched moan. The black wolf lowered his head and ripped out her throat. He swallowed convulsively. Blood poured across the floor and the woman's body quivered.

"Oh God, Oh God," Tom moaned and closed his eyes. He opened them again when he heard the feeding sounds. All six were pressed in tightly over their prey, broad heads moving up and down, jaws working and tearing. One of the beasts bit into the man's stomach and backed away, pulling out a length of intestine. It chewed through a section, gulped it down, and turned to look at Tom; Frank looking at his partner. The stench of hot blood and feces hit Simpson in the face and he leaned forward and vomited. He kept his head down, but from the corner of his eye, he saw the man's heel, drumming on the floor. Now, the wolf-things were bunched even closer, feeding intently. The sound of crunched bones and the wet, sucking sound of tearing flesh filled his ears and brain. Tom cried out and sank to the floor and a beneficent blackness swept over him.

The planet turned and the full moon rose and shed its light. All the vacant warehouses lay like whitened tombs and, in one of them, six monsters turned their faces upward and knew the fullness of Moonspell.

Tom slowly regained awareness and merciless memory flowed in. He took a deep breath and opened his eyes. The creatures stood on the plastic sheet, round eyes watching him closely. Not a sign remained of the carnage. Tom understood why. The Werewolves had eaten the flesh and crunched down the bones and they had licked all the blood away.

The black wolf padded closer and Simpson heard its claws, clicking against the wooden floor. The beast gazed at him intently. Then, without warning, it sank its fangs into his shoulder. Slowly, it backed away and rejoined the others. They waited expectantly.

Tom Simpson felt nothing but pain. Then the pain dissolved and he felt a growing power! Yes, that was it; power in the senses, power in the body. He rose to his feet and spread his bound wrists. The thongs parted like wisps of spider web. He took a step forward and looked around. Oh the senses, the glorious senses. Meyer had spoken of the wonder, and wonder there was. It flooded in through the senses, and the senses were everything. He heard life moving in the walls and he smelled the damp night air and the place where blood had flowed. He looked about the great room and there was no more darkness. Everything shone with a lustrous light and the source of that light hung in the heavens and was a worshipful thing. He looked at his brothers and sisters, so beautiful, so perfect. He walked toward them.

A piece of rough flooring caused Tom to stumble.

He stopped and stared, and lifted his head. All the dwindling perceptions and vanishing memories in his brain, his human brain, suddenly surged forth in a final wave of human thought and reason. In that one clear moment of cognizance, for his soul's sake, Tom knew what he must do.

The Werewolves watched and waited for the change but he put forth his will and, for a little while more, remained a man.

They parted, three to a side, as he walked between them, walked toward the cotton hook that hung against the wall. He was reaching for it before the creatures realized his intention. They pounced, but they were too late. Quicker than he'd ever been able to move before, Tom placed the point of the hook against the side of his neck and yanked it through his own throat. His partially severed head flopped sideways and, just before he died, Tom felt a tugging at his body. The Loup Garou were tearing away his flesh.

The next day, Frank Seeger arrived late at the office. His secretary looked up and went to bring his coffee. He checked for messages, then strolled into his partner's office. There were several memos for Simpson. Frank picked them up and went back to his desk. To all inquiries, official or otherwise, about Simpson's absence, he would merely respond that he hadn't a clue. He would say that Tom had simply disappeared, as indeed he had, and that was all he needed to say. His partner had no family and, as far as Seeger knew, no close friends. Ownership of the business would revert solely to him and that might cause some suspicion, but what could they prove? And what did it matter? They were just cattle anyway. Frank Seeger had lost all his fear; and certainly all of his guilt. He just felt wonderful.

The pretty secretary entered with his coffee and he gave her a smile. "How are you, Sally?" he asked. "Sit down for a moment." She did so and looked expectantly at her boss.

"I've been thinking of letting you get more involved in the business, start doing some outside work. Of course, there'd be a salary increase. How would you feel about that?"

"Why, I'd like that very much, Mr. Seeger."

"'Good," he said, "start looking around for your replacement and, by the way, let's drop this 'Mr. Seeger' business; call me Frank."

''I will," said Sally, "and thank you. When will all this start?"

"Oh, no big hurry," said Seeger. "Get the new secretary trained and I'll prepare a few things for you. We're probably talking a month from now.

"Well, thanks again," said his secretary. "I won't let you down." She was beaming.

"I'm sure you won't," said her boss. "We've got lots of new property to look at. There's a vacant warehouse I may send you out to. That'll be a good place to cut your teeth."

Sally left the office with a spring in her step; and why not? The future looked bright and Frank had become so pleasant. She could still hear him chuckling behind her.

The Dark Gift
By Will Drayton

If you can wait and not be tired by waiting
Or being lied about, don't deal in lies,
Or being hated, don't give way to hating,
And yet don't look too good, nor talk too wise...

— Rudyard Kipling, "If"

Rick Cain hulked over his lunch, politely picking at his food. Blues City Cafe on Beale Street featured some of the finest Southern cuisine in Memphis: choice steaks, homemade hot tamales, sumptuous seafood gumbo, and fresh-baked fruit pies. But the gloom hanging over Rick darkened even his appetite as he sat with his former law partner, B. B. "Braxie" Wardell.

He noticed Braxie eyeing the half-finished T-bone and two tamales—still in the shuck—on Rick's plate, then gazing back at his own empty one. Smiling weakly, Braxie said, "You're letting a mighty good lunch go to waste. I'm buying. Eat. You look thin and pale, like you've been bitten by a *vampire*." He laughed, obviously pleased with his little joke.

Rick glanced around the room then back to Braxie. "Count Dracula hasn't bitten me. I'm just not hungry. Must be the July weather—heat and humidity kill my appetite."

"But this place is air-conditioned."

"Doesn't matter. It still gets to me."

"Are you sure it's not *something else*?"

"Such as?"

"Your new practice? Stress? Worry? Too many highballs after work?"

Rick returned a wry smile. *New practice*, he thought, stifling a bitter laugh. He had been out on his own for three years now, after leaving one of the city's biggest and most successful firms, and had nearly starved to death. Of the many clients he had felt sure would follow him, few did.

When the large fees dried up, so did his wife's affection. Within six months after his "career move," she filed for divorce, took their home and his life savings.

Somehow, Rick had managed to remain stoic, never letting anyone know how bad things had become—it had taken the entire inheritance from his mother's estate, to keep his office open. With that boost, he had held on to his private club membership and maintained his suddenly-meager practice. And that was about all. Braxie didn't need to know.

Rick had been hitting the sauce pretty heavily, too. But he wouldn't admit it. Braxie was a friend, but also a competitor. Everyone at Rick's former firm, O'Rourke, Rizzio, and Dillingham, knew he had challenged the senior partners and failed. With their positions at the prestigious firm intact, they could afford to be charitable. Especially Braxie. All too quickly it seemed, Braxie had filled Rick's place—enjoying the good life Rick had hoped for ever since he had graduated as valedictorian of his law school class.

"No," Rick replied defensively. "I watch those 'shooters.' We know *John Barleycorn* has ruined too many of our professional brethren. I'm okay."

"You're sure? I want you to be— *really*. The firm has some case conflicts to refer out and—well, I'm trying to get the Conflicts Committee to send those clients to you. I know you'd take good care of them."

Rick wondered if Braxie meant that. "Thanks. I can always use new business. They'll get super-special treatment, especially since you're sending them."

Thanking Braxie for lunch, Rick headed out the door, to walk alone amid the tourists, down sweltering, recently-renovated Beale Street, where musician W. C. Handy had given birth to The Blues, reflecting about his life and plans, struggling to overcome his own "blues." Almost immediately, the old emotions of anger and wounded pride, coupled with the desire for revenge began gnawing on him. They fed upon him from within, constantly. He could never forget or forgive the three monumental, career-threatening slights he had suffered. Lost in thought, he blundered into a folding metal sign on the sidewalk.

"Damn!" he yelled, and grabbed his knee. The blue-and-white seersucker suit trousers he wore had done little to shield his kneecap. While rubbing his leg, he examined the sign. Why hadn't he seen it?

A painted hand pointed toward the open doorway of an old brick building, so old it must have withstood everything from Memphis' three yellow fever epidemics to the civil rights riots. It had also definitely escaped renovation. Beyond the doorway a flight of stairs led upward. Beneath the sign's painted hand, antique letters read:

SISTER MAGDA
Advisor & Counselor
Fortunes told. Palms read. Tarot.
Your fate in her hands.
Strictly Confidential.
(UPSTAIRS)

At first it seemed silly. After avoiding normal, professional counselling to cope with his negative feelings, here he was now, seriously considering going to an occult advisor. If she turned out to be bogus, like all the other fortune tellers he had heard about, he could at least have a good laugh telling his buddies about it over drinks.

He bounded up the worn wooden stairs which appeared not to have been painted in his lifetime. He heard them creak with each footfall. Dry rot had probably set in.

At the top, with dim illumination provided from the weak, reflected sunlight at the bottom of the stairs, he found a narrow, empty, windowless hall with a single, closed, wooden door on the right. An undefinable scent permeated the hall. It went beyond the pungent odors of spilled alcohol and countless micturitions—something much older, more potent, more evil.

There was no sign on the door. Rick tried to turn the knob, but found it locked. Making a loose fist, he rapped his knuckles three times.

Nothing happened. He knocked again. A few moments later he heard movement. The latch clicked and the door opened about eight inches. A veiled female figure wearing a long-sleeved, ankle-length, dark dress of antique design peered through the crack and asked, "Who knocks?"

"A potential client. May I come in?"

"You're not police or health department, are you?" Her voice carried the slightest trace of a foreign accent.

"No."

She fully opened the door, revealing that it was darker inside than in the hall.

She lifted her veil, seized his right hand, and, leaning forward, looked closely at his palm. She made a strange humming noise, then released him, straightened, and looked directly into Rick's face. As she did, he studied her features, wondering what her nationality was.

Her brown skin and wrinkled brow made her first appear of Asian Indian extraction. But this was dispelled by her piercing blue eyes. She had thick lips and a flat nose, indicating African ancestry. But this also was contradicted by her high cheekbones and straight white hair. As for her age, it could have been anywhere from around her late fifties to early seventies.

In her youth she must have been beautiful.

"How did you find Magda?"

"Your sign—I literally ran into it." He laughed nervously, apologetically. "I figured I might try having my fortune read. Maybe let you *advise* me. That is what you do, isn't it?"

"Come," she said, her sapphire eyes widening like Svengali's. Before he could resist, she drew him inside.

He noticed that, as he entered, a pesky, rather large black housefly flew in behind him and buzzed around the room. He hated flies, but ignored this one because he was so intrigued with the gypsy.

The dank and musty interior was cooled by a window air conditioning unit partly concealed by heavy drapes that shut out all sunlight. The only light came from the flame of a short, thick candle on a small, round table in the middle of the room. By the table stood two chairs. Beside the candle, on a brass stand, sat a crystal ball. The candle gave off a sweet fragrance which partially masked other, unpleasant odors.

Magda pointed to the nearest chair and said, "Sit."

Rick obeyed, then asked, "What are you going to do?" He became fearful when he realized he had acquiesced like a five-year-old.

"Did you bring money?"

"Yes."

"Give me twenty-five dollars."

He paid her and she stuffed the money into her bosom.

"Place both hands on the table and close your eyes," she commanded. "No, palms up!"

He obeyed. Once more she made the strange humming noise.

She continued her humming for perhaps two minutes, then spoke again. "Open your eyes and gaze into the crystal."

When he did, he gasped. The crystal had turned a bright, deep, ruby-blood red. Together, they watched the crimson ball. After a moment Magda laughed like a witch out of some fairy tale.

"What's so funny?" Rick asked.

"Silence!" she hissed. "The crystal speaks to me."

A few moments later, the crystal cleared. Magda then looked at Rick.

"You are an unhappy man," she began.

"So, what else is new?"

"Do not interrupt me again before I finish."

He shook his head to indicate he would not.

"I see burning within you the desire for revenge—upon three whom you hate."

He nodded.

She resumed. "They wronged you—all arrogant, unrepentant sinners who should suffer and die."

Once more he nodded.

"But you cannot risk your own reputation to avenge yourself, for fear you might be caught. Your prominence inhibits your bloodlust. If you knew you could do it with impunity, you would destroy them. Am I correct?" Her smile widened and became almost diabolic. He could see rot in her teeth and smell her foul breath.

"Yes," he whispered.

"Then I can help you—for a price."

"What? My soul?. Sorry, can't afford it." He laughed at his own weak joke.

"A better deal than that. I wish to extend my own life—by taking *five years* from yours." Rick laughed again. This exchange was sillier than the worst B-movie he had ever seen. He was still young—thirty-five. Hopefully more than half his life lay ahead of him. What would the last half-decade mean anyway, when he would be an old fart rolling around in a wheelchair in some nursing home?

No, the insults and injuries he had suffered had been all too real. Too grievous. This lady might not even be serious, but he *was*. If he could avenge those three great wrongs, it would be worth the five years. His hatred was that strong.

"Can they be the *last five*? I don't want to age now."

"Surely."

"What will you give me in exchange for those years?"

"The power to destroy three whom you hate—without being caught."

"I will agree, but only if you show that you can give me the power."

"Gladly."

She took his right hand in both of hers, opened it, and held it palm-upward. As she released it, she opened a paper packet, and poured the contents onto his palm. "Sugar," she whispered. "Keep your hand open."

He obediently held his hand and arm in the set position.

Around him the fly buzzed obnoxiously, in slower and tighter circles, until it finally landed in his palm and began greedily lapping at the sweet treasure placed there.

"Repeat after me," the gypsy whispered, "*Animam tuam devorabo*—that means 'I shall devour your soul'—three words, three times, for three enemies."

With great care he repeated the three words. To his amazement, sparks crackled in his palm. A blue flame consumed the fly in an instant. Only a tiny dry cinder remained.

"That's incredible!" he shouted.

"Yes, but true," she replied. "And now we have a *bargain*."

All of this suddenly seemed too much to believe. Moreover, the gypsy was already beginning to look younger. Rick could have sworn that, when he first saw her, her eyebrows had been gray. Now they looked dark brown. Her face was less wrinkled, her hair no longer white but distinctly gray. Had something actually happened when he made the agreement?

She pushed him toward the door. "Go now. We have made our pact. Remember the words of power: *Animam tuam devorabo*."

An instant later he stood alone in the upstairs hallway. As though dazed, he made his way slowly down the steps, back to the real world of Memphis in mid-July—where the summer heat is total reality. But even the sweat it provoked could not dispel his belief that now he might be able to avenge wrongs that had seemed unrightable an hour before.

* * *

The three cases had each involved a woman. But Rick's sainted mother had taught him not to ever hurt a woman. Their lawyers had been men, each of whom had wronged him, each of whom he could now punish.

The first slight occurred shortly after Rick had become a partner, after five long, grueling years of establishing himself, when Imelda Dresch, came to him, furious that her late husband Saul had intentionally cut her out of his will. Rick carefully studied the law and drafted a petition in order for Imelda to file her dissent before the probate court.

Imelda had signed the petition and Rick had promptly filed it. Unfortunately, he forgot at the time to ask the clerk for a hearing date. That oversight caused a month's delay. Even more unfortunate was Imelda's insatiable appetite for money. She did not take kindly to hearing she would have to wait longer.

An aged former beauty queen, whose face had been lifted more often than Woolworth's Department Store, Imelda had married five times. Each husband had been rich, elderly, and in poor health. The first three of her previous marriages ended with Imelda becoming a wealthy widow. The next-to-last one had ended in divorce, but she had received a handsome settlement. Although Imelda had a knack for acquiring fortunes, she possessed an even greater talent for dissipating them. This lifestyle transformed her into a spoiled diva, quite accustomed to having and getting her way.

Imelda's personality could not jibe with Rick's. Recognizing this, he still believed he could handle her professionally and tried even harder to please her whenever she contacted him. Too late he realized his mistake. When Rick became involved in the trial of an unrelated case and did not promptly return two telephone calls from Imelda, she went in a huff to see Simon Whitethrush, the senior partner of Whitethrush & Cheatham, another Memphis silk-stocking firm, for a second opinion.

Even at that time, gray-haired Simon had seemed old. He had practiced some forty years and had served as president of the state and local bar associations. Although he had a very cold personality—it was often said he never smiled except when he collected a large fee— he was generally well thought of in the professional community, even if not personally liked.

For, it was reputed, he would stop at nothing, short of getting himself caught doing something unethical, to make money. Simon had promptly informed Imelda that although Rick may have properly advised her about pursuing an elective share of her husband's estate, he hadn't demanded enough money for her. By saying the magic words, "more money," Simon effectively weaned the client away.

At first Simon coaxed Imelda into bringing him and his firm on as co-counsel. Simon told Rick, "She wants us to help you. We'll work together nicely."

But Simon and his *three assistants*, all of whom were charging an hourly rate equal to or in excess of Rick's, kept a chilly distance as they reviewed his files and work product from the past two months, then sent Imelda a bill for more than four times anything Rick and his firm had charged her. When she questioned Simon about his firm's statement, he responded that they suspected Rick of malpractice. Then, Simon told her they could get her twice as much as Rick could, *and*, by alleging malpractice, they could scare Rick's firm into not charging her and also to pay Simon's fee.

It was an offer that Imelda couldn't refuse. She quickly sided with Whitethrush & Cheatham, who, in a letter, dismissed Rick and his firm, and made a claim against their malpractice insurance carrier. Rick was summoned to the office of his senior partner, Fred O'Rourke, who, along with Mark Rizzio and Click Dillingham, interrogated him about the letter.

Rick explained that it looked like a set-up. They agreed that it was a set-up. But they did not want the publicity—it seemed better to them to let the case go, write off their fees (all of which Rick had already earned), and pay Imelda and Simon out of Rick's gross production, than to involve themselves in a nasty, highly publicized, and protracted malpractice claim, even though one of questionable merit.

Their decision shattered Rick's faith in the firm. It also left relations quite strained. It was then he vowed to get back at Simon. Still there was money to be made, and opportunities abounded for Rick and his colleagues. He stayed with the firm despite the Imelda Dresh fiasco.

It took a second crisis to make Rick leave. This occurred when he became involved as counsel for Sunny Dell's estate. Sunny Dell and the Delta Rockets were the hottest rock group to come out of Memphis since the Gentrys. Their second album had gone platinum and they soon found themselves booked for concerts across the nation, television appearances, and their own movie. Unfortunately, like Elvis and Ricky Nelson, the Delta Rockets liked to fly private planes. More unfortunately, like Ricky Nelson's last flight, theirs also ended in a crash with no survivors.

Within days after Sunny Dell's death, his pretty young widow Charlene, who had been a friend of Rick's in high school, contacted him and asked if he would handle Sunny's estate. A preliminary review showed that the estate might generate some extremely lucrative fees, if an astute attorney could handle the quite complex problems associated with it.

One of the biggest potential assets, as well as one of the greatest challenges facing the Dell estate, involved its claim to the late entertainer's right of publicity—an exclusive proprietary right to the reproduction of Sunny's name, likeness, and image. License royalties from sales of tee shirts and posters bearing Sunny's face had, during his brief career, brought substantial revenues. They might now bring the estate a fortune, unless the exclusive right to issue such licenses had become public domain because of Sunny's death. Street vendors, capitalizing on that assumption, were already hawking bootleg tee shirts and souvenirs.

At the time, the law in Tennessee was uncertain. It seemed there was case law to support either position. The Elvis Presley estate had met with some success in establishing the right for Elvis' daughter. It had sponsored a bill in the state legislature which established an inheritable property right and provided for its legal protection, but there had been no case law to support it.

Rick had accepted the job as attorney for Sunny Dell's widow and estate knowing he would have to fight for these rights. Almost at the same time, a group of businessmen, wanting to promote tourism, and rock fans formed the Delta Downtown Development Corporation (the "D.D.D.C."), a nonprofit corporation to build a public memorial in downtown Memphis to honor Sunny and the Delta Rockets—a white granite obelisk with a life-sized, raised bronze relief on the front, depicting Sunny and the band performing. That alone might not have presented a problem.

However, when the D.D.D.C. also announced its intention to fund the project through sale of miniatures of the monument, trouble started. It was for charitable purposes and none of the proceeds would go to Sunny's estate. The story appeared in the morning paper. Charlene called him, obviously upset, just as he arrived at work.

"The monument. It's ugly. I don't like the way Sunny looks. Please stop them. Don't let them walk over us."

Rick tried to sound reassuring. "As your lawyers, we'll stop them."

"That's what I wanted to hear.   How soon can you do something?" Her voice became calm and cheerful again.

"I'll start right now."

Rick buzzed Braxie on the intercom and politely summoned him to Rick's office. Braxie listened attentively as Rick went over the case. Before Rick could finish, Braxie said, "There's another fact you may not know—Mariah Dillingham is the president of the D.D.D.C."

The muscles in Rick's athletically trim stomach tightened involuntarily. Mariah was the wife of his senior partner. "You're kidding."

Braxie wasn't smiling. "I wish I were."

Like Simon Whitethrush, Cleghorne ("Click") Dillingham was known for his cold personality and was not very popular. He had a computer for a brain and a cash register for a heart. Because he was well-connected and brought new and wealthy clients to the firm on a regular basis, his partners respected him as a "rainmaker." The large fees he consistently produced forced them to overlook his other faults.

Click was tall and pale, Rick's senior by seventeen years. Although quite thin, Click was surprisingly muscular and strong, partly due to his mother's having put him through boxing lessons as a child to save him from the scads of bullies that had tormented him. His thin, sandy hair was always oiled, combed back, and parted down the middle. Thick, black horn-rimmed glasses perched low on his long nose shielded his watery blue eyes.

Some speculated Click had been born middle-aged. He wore expensive suits, but never had them cleaned for fear it would cause them to wear out sooner. He and Mariah both belonged to Mensa and proudly reminded others of this fact at every opportunity.

Click seldom communicated directly with his partners or associates. Instead he would dictate memos and circulate them. He was nicknamed "Click" for the sound he made turning on and off the dictation equipment.

Click's devotion to his wife was the only thing that equalled his love of money. She was perhaps the only adult human being he cared anything for, and he was blindly loyal to her. On any other subject, Click could equivocate with the best of sophists. But if the issue concerned Mariah, there was no relativity—everything was absolute—either you supported Mariah and were a friend, or you did not, and became the enemy.

Rick felt a troubling lump growing in his throat. "I guess we'd better speak to Dillingham."

Braxie gave a nervous laugh. In Hollywood-style American Indian dialect he responded, "What you mean 'we,' Kimosabe? You the Lone Ranger on this one. Tonto's outta here."

Anxiously, Rick searched for another senior partner to sound out for support. All were unavailable. Click, who usually would have been in conference or on the telephone, sat at his desk, in his office, reading, with the door wide open. When Rick knocked, Click Dillingham gave one of his rare smiles and motioned for Rick to enter.

"Do we have some business?" Click asked.

"Actually, it concerns your wife."

"What about her?" His voice immediately took on a defensive tone.

"She does so much for charity. Everyone appreciates her work, but—"

"But what?" Click had a natural talent for getting to the heart of any problem.

"Well, it seems like she wants to do something that's not in the best interest of one of our good clients."

Click stood up. His watery blue eyes boiling. "What do you mean?" His tone was civil, but rumbled with threatening undercurrents.

Rick swallowed hard and blurted out the rest. "She intends for the D.D.D.C. to sell miniatures of a monument with Sunny Dell's likeness on it. Our client's widow doesn't want that."

As soon as the words escaped Rick's lips he saw the red tinge rise from Click's neck like a thermometer on a very hot day. In an almost inaudible but threatening whisper, Click asked, "Are you telling me what my wife can and can't do?"

Trying to sound as calm as possible, Rick replied, "No. I'm merely pointing out we have a conflict. It doesn't look good for a partner's wife to be acting contrary to our client's best interest."

At that Click pounded the desk with his fist. His voice rose as he spoke. "Just when does a junior partner get off telling me about any conflicts?"

By lunchtime Rick ended up in Fred O'Rourke's office, in another dismal conference with the senior partners. By one o'clock it was clear to Rick that, although most of his partners righteously hated Click Dillingham, they loved too much the regular income he produced to side against him.

When Fred O'Rourke told Rick of the partners' decision to withdraw from representing Sunny Dell's estate, Rick became livid. Before resigning, he accused his partners in general and Click Dillingham in particular of being spineless moneygrubbers of dubious ancestry and conjectural progeny.

A month later, Rick opened his own law office and got his first eyeful of what the real world for young, solo practitioners was like—cold, hard, and slow.

He had vowed, "You'll get yours, Click."

The third slight had been less about money, more about honor. Julien Tubman had been a loyal client who had followed Rick when he opened his new office. Julien's fat, ugly daughter, Gabrielle ("Gabby"), had a hundred-dollar-a-day cocaine habit that Rick didn't know about and Julien apparently had tried to remain ignorant of until he died. His will appointed Rick as trustee over a substantial trust that would have supported most normal young ladies' wants and needs, but not Gabby's.

Within weeks after Julien's will was probated, Gabby began calling Rick, asking for more money than the trust's income could produce. At first Rick accommodated her. But, as Gabby's needs became greater and her demands and reasons more suspect, Rick started scrupulously questioning her. When he became convinced Gabby was a drug addict, he cut her off from all but her minimum entitlement.

In a fit of addiction-induced rage, Gabby stealthily followed Rick around for a week and learned who his current girlfriend was, then phoned his already-estranged wife. When his wife's attorney contacted Rick and informed him the pending divorce petition was being amended to include adultery, and of his source, Rick immediately petitioned to withdraw as Gabby's trustee and to be paid a final fee.

Not content to have a mere parting of the ways, Gabby retained Otto McCurdy to represent her. It was common knowledge that Otto, long regarded as the nadir of the legal profession, would do anything for a fee, including represent Gabrielle Tubman. His two obsessions were money and sex.

Short, bald, and excessively fat, Otto had never married. He frequented the topless bars in south Memphis near the airport and was renowned for supporting the local ladies of negotiable virtue. He obviously accepted Gabby's last $400 as his retainer in hope that he might be appointed her successor trustee, earn a handsome fee, and do relatively little work, apart from helping his beneficiary prematurely deplete her trust fund.

At the hearing, with no proof whatsoever, Otto accused Rick of embezzling trust funds, spending inappropriately, and acting maliciously—words that stung Rick like angry hornets, despite their obvious falsehood. Rick proved he had been totally honest and prudent as trustee. The Chancellor sustained Rick's claim for compensation, but did nothing to admonish or chastise Otto for the scurrilous attack he made upon Rick's character.

To Rick's surprise Otto was also appointed successor trustee. After the hearing was over, Rick confronted Otto.

"Look," he said in a loud, angry voice, "you told some baldfaced lies. They backfired on you, like you deserved, but I still want an apology."

Otto looked at Rick like he had just landed in a spaceship from Mars. "Get real," he said in a voice full of cold contempt.

Rick sprang at him, hoping to pummel Otto into a pile of suet, but two deputy sheriffs restrained him.

That was when he vowed vengeance a third time.

* * *

Rick decided to test his new power. He walked from Beale, straight to the office building where Otto McCurdy worked. He disembarked from the elevator and entered Otto's suite. A receptionist with dyed red hair eyed him quizzically.

"May I help you?"

"I'm here to see Mr. McCurdy."

"Is he expecting you?"

Before he could answer, Otto McCurdy waddled into the lobby. As soon as he saw Rick, he bristled. "Look, Rick," he said, "I don't want no trouble."

"It's okay," Rick responded in a soothing, reassuring voice. "I've found religion. I came by to forgive you."

Otto looked curiously at Rick. "What do you mean? I didn't do nothing wrong."

"It's okay. Let's just shake hands."

"You really mean it?"

"Sure."

"Okay."

As soon as he accepted Otto's pudgy right mitt, Rick whispered, "*Animam tuam devorabo.*"

No sooner had he spoken the words than he felt the crackle of sparks—raw energy surged from Otto's body as Rick consumed his hated enemy's very life force. Like some insect impaled on a pin, Otto was caught in Rick's grip and could only wiggle spastically, helplessly-—dying, as his life drained away. His eyes bulged out as though they would pop, and he chewed completely through his own tongue. In an instant it was over. Otto lay dead on the floor, blood smeared around his mouth, his stomach protruding upward like a corpulent mountain of rancid gelatin encased in a wrinkled white shirt.

"What happened?" the receptionist asked in a loud, panicky voice.

"He's had a seizure," Rick answered. "Better call an ambulance."

The medics arrived soon and whisked their macabre cargo away. No one raised any questions about it being anything except a heart attack.

As the middle of the afternoon approached, Rick knew he would find Click Dillingham on the tennis courts. He drove to their private club, suited out, and located Click on court number four, where he was engaged in a doubles game with Braxie and two younger lawyers from the firm. Ironically, the player with Braxie had just sprained his ankle. Rick volunteered to substitute. Click reluctantly agreed.

The game went down hard and close. Click and his young partner finally succeeded in breaking a tie and beating Rick and Braxie on the third set. That was when Click—in a mechanical gesture of obligatory sportsmanship—jumped over the net, offered Rick his hand, and said, "Good game."

Rick gripped the hand of his enemy and replied, "*Animam tuam devorabo.*"

Click Dillingham succumbed on the spot, dead from an apparent heart attack.

It must have seemed most unusual to the authorities that Rick Cain had witnessed two fellow lawyers die from heart attacks on the same day. Still, everyone knows that law is a stressful profession. Nobody suspected him of *causing* both deaths.

Rick's last score would be the sweetest to settle. By early evening Simon Whitethrush could usually be found at the club bar, where he normally stopped for a drink or two on his way home.

It was still light outside, so Rick decided to kill some time by driving down to view Beale Street once more. He came around Front Street and turned east. As he proceeded across Second, he noticed Blues City Cafe at the corner. But, to his surprise, when he looked where the building with the gypsy had been, he beheld a vacant lot, overgrown with knee-high weeds. Had it all been a daydream? No. He was sure it was all real.

Soon he would kill Simon, too.   And Rick could hardly wait. Almost as soon as he entered the club's subterranean cocktail lounge, he saw Simon Whitethrush standing alone at the bar, his back toward Rick. Tom the bartender waved and said, "Good evening, Mr. Cain, what'll it be?"

Rick replied, half-laughing, "Make mine a Bloody Mary, Tom. I'm in the mood for *blood*." He said, "Hello, Simon," then, glancing dramatically around the empty bar for emphasis, added, "Having a drink with all your best friends? Or, were you simply exposing your prettiest side to me?"

Simon ignored the jokes.

Tom interrupted, "I'm sorry. I've got to go back to the kitchen for more tomato juice. Won't be but a minute."

"Take your time," Rick responded with a chuckle. Perhaps he was beginning to enjoy this work too much.

As Tom exited, Rick moved toward Simon. Now he would settle the oldest score. He held out his hand in an apparently civil gesture, and asked Simon, "How've you been?". When Simon said, "Fine," and accepted his grip, Rick muttered, "*Animam tuam devorabo.*"

Nothing happened.

"What did you just say?" Simon asked.

Desperately, Rick squeezed his enemy's hand more tightly and repeated the phrase. Still nothing happened. Why didn't the deaf old fart drop dead?

A funny gleam appeared in Simon's hazel eyes. "Ah, I thought I heard you right the first time," he exclaimed. Then he squeezed back upon Rick's hand and said, "That's the right phrase! *Animam tuam devorabo!*" The blue flames crackled, but this time the force flowed *from* Rick to Simon.

Rick gasped and struggled to free himself. Simon gloated, in a mock-sympathetic voice, "Poor Rick. My colleague Magda took the last five years from your life—you were to die on the fifth anniversary of this date, in the Great Memphis Earthquake!"

Rick felt as though some cosmic pump was sucking out the life force from his body. Damn that gypsy! Why hadn't the power worked for him the third time?—unless it had, and—Oh God, NO!-- Otto McCurdy had been his *second* victim and the first usage had been wasted on that goddamned fly!

He wanted to scream at the top of his lungs, but found he couldn't.

As he sank into oblivion, the last thing he heard was Simon, laughing like Satan, and asking, "Did you think you were the only one with The Dark Gift?"

Nurse Bann
By Will Drayton

Lust. One of the last sins to quit us. Danny O'Flynn remembered what the padre had warned him. It had been his one serious weakness all his adult life. For the last four years, however, except for an occasional high-priced call girl, there had been no sexual encounters, and he'd missed that. God how he'd missed that. T h e beautiful singing from down the hall had wakened him, just in time to watch the nurse's shapely bottom bounce saucily within the restrictive confines of her white uniform as she left his room in the new Catholic hospital. The one he had practically built. It was named for his patron saint, but dedicated to him.

He felt the stirring of an erection. A rare, but welcome thrill. Especially at his age, when his old body was becoming less and less responsive to young thoughts.

"Oh, Danny," he thought, *"even in your condition, you're still preoccupied with the ladies."* Not proper for a seventy-four-year-old heart patient, but *his* thoughts nonetheless. He had wondered at the hospital's dedication ceremony if such a good deed might wash the black record of his life clean, after the countless infidelities and affairs that his patient, loving wife had blindly overlooked for fifty years. Or after the thousands of nights he had drunk himself into oblivion while engaging in such debauchery.

That was the nice thing about his faith. The Monsignor acknowledged that the spirit was willing, but the flesh weak. Danny knew the flesh was also sweet. Oh so Goddamn sweet! But because he had made generous contributions to the parish and the diocese, the priests were inclined to grant Mr. Daniel O'Flynn forgiveness and absolution for his sins whenever he confessed.

And, sweet Jesus, they were venial sins, weren't they? Oh, he knew himself for an Irish rogue, but surely not a damned one. Danny had never intentionally hurt anybody. He'd taken great care not to.

Thirty years ago, after bearing him four beautiful, healthy children, his wife Rose announced she was through with sex for good. She refused even to talk about it. That was how lace-curtain ladies handled such matters. He had to deal with his legitimate biological needs, didn't he? Any adultery had been with a willing partner, discretely so no one else would ever know. Nobody would suffer for a little harmless fun. And there would always be the special presents at Christmas to let each special lady know much such friendship was appreciated.

Oh, how he had loved those ladies! Oh, how he missed them now!

After those dedicated doctors and nurses had brought him around from his first heart attack, they'd ordered him to quit doing almost all those things that still brought him pleasure: no more cigars, no more Old Bushmill Irish whiskey, no more rare, prime T-bone steaks. When the doctor had said he could still practice sex with his wife, he broke into hysterical laughter. Three months later he suffered the second M.I.

He'd drunk more heavily and gone back to cigars. That was when his ticker rebelled, which landed him in the intensive care ward.

What was the music that woke him? It reminded him of the Irish countryside of his youth. The haunting, lyric soprano was the voice of a girl on the brink of womanhood. It had to have been a recording. Nobody in Memphis could sing like that. It reminded him of that time, over half a century ago, when Colleen had sung to him. Colleen... the first girl he'd ever kissed. The first girl he'd ever loved. The first he'd ever lost. She had died in the flu epidemic of '36.

The pain from losing Colleen had left him emotionally scarred. Although he'd told himself he loved Rose when he married her, she always had to compete with the memories of Colleen. They haunted him, especially whenever he heard any young woman sing an Irish ballad.

A knock at the door brought Danny around from his thoughts. Dr. Jack Pedersen, Jr. entered. Unlike his father, the younger Dr. Pedersen was all business. "That last heart attack was pretty rough, Mr. O'Flynn. Some serious damage to your aorta. We may have to do bypass surgery."

"Oh, baloney! I'm fine. Just go ask your father. He should know after treating me for forty years."

The doctor shook his head. He managed a weak smile. "I wish I could. You've forgotten he's a patient here, too. Been in a coma since his stroke six weeks ago. Life support system's all that keeps him going. If he had a living will like yours, I could let him die peacefully. As it is, my hands are tied."

Danny felt the flush of embarrassment rising to his cheeks. How could he have forgotten that his old friend, golf and poker buddy was now in even worse shape than he? Was his mind failing him as well as his body?

"What was that singing I heard, Jackie?"

"Singing?" Dr. Pedersen gave a puzzled look.

"An Irish folk tune. Beautiful. It was just outside my room. Somebody's radio or CD player?"

Dr. Pedersen shook his head again. "Mr. O'Flynn, we don't allow music or loud noises in the hall."

"But I heard it. Not loud. Soft and sweet. Sounded like `Danny Boy.' I'd swear to it."

"I didn't see anyone in the hall. You don't still hear it, do you?"

"No." The sound had stopped. The thought saddened Danny. He wanted to know the source.

Dr. Pedersen felt Danny's wrist, checking his pulse. "Feels stronger. Your vital signs are somewhat better. I'll tell them to bring you beef broth with crackers and some Jell-O. We'll move you to solid food as soon as possible. How's the chest feel?"

"Still hurts, but not nearly so bad."

"We've got to be careful with the medication. Don't want anything to interact. Let me know if you need anything."

Then he was gone.

Danny figured all the doctors said the same things, but at least this one would take special care of him, as his father had before him.

There it was again. The music. Growing louder. Coming closer. A beautiful rendition of "Danny Boy," his favorite song, and without any instrumental accompaniment:

"Oh Danny boy, the pipes, the pipes are calling
From glen to glen, and down the mountain side
The summer's gone and all the roses falling
It's you, it's you must go and I must bide . . ."

What a voice that lady had!

Somebody knocked.

"Come in," he said.

The shapely young nurse that entered caused his heart to flutter, then race. He had never seen anyone so attractive in his life, except.... No. It had to be a coincidence. A cruel trick that fate was playing on an old man. The face looked so familiar, but of course it couldn't be—despite the first name on the badge that said "Colleen Bann, R.N."

Her green eyes sparkled and her perfect teeth shone when she smiled. "Hello, Mr. O'Flynn. I'm here to check on you," she announced, brushing her auburn hair back behind an ear with one hand. There was a lilting trace of an Irish accent in her voice.

"Colleen," he asked, "would you or your folks have come from Erin, *Fiadh Fuinidh* (Ireland, Land of the West)? Possibly from County Clare?"

Her smile broadened. "Such a wise man you are, Mr. Daniel O'Flynn. Indeed I was born there."

"Near Ennis?"

"For certain."

"I didn't be knowing any Banns when I lived there. But I did know a Colleen O'Dwyer. You could pass for her daughter. Would you be acquainted with the clan?"

"Aye. And the wicked O'Flynns, too. We've had regular dealings with those folks for as long as time." She had chuckled when saying "wicked" to show she felt exactly opposite.

He took the hint. "I'm the only one that might qualify as wicked," he confessed.

She laughed. "Then I'll be keeping an eye on you to see that you behave." She fluffed up a pillow and placed it behind his head. He admired her full breasts as she leaned over the bed. Her scent made his head reel. In it he caught the fragrance of new mown hay and the sweetness of the Irish wind before an early fall thunderstorm. Such sweet relief from the usual hospital smells of rubbing alcohol and antiseptic.

As she finished, she winked at him, as if to let him know she was on to his secret. "Oh, I've heard you were a bad boy, but never an evil one." Her face was close. He so wanted to kiss her. But how, with his body hooked up to a heart monitor, with oxygen tubes in his nose? So he reached for her hand and squeezed it. And she squeezed back, her smile growing broader, even sweeter. He could feel his pulse racing.

Her eyelids fluttered. Was her interest more than professional? She seemed so kind and dear. He didn't want her to leave.

As if she'd read his mind, she announced, "I'm sorry, Mr. O'Flynn, but I need to get about my rounds."

"Danny. Please call me Danny. Will you be coming back soon?"

"Aye. Count on that. It's 'I'll be there, Danny boy, in *sunshine* or in *shadow*....'"

Once she was out the door Danny heard her singing again, her own special rendition of "Too-ra-loo-ra-loo-ral." *"A lullaby,"* he thought, *"to put an old Irishman to sleep. Colleen Bann, come ye back, come ye back,"* he mused, and drifted happily off to dream.

2

When he awoke, Rose, dressed to the nines in a smart gray wool dress and wrapped in a black llama mink stroller, was standing at the foot of his bed. With her was attorney Simon Whitethrush. "He's coming around, Simon," Rose said. She moved close.

"Wh-what's he doing here?" Danny asked, puzzled because he'd fired Whitethrush after their last fee dispute. The wheezy old fart had grossly overcharged him, putting three lawyers on a case that one could have easily handled.

Danny caught the antiseptic smell of Rose's denture-breath as she spoke. "Dear, I brought Simon here to help us with your business. He's prepared some papers for you to sign. After all, he's so familiar with your affairs."

Too familiar. That was the problem. Danny had helped make Simon rich, but no matter how much he paid the lawyer, it was never enough. He'd told Whitethrush to turn over the files, two days before that damned second heart attack.

Simon's bloodless lips curled back in a contrived smile. "How you doin', old chum? Good to see you're better. Can't wait 'till we get you back on the golf course at the Country Club and...."

"Cut the baloney, Whitethrush. You were supposed to return my files to me. Didn't you tell Rosie that?"

Simon nervously smoothed back his thinning white hair. "There wasn't any time. Besides, you need me now and I'm *here* to help."

Like a vulture to help pick a carcass, Danny thought. "What kind of papers have you brought?"

"A durable power of attorney. It has both health care provisions and general business powers which you confer upon Rose. This way, if you're in here for long, she can attend to your business while you're recovering."

"Let me look at it."

Rose passed Danny his reading glasses and he examined the document. His eyes were still pretty good, but he knew Simon too well to skip reading the fine print. In a moment he found what he was looking for. "What's this gobbledygook about *you* being her successor, Simon?"

Simon focused his eyes upon the document and didn't meet Danny's stare. "Oh, that's just in case Rose can't be reached. Somebody has to be available. Since we go back so long, I didn't mind volunteering."

"*Volunteering*, is it now? What about this part that says, '...notwithstanding anything else to the contrary, my alternate attorney-in-fact shall be compensated at his usual and customary rates for legal services.'

"Weren't your rates the main reason I fired you? Such as billing me for even the times when your associates went to the bathroom? Do you think I want to be charged again for `potty time'? Well, think again."

"But Dan, you need this document in case..."

"I'm going to be fine. I don't need you or your stupid legal papers. I made my way through the world on handshakes and keeping my word whenever I gave it. If I hadn't gotten rich I wouldn't be needing a lawyer, but since I do, it won't be the likes of you."

"Danny, dear," Rose interceded. "What about me? Will you sign that for me? I'll feel a lot better if you'd execute that power of attorney for my sake. I won't use it unless I have to."

"Simon," Danny asked, "how does this affect my Living Will?"

Simon cleared his throat and stared at some imaginary spot on the floor. "It doesn't, except that your Living Will only provides not to keep you alive by artificial means or heroic measures where there's no reasonable chance of recovery. This addresses those gray areas in between."

"So, if I become a vegetable, I won't be kept on life support like my poor friend Dr. Jack Pedersen?"

Handing Danny a pen, Whitethrush assured him, "No, you won't."

Danny crossed out all the references to Simon as an alternate or successor, and to his compensation. He signed the document and passed it to Rose. "Does that make you feel better, Rosie, old girl?"

Her eyes were misting. "Yes, Danny, dear."

Even though she had denied him sex with her for so many years, Rose had otherwise been a devoted mate. He cherished and trusted her. Simon was another matter. That bastard would squeeze a nickel until Thomas Jefferson screamed. "Pay Simon for his services, Rosie, but don't bring him back anymore. When I get out, I'm finding me a new lawyer right away."

Having exhausted himself, Danny let his head sink into the soft pillow to which Colleen's enchanting scent still clung, and closed his eyes.

3

The haunting sound of Colleen singing his favorite tune awakened him:

"But come ye back when summer's in the meadow
Or when the valley's hushed and white with snow
It's I'll be there in sunshine or in shadow
Oh Danny boy, oh Danny boy, I love you so."

Standing at the foot of his bed, she expertly carried and finished the last note. Colleen immediately reached for a facial tissue and dabbed tears from his eyes. "What saddens you, Danny O'Flynn?"

"Nothing. It's just that I love your voice. I'm also afraid I love you. Am I not a foolish old coot?"

Her emerald eyes shone with compassion. "No, not at all. A dear and fine man. And I have good news. There's somebody here to see you." She spoke with warmth and cheer.

Dr. Jack Pedersen, Sr. entered the room. He was dressed in his white physician's coat over regular clothes and looked the picture of health. Danny could not believe his eyes. More tears of joy flowed from them as he beheld his closest old friend, up and about.

"Jack, is it really you? I thought you were a goner."

Jack sat at the foot of the bed and gave Danny's hand a gentle squeeze. Danny shivered, noticing that the room had become unexpectedly chilly. "I'm fine now, Danny," the physician said and smiled. "You will be, too. Soon. Colleen's going to bring you around. We'll be back to our poker and golf games in no time. But I have to go now. .Goodbye."

"Jack, Colleen, don't leave!" Danny pleaded. But they were gone.

Anxious footsteps approached from down the hall. Dr. Jack Pedersen, Jr. entered with two unfamiliar nurses, one about sixty and another in her mid-thirties. He looked distraught.

"Did you see your father?" Danny asked. "He was here. You must have noticed him in the hallway."

The younger Dr. Pedersen swallowed hard. "Mr. O'Flynn, he couldn't have been on this floor. The good Lord took him half an hour ago. I only stayed here to make the final arrangements."

Danny felt his head spinning. "What about Colleen?"

"Who?" The doctor's face looked puzzled.

"Nurse Colleen Bann. Isn't she working this shift?"

"There's no one here by that name," the older nurse declared.

Danny felt new pain bursting within his chest. His heart monitor beeped alarm. The air felt thick as soup, impossible to breathe. The younger nurse turned up the dial on his oxygen tank. The older one pressed two nitroglycerine lozenges between his lips. Dr. Pedersen pressed the call button. He shouted into the intercom,

"Get the Harvey team up to Room 1010, *STAT!*"

4

Danny awoke to see Colleen in her nurse's uniform standing at the foot of his hospital bed. "Well, I made it, didn't I?" he asked.

"So far."

"Colleen, they say you don't work here."

"I'm not on the staff."

"You are *real*, aren't you?"

"As real as a leprechaun."

"Oh, blarney! Don't play games with an old Irishman."

"I'm not. What do you want from me—from this Colleen?"

Danny could not believe the words he blurted out. "Could it—would it be possible for you to be... my lover? The one who left me as a spalpeen, who swore she wouldn't go away, but did. The love I never got over. Are you she? Have you now come back to me, Colleen dearest?"

Her smile was enchanting, overpowering. "Close your eyes and I'll prove it."

When he opened his eyes, the hospital had vanished. He was lying with Colleen in his arms. They nestled together naked under a haystack in the Irish countryside. He was young again, strong, fearless, and lusty. She pressed her full bosoms against his chest, kissed his lips sweetly and passionately, and embraced him. It was an ecstasy he had never known before or since. Somehow he knew, though, that it was just a dream.

Darkness washed over him again.

5

The argument awakened him. Simon was chiding the younger floor nurse who was standing up to him. Defiantly, she protested, "But, Mr. Whitethrush, Mr. O'Flynn's Living Will gives explicit instructions not to keep him alive if there isn't any reasonable hope for his recovery. That stroke he suffered in surgery almost finished him. The odds are completely against his recovering."

Simon retorted, "I don't care what his Living Will says, my Power of Attorney preempts it. As attorney-in-fact, I'm ordering you to keep him on life support. Do you understand? If you don't, you'll lose your job!"

"You bastard!" Danny thought. Whitethrush must have replaced the two pages Danny had altered with two more that contained the original wording. Easy enough to do on any word processor. He'd recorded it and now was using it as his meal ticket. Rosie didn't realize it. Now Simon was in the driver's seat for all Danny's business. He could run the meter and ring up an exorbitant fee.

Desperately, Danny tried to speak. He strained to shout that Simon was a liar. But nothing happened. He tried to raise his hand and draw the nurse's attention, but his limb refused to respond to the command that his brain sent. His body had failed him.

Simon haughtily held up the papers. "The doctor sent Mrs. O'Flynn home to rest; he's given her a sedative to make sure she sleeps. She'll be out for at least a day. These entitle me to decide, in her absence, what measures are to be used to keep Danny alive. I'm ordering you to move heaven and earth to see that he lives, understand?"

"Yes, sir." The nurse's controlled politeness could not conceal the indignation in her voice. She left. Then Simon approached Danny.

He bent over the bed until his pasty face was almost against Danny's, and gloated, "Well, Danny boy, let's see who has the last laugh now. You thought you could get rid of me, but you weren't as smart as old Simon, were you?

"Lot's of folks pay my bills without question, but you—oh, you always had to haggle about my fees and make lots of jokes about how lawyers will do anything for money. Now, you shanty Irish trash, look who's in charge! I'm going to enjoy watching your body waste away as you lie there and shit all over yourself. All that time I'll be making myself richer from looking after Rose."

Colleen's voice interrupted Simon. "Except you've forgotten one thing, Mr. Whitethrush."

Danny saw Simon jump, startled to find he was not the only person in the room with Danny. Simon eyed the pretty, auburn-haired girl in the nurse's uniform. "What do you mean, Ma'am?"

There was no longer any sweetness in her voice, only menace. "When his time comes, it comes. Nobody can prevent that. Just like nobody can prevent your death."

"Now see here, young lady, just who do you think you are?" Simon scolded self-righteously and shook his index finger at Colleen.

Responding, both Colleen's voice and physical appearance changed with each word she uttered. Her tone became deeper, more menacing, sibilant. "I am known by different names to different people. Innocent little children call me the Angel Elizabeth. A lusty Irishman like Danny O'Flynn might consider me his Colleen. But, to you..." her voice took on a thunderous resonance, "I am AZRAEL!"

Something else stood in the place where the beautiful young nurse had been. Something dark and predatory, with wraith-like indistinguishable features, except for two huge, flaming red eyes. Something obviously intent on Simon's destruction.

Lacking any definite form, like a cloud of black smoke, the shade nevertheless had substance, as evidenced when it picked Simon up and shook him like a rag doll, then tossed him violently against the wall. He hit with a resounding thud, screamed, and clutched his chest as he slumped to the floor.

A dry rattle came from his throat, then his breathing stopped. His eyes stared vacantly into space.

"Danny," Colleen's voice, sweet and feminine again, whispered from the opposite side of the room. Once more she appeared as a beautiful young nurse. "They'll be coming to check on the noise. It's time for us to leave."

Danny found his vocal chords responding, so he could speak to her. "Colleen. I know who—what you are: the Banshee, the Angel of Death, Azrael—come *for me*."

"Yes, my dear Danny, I am. But you have nothing to fear. What you saw a minute ago was how Simon perceived me. To an evildoer, I can be quite frightening, even to the point of fatality. However, to you and your friends, like Dr. Pedersen, Sr., I am pleasant and kind."

"And how will you take me?"

"Why, Danny boy," she said with a smile, slipping out of her uniform and crawling beneath the sheets, nestling against him, making his arms and the rest of his body respond as that of a young man again—eagerly, in sublime pleasure, and free from any pain— "I'm going to love you from here to eternity."

Snare of the Fowler
By Lance Carney

I'd never been to Memphis, not in my adult life anyway. Hell, I'd never been on a Brazilian 120 turbo prop either for that matter. But here I was on one headed for the other.

The plane climbed toward the clouds; the noise of the propellers was deafening. I looked out as my city, my state became small and insignificant. I waited for the tension in my shoulders, back and neck to be released, but instead it remained, a constant reminder of my troubles. Troubles, it seemed, I could not leave behind.

The pain weighed heavy on my heart, as if hundreds of tiny acupuncture needles had been implanted in my chest. I thought now, and not for the first time, that the only pain that could possibly be worse would be suffering through the death of a child. But then again, this pain had the extra ingredients of humiliation and betrayal. Something I might expect from my brother, but God, not from my daughter. Not my own flesh and blood.

I tried to think of my father, happy thoughts, the reason for this sojourn to Memphis. Or escape to Memphis, if you will. Nobody knew I had left, let alone where I was going.

I closed my eyes and leaned back against the headrest, trying to purge all thought from my head. A peck on my shoulder interrupted me before I had time to gauge if I still had the ability to relax successfully.

"You okay?" the man across the aisle shouted at me.

"What?" I shouted back over the roar of the propellers.

"I said, are... you... okay?"

I wanted to answer with the usual "I'm fine" and sink back invisible into my seat, but for some reason I didn't. Silently, I looked the man over. He looked like any other sixtyish, rotund, generic man, the kind you overlook a hundred times a day. But his face... It wasn't any particular feature, it was all of them put together. A gentle kindness radiated from him. A kind of glow.

He continued when I didn't answer. "I'm sorry. It's just that you looked so... troubled."

I laughed. I couldn't help myself. I'll admit it had a tinge of a maniacal quality to it, but damn, it felt good. It had been a long time.

I reached over and extended my hand to him. "I'm Ralph Hutchins."

He smiled, seeming not the least bit offended at my outburst, and took my hand. "My name is Paul, to my friends. Pastor Paul to my church friends and family."

I laughed again. Wonderful. A preacher. Perhaps that was just what I needed. A preacher, a priest, a rabbi. Anyone that could possibly exorcise my demons.

With much difficulty, he shifted his bulk over and placed a large hand on my shoulder. It was the most comforting touch I had felt in many years.

"We can talk more when we land, if you wish," he said, just loud enough to be heard over the noise of the plane.

The sadness suddenly flooded back over me. I weakly nodded my head.

It turned out Pastor Paul was headed to Memphis also, for a ministry revival. He said it was a good time for him to reaffirm his faith. Ha! It would take more than a week of preaching and praying to renew my faith in anything or anyone ever again.

Funny thing was, he seemed to sense this about me, even before I started opening up to him. It so happened we had the same connecting flight in Atlanta, and we accompanied each other to our gate.

He was easy to talk to. We talked the entire time of our fifty minute wait, or rather, I talked and he listened. He listened, gently prodded, smiled at the right places, and was empathetic when I needed it. He was an amazing cross between a minister and a psychiatrist, putting me completely at ease. I told him more than I had ever told anyone, and yet, I couldn't bring myself to tell him everything. Janey. I didn't tell him about Janey.

But I did tell him everything about Josh. I couldn't keep the venom out of my voice when I talked about my older brother.

I started by describing to him our mother, a gruff, tough old bird with the heart of a lion and a little dash of Donna Reed. How, after our father died before either of us had reached the age of fourteen, she had gone to work to support us. I admitted that it probably wasn't much different from most hard luck stories he had heard; however, I tried to impress upon him the flair with which my mother handled all her burdens. The time, for instance, she had worked all Friday evening and stayed over for the midnight shift. Instead of acting dog-tired on Saturday morning, she had bounded in to wake us up and take us to the county fair. All day she remained on her feet, laughing with us, shouting as we rode the rides and played the games. As with most kids, it's not until you are grown that you appreciate the sacrifices your mother made on your behalf.

I tried to hold the emotion back as I told him of her illness: a debilitating stroke that left her half paralyzed. I considered it my duty, nothing more, nothing less, that I should look after her. Yet Josh never saw it that way. I was "sucking up" as he put it. He had paced and fumed and ranted and searched until he had finally found the lawyer who had handled Mom's will. I didn't know there was a will, let alone what was in it. Mother certainly wasn't rich, but the farm house and the hundreds of acres of pastures were now in a prime development area. The city was full up and the people were starting to overflow into our area. Subdivisions were popping up all over. Other farmers around us were getting out and getting rich. And, she was going to leave it all to me.

I described to him all the things Josh had done to me after he found out about the will, except the last one.

Instead, I changed the subject. I told him of my father and our trip to Memphis. Pastor Paul immediately sensed the change in me and began smiling and nodding his head. It was when I was five years old and Dad was going to visit his brother in Memphis. Mom was deathly afraid of flying, so she didn't go. Josh was heavily involved in minor league baseball and didn't want to miss a game. So it was just Dad and me. I tried to put into words the wonder of it all for a child of five. The fact that I could recall it all vividly impressed upon him the significance of the event in my life.

He only interrupted me once. That was when I told about the ducks and the hotel.

"You mean, there're ducks, and they live on the roof?"

"Yes, they have a sort of cage they keep them in on the roof."

"And they let the ducks—they let them inside the hotel?"

I told him the whole story, as I remembered it. The ducks arriving at the first floor in the morning, emerging from the elevator and parading to the great marble fountain in front of a huge crowd.

"It was one of the happiest days in my life. My dad laughed and laughed with his arm around me as I squealed at every duck that passed. He even let me hang around after the crowd died down to watch the ducks swim in the water of the fountain."

I hung my head suddenly. "He died six years after that. That was the best moment I ever spent with my dad. I guess I'm going back to see if I can recapture that feeling... or at least figure some things out."

He laid his hand on my shoulder again, and again I felt the tingle. "My congregation always tells me there is one true gift God gave me, and that is the ability to listen to their troubles and then quote scripture. They say the scripture always hits home and helps them to overcome. I claim no responsibility, you see, because the scripture just jumps into my head with no conscious thought on my part. If you will allow me..."

"Please, please go ahead."

"Psalm 91, verses 2 and 3: 'I will say of the Lord, He is my refuge and my fortress; my God, in him I will trust. Surely he shall deliver thee from the snare of the fowler, and from the noisome pestilence.'"

* * *

Once we boarded the Boeing 727 Pastor Paul and I were separated. I reclined my seat back and closed my eyes, feeling better. At first it seemed I might drift into one of the first peaceful sleeps I'd had in awhile, but then the thoughts of Janey came back.... Janey, oh Janey, how could you? How could you do this to me?

* * *

The jolt of the wheels touching down at Memphis International awakened me from my stupor. I stood, impatiently waiting my turn to exit the plane. When we finally started moving I could see Pastor Paul ahead talking with a tall man, another weary soul no doubt. I didn't try to catch up but just let the crowd push me along as we left our gate and headed for the baggage claim. It seemed the weight of all my problems had descended upon me again; I walked with head down, shoulders slumped.

Looking up suddenly, I found my progress impeded by a steel door. I glanced around and didn't see any of the other passengers. I shrugged and opened the door. I must've drifted to the back of the crowd and hadn't noticed them go through the door. It must be the way to the baggage claim.

The stairway on the other side of the door was dimly lit. I stopped, listening for other sounds from below; there were none. I shook my head hard. Must have been in a real trance to let them get that far ahead. I descended the stairs.

At the end of three flights I opened another door and entered a large room. A large empty room. I was confused. Where did they go if they didn't come down here? Then, over in the far corner I spied a rusty baggage conveyor belt. It wasn't moving, but on it rested my lone suitcase. Seeing my familiar ragged possession put me at ease and I went and grabbed it.

Taking the only exit I saw, I walked out. The street was strangely quiet, except for a single taxi that pulled up to greet me.

I opened the door, jumped in and sank back into the well-worn seat. As the taxi began to move I tried to act the part of excited tourist and strain to see the sights. Instead, I found my mind drifting to Josh. Although there'd been four years between us, I had always believed we were close. Then again, maybe it had just been wishful thinking on my part. One thing for sure, our one common thread was competition. The same sports, the same girls, and later the same cars. It seemed okay then, but in adulthood it had become something vile and shameful.

The taxi bounced over a speed bump and surprised me. I looked out and saw we were pulling under the entrance way to the hotel. The driver motioned for me to get out. It wasn't until much later that I realized I hadn't spoken a word to the driver the whole time.

With bag in hand I glanced around at the side of the large structure. She sure didn't appear to be much on the outside. But, when I went through the glass doors, I was truly amazed. She was a grand old dame on the inside. Tradition seemed to ooze from every corner. There were marble columns and antiques everywhere. I stood in awe until a crowd bumped me from behind, pushing through the doors. Whatever became of good, old fashioned Southern hospitality? Not a one of them said a word.

There were more people coming in, so I decided to have a look around the hotel before I went to the front desk for my room. I quickly checked my bag and took the nearest staircase I could find to escape the crowd.

I arrived on the second floor, which was more of a mezzanine overlooking the entire lobby. There was a huge ballroom, and several meeting rooms lining the outside, but I was drawn to the inside rail and the view below.

Right below me, was the fountain—the magnificent marble fountain I had so often evoked from memory. I thought of my dad, standing near it, holding my hand; me literally twitching and jumping with anticipation while we waited for the arrival of the ducks. Oh, the love I had felt for my dad that day!

With a start, I realized I didn't even know if the hotel still put on the show with the ducks. I had failed to ask about it when I made the reservation. Was it that important anyway, or did I just need to touch base with the place where I had felt the happiest with my dad?

Just as I noticed there was a crowd forming around the fountain, I realized it was important. Quite important, for some reason I couldn't quite grasp.

I thought of my father placing his large hand on my shoulder and giving me a squeeze and a smile as we waited. We were right down there, part of the line forming between the fountain and the elevators, on the front row. Beyond, I could plainly see three elevator doors on the far wall. There were also more people assembling at the rail of the mezzanine around me to watch.

Suddenly music blared from the loudspeakers. As if in reaction, I felt the palms of my hands grow moist as I gripped the rail. It was familiar music, marching band music. Sousa's March, I think. Just as suddenly it stopped.

A microphone squelched before a deep voice began: "Welcome one and all, in a long and glorious tradition here ..."

I didn't listen to what was being said, I was too busy scanning the faces of the children and parents lining the imaginary path between the elevators and the fountain. Each face held a smile, of varying degrees. It seemed to me each person had left whatever troubles they faced in the world outside. In here, there was nothing but happiness and breathless anticipation.

A bellboy appeared at the elevators with a red roll in his hands and proceeded to roll out a red carpet down the middle of the crowd. He used a stick to roll it and it ended right at the foot of the fountain. There, another bellboy placed a set of three wooden steps so that the top step was flush with the lip of the fountain. A great shudder of anticipation rippled through the crowd.

That's when I saw him. Down on the front row, half-way down the red carpet. I grasped the mezzanine rail with whitened knuckles, trying to maintain my balance, trying not to topple head-first down into the crowd in my dizziness. He was in the same place that we had stood all those years ago. My dad.

I took the steps down four at a time. The man on the loudspeaker was still reciting his speech as I pushed my way roughly through the crowd until I reached the spot where I had seen him. I couldn't find him! I looked around frantically. Suddenly, the man's voice on the loudspeaker boomed, "Ladies and gentlemen, please direct your attention to the middle elevator!"

Sousa's March began playing again, louder than before. Everyone was clapping. The door to the middle elevator opened and everyone cheered.

Dead silence from the crowd followed as the mangled, bloody body of a bellboy rolled out. From where I was standing I caught a glimpse of the ... something that must have done it before it retreated to the back of the elevator.

Sousa's March still blared throughout the lobby. There were no other sounds.

Tentatively another bellboy approached his bleeding comrade. He reached for his wrist, presumably to feel for a pulse, when he happened to look into the back of the elevator. His screams could be heard above the band music.

None of the crowd had moved from their places. It was as if we all still waited for the parading of the ducks to the fountain.

The parade we eventually witnessed was one of the devil's own.

Something slithered with lightening speed from the elevator, used the bleeding bellboy's body as a sort of ski jump and attached itself to the screaming bellboy's neck. I remember thinking stupidly that it must have hit his jugular as blood spurted out in an arcing stream.

The rest emerged from the elevator then, pulling themselves forward on muscular fore-limbs that ended in webbed feet. Their fat, snail-like tails dragged behind them leaving a trail of green ooze-like substance.

They came one after another down the red carpet, their tails seemingly twitching in time to Sousa's March. Women screamed. Children screamed. Men screamed. The lead creature veered off the carpet and, opening jowls that did not seem to be restrained by any bone structure, engulfed the head of a small child on the front row. I remembered watching the little girl from the mezzanine, determining her age as no more than three. She had been hugging a small doll protectively to her chest.

The crowd started moving as one then, running for the exits, screaming. But not before one of the last creatures sank two sharp incisors into a young boy's calf. He had just turned to run, his mother clutching his hand. She kept running but the boy's hand was ripped from her grasp. The thing dragged the boy, screaming and crying, toward the fountain.

That was more than enough for me. I turned to run for an exit but they were all blocked by a solid wall of people. Several people lay bleeding and moaning on the floor, obviously trampled in the mad rush to the doors.

I quickly decided the best escape was up and bounded for the stairs to the mezzanine. Surely those things couldn't climb stairs. When I neared the top, I tried to take the last five steps in one leap, catching my toe on the top one and losing my balance. I slid and crashed head-first into the rail overlooking the lobby. I groaned as I reached and felt my forehead and the knot that was already forming. But what was worse, I had plain view of the horror below. I saw the creature leaving the bodies of the bellboys and I got my first good look. Its skin was gray-green and slippery in texture, its body about the size of a sea lion. But its face, its face caused my heart to race even faster when I did not think that was possible. It looked positively vicious, a true carnivore. Its head swayed from side to side as it alternately hissed and emitted low guttural moans. Blood, saliva, and tissue dripped from its sharp teeth.

A shrill scream drew my attention to the fountain. I grasped the rails with both hands and pulled my face painfully into the bars. "Noooo!" I screamed. One creature had the young boy in the fountain and was maliciously dunking him under the water and then tearing at his skin when he came up sputtering and screaming. The water in the fountain was slowly turning red. Over in the lounge area on the other side of the fountain, another creature had a woman's body pinned under its tail while it snacked on the side of her face. Then, I spotted the decapitated body of the little girl just below me.

I stood too quickly and had to hold onto the rail as I made my way to the far wall on the other side. I wasn't sure where I was going, just that I had to get away fast. I paused near the elevators. Suddenly I heard that familiar "ding." The doors started to open, the ones on the middle elevator. A chill ran down my spine. I pushed myself flat against the wall and quickly slid around the corner. But not before I caught sight of one of the creatures sliding out across the floor.

How can this be happening? My heels bumped against steps as I backpedaled, and turning, I climbed three steps and opened the door at

the top. I found myself in a small room filled with shelves and desks. I fumbled with the door a minute before I realized there was no way to lock it. I put my ear to the door. Was that the slap of the creature's front limbs I heard, the low hiss as it slithered toward me? I dived under a desk on the far wall and quickly pulled my legs in under me. I looked around for something to defend myself with, but all I could see were newspaper clippings and old photographs. It seemed I had stumbled on the room containing the history of the hotel.

The doorknob turned. But how...? The door opened slowly. Suddenly I was five again, and there Dad was. He looked the same as I remembered him on that day. Tears blurred my vision.

"Dad?" The words seemed to come from somewhere outside of me.

He looked at me with that wonderful face; soft features set against a rugged background and a days growth of beard.

He took me by the hand and I stood. Though we were standing eye to eye, I felt I was looking up at him.

"What is it, Ralphie? What's wrong?"

"Oh Dad, I'm in a real bind here. A terrible bind."

I couldn't stop the tears from streaming down my face. The sound of his voice, the touch of his hand...

His voice was soft, almost a whisper. "Tell me about it Son."

"Well Dad, outside, " I pointed frantically toward the door, "There's these... these..."

He squeezed my hand hard. "Tell me what the problem is Ralph."

Suddenly, I forgot all about the present horror.

"Dad, it's Josh and Mom and... and..."

"Joshua? What's that boy into now?"

"Well, Mom is... she's..."

"I know. She is dying. I can hear her calling to me. I asked you about your brother."

I took a deep breath and grasped his hand tighter. "He wants it all, the money, the farm. And he's turned them all against me, my wife, even my daughter. Oh Janey!" I sobbed.

"What's he done?" my father asked in that stern voice I had always feared.

"Somehow he, well, Janey is seventeen and he convinced her to..." I took a deep breath and for the first time said it out loud. "He convinced her to file sexual assault charges against me. Against her own father."

I bowed my head in disgust and continued. "I know I was never a great father, but I always tried to be there when she needed me and give her distance when I thought that was what she wanted. Maybe I gave her too much distance. Maybe she drifted away. But I've always been honest. And I've never, ever touched her like he said. These... charges are really much more than I can handle. I don't know what he's promised her. But I just can't, just can't face any of them. It was in the newspaper. The whole town knows and they look at me like I'm some kind of pervert. I had to get away."

"You mean, deep inside, you felt you had to run away. Deep inside."

I wiped the tears and looked at my dad. He had said those very words to me two months before he died. Barry Boling had knocked me down every day for a week on the playground. My dad had listened to each excuse silently, until I didn't have any more to give. And then he had said those words to me.

He smiled then, and tussled my hair. He turned and walked from the room.

I stood there a minute, then took a deep breath and set my jaw. I looked around and above the desk I had cowered under were a pair of crossed swords. The plaque beneath said something about an ancestor of the hotel owners and the Civil War. I grabbed them both and headed for the door.

I knew it was still out there, somewhere. I also knew my best weapon would be surprise. I slowly turned the door knob and peeked out.

Luckily, the creature was around the corner, near where I had fallen into the rail, facing the opposite direction.

Brandishing both swords, I charged through the door like a Confederate soldier at Bull Run. The creature half-turned toward me as I reached it. The first sword pierced straight through the meat of its tail; the second grazed its neck and penetrated one webbed fore-limb. It emitted a loud roar, unlike any of its previous sounds, and its tail reflexively snapped around, catching me in the back of the legs just above the knee. The force of the blow sent me flying into the wall by the stairs. I crashed down over a chair. It rolled on top of me. Stunned, but still lucid, I realized I still had a vicelike grip on one of the swords.

The creature came at me, its tail propelling it, but somewhat slower, probably because of the other sword, which still protruded from it. I managed to pull the overturned chair around to shield me just as the creature snapped at my head, so close that I could smell its fetid breath. I quickly boosted myself on the chair to my feet but the creature was faster. It clamped its terrible jaws on my calf. I screamed loudly, half from pain, half from anger. I raised the chair over my head and brought it down with all my strength on its head. It released its grip at the same moment I jabbed the sword just beneath its mouth, and with both hands, drove it in at a downward angle.

I must have hit at least one vital organ because with an explosion of blood from its mouth and a final shudder, it collapsed at my feet.

I carefully extracted both swords and started for the stairs. After a moment's hesitation, I turned back and retrieved the chair.

At the bottom, most of the people had escaped. A few, however, weren't so lucky. The creatures had dispensed with their original victims and were now preying on the unfortunate ones who had been injured in the mad dash to the exits.

The creatures seemed to have no protective instincts for their own kind, which was to my advantage. One by one, I pinned their heads with the chair and drove the sword through their necks. Not one of the creatures stopped their carnage long enough to come to the aid of another.

When the last one collapsed, I had to will myself to release the chair. Exhausted, I turned to face the doors I had entered several hours before. With one last look back, I raised the sword in triumph, reared back my head and yelled. I slammed the sword down; it bounced off the marble floor and came to rest beside one of the slaughtered creatures.

* * *

Outside, I wasn't surprised that the same taxi was there. I collapsed into the back seat. Without a word the driver pulled out. This time, as he made his way through Memphis, I paid more attention and noticed there wasn't any other traffic, anywhere. The sky was a strange grayish red; the buildings had a peculiar slant.

He delivered me back to the airport at the same door. There was no one around. I went inside, retraced my steps, and after ascending the darkened stairway, opened the door at the top.

"Ah, there you are Ralph."

I looked around, stunned. There was Preacher Paul, calling to me. He stood next to the baggage claim conveyor belt. Many other people were gathered around it and I recognized a couple of them from the plane. Slowly I made my way to the preacher.

"I'm glad to see you again, Ralph. I was beginning to wonder if something had happened to you."

"Yeah, me too," I mumbled. I was watching my ragged suitcase go past me on the conveyor belt. I watched it go all the way around, until it disappeared from sight.

"Well, we're here in Memphis," he said jovially. He then became quite serious and put a hand on my shoulder. "Son, I really hope you find peace of mind and what you're searching for while you are here."

My bag came back into sight and I grabbed it.

"You know what, Paul? I already have. I'm going back home. I have a lot of problems to iron out. It's time I look inside, deep inside, to figure out what to do."

For a split second he looked at me like I was crazy, then his face broke into a big beaming smile.

"I'm happy for you. Real happy." He took my hand and shook it hard.

I started to turn and head to the nearest ticket counter, when he added, "I think I'll go to that hotel and see the marvelous show with the ducks. You made it sound so wonderful."

I froze. I looked past him through the two exit doors I could see. The sun shone brightly. There were taxis, cars and buses everywhere. And everywhere there were people.

I smiled at him. "That'd be all right, Preacher. I think now, that'd be all right."

Tokhtamysh
By Vassar W. Smith

1

At eleven o'clock on a bright Saturday morning in May, a blond boy knocked on the door of the rented cottage behind his home. There was no answer. The boy knocked again. When there was still no response, he called out, "Mr. Hammadi?" Now eleven-year-old Timmy Lane knit his eyebrows in a worried frown and muttered almost inaudibly, "Gee, I hope Mr. Hammadi's OK." Deciding to try the door, he found it unlocked.

Hafiz Hammadi, lecturer on Middle Eastern Studies at Rhodes College, had been renting these quarters for seven years. From their first meeting a cordial rapport had developed between this Oxford-educated Egyptian scholar and his colleague and host, Charles Lane, professor of history at Rhodes College. This warm rapport with Hammadi soon extended to Lane's wife Ellen, and their son Timmy.

Although he was taking a sabbatical this spring, Hammadi had been oppressed with sinusitis and so immersed in a research project that sometimes the Lanes did not see him for days. This morning, when Ellen had telephoned, Hammadi had told her that he was feeling much, much better. Soon thereafter she sent Timmy to him with a basket of chicken-salad sandwiches and freshly baked cookies.

Stepping inside, Timmy called out cheerfully, "Mr. Hammadi! Mom's sent me over with a Care package!"

Then Timmy fell into an abrupt and bewildered silence. Not only did he hear no sound from Mr. Hammadi (who had always addressed him with courtly words when pleased, and patient words when disappointed), but indeed the man was nowhere in the four-room cottage. Timmy's bewilderment gave way to alarm when he realized that he now saw nothing in the cottage to indicate that Mr. Hammadi had *ever* lived there. The vases and books that had filled the shelves and cases along the walls of the front room and hallway were gone. So were the beautiful rugs which Hammadi had spread over the hardwood floors. Even his Macintosh, Apple printer, desk, chair and reading lamps were gone. Remaining in the cottage were only the linens and furniture provided with the premises.

Not entirely true. Upon a second inspection of the bedroom, Timmy noticed the bedclothes: their slight disarray, indicated that someone had recently occupied the bed. That someone no doubt had been the ailing Mr. Hammadi. However, instead of the odors associated with a sickroom, the only distinctive aroma was the fragrance of fresh apricots.

On the bed there was something else... more than a wrinkle, more than a lump in the bedspread... Nestling amid the folds of cloth was an object that caught the eye both with a silver gleam and a contrasting blackness of extraordinary opacity.

Setting down the basket, Timmy approached the bed and picked up the object. It was a vessel of some sort, very old, of some strange metal alloy, and etched with a geometric Middle-Eastern design. It weighed no more than a pound. The feature that most caught the boy's curiosity was the contrast in its surface: perhaps one fourth of the object reflected light with the brilliance of the most highly polished silver, while the rest reflected no light at all, but absorbed it as totally as the opening to a coal chute. Elongated, with a handle on one end and a sort of spout on the other, but no opening at the top, it resembled a teapot or a gravy boat, but obviously was neither.

As Timmy investigated further by rubbing the silvery surface of one side, suddenly, the vessel began to shake in his hands. Cool to the touch at first, it was now the temperature of very warm bathwater. Had he not recognized the object as something extraordinary and valuable, Timmy would have dropped it at once. Instead he set it down on the floor. As he did, he smelled again, much stronger now, the aroma of fresh apricots, and saw a pale orange vapor begin to billow from the opening. Then, instead of pervading the room, the mist coalesced in one spot. Four feet in front of Timmy it began to take the shape of a man.

The man who materialized was anything but terrifying. He was, for one thing, a small man. He seemed taller than Timmy only because of his turban. His headdress was only the first strange article of his apparel. While Mr. Hammadi had always dressed in irreproachable style for a Western professional gentleman, this fellow wore the curled slippers, baggy pantaloons and flowing robes of a Middle-Easterner of several centuries ago. For another thing, amid the short, dark beard and mustache, the man's full lips drew back in a slight smile. A kindly gleam appeared in the calm, brown eyes, and the man acknowledged Timmy with a bow.

Then he spoke to the boy in an incongruously high-pitched voice:

"Salaam! Peace be unto you!"

Timmy found his tongue at last: "Uh, hello... You speak English?"

"Of course. All languages are known to us of the Lamp."

"Oh, wow, is that what that is? Does that mean you're a genie?"

"The proper word is *djinn*. The answer to your question is *yes* and *no*."

"Sorry, I don't understand. I mean, are you a *djinn* or aren't you?"

"I shall explain," the man replied in precise but accented English. "I have served as a *djinn* for six hundred years. I am being released from that capacity. It is a most onerous commission, and my heart rejoices to be free of it."

"Mister," Timmy asked, "if you were a djinn for six hundred years, then what were you before that?"

"Very sensible questions, young Sir," the man responded, "but first let us become properly acquainted. You are Timothy Robert Lane..."

"Timmy or Tim, please. I hate being called Timothy and don't like Robert much either."

"Very well," the man continued, "I am Abdullah ben-Ayoub. You may call me Abdullah. Six hundred years ago I was the most renowned clothier—you might say "tailor"—in the city of Damascus. At one time every man in the city, every man great or small who desired the best new slippers or finest new cloak would come to me to be measured and have the items made. I had the greatest assortment of leathers and woven cloth in the city. I knew how to make items of the finest quality. Alas, being a master of my trade I also knew how to make items that looked good at first, but were of defective material and did not wear well.

"My neighbor Mordecai the Jew was an apothecary—you would call him a pharmacist. He was the stingiest man on earth, but terribly vain. When he stopped by my shop and chanced to see the cloak that I had just made for the Emir's physician, Mordecai inquired whether I might be engaged to make one of similar design and materials for him—though of course he was unwilling to accord me anything close to the fair price offered by the noble physician. Still, I agreed to the sum he offered, letting him think me a fool until I could show him the greater fool.

"And by the Prophet's beard, I did exactly that. One day the stipulated silver dinars went into my coffers and the vain Mordecai walked out of my shop, strutting like a peacock in his new cloak. A week later he was back, throwing the cloak in my face and demanding the return of his money, howling a thousand complaints about the material and workmanship.

"First I protested, then laughed at him, finally I threw him out of my shop. When he threatened to take me to court, I told him not to insult the faithful of Allah with his miserable whining. When he did take the matter to court, the judges ruled against him. I heard no more from Mordecai the Jew, and all my friends and relatives and I laughed about the matter until my dying day.

"I have not laughed about it since. Woe to me that I forgot the all-seeing angels of Allah! No sooner had my soul left this world than I was brought before my two sentinel angels, the radiant Gibril (you call him Gabriel in your language) and the dark Azrael. Every good and virtuous deed of my life had been recorded by the former; just as dutifully had every evil, reprehensible one been written down by the latter. Every entry that either of them had made on the scroll of my life became a weight on the scales of Allah's justice. Great was Gibril's record of my faithfulness to the Law, my regular prayers and dutiful fasting, my pilgrimage to Mecca, my generous alms-giving and other deeds of kindness. It seemed certain that my merits would outweigh my failings—until Azrael laid onto his scale the grievances of Mordecai the apothecary and other offended Jews, whereupon the balance was tipped in the other direction.

"'Allah is just and compassionate!' Gibril declared. 'A man of your virtues could go to the Sixth Heaven—as you may, after atonement through service.'

"Then he told me that until it had served Allah's purpose, I must serve as a djinn: Into the lamp, out of the lamp, granting the wishes. Everybody knows the routine from Scheherezade's stories. I believe you call them *A Thousand and One Arabian Nights.*"

Timmy, who had not dared interrupt, now spoke up, "You mean, *they're* for real, too?"

Carefully, the djinn Abdullah replied, *"Elements* of them are. You see, just as your stories of King Arthur get tangled in pagan myths, so the fabulous Arabian stories often echo facts and fancies from the times before the Prophet's rise at Mecca."

"But the part about the Djinn of the Magic Lamp is real?"

"In a word, yes."

"Will you grant me three wishes?" Timmy asked eagerly.

"Formerly I would have, but, you see, my service is ended, with one exception."

"What's that?"

"I must warn you about Tokhtamysh."

"Who's that?"

"The one becoming new djinn of the Lamp."

"Is he very different from you?"

"Exceedingly," Abdullah affirmed with a sigh. "He was Khan of the Golden Horde. He sacked and burned Moscow. Then he did battle with Tamerlane and lost."

"Wait a minute!" the boy protested. "Are you telling me that the new djinn is some guy like Genghis Khan?"

"Alas, less intelligent, less methodical."

"But I thought djinns had to serve whoever summoned them."

"Absolutely, they do, but they can do so quite perversely. A djinn is not required to protect his master, can even deceive him unless specifically commanded to tell the truth, and takes boundless delight in tricking him into wasting precious wishes on the basest trifles. You must be very, very careful..."

* * *

"So what happened to Mr. Hammadi?" Timmy asked.

"He is in Alexandria, married to Fatimah, the love of his life," explained Abdullah. "They own a coffee house. It prospers. They now have seven grown children and thirty-five grandchildren..."

"Wait a minute!" Timmy interrupted. "Mr. Hammadi's divorced from his only wife and has no children..."

"But it's very simple," the djinn said beatifically. "Hafiz Hammadi loved children. He always wished that he had had some of his own, just as he always wished that he had married Fatimah instead of the wife his parents arranged for him. So when he brings me out, he makes the wish official. I actually put him back in his young body in the 1960's and let him live anew and differently the last thirty years."

"So how come I know about him?"

"You entered this house just as the time/space alteration took effect. You are now the only person who remembers Hammadi's existence here. If you spoke of him now, others would have no idea of whom you were speaking. They might even question your sanity."

"Hey, that sucks! Mr. Hammadi was like a member of our family! You're saying we'll never see him again, and I'm the only one who knows he's gone or that he was here? That really sucks!"

Patiently Abdullah replied, "I do not understand this use of the word 'sucks.' I take it for some expression of great annoyance, and I sympathize. May it help you to know that even as Hammadi pursued his own happiness, he regretted leaving you and your family. He leaves you a great gift and entrusts you with a mighty task."

"What gift and what task?"

"Look on the bed again."

Timmy did, and saw something he had overlooked earlier. In the folds of the blanket was a small velvet bag with a drawstring. When Timmy opened it, he found a man's gold ring ornately wrought with a geometric design identical to the pattern on the Lamp.

"Hey! Cool! What's this?"

"The ring is yours now—a gift from Hammadi..."

Timmy tried it on his left hand.

"Awesome! It fits the middle finger. "

"Good. Treasure that ring, and remember it in time of extreme trouble."

Then the djinn addressed him most gravely, "Trust me. The only thing that you must do with the Lamp is put it out of harm's way. It cannot be destroyed. It could be used for good, but with Tokhtamysh in it there is too great a chance it will not. It is best that you put it in an inaccessible place, where no one can find it for the foreseeable future."

"Well, I could just bury it somewhere. But hardly any place is safe any more. If some kid or dog didn't dig it up by accident, some gardener, building crew or utility workers would probably come across it. So, what do I do? And how did it get to Memphis in the first place?"

"The writer Richard Halliburton found it in his travels around the world and brought it to America. In the 1960's, when Halliburton Tower was built at Rhodes College—then called Southwestern—a number of Richard's effects were kept on display there in a locked case. This was among them. Someone examining it closely enough might have discovered its extraordinary properties, but no one did. Hafiz Hammadi was the first person here to recognize it for what it is. When he changed the configuration of time/space with his wish—that is, when he went back in time and changed his life—the

Lamp did not go with him, but all record and memory of it at Rhodes College disappeared."

"So nobody else knows about it or wonders where it is?"

"Correct. Here, then, is what I propose. Tomorrow afternoon there is a ceremony at the college, the sealing and setting of the cornerstone to the new building..."

"Yeah, the Wood-Jolly Humanities Center, where my Dad's new office is going to be. He's going to make a speech. Mom and I have to go to the party too."

"So, then, before the cornerstone is sealed you must conceal the Lamp inside it. Once the cornerstone is set in place, the Lamp will be safe indefinitely, at least for the next few centuries..."

Then, infinitely faster than he had materialized, Abdullah ben-Ayoub vanished.

2

Several hours later, the treasure inconspicuous in his backpack, Timmy headed for Rhodes College through Overton Park. Suddenly, at the spot where a small trail met the main path, he had the misfortune to encounter D'Aragon Johnson and his slightly younger but much heavier cousin called Termite. Hearing movement behind him, Timmy looked over his shoulder. Blocking his escape stood the Johnsons' buddy R.C.

The only fifteen-year-old in the sixth grade, D'Aragon Johnson was the archetypical class bully. Behind his back countless boys reveled in the mispronunciation of the name by its bearer (Duh-Aragon rather than one graceful dactyl), but no one dared to pronounce it correctly to his face. None of Timmy's friends even knew Termite's real name, but there were two schools of thought about the derivation of his moniker: one stating that it arose from his insatiable and indiscriminate appetite; the other postulating that it had been applied—and stuck—because,the boy with his enormous nose, bulging eyes, and severely receding chin had, to put it kindly, a face that only an entomologist could love. Although the letters R. C. did stand for the third boy's name—Raphael Congdon—they also bespoke his legendary fondness for Royal Crown Cola.

In the school lunch line yesterday, D'Aragon had told Timmy to let him borrow three dollars. Since D'Aragon had never repaid—and had no intention of repaying—the last three dollars that he had "borrowed" from him, this time Timmy had refused. D'Aragon, compelled to put back the milk, sandwich and custard that he could not pay for, had sworn to make Timmy pay heavily for this humiliation. Finding the opportunity at hand sooner than he had thought possible, D'Aragon grinned in malicious ecstasy:

"Well, well! Look who we got here! You got fifteen dollars for us today, punk?"

At that, Timmy's alarm was superseded by his sense of outrage. Still he struggled to maintain self-control, to betray neither fear nor anger in his reply: "Fifteen dollars? Yesterday you wanted three."

"Yeah, well now there's three of us to feed, and food costs more than in the school cafeteria. Plus, you owe me big-time for dissin' me in front of everybody yesterday. So now you're gonna loan us fifteen dollars," D'Aragon stated his case as though it were gospel.

By now the trio of older boys had hustled Timmy down the trail to a small clearing out of sight of the main road. Yelling for help seemed pointless. The early morning ball games were all over by this hour. Also, today was the day of the Cotton Carnival parade. Most people who were about at leisure today would be downtown watching the procession of bands and floats. Besides, yelling would have shown that he felt intimidated and helpless.

"Listen," Timmy persisted: "I can't lend, can't even give you what I don't have. I don't have fifteen dollars!"

"Punk, if you're lyin', you're dyin', and if you ain't lyin', pretty soon you're gonna wish you was dead," D'Aragon replied, then ordered his companions: "Search him."

* * *

The two rubber bands, three scraps of paper, and coins totaling thirty-seven cents were of no interest to the trio. The backpack's contents were quite a different matter.

"What the fuck is this?" D'Aragon asked, holding the Lamp. "This ain't no Cotton Carnival gewgaw from the Midway, so what the... JESUS!"

Even before Timmy could have warned him, D'Aragon had rubbed the lamp, in the unthinking, offhanded way that children and bumpkins finger and paw objects of great beauty or fascination. Instead of the pale orange mist that emerged before, from the lamp's opening now billowed a thick, copper-colored cloud with a pungent odor like the combined scents of musk, leather and sweat. D'Aragon's last word had come out almost as a prayer rather than an expletive, and only the urgency in Timmy's voice had kept D'Aragon from dropping the Lamp on the spot. Instead he set it down as quickly as possible, then stepped back several paces.

This time the smoke coalesced into only the upper half of a human figure. From the waist down the figure remained not just shrouded in vapor, but vaporous itself, tapering downward ever thinner until its lower extremity disappeared into the Lamp. Still, the face and form manifested were formidable: In contrast with a well-shaped, completely shaven head were beetling brows and thick, foot-long mustaches. The almond eyes and high cheekbones looked Asiatic. The expression on the lips was something between a sneer and a scowl. Besides a leather vest that revealed both mighty biceps and powerful pectorals, this unmistakably male creature wore several heavy gold chains around his neck. With a thunderous voice he asked:

"Who dares summon forth the great Khan Tokhtamysh?"

Now D'Aragon stood his ground: "Hey, I seen cartoons about Aladdin. Ain't you supposed to say, 'I am the genie of the magic lamp,' or some shit like that?"

"Beware," Tokhtamysh answered gravely. "Yes, I am now a djinn, bound to serve the holder of the Lamp, but only with three wishes and only if your words are respectful and not *ayeeb*. Disregard these conditions, and your wishes will bring you great sorrow. So, who is the master of the Lamp now? Who gets the three wishes? Do you get them all, or do you share them among your comrades, so that each of you gets one?"

"We share," R. C. said firmly.

"We share, don't we?" said Termite.

After the briefest hesitation, D'Aragon assented.

Timmy had taken advantage of their confusion to escape. However, concerned with the fate of the Lamp, he remained nearby, hiding in a grove of oaks. Even if they spotted him, he was confident that he could outrun them. Meanwhile, from his present position he could not only observe but even overhear them clearly. He had had to restrain himself from laughing when Tokhtamysh had mentioned the word "ayeeb." Duh-Aragon & co. had missed this one, not even asked about it, but from somewhere—maybe from Mr, Hammadi, maybe from stories or the movies—Timmy had encountered this Turkish word that meant the Moslem equivalent of "un-Kosher," "obscene," "shameful," or simply "dirty." There was no doubt—at least one of these guys was going to do himself in.

So it happened with R. C., whom D'Aragon allowed to go first, more out of caginess than consideration. It turned out that his legendary craving for cola was insignificant compared to his desire for wealth and sexual fulfillment. Facing Tokhtamysh, the gangly, pimply adolescent declared that his one wish was to be surrounded with "riches and pussy" for the rest of his life. Tokhtamysh, who had listened impassively, arms folded on his chest, now nodded his head, clapped his hands once. and declared, "So be it!"

In an instant R. C. was gone, and Tokhtamysh threw back his head and laughed heartily. D'Aragon stared at him suspiciously and finally demanded, "Hey, where's R. C.? What'd you do with him?"

"Do with him? I simply granted his wish. He asked to be surrounded with riches and pussy for the rest of his life, so I made him the head chamberlain—the chief eunuch in the harem of Selim the Sot, who ruled the Turkish Empire centuries ago. He will be surrounded by all that he desires—and able to use none of it."

D'Aragon was outraged (he knew the term *eunuch* not from books but from schoolyard parlance). "You mean he ain't got no nuts now?" he shouted. "You butt-headed, smoke-assed son of a bitch! Why'd you do that to him?"

No longer laughing, but still enjoying his handiwork, Tokhtamysh replied, "I already told you. I simply granted his wish. I warned you all against making vulgar, foolish wishes. He did not heed me. He made a fool's wish. He reaped a fool's reward. Be careful lest you do the same."

"Uh-uh, not me!" D'Aragon declared seriously, resolutely, as though everything that had happened before now, even the loss of his associate, were utterly inconsequential. "What I want is power. So give me a army, say a million men with all the latest weapons, technology, supplies and equipment. That means tanks, jets, APC-s. You know what I mean?"

"Of course I know! I *commanded* armies. Well, then… So be it!"

He nodded. He started to clap his hands, but did not. For a second he looked at the sky, and a vacant look passed over his face. Finally he briefly pressed his palms against each other.

"Behold!" he declared.

There was a sound like a thunderclap, and at once space and time became bifurcated. Not only D'Aragon and Termite but also Timmy saw two different worlds before them. One was the familiar, ordinary sight of Overton Park: lush deciduous trees, the small clearing, and the trail between the road and the golf courses. In the other, the clearing and even the surrounding trees were gone. In their place was a huge stone building—a towering monument with a railed observation deck on the roof. D'Aragon, Termite and Tokhtamysh stood at the eastern end. Here Timmy was hidden by ornamental columns instead of trees. Although Timmy's clothes and shoes remained the same, D'Aragon and Termite were now wearing the gold-braided dress uniforms and gleaming boots of commanding generals. Below, the first battalions of infantry stood ready in formation. They covered the fields of the golf course, the pavilion, the baseball diamonds...

And beyond the park? As far as the eye could see, Poplar Boulevard and the North Parkway-Summer Avenue thoroughfare were occupied by an unbroken, rumbling column of armored vehicles—tanks, jeeps, personnel carriers, even missile launchers—all bearing their assigned complement of soldiers. With a gloating smile, Tokhtamysh turned to D'Aragon:

"Well, *Gen. Johnson,* is this the army you wished for? Your army of a million men?"

Even to one of D'Aragon's limited capacity, the problem was obvious:

"What's happenin', Tock? Is this for real or ain't it? It's like I see a army and other stuff, but it ain't there."

"Allah is compassionate," Tokhtamysh replied. "By the laws of the Lamp one's wish itself may not kill people—not *directly.* I shall grant you your army, and it certainly will kill multitudes. But not one soul may be killed at the moment that I make your army materialize. With the quantity and the speed of the automobiles and other vehicles on the streets at this hour, fatalities would be unavoidable. The granting of the wish must be delayed, then, until 2:23 tomorrow morning. Only then will the required area be free of traffic."

Here Tokhtamysh pressed his hands together again. The chimerical vision vanished. They were all back in Overton Park on a beautiful spring afternoon. Only one detail had changed: the Johnsons were wearing generals' uniforms.

"Tock, there's another problem," D'Aragon said gravely.

"Not *Tock*—I am TOKHTAMYSH!" the Khan thundered.

"OK, OK, Tokhtamysh. So at 2:23 tomorrow I'm gettin' this army. It ain't gonna do me no good. Oh, we could take over the place with no sweat... But just puttin' a army that big here is gonna tear up a lot of stuff... And if there is a fight, a lot of Memphis is gonna be leveled, not just schools and offices and stores, but people's homes and apartments. And Memphis ain't some place off on a island. It's right in the middle of America. We take over part of America—we got a *war* on our hands. You can't win no war against America. We gonna die!"

At this Tokhtamysh laughed uproariously. So did Termite. The latter, in his high, wet voice declared, "D'Aragon, where you comin' from? I ain't never heard you talk like a pussy before. I guess you just don't know how to use a army like Tokhtamysh. Look at him laughin' at you. 'Stead of him sittin' there with his ass buried in a cloud o' smoke, I wish Tokhtamysh was a regular man again, so he can put this army to use when it comes!"

Before Termite realized the import of his words, Tokhtamysh had bowed, clapped his hands, and declared: "So be it!"

* * *

There was a flash like heat lightning. The cloud of smoke from the Lamp had vanished. Before D'Aragon and Termite stood a tall, powerful brown-skinned man with the face of Tokhtamysh. He wore a general's uniform too, but his had five stars, theirs only four.

"Thank you, Terence!" he beamed. (So that was Termite's real name, Timmy realized.) "How generous of you to use your wish for my sake! Oh, boys, you are but poor boys and have so much to learn. Yet I am so grateful for the service you have done me, that I shall let you live to serve me, perhaps even command forces—once you learn military strategy..."

"That ain't fair!" Termite protested. "You cheated me out of my wish!"

"Nonsense!" Tokhtamysh rebuked him. "You made the wish yourself—after I warned you all to be careful of your words. Besides, we now have a common cause. In a few hours the army will arrive. Then we can simply take whatever we desire."

"Wait a minute!" D'Aragon spoke up. "You mean, even though you ain't a genie no more, that army is still comin'?"

"But of course. After all, a djinn is not the source of the magical power, merely the key that unleashes it. All has been set in motion for the fulfillment of your wish. What's done is done! Oh, how glorious it shall be to ride into battle again! To receive homage and tribute from the vanquished! To offer all opposition but one set of terms: Surrender or die! By tomorrow night this whole city shall be ours—or it shall be no more!"

Overhearing these words from his hiding-place, Timmy Lane clenched his fists in outrage and frustration. What was he going to do? If he told anyone that Memphis was going to be destroyed or conquered by an army led by the worst butt-head in Asian history plus two of the domestic variety, nobody would believe him. If he did nothing, then, one way or another, tomorrow his home town—maybe his home itself—would be ruined beyond recognition. What could he do?

* * *

Looking down, he found his gaze resting on the beautiful gold ring with the strange geometric pattern—the pattern identical to that on the Lamp. Then he recalled Abdullah's words:

"Treasure that ring and remember it in times of extreme trouble."

And just as he had rubbed the Lamp, gently and firmly he rubbed the ring three times.

At once the gleam of sunlight reflected by the gold leapt up like a tongue of flame without heat. Ever growing as it moved away from Timmy, the flame assumed the size and shape of a man, then dimmed and coalesced into—Abdullah ben Ayoub.

"Salaam!" he greeted Timmy with a smile and a bow. "I could not tell you outright, but you did catch my inference."

"Be quiet. They'll hear us."

"Not to worry. As the djinn of the Ring I may grant only one wish, but except to you I am invisible, and while I am present our conversation is inaudible."

"Cool. You mean, they can't see you or hear us?"

"Correct."

"And you can grant me *any* wish?"

"Any wish except—"

"You can't kill anybody, make anyone fall in love, or bring anyone back from the dead."

"Precisely. And remember: only one wish, so choose your words wisely."

"I don't have any choice, Abdullah. We've got to save Memphis. So here's my wish: Take Tokhtamysh, D'Aragon, Termite and all their forces—wherever they are—and put them ten thousand miles from here. Put them all on the other side of the world!"

Abdullah bowed, clapped his hands once and declared: "So be it!"

In the clearing Timmy saw the Lamp still on the ground where D'Aragon had set it. Other than that and their footprints, there was no trace of either Tokhtamysh or his new adjutants. As he reached for the Lamp, Timmy heard Abdullah's warning:

"Timmy, beware the Lamp!"

"But Tokhtamysh is gone."

"No matter. The next djinn could be someone or something even worse. Even with a good djinn, in the hands of a foolish or evil master, the Lamp's potential for harm is enormous. Please, let us proceed with our original plan. Let it be sealed in the cornerstone."

"OK." The boy hesitated, then said, "Hey, it's not a wish, but there's something I need to ask you, two things in fact."

"Ask."

"First, does the Lamp ever bring *anybody* happiness?"

"It is extremely rare, but, yes, it happens. It happened for Hammadi,"

"Because he only made one wish?"

"No, he made three, but only one was for his own benefit, and that not entirely selfish. The other two were entirely for the benefit of others."

"But what were his other wishes?"

"Hammadi knew the Lamp better than anyone else. Once he learned of Tokhtamysh his first two wishes were for the safety of his favorite family—yours—and for the protection of his adopted city. For this he created the Ring and gave me my instructions. Only then did he seek his own fulfillment. Allah will bless him beyond measure!"

"Abdullah, I can see through you! You're fading!"

"Yes, my work and my atonement are done. I go now to the Sixth Heaven. Farewell!"

3

Prof. Charles Lane's bright, well-mannered son was seen on campus often enough to be well known to most of the faculty and staff, at least to those who worked in Palmer Hall and Burrow Library. Hence, no one stopped or questioned Timmy when he reached his destination at Rhodes College. Using his father's extra set of keys, Timmy was able to find and enter the room where the cornerstone was kept until tomorrow's ceremony. The open side had been neither sealed nor set in place yet. Checking the list beside it, Timmy ascertained that the inventory of contents was complete, and he managed to insert the lamp in such a way that it looked as though nothing had been added or rearranged. Then he left as quickly and quietly as he had entered. His father, having played tennis all afternoon, never noticed the keys' temporary disappearance.

* * *

Although he tried to follow his father's speech at the ceremony the next day, it was preceded and succeeded by so many other speeches, that Timmy felt lost in a sea of words. He did follow attentively the sealing and setting of the cornerstone. The reception afterward would have seemed deadly dull to Timmy on any other day, but after the events and prospects that he had witnessed yesterday, this normal world of safety, order, even dullness was not just bearable but welcome. No doubt about it, college receptions were BORING, but usually the cookies and punch were pretty good...

Nearly dozing in the back seat as he rode home with his parents, Timmy snapped awake when he heard the news broadcast on WMPS:

"Governments around the world are proceeding with extreme caution in expressing their position in response to the sudden coup in Baghdad that toppled the government of Iraq and replaced it with an 'Islamic Military Republic' under the command of Marshal—now President—Mohammed al-Tokhtamysh, who, despite his obscure and mysterious origins, was welcomed by soldiers and civilians alike exasperated by the tyranny and corruption of the former regime. In Washington, Moscow, Jerusalem and Tehran alike, there may be little regret over the demise of the former dictator; however, there is universal concern over the official statement issued this morning, namely that the new Iraqi government indeed 'possesses nuclear capability and, if provoked, will not hesitate to use *any necessary measure*' against their country's enemies.

"Meanwhile, Memphis police and other agencies have been unable to locate the three teenage boys missing since yesterday afternoon and last seen in the vicinity of Overton Park. Anyone with information as to the whereabouts of fifteen-year-old D'Aragon Johnson, fourteen-year-old Terence Johnson, or fourteen-year-old Raphael Congdon, please call any of the following numbers..."

Jim
By Beecher Smith

1

Lee Ralston-Smith examined the diminutive package the postman had brought special delivery to his office that Monday morning in Memphis. He hoped it contained something valuable or good news. God knows there had been enough of the bad lately.

The New Orleans law firm on the return address represented his late Uncle Silas' estate. Was this about a possible inheritance?

Ripping off the packing, he found a letter labeled "READ FIRST," folded around a small, blue, sealed jewelry box. The attorney had written:

"Enclosed is the bequest your Uncle Silas left you under his will--his lucky ring. He purchased it on a trip to Baghdad in the 1960's and felt it changed his whole life. Your uncle instructed me, in delivering this, to caution you: *Be very careful about anything you might wish for when wearing the ring. You might get it.*

Respectfully,

. . ."

He broke the clear plastic seal and looked at the contents. Inside he found a massive gold man's ring with a solitaire, square cut three-carat ruby surrounded by pave diamonds.

Removing the ring from its box, he tried it on his right hand. A perfect fit. It felt as though it belonged on him. He found himself unable to keep from rubbing his other hand across the blood-red ruby and fingering the simple, yet elegant square-cut face of the large gem. He compared the ring with the solid gold wedding band on his left, which he had continued to wear even after cancer had claimed his beloved Lucy a year ago, three weeks before her forty-third birthday.

Not believing in magic, he was disappointed that his fabulously wealthy uncle had not chosen to remember him with a large financial bequest. Silas had always referred to him as "my favorite nephew." Even though the ring and gemstone setting in it were probably worth several thousand dollars, that was only a pittance compared to the millions in the deceased tycoon's estate. Still, the ring was certainly beautiful to behold—an addition to the small list of things that gave him pleasure, a list that had been critically shortened by Lucy's death. Sometimes Lee felt that their daughter DeLynn and his business were the only things that kept him going.

DeLynn was both exceptionally beautiful and bright. She had earned a full scholarship to Yale, where she was a freshman, and would be home soon for Thanksgiving. There was a young man in her life now—Sam—and he would be accompanying her.

2

After a few moments' indulgence, Lee directed his attention from the bedazzling jeweled ornament back to the office work. So far the day had not been productive. His elderly assistant Tom, who had run Lee's real estate appraiser's office for the past fifteen years, had suffered a mild heart attack two weeks ago. Although predicting a complete eventual recovery, Tom's doctor had forbidden him to return to work for at least six weeks. Lee had explored alternatives for support personnel and decided to try a local temporary service. Tom's fill-in was due this afternoon, but so far had not shown. Lee looked at the mounting pile of papers that needed processing—mostly typing and filing—things he was used to having his trusted assistant handle while he took care of the appraisal work.

Most of what needed immediate attention was "piddly" stuff. Even though appraisal work had slowed down somewhat lately, Lee would much rather pay someone else to handle the small matters and leave him free to work on the big ones or else go to the country club and play golf. Where was the "temp" he had ordered, anyway?

In exasperation he blurted, "I wish my help would come!" He involuntarily rubbed the ring.

At that moment the door from the hall opened and a tall, tan skinned man with Oriental eyes, entered. He was wearing a three-piece gray business suit accented with a red silk tie. He immediately flashed a white-toothed smile and said, "Good morning. I am Jimal. 'Jim' for short. You sent for me."

"Yes. I believe so. You're from the agency, aren't you?" There had been a recent influx of foreigners in the city. Lee had always been tolerant of other races and ethnic groups and had likewise encouraged DeLynn to be open-minded. But now it seemed that minorities, especially blacks, had taken over Memphis. He didn't feel any too comfortable with this fellow, but the labor laws being what they were—everybody being sue-happy over their civil rights—he figured he'd better give Jim a chance.

Jimal declared, "I am here to serve you, Master—for as long as you require."

Lee laughed. "Sounds like you haven't been here long, Jim. The only 'masters' we have anymore are at golf and bridge tournaments, and in college degree programs. Nowadays we call them 'bosses.'"

"Then," Jim replied, his smile growing to encompass about a third of his face, "you are my new boss."

Lee motioned toward Tom's desk. It was piled up high with the backlog. "Can you type the reports from my scribbled notes and tabulate the columns of figures for the appraisals in the folders there?"

With a courtly bow Jim replied, "As you wish." He then removed his coat and sat behind the desk.

A good start, Lee thought. *Pleasant but businesslike. This temp should work out fine.* "Jim, I'm going downstairs to check the post office box for mail. If anyone calls, tell them I'll be back in a minute."

Because of the antediluvian elevators in the office building, Lee's "minute" expanded to ten. When he returned he found Jim seated before an immaculately clean desk, whistling an unfamiliar melody that sounded like a snake charmer's tune, his hands folded lazily behind his head.

Stifling nervous laughter Lee said, "Don't tell me you're finished already?"

His face reflecting casual self-confidence, Jim responded, "But of course, Mast— er, Boss. I have put the files on your desk."

Entering his private office, Lee found the six manilla folders stacked neatly on his desk. Opening and examining the top one—the McClusky Estate appraisal—he found it perfectly typed and tabulated. Each of the other five files had likewise been thoroughly and professionally prepared, and all in the course of not more time than it had taken for him to ride the elevator!

But that was impossible. Tom, in good health, would normally have required three days to complete that work.

Shaking his head in disbelief, Lee asked, "Is this a joke? How did you do it so quickly?"

Jimal beamed, "Because you asked me. What is my next task?"

Lee thought but could not come up with an assignment right away. He had been so sure the paperwork would have consumed at least three to four days for an average clerk, especially one lacking Tom's familiarity with the figures and methodology. Had Tom been goofing off all this time? Surely not.

He did not want to penalize the man by dismissing him early.

"Why don't you stick around and answer the phone. Take messages if anyone calls. I'm hoping we'll have lots more work when I get back from my meeting with the bankers."

3

The bank had taken over two defunct savings and loan associations from the Resolution Trust. It needed market appraisals for seven commercial properties that had to be sold before the really bad winter weather set in and slowed real estate activities to a snail's pace. The chairman gave two reasons why the directors had awarded the business to Lee: his reputation for proficiency and his promise to have the work completed far ahead of his competitor's bid.

Lee set out on his field work immediately, leaving Jim to answer the phone and attend to minor details at the office. The appraisal data was not complete until 4:00 P.M. Wednesday. "Okay, Jim," he said, handing over his handwritten notes, "You need to have these appraisals ready by the first of next week. Tomorrow is Thanksgiving, but you can work Friday. I need them Tuesday morning at the latest. Can you do it?"

His clerk bowed deferentially and said, "As you wish, so it shall be done." Lee left for happy hour at the country club.

4

Lee had two hours to kill before he had to pick up DeLynn and Sam at the airport. Since he had already made sure the homeplace was immaculate, he decided to spend his wait at the men's bar.

Dr. Grady Tate, the first face Lee saw when he entered the bar, was an old acquaintance who had all but retired from the practice of medicine. The doctor's drinking problem had come to the attention of the state medical board, which had ordered him to seek treatment or withdraw from practice. He had chosen the latter.

Dr. Tate found a second profession at his club bar—gambling. The members often played friendly games of gin rummy for modest stakes. One evening, soon after his involuntary retirement, Grady suggested to his fellow players that they up the stakes. To everyone's surprise, Grady ended up winning $15,000 that night.

After that, the doctor became a regular fixture in the bar—sometimes losing, but garnering large sums when he won.

"Lee," Grady hailed. "Haven't seen you in ages. Pull up a chair. Can I buy you a drink?"

Appreciating the offer of hospitality, Lee replied, "Sure." The bartender set an Old Charter and water before Lee.

"What's happening?" Grady asked.

After a long sip from his drink, Lee answered, "DeLynn's coming in for Thanksgiving with her new boyfriend. I'm to meet them at the airport in two hours. Just killing time till then."

Grady smiled like the snake at the bird. He ran his thumb down the side of a deck of cards he held, making the edges buzz. "Why don't we kill it with a friendly game of Gin Rummy—ten cents a point, Hollywood rules?"

Lee hesitated. This variation would triple the score for the winner and garner a prize equal to a week's wages or more. For some unexplainable reason Lee felt lucky, even though he hadn't played in years, so he responded, "How about a quarter a point?" Grady's eyes narrowed like John Wayne's. "Are you sure? I meant for the game to be *friendly*."

With a smile Lee said, "So do I. It's just that I can't play long, so we need to make it worth our while."

"Okay," Grady agreed.

They cut for the deal. Grady lost and dealt. Lee examined the eleven cards he received: a four, five, and six of clubs; three kings—hearts, spades, and clubs; two jacks—hearts and diamonds, two eights—spades and diamonds, and the Queen of Diamonds. A good start. He discarded the Queen.

Grady picked it up, tossed a card face down, and declared, "Gin!" He proudly displayed three Aces, and the seven through the king of diamonds! He had won fourteen dollars from Lee in four minutes. If Lee hadn't believed in the gentlemen's code of the club, he would have sworn the doctor had cheated.

Lee rubbed his ring in frustration, and thought, *I don't deserve to lose to this bum. I wish I could clean him out!*

To his surprise, inside Lee's head he heard Jim's voice respond, "As you wish!"

Lee shuffled, Grady cut, and Lee dealt the next round. Lee held three Aces; two Kings—diamonds and spades; the three and the five through nine of hearts; plus the Jack of Clubs. He discarded the Jack.

Grady drew a card and discarded the King of Hearts. Lee snatched it up and discarded the Three of Hearts face down. "Gin!"

A red hue moved up from Grady's neck to his forehead, like an oven thermometer heating. In a forced tone he laughed nervously and said, "Ya got lucky on me that time." He laid his cards down—only a set of three fours and the balance was all high cards—a net win for Lee of $16.75.

Lee won every hand of the set and the next four, garnering a total of over $1,250 cash—all Grady carried on his person.

"That can't be right! You must have cheated," Grady stormed. He rose from his seat, half drunk, angry and threatening. Several cards, identical to those in the blue Bicycle deck they had been playing with, fell from the cuff of Grady's jacket to the table. Audible gasps emanated from the few members who had gathered to watch the game.

Fortunately for Lee one of the spectators was the club manager, Herc McCord, who interceded. "That's enough, Grady," he said in a normal but forceful voice. "It looks like you're the one who's the cheat. So you're suspended from coming here until I have the board act on the complaint I'll be filing Friday morning. Your membership will be history."

As he turned to leave, Grady snarled at Lee with unbridled rage. Anger and alcohol had released all his inhibitions. "We're not through, buddy-boy. Not by a long shot. I know people who will deal with you—people who break both legs at the knee-caps, who kill slowly and enjoy it. You'll be sorry for this."

Lee believed the threat and it frightened him. *Oh, Lord*, he thought, rubbing his ring unconsciously, *I wish Grady would forget everything.*

Jim's voice echoed inside his head, "As you wish."

Seconds later he heard a horrendous crash. Lee and several others rushed outside, where they found a police car driven at a high speed had crashed into Dr. Tate's automobile. The officer had apparently been racing without using his siren or warning lights. When Grady pulled out into the street the squad car had crested the hill and plowed into him. He was thrown from his vehicle and knocked unconscious. When someone applied smelling salts, Grady said, "Who am I? Where am I?"

"Oh, God! Total amnesia," Lee exclaimed. He thought, *I wanted, even wished for this*. Was his uncle's ring really magic? Was Jim the legendary genie of the ring? But, of course that was preposterous!

5

Lee dispelled his depressing thoughts as he approached the arriving passenger's curb at Memphis International Airport. DeLynn would be there, and from that moment everything would be all right.

True to her promise, she was waiting—wearing a tan trenchcoat—smiling, her chestnut brown hair falling over her shoulders, blue eyes sparkling and radiant. She waved as he approached in the Jaguar, and crawled in to kiss him the moment he stopped.

"Where's Sam?" Lee asked. "I'm looking forward to meeting him."

"He's bringing our bags. Oh, Daddy," she beamed, "I know you'll love him. Just like I do."

He noticed some hesitancy in her voice. At that moment a handsome young black man in a fashionable dark suit appeared at the door by DeLynn, carrying luggage. "Daddy," she announced, "This is Sam Dobbins."

6

At La Tourelle, the exquisite Country French restaurant off Overton Square, Lee hardly touched his dinner. He struggled to remain polite toward Sam until a moment came when DeLynn's boyfriend had to excuse himself.

As soon as Sam was gone, DeLynn squeezed her father's hand. "Oh, Daddy," she said smiling, "Thank you for being so understanding. You always encouraged me to be liberal in my thinking and to despise racism. I hope there's no problem about Sam being black. He's so wonderful. He's on a full scholarship and plans to be a doctor."

Lee avoided looking in her eyes. "Honey. I'm sorry. There *is* a problem." He returned her squeeze to let her know his sincerity. "It wouldn't matter if he were the President's son: he's black, you're white, and this is Memphis, Tennessee, not Paris, France. If you loved him—enough to marry him and have children—there'd still be real problems. Few, if any of our friends would understand. None of your relatives would.

"As your father, who loves you so much, please end this relationship before it gets too serious. There's only trouble ahead. Believe me. Can't you see?" He managed to bring his eyes to meet hers, only to have her avert her gaze.

Tears welled up in her eyes. "I'm sorry. You don't understand. We *are* serious about each other. I'm not a baby anymore, but a grown woman. Sam *made* me one. He loves me and wants me to marry him. That's why he came here: to ask your permission."

Lee found himself choking. He squeezed his precious daughter's palm tighter and lifted her chin with his free hand so he could look into her eyes again. "Darling, don't you know that all I want is your happiness? You won't find it in an interracial marriage."

Her eyes grew dark, stormy. "Daddy! I thought you were a liberal?"

"I am," he snapped hoarsely, "but I'm also a realist. Statistics show most mixed marriages don't last. All I want is your happiness." Struggling to maintain control, he was repeating himself.

"Then give me your blessing when Sam asks."

Lee gritted his teeth. "When will that be?"

"Anytime."

"No matter how much this pains me, I'll search my soul to do what's right. I love you so much."

She smiled through her tears. "I know, Dad. It'll work. Keep trying and keep on loving me."

Sam returned to the table.

7

At the house they unpacked the bags. Lee showed Sam the guest bedroom downstairs.

Instead of carrying her luggage to her room, DeLynn brought them to Sam's.

"Why are you taking your bags to the guest room?" Lee asked.

DeLynn rolled her eyes. "Daddy, we've been staying together for the past month. It would be hypocritical of us not to do so here too."

Lee's heart pounded painfully. Was his daughter going to cause him to go into cardiac arrest? She'd already given up her virginity to a black man she intended to marry. He'd never thought of himself as a racist—until now. Could he cope with her continuing that relationship... under his own roof?

He tried to sound calm, reasonable. Thank God poor Lucy wasn't around to suffer through this. "I'm sorry. As your father I demand proper decorum.

"Sam, as a visitor in my home, you will stay and sleep in the guest bedroom and DeLynn will have to sojourn upstairs."

Defiance blazed in his daughter's eyes. "I'm a grown-up. Don't treat me like a child."

"I'm your father. I decide what the rules are under my roof."

"Then we won't stay under your roof." She headed for the phone and called a taxi.

8

As DeLynn and Sam pulled away in the cab, Lee thought, unconsciously rubbing his ring, *Damn that ungrateful little slut, I wish she and Sam were both dead!*

No sooner were Lee's words out than he heard Jim's voice, ringing inside his head, "As you wish."

"No! No!," he shouted into the night, waving his arms frantically. "I didn't mean it. I take it back. It was only a thought, not a real wish. Please!"

No response from Jim.

To Lee's horror he saw a car approach from the far end of the block, weaving wildly as only a drunk driver would. The cab's driver tried desperately to avoid a wreck, but, as he veered at the last minute, so did the oncoming vehicle, resulting in a head-on collision. Seconds later the cab exploded into an orange fireball that ignited both automobiles, killing all involved.

Too late Lee realized that he had forgotten to rub the ring. "Oh, Jesus, Jesus—no. It can't be," Lee wept.

In the light from the fire he examined his new ring. If it did really have the power hinted at by his uncle's lawyer, was there any limit? There was one way to find out.

"I wish," he declared, remembering to rub, "that none of this had ever happened."

Once more, the familiar voice responded, "As you wish."

9

Lee Ralston-Smith awakened at his desk on Monday afternoon before Thanksgiving and examined the diminutive package the postman had brought special delivery that morning. He hoped it contained something valuable or good news. God knows there had been enough of the bad lately.

The New Orleans law firm on the return address represented his late Uncle Silas' estate. Was this about a possible inheritance?

Ripping off the packing, he read the attorney's letter, then opened the box and examined the ring.

A second chance?

Or would he only be repeating the nightmare?

A Time For Crosses
By Frances Brinkley Cowden

It is strange that one is never quite as clever as she thinks she is. By the middle of the next morning, I regretted my ingenuity in suggesting that we needed more students on the night watch since it produced another difficult situation. True, we had not sighted any vampires as yet in Shelby Forest, but the rumors could still be proven true. I was not sure what the strange figures were I saw last night; that is why I wanted someone else to look out.

According to the schedule, Dr. Frederick Attar and Dr. Sam Gregg split the night shift and day shift. Dr. Attar managed to have me in his group on the morning search. Moreover, somehow we had ended up in the same corner of the cave our party had been exploring.

"Stella?"

"Yes, Frederick?" We were on a first name basis after last night when I had looked out and seen the ghost-like figures. I ran into his arms out of fright, but apparently he had thought it was something more.

"I talked to Gregg. He agrees that there ought to be more on each night shift. So from now on, you can have the same shift as I."

"What?" I gasped, feeling the walls caving in. Okay, Stella, I said to myself, you got yourself into this, how do you get out of it? I had had such bad luck with relationships in the past, I was not interested in developing another one. In fact, I was almost as frightened of that as I was the alleged vampires.

"What's the matter?" Frederick gave me a perplexed look, "I thought you wanted to be with me so that I could reassure you."

"But what will the others think?" I muttered, trying to salvage my common sense, "and my sister... I wouldn't want to give Lora the wrong idea."

"Stella, this is the twentieth century. Wake up, dear. Other people don't care what you do."

Suddenly I realized I had misjudged this man. But what kind of middle-aged man, college professor or not, would bring a group of students on a vampire hunt? They were not even real psychology students; most of the watchers were taking the introductory course or had been invited by a friend and had come along for the adventure. I am sure that neither instructor really believed the vampire rumor, but wanted instead to record the reactions of the participants. Why would we have burlap on the windows instead of boarding them up—if there really were vampires? It was all a hoax. They probably had somehow staged the weird things I saw when I wasn't supposed to look out the window. If we were watching for vampires, why couldn't we look out the window? Stupid! I should have stayed at home. But who would look out after Lora?

My sister Lora was here because her high school sweetheart had flunked out of college when he joined the vampire club. The club had caused more than a few students at the University of Memphis to drop out. They would act out vampire games in a manner similar to the Dungeons and Dragons ritual. Like the others, he couldn't stay up all night playing the games and also keep up with his courses. His obsession had included drugs to stay awake in class. When he disappeared from Lora's life, she changed her major from English to psychology. I was there with my sister.

"Okay, we'll discuss it later." I cut him off, unable to decide whether to be more angry with him or with myself. But maybe I could turn this into an advantage.

"Okay, if you will get permission to let us look outside." I really wanted someone else to look out to see if it was my imagination or if there were real monsters lurking in the trees.

"Get permission? I made the rule. Gregg and I are in joint command here, you know that."

"Then change the rule." I tried to look at him in such a way that would melt his old attitude enough, but not too much, for such close quarters.

"Rules are made to be obeyed, Stella dear," Frederick said softly, touching my hair. "We have to find the monsters during the day while they are asleep—if they exist—that's the only way."

Maybe he's not so bad, I thought. "But it wouldn't be against the rules if you added an amendment that all those on night watch could look out the window from time to time... just to be safe."

"That rule was made to keep people with flighty imaginations from causing panic with false alarms. Mass hysteria would abort our experiment. Moreover, it could become dangerous."

"I can't stay with you if you don't get Dr. Gregg to let you amend the rule."

"Let me!"

"Well, do you think you could persuade him?" I baited the trap further.

"Let me! My dear, you forget that I have just as much authority as he. If it were merely a question of that, it would be easily arranged at any rate. After all, this experiment was my idea in the first place."

"Wonderful, I'll see you tonight," I said sweetly as I squeezed his hand quickly and turned to leave.

"But I didn't say... oh, well, I will think about it."

"Hey, Stella, where are you?" It was Lora calling, and soon the others had joined us. I could hardly wait for dark so I could get a chance to look out the window again.

* * *

When the chance came at last, I wasted no time. Trembling, I opened the burlap flap. This time a scream locked in my throat. On the other side of the window was a face—a human face staring at me.

Clutching my hand over my own mouth in a reflex gesture, I stood there looking at that face. Why didn't he move? Why didn't I move? You would think that I would have scared him away. Peeping Toms usually run, but he wasn't exactly a Peeping Tom. He looked like the self-portrait of Van Gogh, except the bandanna was a sweatband instead of bandaging his ear. His eyes were much duller and there were more whiskers on his unshaven face. And he had that angular, rebellious look. But I wasn't thinking about art at the moment—I wasn't really thinking at all.

Then I knew. Summoning all the courage one is supposed to have in a moment like this, I moved closer and looked beyond him. I could have reached out and touched him, or he, me—but neither of us did. In the moonlight I saw other figures—not the ghostlike wisps of the night before, but men. My last bit of courage left me.

I pulled the flap down and started screaming, holding on to it in a weird effort to keep out the invaders. Frederick came to me, and I ran into his arms.

"Stella—what?"

"They are out there; tell the others," I moaned.

"Calm down, dear, and tell me what's wrong," Frederick tried in vain to reassure me.

"Look outside. No! Don't go out there! Warn the others. They've come for us. And these are real... not like the ones last night."

"You are not supposed to look outside. Listen," he pulled me into his arms firmly, "this is the reason for making the rules in the first place." He added, half-scolding, half-consoling.

"You didn't see..." I begged.

But it was already too late. No one knew where all of these men had come from, but they were there. Some had climbed in the burlap-covered windows and others had broken in the flimsy doors of the cabins. They were armed with knives and shotguns while we had only our crosses.

Soon we were all assembled in the dining area. Everyone was both dazed and frightened. From where had all these human fiends come? More important, what did they want with us? It was some consolation that they were human beings; and had not come through the walls as we would have expected. I wanted to believe that the previous night's visual encounter was an illusion.

"It's too late to run. If these are not vampires, what are they?" I asked Frederick, who was only slightly less anxious than I.

Knives flashed in warning. A fat, greasy man seemed to be the leader. "Shut up on the yack!" he screeched. "Everyone, line up."

But there was one young man that didn't seem to fit in with the rest. In contrast to the crude appearance and manners of the others, he was well-dressed and had a debonair glow to his strikingly handsome countenance.

He smiled, and I forgot Frederick and walked over to him. "What are you going to do with us now?" I asked.

"Oh, they thought you people were the ones who had been spreading the vampire rumors. Three of them were hunting this afternoon and saw you prowling in the caves. They came to make you leave."

"You are so wonderful... to explain," I said, plainly enamored, in spite of myself. This man was magnificent. I had never seen such fascinating—almost metallic—eyes. I got that helpless feeling that starts deep in the stomach area and dries out one's throat. I felt really stupid, but I knew he was taking mental control of me. I couldn't stop whatever was to happen.

"The moon is so beautiful tonight. It looks like it has spilled across the lake." I couldn't believe I said that. Everything that came out of my mouth sounded like it was being said by someone else.

While he and I were talking about the beauty of the moon on the lake, Dr. Gregg and Frederick were convincing the local men that we had not been the cause of the rumors. In turn, the men assured the professors that the Dracula idea was a hoax. Some college kids had come out here to play their vampire game until they had been run off.

Someone probably saw them. Since it wasn't Halloween, there had been joking that they were real. The locals had never taken the rumor too seriously, but they were not about to have interlopers causing problems.

I don't know whether everyone was disappointed or relieved, but it was agreed that we would all leave tomorrow.

"Well at least we won't have to sleep with these tonight." Lora remarked as she threw her wooden cross on the floor. Everyone else soon followed suit. They even took the garlic back to the kitchen.

"I'll be glad to get out of this place!" one student laughed. "Never did think we would find anything."

"Now, what are they going to do?" I asked the stranger, pointing to the local men.

"Oh, they'll all go home," he smiled.

"And you?"

He continued to smile. It gave me no reassurance.

A vision flashed across my mind... all those people sleeping without a single cross.

The Big Chill
By Cynthia Ward

"That was the Doors with 'Riders on the Storm,' an appropriate song for this rainy Monday morning—hey, is the drought over?"

"Nah!"

"At the top of the set we heard Jimi Hendrix and 'The Wind Cried Mary.' Then we had 'In My Life' by the Beatles, 'Not Fade Away' by Buddy Holly, and Big Brother and the Holding Company doing 'Piece of My Heart'—oh, Janis, *baby!*

"It's 6:51 a.m. and you're listening to Renegade Rawlins on KMRK, the Masters of Rock, San Francisco's premier classic rock station."

"Renegade" Rawlins wasn't the highest-rated disk jockey in the Bay Area, but he had a sizeable and devoted following. His extensive knowledge of rock made him equally attractive to kids who idolized the old guitar gods and to Baby Boomers who loved hearing the music of their youth and pretending they were still young and rebellious. Rawlins cemented his appeal with his irreverence, which made younger listeners think taboos were being broken and older listeners think they were still hip. Rawlins was no shock jock; he didn't scare away the advertisers. Quite the contrary.

Rawlins picked up a printout. "For those commuters who are actually *moving*, let me update you on road conditions. The pile-up on the upper deck of the Bay Bridge has been joined by a fender-bender on the lower, so traffic in *and* out of the East Bay is backed up. On Highway 101, a truck has jackknifed at the 280 interchange, so expect delays there too..."

Unlike most drive-time disk jockeys, Renegade Rawlins wasn't half of a duo of wits teamed to ease commuters into deadly-dull jobs in the Financial District and Silicon Valley. Solo, Rawlins carried the morning show so ably he was the jock featured on KMRK's billboards near Candlestick Park, billboards that made like Burma Shave signs, only as irreverent as the D.J. they promoted:

Pedal to the metal

Balls to the wall

Ride with the Renegade

Spring Summer and Fall.

Renegade Rawlins—6:00 - 10:00 AM—KMRK-FM 108.7

The last billboard showed Rawlins's face wearing a wild expression, as if he were screaming with all the energy and passion of rock music. It showed he actually *looked* like a disk jockey, with long wavy blond hair and a ruggedly handsome face, youthful but crinkly-eyed. It showed he was old enough to remember when rock *meant* something.

Rawlins laid the printout aside as he concluded the traffic update. "We've just learned that a car has collided with oncoming traffic on the Golden Gate Bridge. In other words, all routes in and out of San Francisco are constipated. *Everyone's* late for work today! What a way to start the week!" He glanced at the monitor, making sure the signal was going out. "So, you yuppie overachievers who by some miracle haven't left for work yet, get in some quality time with your kids. What's that? Fifteen minutes last night was *enough?* Well, hell! More time for the Stairmaster!"

The lamest yuppie joke was guaranteed to go over big. Everyone hated yuppies, including yuppies, who always assumed the abuser was referring to someone else.

"We'll be right back with more classic rock."

During the commercials, Rawlins loaded new disks in the CD player and programmed the tracks he wanted. When the last commercial ended, he flipped on the microphone. "Here's an Elvis tune from 'way back when the King was *good...*"

Renegade Rawlins fell silent, but no music started. Rawlins sat motionless, his finger frozen on the PLAY button. He was staring at the studio door. Staring at the man walking *through* the closed door like some Hollywood special effect. Staring at a man who looked exactly like Elvis Presley.

"Uh, folks—folks, Elvis has *just* walked into the studio," said Rawlins. *What the hell is going on?* "I think Elvis wants to dispute my assessment of his work."

Somebody was pulling a prank—Hoffman. It *had* to be Hoffman, his engineer, paying him back for stunts like peppering the Kleenex box during allergy season, swiping the remote control of a TV with no other controls, and scratching "Butt Pirate" in the mud on the back of Hoffman's 4Runner. Why did Hoffman pull a prank like this one? Rawlins wasn't really an Elvis fan. And how had Hoffman made it look like Elvis had walked through a closed door? Pretty fucking sophisticated hologram!

The hologram looked so solid Rawlins could almost believe someone was in the booth with him. And the hologram was not the fat, clownish, irrelevant Elvis in the scarf and the rhinestones and the white jumpsuit, but the Elvis who had appeared on the "Ed Sullivan Show," young and handsome and vital, almost a force of nature. A force to change the world.

Hoffman must have hidden a tape deck in the booth, because the hologram spoke. "Let... me... rest." The Memphis drawl, a perfect Presley baritone, sounded like it came right out of the hologram's mouth, the full lips moving in sync with the words. "Let me rest."

"Let you 'rest'?" Rawlins said. "I'm not sure what you mean."

"I'm dead."

Rawlins glared through the glass at Hoffman. The engineer raised his hands and shook his head violently. *Yeah, right*, Rawlins thought. He'd made the right call, reacting on-air to the prank. Let Hoffman catch the shit from the station manager if a bunch of listeners called in to complain.

"I'm dead," the hologram repeated. "But I cain't get no rest. Thousands visit my grave every day, with more comin' all the time. People keep sayin' they seen me at Burger King or the service station. The tabloids write about me every week. Golden oldies stations around the country keep my records playin' constantly."

"Elvis," said Rawlins, "are you saying you don't want to be remembered? Surely the King of Rock 'n' Roll doesn't want to be forgotten!"

"I wanna be remembered, jes' like anyone else. But you all are keepin' me from my rest. I done too much in too short a time. I'm tired. The dead are supposed to rest." The hologram raised an arm and pointed at Rawlins. "And you people who won't listen to nothin' new, you're makin' yourselves dead while you're still alive!"

"Christ," Rawlins said.

"The country-western stations were too conservative to play my first records. Now it's the rock stations that's too conservative to play new music. New recordin' artists are breakin' in left an' right on the country stations. But there's less pop stations playin' new acts *now* than there was when I was gettin' my first hit records!"

Rawlins laughed. "With good reason!"

"Look at rap music," the hologram said. "Rap is the spirit of youth. Rap is the spirit of the nation the way it is *now*. But there ain't a single big radio station willin' to play the *real* stuff. The pop stations just keep playin' the same ol' music. They're keepin' us from our rest."

"Rap is n-noise!" Rawlins cried. "Obnoxious, offensive, unlistenable noise."

The hologram's lip curled in the classic sneer. "I remember when people your age said that about rock 'n' roll."

"Rock 'n' roll is *nothing* like rap," Rawlins said.

He remembered a rap song he'd heard in a movie his girlfriend had dragged him to. The rap song had thumped over the opening credits of *Do the Right Thing* while a beautiful black girl danced and boxed with the camera. Rawlins tried to figure out what the rapper was chanting (this was *not* singing), but couldn't really make out any lines except two that irritated him so much he remembered them perfectly years later: "Elvis was a hero to most/But he never meant shit to me."

"The rappers *hate* Elvis!" Rawlins cried.

"Naw, they don't hate me—jes' the system."

The hologram was interacting with him. Rawlins felt a chill between his shoulder-blades, as if someone had laid an ice-cold hand on his back. Then he realized he must be hearing the voice of a friend of Hoffman's, coming through a speaker hidden in the studio. Rawlins leaned close to the window, but saw no one except Hoffman, badly overdoing the pop-eyed surprise shtick.

Rawlins glanced at the clock. Top of the hour, time to ID the station. He realized he'd let a few seconds of dead air slip by. Time to bring this prank to an end.

The baritone voice spoke again. "My time is past. I'm bein' held here unnaturally. We *all* are."

"What?" Rawlins stared at the hologram. *"'All?'"*

"Let us rest." Now it sounded like more than one voice. "Let us rest."

Shapes appeared behind the image of Elvis, materializing out of the air. Rawlins found himself looking into a pair of intense eyes under a mass of dark curls, felt himself being drawn by a powerful charisma. He forced himself to turn away from that magnetic gaze and found himself looking through long tangled strands of red-brown hair into a woman's eyes. He looked away, saw a tall dark rangy man with a bushy Afro and long thin mustaches and a white Stratocaster worn upside-down so it could be played left-handed.

The figures spoke again. "Let us *rest!*"

Behind them still other shapes were materializing. Rawlins glimpsed a nerdy-looking pair of black-frame glasses, a pair of round-lensed wire rims. He dragged a breath through his tight throat.

A D.J. couldn't let anyone—or anything—take control of his show.

"Elvis, it's nice having you and your friends drop by for a chat, but we've been talking so long I have to run some commercials." Rawlins leaned closer to the microphone. "This is the Masters of Rock, KMRK, 108.7 FM, San Francisco's premier classic rock station."

He pushed in a cart. A Circuit City commercial filled the studio and the airwaves.

Rawlins looked up and found the booth empty except for himself. He looked through the window and saw Hoffman slumped with his jaw slack. That bullshit artist.

Rawlins switched off the microphone and burst out of the booth. "Hoffman, what the hell did you do?"

Hoffman jerked upright and swiveled his chair around. "I didn't do *anything*, man! They were just *there!*"

"Liar. Pranks are one thing, but fucking with me on the *air* is another." Rawlins closed his hands in Hoffman's tie-dyed T-shirt and jerked him forward. "You tell me right now how you pulled that stunt."

"I *swear*, man, I didn't do anything," the engineer whispered. He was sagging in his shirt, held up by Rawlins' grip. His face was paler than his cornsilk hair. "Those were ghosts, man. *Ghosts!*"

"Right." Rawlins released Hoffman's shirt with a disdainful gesture. He always owned up to *his* pranks when it was time to do so. Still, Hoffman's line of bullshit gave him an idea.

Rawlins returned to the booth and made a phone call. A month later, he was on *Geraldo*. In the intervening month he had invented several additional visitations by the dead heroes of rock. His convincing demeanor, quick wit, and good looks got him on all the other TV talk shows, and brought him a lucrative contract and a collaborator for a book about his meetings with the dead gods of rock'n' roll. *Spirits of Rock* broke all sales records set by previous rock memorabilia books, and Renegade Rawlins's oldies show was syndicated to every radio market in the country. The show was no longer engineered by Hoffman; Rawlins had fired him.

The Sound Of Fury
By Mark Sutton

My grandchildren can't understand why night-time storms scare me so much, why I cannot sleep when lightning tears the velvet sky and thunder shakes my tiny house. I wish I could tell them the truth, but they wouldn't understand. They would say I've lost my mind.

After what I saw, I'm surprised I didn't.

I don't remember my parents, and the desire to locate the people who abandoned me outside of Memphis has never been very strong. Five years after my birth a fever robbed me of my hearing. After I recuperated, I was rarely shown to families for possible adoption; no one wanted a crippled child. At eight, when it was proven that I had normal intelligence, I was taken from a Catholic hospital and placed in the Oakhill Boys Home.

My first sight of the place was the twisted old oak on top of the hill which gave the building its name and cloistered it from the main road. When I saw the grim brick building, my whole body shook in panic. The social worker, a lady who kept her hair pulled into a tight ball at the base of her skull, held my arm like a manacle; otherwise I think I would have run.

The social worker stopped, rigidly hugged me and opened the heavy oak door.

The lobby had a wooden floor with a crimson and emerald Oriental rug in the center. We walked through a smaller door opposite the main one, revealing a hallway with uneven stairs. She led me to the bottom step and placed me on it. I clung to the banister as she walked to the right of the stairs and disappeared under them.

The gray wooden walls and floor made me feel as if I had been locked in a cave. I wanted the social worker to take me away from here, back to the white security of the hospital. The railing bent under my weight.

A rough push jettisoned me from my support and sent me spinning onto the floor. A group of boys surrounded me. Their mouths were twisted into words and feelings I recognized without having to hear them. One yanked me to my feet with dirt-gloved hands. He spat in my face; two of his front teeth were broken into right triangles.

I shook my head and tried to talk with the few words a kindly nun had taught me. Deaf. Don't hurt. Please. The boy who held me threw his head back and opened his mouth wide. Out of the corners of my eyes I could see the others mimicking him.

Someone shoved me from behind; the boy I fell against slapped me towards someone else. They passed me back and forth in a game of keep away. Their faces spun past me, warped in mocking jeers.

One particularly hard toss sent me out of the circle. Landing against the brown-paper package that was sent from the hospital, I watched the boys run out the main door. Stony hands pulled me to the level of a man's chest. A balding head, the pale skin broken by coal-dark eyebrows and strip of hair just above the ears, shook stiffly. He carried me up the stairs mechanically, without either the jaunty or irritated bounce that most people possess.

The second floor was lit by hurricane lamps mounted on bronze holders shaped like bird claws. Eighteen urine-yellow doors, nine on each side of the hall, were the only other things along the unpainted walls. The man banged his fist against one of the doors.

It slid towards me, and a boy with a queer little face peered around it. His eyes had an extra fold of skin around them, and his nose looked like it had been a target for a prize fighter. The man spoke. The door flew outwards, nearly hitting him. He stormed in, knocking my leg against it.

Two beds leaned against the opposing grimy white walls. An unvarnished, splintery dresser occupied the tiny space between them. The boy cowered on one bed, his arm over his face as if he expected a blow. The man dropped me on the other bed. My back hit the slats under the thin mattress.

The man's arms cut through the air. He gestured towards me and said something to the other boy. He stomped out, closing the door quickly behind him.

The other boy uncurled and crawled off his bed. He shuffled across the room, stopping just before my bed. He spoke. His mouth slid along his face strangely, like the lips were not properly attached to his skull. Holding his hands in front of him, he stared at me like he was expecting an answer. I smiled and pointed to the bottom half of the bed. The bed wobbled dangerously when he collapsed in relief.

He began to talk again, face stretching like new bandages. He didn't stop for about five minutes. When he seemed to pause I cupped my hands over my ears and shook my head slowly. He closed his right eye and resumed his conversation. I continued my signaling. After a moment of thought, with eyelids squeezed together until I couldn't see his eyes, he exaggerated the signal back to me. I nodded.

He walked to the dresser, returning with a scrap of paper and a pencil. As he scribbled his tongue peeked through a gap between his front teeth. He showed me the paper, the word "Benji" stood out in large block letters. He pointed to the name, and then to his chest. I slowly copied the motion. Then I reached for the pencil, wrote my name, and held the paper against my chest.

Benji picked up my luggage. He turned towards the dresser and flapped his jaws a little more. I sighed; couldn't he realize why I wasn't talking to him? Benji tossed the package onto his bed and pulled open the top drawer of the dresser. Taking out a navy-colored shirt, he put it on my package and carried it back to the drawer. He repeated this show with two pairs of pants. After several confusing seconds the meaning of his pantomime came to me. I tore open the package, removed my other pair of pants, and handed them to Benji. He put them in the bottom drawer. When we finished he walked around the building with me, communicating through waves and pointing.

My friendship with Benji that started that afternoon proved to be fortuitous for both of us. He let me know when people tried to sneak up behind me, thus preventing several beatings. I soon learned Benji was simple, but he had a good heart.

I discovered from Benji that the man who had brought me into my new room at this home for unwanted boys was the director. He was seen only rarely, and then he usually yelled at anyone who had not done his job properly. The only other adult who worked here, a crone that kept watch over the kitchen and laundry, would stand perfectly rigid whenever he appeared, as if the lack of motion would keep him from noticing her. Benji and I spent most of our time repairing damage to the interior of the youth home. We would often prepare the sticky white porridge and peanut butter sandwiches that were our normal foods. Meat was a special treat, usually once a month. We were not given much chance to receive an education; I had learned how to read at the hospital and would "read," through a made-up sign language, to Benji by candlelight after we were supposed to be asleep.

Despite the hardships I did not think the next year and a half of my life was unbearable. Most of the older boys, the bullies, had to do outside work and weren't difficult to avoid. It was not hard to remain beneath the director's notice, once you learned his unsaid rules. I was not beaten often, on the average once a month, by either set. I was able to surreptitiously borrow magazines and books from the director's library, so Benji and I had some sort of entertainment. Benji often wanted music, but I had never had the chance to properly appreciate it, and the director kept no gramophone. Music would have been heard, and caused us problems.

It did.

The events that still haunt me began at about three on a September afternoon. Benji and I were dusting the banister when I saw the door open. I knew it was too early for the older children to be coming in; the director never let them stop before sundown. Two people walked in, one a boy and the other the same social worker who had brought me to Oakhill. She ignored us and went into the director's office, leaving the boy.

I have read that people who are handicapped developed other, supernaturally acute, senses to compensate for the ones they have lost. A feeling of unease seeped out of my spine when I got a good look at the new boy. He was tall and lanky; his tattered clothes made him look like a scarecrow. His ebony hair was streaked with white, and his eyes appeared, to me, to be a touch too far apart. He waved; his fingers looked like they would break if he moved them too forcefully. He had an... ageless look on him, like I've seen in people who have known great hardship and survive through shutting out part of their youth. My vitals began to compress, and I thought I would vomit. I turned away, concentrating too much on my task.

I had time to wipe the dust off one of the rotting dowel rods before Benji's doughy hands turned me towards the door. Then he moved to the right of the new boy. We had practiced this when someone wanted to talk with me; he would do the talking if I had problems understanding the other person.

Benji's flowing mouth took very little effort for me to read. "This is Aaron. Aaron, this is MR, my best friend."

I rolled my eyes. Benji used only my initials when he wanted to refer to me. I couldn't convince him otherwise. I often thought, in moments of arrogance, he did it because he respected me.

Aaron smiled. It looked perfectly normal, but the rumbling in my stomach intensified. "You must be very important to be a Mister already."

I traced my name on the banister. He nodded. I gave a quick salute; I didn't want to shake his hand.

Benji interjected. "He talks funny because he can't hear."

"I really didn't notice," Aaron said.

I asked, "Where are you from?"

He shrugged. "I've never lived anywhere enough for it to count over my life. The curse of the unwanted. How long have you two been here?"

I held up two fingers, one half bent. Benji added. "I've been here three more years than MR. This isn't a nice place."

Aaron's eyebrows slid up his forehead. "Really? Does the bald guy have anything to do with that?"

Benji never knew when to not talk about things that would get him in trouble. The director had ordered us to remain quiet about the conditions of the home when other adults were around. "He's the big man. He's not very nice; he likes to scream at people."

"The older kids have a habit of beating up the younger ones," I added. "You look old enough for them to not give you much trouble."

"I'll be careful." He patted Benji's shoulder. "Can Benji help me find my room? I think it's somewhere on the next floor."

"If he wants to."

"Otay," Benji said.

"I've got a package and a box in the foyer that I need to put in my room."

"I'll help," Benji raced backwards down the stairs. Aaron followed with much more self-control. When they disappeared through the door I turned to the banister and smudged my name off the wood.

My mind turned over the feelings I had about Aaron. He seemed very kind. Benji obviously liked him, and the feelings seemed reciprocal. However, this new boy made my scalp itch. Perhaps it was the white streaks; they did not look like real hair, but spider webs. Perhaps he was too nice. I was very suspicious of people back then, especially anyone who lived at Oakhill. Perhaps it was...

Benji brushed against me. He carried, with both arms, a wooden box with a quarter-sized hole in the side. I stood against the banister so they could pass. Aaron, his head bouncing on Benji's shoulder, took up the other half of the stairs. I do not know whether they were speaking; I couldn't see their mouths. Benji's head nodded as they walked with purpose, as if he was answering a question.

When he returned he picked up his rag and went back to work. I waited a minute, then I poked his shoulder. "Did Aaron say anything special to you?"

He shook his head, locking it at the edges of the arc like a machine. "He just asked me who the other kids our age are, and where their rooms are."

I nodded.

"He said he would see us at dinner."

For some reason that I could not understand at the time, this upset me even more. I threw down my rag and ran upstairs. Benji must have thought I was crazy. I went to the bathroom and hid for a while. I couldn't understand why I was being so agitated. Young minds rarely do.

Aaron did not join us for dinner, much to my relief. A group of seven younger children clamored around him as he entered the cold cavernous dining room. The director appeared and scattered the group by slapping two of the children. He spoke to Aaron, and left again. Aaron nodded, and stuck out his tongue once the man's back was turned. His new friends struggled to keep silent, their cheeks bulging and lips threatening to burst apart.

Aaron sat in the center of his group of admirers. They moved close together, and covered their mouths in conspiratorial whispering cones, in sharp contrast to the tombstone rigidity of everyone else.

Benji startled me when he stuck his face between me and the group. "I gotta go talk to Aaron real quick. Be right back."

He skipped over and fell into the seat opposite Aaron, blocking my view of the proceedings. I bit a large corner of my peanut butter sandwich. It tasted even worse than usual. I was angry with Aaron; what right did he have to steal my best... my only...friend? I finished my meal alone and skulked up to my room.

I did not normally go to bed early, but that night I fell asleep after an hour of staring at the labyrinthine cracks in the chipped white paint. A sudden shake pulled me from my dreams. After turning on my side I rubbed my eyes. Benji stood in front of me, carrying a tiny candle. His poked-out lip cast a wide black line along the center of his face.

"I need your help," he said.

"How late is it?" I thought. The hall lamps were out for the day. After midnight, I guessed. What did he need now? He knew where

the bathroom was, and we didn't have any books to look at. "What?"

"It's real important." He tried to pull me out of bed. I twisted onto my back. "Please, MR. We really, really need your help. A bunch of us are getting together, but we need you to come, too."

If we were caught out of our rooms it meant we would be beaten, even Benji knew that edict. Yet something in his demeanor begged to me, a nameless sorrow that dripped out of his trembling face, the strongest longing I had ever seen. Whatever it was had to be very important, to him anyway, and he did so much for me. I thought, I can at least keep him from being punished by himself.

I slid to my feet and buttoned my shirt. Benji jumped in place. I snapped my palm flat quickly, and he stopped. The director was a light sleeper, and any little noise could have accidentally woken him.

"Follow me exactly," Benji said. We crept down the hallway. He dodged around numerous loose floorboards. If the director heard us as we sneaked downstairs—his chambers were directly under the staircase—he did not come out to get us. The main door opened without protest.

Once Benji reset the door he jumped off the porch and ran into the night. It seemed darker than usual, without stars. The full moon was dull, as if someone had covered it with cotton cloth. A violating wind rustled my hair. The special sense that warned me about Aaron was pulsing in my neck, stronger than before. I staggered along the way Benji had gone.

I could see a group of people gathered around the oak, including Benji. I scrambled up the dew-slicked grass, my anxiety of being caught and the bizarre... unreality of the night twisting my perceptions. The hill stretched above me, almost to the moon. It felt like it took hours to reach the top, even though my rational mind knew it only took a couple of minutes.

A wave of dizziness assaulted me when I hit the apex. I teetered backwards, over the empty space. A patch of reddish cloud loomed above me, pressing down like a suffocating pillow. Benji caught my armpits. He shook me briskly, and set me down.

Ten other boys, all between the ages of six and ten, stared at me. I knew them, but none were good friends. They watched me like starving dogs watching a dying squirrel. Aaron knelt in front of me, a wolfish smile on his face. "Glad you could join our party."

For a moment I didn't understand what he said. "Party?"

"We decided to have a little dance, to celebrate life and surviving to another day." He flicked his hand behind him. "Benji said you could play the music."

I looked where he had gestured. Aaron's wooden box sat just to the left of the ancient oak. A wooden board, the same color as the box, was propped against the box. Metal rods, each about six inches high, were attached to the top. An L-shaped handle curved out of the hole I had noticed earlier.

I crawled to the machine. As I ran my fingers along the polished edges, I detected cracks—carvings actually—that seemed to form letters, almost. Other carvings seemed to be shapes: a star in a circle, two circles side by side, and others I could not recognize. I could not detect any nails or gaps around the edges of the box; it seemed to be one solid piece of wood.

I twisted back around and tried to sound angry, "You're going to get us in trouble."

"This isn't a loud machine," Aaron replied. "They won't hear it from the house. The director won't know; we'll be back inside in an hour. I do this every place I've been, and no one in any of my groups has ever been caught by the people in charge. I just want us to have a little fun; you all could certainly use the release."

The other kids nodded. Benji loped to my side. His tears dropped on my shoulder. "Please, MR."

Aaron smirked. "I promise, no trouble. If there's any I'll take all the lashes."

I sighed. If I refused to help them they would consider me as bad as the director, and Benji would probably hate me for the rest of his life. I didn't want that, or to have to deal with every child in the youth home alone. He was probably right about the noise, I thought, after all I certainly couldn't know for sure how loud it was; I only knew sound as a concept. And Benji wanted to do this so badly. Most likely, I thought, I could get us out of serious trouble.

As I closed my hand around the handle it dug deeper into my grip. My arm moved without direct order. The box pulsed beneath my other hand like a diseased heart. Stinking air from the pipes anaesthetized me.

I don't know how long I was enthralled by the motions of my task. I can remember a dull pulsing... sound, just on the edge of my awareness. It put pictures in my mind of fire and feverish emotions. It reminded me of the director's voice, demanding action. Unlike the director—and my fear of his wrath—something gave me the power to resist. I assume it was my deafness. My curse.

Someone brushed against me, and I looked up. The others were running in twisting circles. Their mouths shook in wordless screams. Their faces gave no recognition of consciousness. They repeatedly threw their hands upwards, as if they were offering thanks in a pagan ritual.

A large drop of rain bounced off my hand. More followed with unnatural speed. Thunder jarred the hill. Reflected bursts of lightning on the pipes kept my vision blurred. I couldn't let go of the handle. It spun my sweat-soaked arm faster and faster. My thoughts raced as fast as the wind around me. Why are we not being struck by lightning? We're on the highest location within miles, under an old tree that wasn't strong, and that had been struck repeatedly in the few years I'd lived at Oakhill. As it was now...

A clod of dirt hit the box, attracting my attention to the edge of the hill. The director pulled himself into view. Aaron's machine must not have been as quiet as he promised, I thought, panicked, or the wails the dancers seemed to be projecting had awakened him. He grabbed Benji and threw him onto the ground. My friend didn't seem to care; he writhed on the ground and smacked his head repeatedly against a root. I was afraid he would split his head open. Somehow he didn't. I said a prayer for him, but I think another power was protecting him.

The director repeated his attempts at discipline with the other children, with similar results. I tried to run, or curl against the oak and hide, but the handle kept me in one place. The director began to stalk towards me, his face twisted and distorted by the wind and rain. He reached for me as a bolt of lightning split into five deadly fingers, one of which hit the tree behind me. The force and heat threw my head forwards, knocking it against the box. I was prepared to die as my thoughts fugued away.

* * * * * * * *

The dawn burned my eyes as I woke up. I was suspended two feet off the ground in a crib of roots. I didn't dare move, for fear of hurting myself. I saw Benji and two other children curled, asleep, by the singed trunk. Benji was sucking his thumb. After turning my head, I saw—at the base of the trunk, next to a dull red strain—the black slippers and pajama bottoms that the director wore when he slept.

Sometime later a group of men drove up in a police car. They collected the others and fished me out of the roots. Once I was safely in his arms I saw the charred fragments of the youth home. "Struck by lightning," one of the men said. There was a strange calmness in the other children's faces, a look of forgetfulness and drowsiness. They shook their heads to any attempt at questioning. I ignored the men; they wouldn't have believed me.

I was immediately transferred to another youth home, this one much nicer, where I was allowed to learn and play like a real child. I never again saw Benji or the other children who had met and "celebrated" on the hill. I did, however, receive one short letter from Benji about a year later:

MR,

Hope you are doing all right. I miss you a bunch. My new home is so much nicer than the other one and I really wish you could be here with me. I hardly ever think of the bad place any more. It's going away in my mind, just like Aaron said it would. Thanks a bunch for playing the music. It helped me feel a lot better.

benji

After that, in spite of all the time we spent together, he must have forgotten me.

After I graduated from college I found a job as a teacher at a deaf school. My children—both those I teach and those I helped bring into the world—don't believe anyone could turn out as normal and happy as I did living in those conditions. I don't tell the story often; it usually brings my younger students to tears. I never mention that night.

The questions about that night never left me, and I eventually got up the courage to check the newspapers. They called it the worst storm in the state's history. Seventeen adolescents died in their beds when the orphanage burned to the ground. They could never be positively identified; the records—the only way to trace Aaron—were destroyed with the building. The director was reported to have died when he "tried to take the younger children to safety." The old woman who worked at Oakhill lived nearby, and said that she heard faint music, like that of a pipe organ, before the storm began. She died soon afterwards, when she slid into a ditch after a rain shower.

I suppose I will never know the truth about that night, but if I could it would make it easier to sleep at night during the storm. I have to have someone else in my room to be able to sleep at all. Even though they don't understand, my grandchildren take it in stride; it proves to them that adults are human too. They hold granddaddy's hand and pretend to be super-heroes, keeping the bogeyman away. But they can't. My mind always recalls the images of Benji and the others dancing in the storm. It twists my heart, for I wish I could have heard the music, and joined them.

The Camping Trip Incident
By Stanley T. Evans

The children began to fidget and nudge one another as they watched the campfire crackle in the night air. It was dark now and the full moon was beginning to rise. They looked around at the deep and mysterious woods around them. Walking toward them from the tents was a large man. They all looked up expectantly at his approach. The children all got very quiet as he sat down. His normally boyish face now looked faintly sinister in the light of the fire. He leaned forward and gazed at his audience with a cold glare. He smiled in satisfaction that he had their complete attention.

The children huddled together to hear tonight's tale. The man smiled. The effect of story telling over a campfire would never change. He pointed his finger at the children as he began his story:

"This happened back in the seventies, when I was about your age and in Boy Scouts. Things have changed since then," his voice grew deeper with the mood of the night, "but I wonder how much. I have sons of my own in Scouts now, and I hope that they never have an experience like the one I'm about to tell you."

* * *

It started out like any other camping trip. We already had the trailer loaded with our gear. All that remained was for us to put in our personal bags and leave for the weekend.

Everyone was excited about this trip, because it was the first trip of that spring. Of course the weather was threatening rain, but we didn't care. After all, what was a little mud? This was supposed to be a really warm weekend anyway. You know the weather in Memphis tends to change hourly. Woody and Paul finally showed up so now we could leave. Everyone hated setting up camp in the rain or on wet ground, so we were anxious to get there.

We planned to spend the weekend camped at Shelby Forest. We always had a lot of fun there. Even had a night hike planned for Saturday evening. Did that ever turn out weird!

Anyway, we arrived at the campsite about 7:00 p.m. Everything was going fine. I had the coffee going for the adults about fifteen minutes after we got there. Everyone was setting up their tents, and all the patrols were setting up their areas. We still had enough light left to get everything in place.

Once we were established and had finished dinner, we all gathered by the campfire. We were doing the typical scout thing—you know, telling ghost stories while roasting and munching marshmallows.

My dad could really tell stories. He got going on one that had us enthralled. It was a story about a Chickasaw Indian who was killed in the park area. Of course this happened two centuries ago, but the legend lives on. It seems that this brave—Walks-in-Wind—was murdered by a rival from another village. Walks-in-Wind was the son of his tribe's medicine man, and was studying to succeed one day to his father's place. Walks-in-Wind was a strong and brave warrior who had already proven himself in battle. He was to marry Little Deer, a beautiful maiden, the daughter of a very good friend of his father's.

Walks-in-Wind did not know that another brave coveted his bride to be. This brave's name was Bear Killer, as he had killed a bear during his ascension rite. Bear Killer wanted Little Deer for his wife also, but had not told anybody this.

One day Walks-in-Wind was gathering medicinal herbs for his father, and Bear Killer went along with him, supposedly to help. While Walks-in-Wind was bending over to get at a hard-to-cut herb, Bear Killer struck—like a coward—from behind, never giving Walks-in-Wind a chance to defend himself. Then Bear Killer carried Walks-in-Wind's body to the bluff and threw it off.

Bear Killer went back to the village later with a very convincing story. He told the Chief how they had been attacked by warriors from another tribe. As they were trying to get away, he lost sight of Walks-in-Wind. A few minutes later he had heard a scream and assumed it was Walks-in-Wind's death cry. Everyone believed his story. War was declared on the neighboring village.

Bear Killer did marry Little Deer and persuaded her to leave the village with him. Unbeknownst to his murderer, Walks-in-Wind had already learned most of the ancient medicine of his people. He had stumbled across a very ancient and almost forgotten rite, one he had already performed upon himself, which would not let his spirit rest until he avenged his own death or his murderer was executed. Bear Killer escaped his fate by fleeing the vicinity. He later died, along with his wife, when they contracted smallpox, a disease brought from Europe by the white man. Because Walks in Wind never learned of his murderer's fate, his spirit is stuck in the forest, forever hunting the one who killed him.

We had heard rumors of some strange things happening up this way for a couple of years now. Legend has it that Walks-in-Wind required the blood of a living being at each full moon in order to stay this side of the spirit world and look for his murderer. Walks-in-Wind was supposed to haunt the swamp at the base of the main lake in the park. We were going to hike through this area the next night. Most of us were thrilled with this idea. Maybe we'd run into a real Indian ghost!

We were camped about a mile from the swamp anyway, and a few of us wanted to sit up through the night and keep the fire going. That idea was vetoed by the adults who said they would take care of it for us. I went to bed a little apprehensive. There was a full moon that weekend, and with it being partly cloudy, we had a perfect horror movie type of sky. Everything was coming together in a pattern to scare the bejeesus out of us.

Luckily we all made it through the first night without any mishaps. Everyone was present and accounted for on Saturday morning. We started cooking our usual breakfast of scrambled eggs, bacon, biscuits, etc. No one was in a big hurry because the hike wasn't until that night.

After breakfast we broke up into our separate merit badge groups. Steve, John, and I headed for the lake to "work" on our fishing merit badge. I must say that we did very good work. We caught enough fish for our entire patrol's dinner.

While we were at the lake, we worked our way down to the end by the swamp. We just had to look for any sign of a ghost. You know how kids can be real brave in the daylight, and especially since we thought we were professional trackers. There was absolutely no sign of a ghost or anything amiss. Luckily, the fish were biting and we didn't have to come up with a cover story.

Around four-thirty that afternoon, we headed back to camp, cleaned the fish and helped start supper. The plans were to hit the trail about eight o'clock that night. Supper was great: barbecued chicken, baked fish, garbage bag salad, veggies, and peach cobbler for dessert.

Of course the conversation turned to the hike and Walks-in-Wind. The new kids were getting a little edgy about the hike and the possibility of seeing a ghost. We "older" guys weren't too worried after the "trackers" had been out and hadn't seen anything.

Once the dishes from supper were clean, we started getting ready for the hike. Most of the guys had flashlights with them. No one was going to get lost tonight, not that anyone ever did. This was the first night hike any of us had ever been on, so we were being careful. Everyone was really hoping at least to see some animals tonight.

None of us kids had been paying attention to the weather. You know how the heat lightning gets going around here? Well it had been a really warm day and we started to notice the lightning along about eight-thirty or so. It really added an eerie feeling to the night. There is nothing quite like walking around in the woods in the dark with the night sounds all around. Throw in a little heat lightning and a full moon peeking through the clouds, a couple of dozen kids with their over-active imaginations running completely wild, and you have the makings for a really fun evening.

The things your mind can conjure up in the dark are amazing and innumerable.

The hike was actually going great, and we were making really good time. It was only a ten mile hike, half of it uphill. About a fourth of the way into the hike, we were strafed by this really *big* barn owl. That owl came in low from out of the clouds and hooted right over us. I thought my heart was going to stop right there. The adults about busted a gut laughing at the looks on our faces.

Part of the hike was along the park road—good, hard topped road, easy to walk on. It also provided plenty of space for us to walk between one another, free from the brush and branches. We weren't scared walking in that area, oh no, not us big brave scouts.

From the sounds in the darkness, there were obviously some animals out and about that night. One of the guys spotted a pair of raccoons in a tree. And that owl was still flying around. We kept hearing something in the woods shadowing us but we never could get a glimpse of it.

About half way into the hike we checked out watches. It was 10:30. We left the road and followed a path through a field. The grass and weeds were about seven feet tall. You could not see anything through the grass. The trail didn't look like anyone had been on it in quite a while. None of the guys knew where we were or how near our campsite might be.

As fuel to fire our imaginations further, we found a dead whitetail deer lying across the trail. It was lying beside the trail, looking like a broken toy. It looked like it had been dead a few days and something had been gnawing on it. What, we could not tell. This was a young buck; there was no indication of how it had died.

Everyone was kind of quiet for a while, and it was obvious we were all starting to get a little worried. Walking from the site of the deer's carcass, all anyone could talk about was that deer and Walks-in-Wind. This had not gone unnoticed by the adults, especially my dad. Pop started talking about ghosts. Then he got off on how magicians believed someone could conjure up something just by talking about it. That shut us up. Please don't take this wrong. I really do love my dad. There are also times when I would dearly love to throttle him. This was one. Especially with everybody thinking about that dead deer, and Walks-in-Wind. Then, he got off on how you could conjure up something just by talking about it.

For those of you who have never been in or around a swamp in the warm part of the year, it has a very distinct odor. Sort of a fetid, decaying type of smell, which is hard to describe. It's not too bad if there's a wind blowing. The wind died about eleven o'clock. So the smell just hung too low to the ground for our enjoyment.

About midnight we entered the swamp part of the hike. Our imaginations had been running rampant for some time now. We had been hearing all kinds of noises and attributing to them something dire and strange. I knew that the adults had to have timed this just for our benefit. Our fearless leader called a rest break right there in the middle of the swamp. We didn't understand why he was tired, especially when we wanted to press on. After all camp was only a couple of miles away. We didn't at all like being in a smelly swamp at midnight—a swamp haunted by the ghost of a dead, vengeful Indian warrior. We were more than ready to get back to camp. To top it all off, at that moment they made us turn off our flashlights and listen.

The Park Service had put boardwalks through the swamp to keep folks from getting stuck in the mire. These boardwalks included an occasional bridge across a stream. We had stopped on one of those bridges that appeared to be right in the middle of the swamp.

You can hear all kinds of noises in the middle of a swamp about midnight: the water running underneath the bridge; the soft splashings and rustlings of the animals, who live nearby; the angry and hungry buzz of mosquitoes in your ears; the call of the night birds; and the chatter of small animals. Also the chirping of the crickets and hum of the locusts.

What really gets to you is when all of the noises suddenly stop! Because you know, in your heart of hearts, that there can only be one reason for the deathly quiet: There is a ghost out hunting for blood.

About this time the adults went into a huddle whispering about bears and cougars. They do live around here because I have seen their tracks. Surely this was just to take our minds off the ghost.

All of a sudden we heard a very loud splash not twenty yards away from us. Of course all the flashlights immediately came on and were pointed in that direction. All we could see were ripples coming from upstream. No sign of anything. No other sound—just the oppressing silence.

Then on the other side of us we heard a bone chilling noise. To us it seemed like the type of sound a tortured soul would make.

Let me back up a moment. Four or five of the guys were sitting on the edge of the bridge with their feet hanging over the edge. Tim, one of the newer members of the group, was sitting in the middle of the bridge, on the edge. Suddenly he started screaming that something had grabbed his leg. We believed him, as he actually began to slip off the bridge. Steve and I grabbed him and yanked him up onto his feet.

Everyone jumped up and rushed to the center of the bridge. Looking under the bridge with our flashlights, we couldn't see anything.

Then we heard that same screaming coming from the brush again.

When our flashlights zeroed in on the area where the noise came from, there appeared two red glowing objects that looked like eyes. We were not really sure, until they blinked at us. Then we knew we were in deep trouble, and we were still over a mile away from camp.

Turning "chicken," we, including our adult leaders, all huddled together for "protection." We had no idea what to do against the supernatural, so we just did next what came natural to us. En masse, we bolted for camp. Whatever was doing the yowling, it just seemed to stay right with us. Sometimes it would be in front, sometimes behind us. The pitch would change like it was calling out to someone or something. Every once in a while we would see those eyes, reflecting the glow of flashlight beams, out in the darkness. After about another fifteen minutes the yowling and the eyes seemed to fall behind us.

Woody, one of our adult leaders, being a brave and wonderful soul, took up a rearguard position. He was nicknamed "Reverend Joe" because he was studying to be a priest. At that time he was twenty-two years old, six foot three inches tall, and weighed about two hundred twenty-five pounds. He wore his blond hair at shoulder length. He carried a quarterstaff as a walking stick whenever he was in the woods. This being the closest thing to a weapon any of us had, we didn't argue with him when he dropped behind to "defend" us.

The terrain became familiar again and we could tell we were less than a mile from camp. We were within sight of the main road again, when a horrible, blood-curdling scream came from behind us. The second we heard it, we knew it was Woody in trouble. Praying that our flashlights wouldn't confirm what our ears told us, we shined them behind us. Woody was nowhere to be seen.

We couldn't abandon him. Our concern for him was stronger than our fear. But the adults wouldn't let us go. So Paul, David, and Pop headed back after him, while the rest of us high-tailed it to camp, and went for help. About this same time we heard a very loud "crack" from the direction where Woody had last been seen. We feared the worst. Even though we were almost back to camp, we could still clearly hear the screams and howling, with the voices of the three grown men being added to the din. We were some scared kids, who didn't know whether to go back to them or on to camp.

Obviously they'd found Woody. They solved our dilemma as they dragged him back to camp with his clothes all badly torn and bloodied. All the hair, even the skin from the top of his head, was missing. He looked like he'd been scalped.

David, Paul, and Pop were white as sheets and badly scratched up. Paul was carrying what looked like a bloody Indian war club in his hand. Gasping for breath, he told us that Walks-in-Wind had tried to take Woody that night, but they were able to rescue him in the nick of time. They wouldn't let any of us get a closer look at Woody.

Down the road toward the swamp, we heard that hellish howling again. All of a sudden there was a bright flash of light followed by a loud noise. It sounded like an explosion, could have been thunder, or possibly the closing of the gate to another world. Then, again came that unearthly silence. We noticed the breeze had started up again.

With Paul accompanying him, Pop drove Woody to Memphis, presumably so Woody could get medical treatment. David watched over the rest of us, as we sat around the campfire talking about what had just happened and drawing our own conclusions. We felt like the adventure was over, at least for the night. But no one wanted to go to sleep. So we roasted marshmallows and hot dogs, and talked. A few finally gave up and went to bed. The rest of us stayed up and dozed by the fire, under the watchful eyes of the adults. The only sounds we heard the rest of the night were the normal night noises of the forest.

When morning came, it seemed like we had been sitting there forever. We went ahead and fixed breakfast, even though there wasn't much coffee left. Pop returned about eight o'clock from the hospital. He told us Woody should be fine in a few days. Except for the loss of his scalp, he hadn't suffered any other permanent injuries. Apart from the trauma, he should recover.

In the safety of daylight, a few of us decided to go check out the site of the previous night's happenings. Not having seen Woody up close after the incident, some of us suspected that the adults had just pulled off a major hoax and done a first-class job of scaring us the night before. Six of us went back to where Woody supposedly got hurt.

We looked around really well and found a broken staff lying on the ground. It had carvings on it and looked ancient. The surrounding area was pretty torn up, like there had been a serious struggle there. We even found a couple of footprints that looked like they had been made by moccasins.

Doubts began to arise as to our earlier conclusion about the hoax. Maybe something really had happened the previous night.

Since then, nobody will talk about it. I can't get Pop to level with me, either. Except he told me that Woody had to be sent off to a mental hospital. Seems he had a complete nervous breakdown and still hasn't recovered.

Since then, we all quit the Scouts and I didn't get interested again until my own sons joined. I lost touch with the other guys. So I can't find out from them any more about what went on that night. David, who seemed such a good friend to my father, doesn't come around. Pop is running true to form and not talking, either. He claims he's forgotten the details, but I think that he's just not talking. I won't bring it up to him again because, when I have before, the look on his face and the glint in his eyes tell me *there is something else.*

To this day, there are still reports of strange happenings— mysterious deaths and disappearances—in that part of Shelby Forest. Nobody seems to know what causes them. I don't have the answer, either.

If you're up that way, camping during a full moon, stay away from the swamp.

My House
By Allan Gilbreath

Brian could not believe his eyes. His new house was a wreck. Not the usual mess of moving, someone had trashed the place. Walking inside, he looked over the shredded paper, dumped boxes and broken glass. He sadly shook his head and walked back out to his car. He searched through more boxes until he found his cellular phone.

"Hello. I'd like to report a break in. I'm just moving in. I stayed at a motel last night. When I got here this morning, the place was a disaster." Brian walked back into the house as he talked. He walked through, shoving boxes with his foot as he described the damage. "No. It doesn't look like anything's missing. It looks like someone just dumped everything."

He finished giving his information to the police dispatcher as he walked up the stairs. He carefully stepped around the clothes strewn down the stairs. He said, "Thank you, and goodbye," as he reached the top landing. He put the phone in his pocket as he passed more overturned boxes. Stopping to look back at the stairs, he remembered clearly that he had unlocked the door this morning.

Brian stopped when he saw the attic stairs were half down. He wiped his mouth nervously. He stood very still, listening for any noises. There was nothing except his own heart's beating. Quietly, he crept over to the stairs and listened again. Again he heard nothing. He reached up, gripped the dusty steps and pulled. The loud groan of rusty springs made him jump in spite of himself. Brian exhaled loudly and rubbed the back of his neck to relieve the sudden tension.

Having decided, Brian began to climb the creaking steps, up into the darkness of the attic. Gingerly he raised his head above the floor level and looked around. The first thing he noticed was the heat. The attic was very warm and humid. As his eyes adjusted to the gloom he saw the locked trunks were untouched, but boxes of Christmas decorations were scattered all over the place. The bulbs were broken, all of the cords were tangled. The little bits of broken glass glinted in the low light. A tingling feeling, as though he were being watched, crept down Brian's neck. He looked behind, but couldn't see anyone. He next looked up toward the roof. There was no one else here.

The feeling of being watched grew. A nervous sweat, caused by more than the heat and humidity, began to break out on his forehead. He forced himself to take one more step. Sweat was beading up on his forehead and beginning to roll down his face.

"Hello. Anyone up here?" Brian's voice was dry and weak. There was no answer. Nothing moved. The hair on the back of his neck began to stand. If there was someone up in the attic, in that heat, Brian decided to leave them there. As Brian climbed down the steps, he did not feel welcome in his new home. He went downstairs and then outside to wait for the police. He needed to see sunshine. The gloom of the attic was still in his mind.

He felt relieved to see the police car coming down the street. The massive oaks that lined the way swayed gently in the warm morning air. Brian stood up as the car came to a stop. A large well-groomed man in a sharp blue uniform got out with a metal clipboard.

"Sir, did you report a break in?" He asked in a friendly, but businesslike tone.

"Ah, yes I did." Brian answered as the officer started walking toward the door. "I am just moving in so I stayed at a motel last night. When I unlocked the door this morning, this is what I found." Brian opened the door and stepped back to let the officer enter first. The officer walked around for a moment, then asked, "Do you have an attic?"

"Yes, just up the stairs." Brain motioned to the stairs as he nodded. "Careful, there are clothes all over them."

"Have you noticed anything missing?" The officer asked over his shoulder as he walked up the stairs.

"No, the place is just a total mess as far as I can tell."

"Were there any windows broken or damage to any of the doors?" He asked from the top landing.

"Not that I could tell." Brian answered from the stairs. He followed the officer to the attic. "The stairs were half down when I got here."

The officer seemed to be looking for something on the steps. Brian had a guilty feeling he should not have touched the attic stairs. Then the officer smiled and turned to Brian.

"Sir, you're not from Memphis, are you?"

"No, I just transferred here from Kansas with the hub. Why?" Brian was very curious now.

"Well, sir, I think I know who your prowler was. You have raccoons living in your house." He smiled as he talked.

"Raccoons? Are you serious?" Brian looked around at the mess in disbelief.

"Look, here, do you see this print?" He asked pointing to a spot in the dust on the attic steps. Brian leaned in and saw a small hand print with sharp fingernails. Brian nodded his recognition. "Was this house empty for a while before you bought it?"

"Yes, for about a year and a half." Brian answered still looking at the print. "You mean raccoons could do all this in a night?"

"Yes sir and then some." The officer turned to face Brian. "This is Midtown and the animal control people tell us that there may be more raccoons here than there are people."

"Well, how can I get rid of them? I can't have them wrecking my house every night." Brian looked around at the damage and was beginning to worry. This was serious.

"You can call an exterminator or you can get them out yourself. Most folks put a bright light on in the attic. 'Coons don't like light. I put a radio on a loud station and mothballs in my attic when one moved in a couple of years ago at my house. He left the next day. I just patched up the hole he made to get in." The officer was closing his clipboard and putting the pen back into his pocket as he talked. Brian was listening intently to the instructions.

"That will work?" Brian asked hopefully.

"It should. If not, you can always call an exterminator." The officer began walking toward the stairs. "Just look around the edge of your roof for any holes or loose boards. After they move on, close it up so they can't get back in."

Brian followed the officer down the stairs and out the front door. "Thanks for coming by. I guess I need to go to the store today." Brian extended his hand. The officer shook it firmly.

"If you have any more trouble just give me a call at the station." He handed his card to Brian. "Ask for Officer Dixon. You have a good day."

"Yeah, thanks."

Officer Dixon got into his car and started talking on the radio. Brian turned and went back inside. It was going to be a long day.

Brian finally took a break about lunch time, after he had cleared away most of the mess downstairs. The rest he had shoved back into the boxes. He was hungry and a little cross. The second moving truck had not shown up yet. It had the rest of his furniture, including his bed. Brian looked out the window at the street. There was still no truck.

He muttered, "I know you guys will show up as soon as I leave."

Brian locked the door from outside and pulled on it just to make sure it was secure. He walked around the house looking at the roof's edge. He saw a couple of places that could be loose. He sighed and shook his head. He could see the limb of a large tree extending over the edge of his roof. "So, that's how you guys come and go. Well, I'm going to fix that." He challenged the raccoons as though they were listening.

The movers were sitting in front of the house when he got back from the hardware store. He unlocked the door for them. Brian then sat on the hood of his car to eat his sandwich. He watched as they moved in his book shelves, more boxes and finally his bed. The moving team worked quickly. Within thirty minutes the rest of Brian's stuff was in the house. Brian sat for a few extra minutes of sunshine, then went back inside.

He was hot and tired when he realized that the shadows were getting long outside. Brian looked around downstairs. Most of the kitchen was in place. The furniture was where he wanted it. He had even put most of the books on the shelves. Brian looked at the mound of boxes and packing in the front room—trash to be thrown out tomorrow. He looked at the bag from the hardware store and decided it was time. He picked up the bag and went up the stairs. He had found his portable radio earlier and put it at the top of the landing. He took the extension cord out of the bag and plugged it in. He unwound it as he climbed up the attic stairs. The mess from last night was still there. He would clean this mess up after *they* were gone. He set the radio down to one side and the bag to the other. The heat was already causing him to sweat. It felt like a sauna in the attic. Brian stood up and unscrewed the old bulb from the socket. He put in a 150-watt spot light. The attic lit up brightly.

"This ought to brighten things up." He plugged in the radio, set it to an alternative rock station and turned up the volume. As the sound blared out into the attic, he pulled two bags of mothballs out and opened them. He picked up a loose box top and poured them into it. The smell hit him. "Whew. I think I'm going to leave. Good night, wherever you are."

Brian looked around and did not see anything moving. The feeling of being watched was making the hair on the back of his neck stand for the second time today. He shrugged his shoulders and went back down the steps with the bag. He closed the steps and pulled a screwdriver and a latch kit out of the bag. With a grim smirk on his face, he installed the latch on the bottom of the steps and locked it. Pleased with the results, Brian turned and went downstairs. One quick check around the first floor and Brian decided it was time for a shower and dinner at the motel. He locked the door and pulled on it. Brian took a few steps out from the house and looked back. He could hear the radio softly in the distance. On an impulse, he walked around to the side where he suspected the loose boards were. He thought he saw something move. It was just a brief flash of white. As he stared, a chill ran down his back. He felt as though he were being watched. Two reddish pink spots that were animal eyes caught his attention. For a brief moment they glared malevolently at him from a space between two boards; then they were gone. All of the hair on the back of Brian's neck was standing again. He shivered involuntarily. It was getting late, Brian decided. He turned and walked away.

As he pulled up to the house, he saw three raccoons disappearing down the storm drain in front of his house. They were huge, not like his childhood memories of small, loveable fuzzy animals with bushy tails and dark masks on their faces. These things were as big as mid-sized dogs. Brian got out of his car and walked over to the drain. As he looked in, he said, "And stay out, you hairy little freeloaders. This house is mine now. Go tear up somebody else's place."

He stood up and walked to the door. He knew something was wrong as he touched the door knob. That same cold chill ran down his back. He shivered as he unlocked the door.

"Oh my God!" he gasped as he looked around. Everything had been thrown around. The tables, the chairs, the book cases and their contents now lay on the floor.

"You little bastards. You little hairy bastards!" He repeated himself with even more anger as he looked around. A noise at the top of the stairs caught his attention and made him inhale deeply. Brian stormed to the foot of the stairs, kicking a path as he went. He grabbed the railing and stopped. A wave of hot, moist air hit him. At the top of the stairs those eyes appeared again. They were reddish pink and glowing with hatred in the dim light. Brian could feel the sweat start to roll. His eyes were locked upon the glowing points of maliciousness. He was not sure he could blink, not sure he could even move. The glowing points went out and Brian could hear something large walking off into the upstairs. Brian looked down at his bare hands as they shook, and he took a step backwards.

Almost in a panic, Brian feverishly looked through his car for a phone book. He ripped it open to exterminators. An ad about animal and pest control caught his eye. The woman on the other end of the phone agreed he had a raccoon problem. She said she had someone in the area who would be by shortly. Brian decided to wait in the car.

About an hour passed before Brian saw a pickup truck with a pest control logo on it pull alongside. Brian got out of his car as the pickup pulled into the driveway.

"I understand you got a raccoon problem. Hi. My name is Dale," the young man said as he got out of the truck.

"Ah, you might say that. They keep trashing the place at night. Nice to meet you. I'm Brian." They shook hands.

"Well, let me take a look and see what we got here." Dale tested a heavy flashlight and picked up a large wire live trap out of the back of the truck. "Let me guess, they're in your attic."

Brian nodded in agreement. "Just up the stairs and then there's another set to the attic."

Brian led the way to the door and opened it for Dale. They walked in and surveyed the mess. "This is the second time in a row that this has happened." Brian said as he picked up a chair set it upright.

"Yes sir, they will sure do a job on a place." Dale agreed, then continued, "I'm going to set the trap."

"You go right ahead." Brian watched Dale as he took the steps. He could not get those eyes out of his head. He could hear Dale walking around upstairs. Brian checked to make sure the air conditioner was on while he waited. He heard Dale coming back down the stairs. Dale was pale and sweating.

Dale looked nervous as he said, "I set the trap up there. Just give us a call if you—if we—catch anything. Here's my card with the number on it." Dale seemed in a hurry to get outside. "I have a few more stops in this area tomorrow. I'll check back with you by afternoon if I don't hear from you sooner."

Brian had to follow him outside to say, "Ok." Dale already had the truck started and was backing out. Dale waved and pulled away. Brian shook his head and walked back inside.

Brian stopped in the doorway. He could hear the sound of something being dragged across the wooden floor upstairs. When something came crashing down the stairs, Brian thought his heart would stop. At the foot of the stairs was the animal trap. Brian scratched his head nervously, apprehensively. He walked over to the chair and sat down, staring at the trap. What in hell was this thing?

The longer he sat there, the madder he got. This was too much. No dumb animal was going to run him out of his new house. He remembered passing a library on Peabody on his way to the house. He would start there. He needed knowledge—much more than his bare hands—to evict this thing.

The moment he walked into the sunshine he felt better. The short drive helped him decide. That animal was going to go today. Walking through the library, Brian found the help desk in the center of the first floor.

"Ah, excuse me." ventured Brian.

"Yes, what can I do for you?" an attractive middle-aged woman turned to face him.

"Well, this may be a little strange, but I need some advice on how to get a raccoon out of my house. I have already done the light, radio and mothball thing." Brian explained. He looked at her with hopeful eyes.

"Let me see if someone here can help you." She answered, then looked around the room.

The young man at the end of the counter leaned over and said, "I can probably help you."

"I hope so. Those things are about to tear my house apart." Brian said turning to the young man.

"I have to get them out of my granny's attic every year. Every so often, you get a tough one that won't leave," he explained. "They are the ones you got to persuade to move on."

Brian liked the way the man said "persuade." After the beating his house had taken the last two days, he was ready to persuade something the hard way.

I have a pair of welder's elk hide gloves. The long ones." The young man was pointing to his bicep as he talked. "My granny doesn't want me to hurt them, so I reach down the wall, grab them and stick them in a carry box. Once I have them all, I take them outside and turn them loose. Then I patch up the hole."

"A carry box? What's that? Something like you put your dog in?" Brian asked.

"Yeah, you can get one at any of the big pet stores around here. There's one on Madison." The young man added, "Be careful. They can bite pretty bad. Just get a good grip and don't let him spin around on you."

"Thank you. I saw those gloves at the hardware store yesterday. That helps a lot." Brian shook his hand. Then he asked, "Can these things have pink or red eyes?"

The woman behind the counter who had been listening said, "Yes, sir, they can. We have a small population of albinos here in Midtown. They are white with pink eyes."

The young man nodded in agreement, then said, "And they're real mean. Good luck."

"Thank you both." Brian said as he got ready to leave. "You both have been very helpful." Brian was beginning to like the soft southern accent and friendly atmosphere of this town.

On the way to the door, a young woman with long, dark stringy hair walked up to him. "There is something more you should know."

Brian stopped and looked at her. "Yes?"

"The Chickasaw and Choctaw have legends about spirits in animal form that can take over man's places. Only the very brave can hope to win over one of them. Here, take this. It may help you." She handed him a crystal of some kind on a leather thong. She turned and walked away into the book stacks.

"Thanks," Brian said as she walked away. "...I think," he muttered to himself as he put the crystal in his pocket and walked to the door. There was obviously more to this town than met the eye.

The afternoon sun shone in the windows as Brian grimly stood in his living room. A couple of new bags were thrown on top of the mess from last night. He began checking himself to make sure he was ready. He retied his athletic shoes and pulled up his socks. Over his blue jeans were white knee pads. After adjusting the matching elbow pads, he put on an old leather jacket. Next, he placed a catcher's mask over his face. He pulled hard on the thin straps. He picked up the long leather gloves, broke the plastic tie that held them together, and pulled them on with grim determination. Brian took a deep breath as he looked at the stairs. He picked up the animal carrier in one hand and a baseball bat in the other. He just felt better carrying the bat.

Brian listened intently at the foot of the stairs. The red eyes were not there this time. He could not hear anything. Slowly, he stepped over the useless trap and started up. A line of sweat trickled down his face. His heart pounded with each step. He reached the landing and peered around. The upstairs was even more torn up than the last time.

"Damn." Brian said softly as he surveyed the damage. He shook his head from side to side. Brian started to feel watched. The hairs on the back of his neck stood up. He shivered in spite of the warmth of the coat and the hot, humid air. Almost without thought, he set down the carrier and leaned the bat against it. With a gloved hand he reached into his pocket and pulled out the crystal the young woman had given him. He slipped the leather thong over his head and dropped the crystal inside his shirt.

He jumped hard, as a Christmas bulb hit the hardwood floor and exploded. "All right, enough is enough, you hairball," Brian growled as he tried to calm himself. He gripped the bat hard and picked up the carrier. He could now hear something moving in the attic. Brian stopped. The radio was not blasting. He could hear it playing, but it was not on the station he had left it on and the volume had been turned down. Brian started to lose his nerve. Perhaps he should call the exterminator again and let them deal with this. He stood there for a moment longer as he listened to it romping back and forth in the attic. It seemed to be mocking him, daring him to come up.

Brian gritted his teeth together and gripped the bat hard. He was getting angry now. Another bulb crashed to the ground. "That's it!" Brian shouted. He walked over to the attic steps that were down, in spite of the latch he had installed yesterday. Brian threw the carrier up into the attic and slammed the bat into the springs on the steps. The ring of metal springs was tremendous. Brian heard the creature jump and cry out in surprise. Brian smiled at the sound. Revenge! He quickly started up the stairs. Just as his head cleared the floor, he was pelted with mothballs. The mask deflected most of the pieces, but they still hurt. Brian leapt up the last couple of steps and turned in the attic. He looked for the raccoon. He held the bat in front of him like a samurai sword. His heart was pounding. Sweat rolled down both sides of his face. The heat was oppressive.

A sound. Brian spun around and batted a wad of tangled cords that had been thrown at him. Brian was breathing heavily now.

"Yah!" Brian shouted. "Go on, get outta here!"

Brian saw a flash of movement. He could hear his own heart beat. He stepped forward, careful to avoid the attic steps. His knees felt shaky, but his anger blazed. There, in the far corner, the glowing eyes appeared. Brian swallowed hard and told himself, "It is just an albino raccoon, they have pink eyes." He lunged forward and yelled, "Yah!" again. The eyes blazed out in dark red light. A box flew into the air toward Brian.

"Oh, Hell!" he shouted, as he punched the box to the floor. It was too late. He saw the animal leap for his face. Brian fell backward, throwing his arms up, swinging wildly with the bat. He missed, and the animal slammed into his chest as he fell toward the floor. All he could see were the flaming eyes and flashing white teeth. Brian tried to roll, but it held him down. The long canine teeth locked on to the face mask. The horrible growling sound it made filled his ears. He dropped the bat and grabbed with both gloved hands for its throat. He could feel the claws through the jacket. His grip on it tightened and he squeezed even harder. He could feel the hot fetid breath of the beast on his face, as it snarled and kept trying to bite him. Its feet were everywhere. He could feel one slide down the side of his neck, until... it touched the crystal! Shockwaves ensued. A blinding flash of blue light burst forth with a deafening thunderclap.

The creature immediately released its grip. Brian seized the opportunity and hurled it out onto the middle of the floor. It lay there stunned. Brian got to his feet and, with a gloved hand, fished the crystal out of his shirt. Brian saw the creature get to its feet, shaking its head. He picked up his bat and stared. The beast was twice the size of the raccoons he'd seen that morning. It had thick white fur and blazing red eyes. They locked eyes. Brian could feel the malevolent intelligence of its gaze. Brian refused to be cowed. It growled low in its throat.

"You didn't like that did you?" Brian asked, feeling braver. "Not at all." It stood up on its hind legs like a human and showed its wicked teeth, as if in direct answer. "Maybe you are one of those spirit things. It doesn't matter." Brian shook his head to show it didn't. "You're leaving anyway. This is my house now."

It lunged for his legs, but Brian got the bat in front of its face to block it. They circled each other slowly, each staying just out of range of the other. Brian stared hard into its eyes as it moved. It glared back. Brian could feel it trying to intimidate him. But his anger was much stronger than his fear. It moved suddenly to the right and Brian swung at it. It leapt into the air and landed on the bat, catching it with its paws. The impact and the additional weight wrenched the bat from his hands. Brian had no time to recover. The beast jumped into his face. Reeling under the attack, Brian grabbed its back and pulled with all his might, screaming as it snarled back. As he pulled its head away from his own, they locked eyes again.

"Bite this." Brian said coldly as he reversed and pulled the beast to his chest, making it connect with the crystal again. The resulting shockwave knocked him down. He fell back over the trunks. He struggled to his feet as fast as he could. The great white raccoon lay there, dazed. He ran forward and kicked it as hard as he could, like a football that he was punting for a field goal. It bounced off the ceiling and crashed to the floor. The creature gave out an almost human moan. Brian grabbed it by the hind legs and spun it around.

"I told you this is my house and I want you out, NOW!" Brian let go and flung it into the gable. The thin wood shattered and the beast passed through it clear to the outside. There was a thunderclap, then quiet. Brian staggered over and looked out the hole and down. On the ground he saw nothing but pieces of his gable, no animal body, living or dead. Brian walked back over to the trunk and sat down heavily. The radio was still playing. Brian leaned back and said,

"Now this IS my house."

Swan Song
By Charlee Jacob

"Kiss him goodbye," Mother ordered Cygne. She lifted the fragile eight-year-old darling into her black-clad arms and onto a chair to reach the coffin. Quicksilver ringlets rolled across her daughter's shoulders, resembling Mississippi river water at dawn.

Many youngsters hated the cliche spitswap that parents insisted be done with passed-on grandstiffs. But Cygne knew she wasn't really related to the dead rock and roller. Daddy had just worked at Graceland, that was all. She'd only met the great man once and that was when Mr. Presley had just arrived in the driveway, stepping from his favorite Cadillac. He'd given her and her sister candy bars. But Ruah couldn't eat hers because she was diabetic.

Cygne gave Elvis a gratuitous bunt, tasting wax. She lingered, bending forward like a child at a summer water fountain, pressing down with a sponge's own momentum. Her parents and little sister waited, puzzled.

But the child took no notice of her family standing behind her. Little Cygne's spirit had suddenly plunged inside the frozen tunnel of the corpse. The journey was crowbait resurgent. There was a dark slowness—rhythmic on an atomic level—unseen by mourners speckled around the draped room. Way down within, cells turning into shadow country were tiny recollections.

There were images of orgiastic fever, shocking as porno and snuff flicks which Cygne wasn't supposed to know anything about at her age but which, of course, she did. It was nothing that would rise often to the surface of a person's life. Just the suffering, the anger and the awkward unbalanced fears that people clutched within themselves. What they never wanted anyone else to see in them.

What she found were the betrayals, which, under the skin carved a man to the bone, and caused him to grasp at weapons that with a single squeeze might make the bearer seem finally empowered. Acts of revenge, contemplated in pain's lowest depths but never acted upon. The shudder at one's own disintegrating image in a mirror.

A thread of music bubbled in a circulatory system, which once ran with blood and now was stagnant with formaldehyde.

Love me tender, love me sweet... never let me go...

And Cygne had a brief moment when she wondered if she'd fallen asleep in the family Olds on the way to the funeral. She often fell asleep in the car rather than listen to her parents bickering and sniping at each other. She'd nod in the back seat and drift, next to that dull lump Ruah.

On those occasions, Cygne never had anything whatever to say to her sister. Not ever, really. She didn't share the obscene little games she played with her own collection of dolls. Nor did she tell Ruah her weird dreams, about gargoyles coming to life on the roof of downtown Memphis's library and carrying her away in their knobby laps. The brat would only have told on her.

Cygne's small rosebud mouth was yet pressed to those of the star's. She knew she wasn't merely dreaming this. Because she'd had a similar experience when her grandmother died. She'd been made to kiss the corpse then, too. And had slipped down through the vortex of forced embrace, into the body—or its spirit—or some sickly softening mesh of both. There had been a rapacious poetry inside the boxed cadaver that none ever suspected of the old bat.

Now Cygne heard the song reverberating in the echo chamber of bones. She understood somehow that a very haunted Elvis was singing to a parade of dead within him: twin, mother, friends, marriage. Their hollow eyes and shadowy backs—*no backs*. It was impossible to say goodbye to memories that couldn't turn their backs on you to depart.

Love me tender...

Its very desperation made her tingle all over. She felt like a nasty little spy, putting his secrets into a child-sized purse to keep forever.

"Enough," Mother commanded brusquely, miffed at the augenblick of a minute's passing. "It's supposed to be just a peck."

Cygne wiped her mouth, grinning, explaining lamely, "Sorry. I fell in."

Father gasped in his charcoal pin-stripe, hoping that none of the family had heard. "That's very inappropriate, young lady."

Cygne felt the thick smear of mortuary lipstick on her mouth. She stared at her palm where she'd rubbed it against her lips. Mother growled and began wiping it off with a handkerchief.

"Necrosis fucks," Cygne replied solemnly, like uttering a sacrilegious yet cogently defensible prophecy.

Because she'd had a tasty vision. And its weight—added to that from Grandmother's funeral—was sensuously carnal beyond her tender age. Mother slapped Cygne's face. "Stop smiling like that. It's disgusting. What's the matter with you?"

Then the woman gave her child a look that warned her not to answer.

Daddy placed Cygne's sister on the chair for the icy adieu. Ruah, two years younger, had veins replete with crow's feet. The ends of her tiny pink fingers were ragged with the punctures that were the diabetic's composure. Her face was whiter than sugar as she glanced back at Cygne nervously.

"Go on, dear," Mother told her younger daughter. "Quickly and get it over with."

She bent and kissed with trepidation. She lingered for a split second until Cygne became jealous that perhaps Ruah was enjoying the same mysterious trip she had. But Ruah only looked up with tears on her pinched face.

* * *

And so it went from the early lichhouse rites.

Cygne discovered power.

The Hindu were correct that cremation was necessary to release the soul, the atman freed only as the skull burst in the flames. These meager Christian inhumations left worlds within... septic pools a death freak could dive into with but a kiss. Finding delicious tomb-fodder.

Inside a reasonably fresh corpse was heaven spread for all to see. It was rather like an open casket funeral, eyelids sewn neatly shut across stars.

Visitations of the dissolve, Cygne ate the memories, which the melting atoms fizzed out. Secrets buried all the way to the electrons and meant to die with the owner, a tapioca of pain and worms, dirty, juicy, tidbits of bondage, the thousand ways innocence could be lost at midnight. Cygne tasted them all, shoving the nonsense of morality to the edge of the plate.

She fondled the pathological anatomy, mephitic with alchemy, death-freak invasive groping the vestiges and the continuums of their despair. Her soul-tongue licked deftly at the necrotic humiliations of the unwary dead as if it were fat white icing on a wedding cake. All the while she delicately dodged the causes of damage: the typhus and biliary calculus, syphilis and cancers and swarming armies of e-coli. Finding the bare kernel of memory like the shaved head of a penitent cowering in a corner because he fears the priests will beat a confession out of him.

The stink was primordial, viscera in the slowly churning swamp. A kiss on cold lips at someone's—anyone's—funeral, and she descended like a gator, spirit mouth steaming, the path of Cygne's consumption through the levels of lifeless contours and spindles of gak traceless.

' And there were always people dying, that was the beauty of it! It was so easy to slip from classes and hop a bus to wherever she read in the papers a viewing or a service would next be held. Arrogant in the presence of condolence wreaths, she danced down the spiral staircases of veins and did the bossa nova across terraces of gleaming moonlight ribcages. She had a midnight supper on the spleen's balcony, skinnydipping in the discharge abandoned in the rectum. Dust was a suffocating sponge pressed against the nose and mouth.

"There goes the child of death," Cygne would hear some preacher say. "Third time I've seen her this month."

"Isn't she a pretty little thing?" a grieving widow might reply, somehow comforted by the sight of the exquisite youngster with gold-white curls appearing like a cherub from Elysian Fields to honor the beloved dead.

An organist would be playing a music Cygne'd always thought to be icky and old-fashioned. But how quickly the child changed her mind about that. Wasn't it lovely and deep, even if jaded in its ornateness? She could close her eyes and simply hear Elvis crooning the hymnal words, the resonant voice making the gospel sensual, comprised of angels naked on black velvet beds.

And she'd hear every sacred word of it in her head as:

Love me tender, love me sweet, never let me go...

Every death had a history. Even the corpses of catatonics had it when they died, brought out of the mental asylums by their long-suffering families to be buried like any other normal corpse needing Christian rites. Even those who lingered in comas for I.V. years had black pearls and ruby nuts of dreams.

Cygne always paused to look behind her after the kiss and the fall into corruption. Her face would move with annoyance, for there was Ruah tagging along at every wake. The little sister never came up to speak to Cygne, to ask if she even knew this cadaver. The two never spoke to one another. If Cygne could truant herself from school easily, so could Ruah. She had only to find the newspaper and see what Cygne had drawn a red circle around to know where she was going.

If Cygne sneaked from the house to go to some cathedral viewing, her sister was sure to sleuth it out. She'd sit in the back pew or at the end of the mourner's line, after—always after.

If the minister and the mourners saw Cygne and called her *child of death*, what did they call Ruah?

"And there's death's shadow," they would say, almost whimsically.

As if the pair of them were a sacred team, even when the girls were no longer small. Even when high school came and the child of death and death's shadow still attended most every funeral held in Memphis—and that was a great many. Occasionally they even appeared at chapels in nearby towns like Raleigh and Oakville. A reporter had once taken Cygne's picture, standing under a willow tree outside a church in Germantown. But the leaves had drifted across her face. Father, seeing the picture in the paper, didn't recognize her.

The fact that their parents never caught on was no surprise, for there was much that children did that their folks never found out. And if the lovely one with the golden hair felt the call to bless the dead with a sweet kiss, then perhaps she was a saint.

Cygne got used to seeing Ruah behind her. She resented it at first but resigned herself to the annoying tag-along. Well, it had been nearly ten years now that this had been going on. They both had breasts and periods by then. Cygne had no idea what her sister got out of the experience. Obviously she wasn't a spy because she never ran back to snitch to the folks. And Ruah didn't glow like she'd just enjoyed a really good backseat screw—which Cygne was sure she'd never done. The plain old mop never dated. Nor did Ruah rush to the ladies room to masturbate the rush off to a more physical climax. Something which—since she'd had her first bleeding—Cygne could hardly wait to do, after pulling back from the coffin before the altar.

The little fool only followed Cygne up—death's shadow. Kissing where Cygne had kissed. Weeping and staggering away.

Soon Cygne's face was known at all the churches and chapels in Shelby County: the visage of every beautiful, clear blue-eyed madonna of the candlelit path. She bent to kiss with red lips. Then fell to experience the unraveling of the libidinous vermin of repressed crimes trapped in the muscles, the dreams of libertines harnessed to good Baptists—unreleased, turgid with the slowly crumbling anxiety of unrequited loves as she lowered her spiritual self down to straddle them.

And the screams of angel outrage, the mutual satisfactory violence of bodies in putrid retrograde which was nature's sin of mutilation on a biological level, of pleasurable nightmares discovered before they could slip away to non-existence. It was one final revel lubricated with corruption. Mortuary date rape, when seventh heaven virgins and stalwart heroes alike gave up their intimate mysteries with a shudder of cells.

The meat rot dance was an addiction. It was bondage within chains of DNA and whips of time drunk on body beer. It was the cool leather of stiffening skin, sadistic with a ghost unable to fight, helpless in the reaper slide. It was as naked as it got.

Cygne mused at this power of internal voyeurism. The little universes of thoughts and personal cavities were once the sole property of the deceased. But no longer.

Cygne indulged, remembering her favorite times. She possessed the memory where Grandmother fantasized about sawing off Grandpa's hands because he used to use his fists on her head. Grandpa *did* have that awful accident with the tractor, losing both arms above the elbows. Afterward *he* was the one with bruises on his face.

And the girl down the block who was struck by a car in front of their high school, a fender dragging her for three blocks before the police chased the driver down. At her funeral, Cygne discovered that the girl used to wonder what it would be like to bite off a hound dog's dick. There was a shadow of some man faceless in the nights of her shallow memory, harsh and reeking of gin, groping and brutal in a way that none of the teachers or kids at school had ever known of.

There had been Cygne's boyfriend from back when she attended Southwestern College. He'd died in the Desert War, to be ceremoniously delivered home in a body bag that clattered like tin cans. But he still had one serviceable lip she could kiss after surreptitiously unzipping the plastic. (Singing while suppressing her giggle, *"Love me tender, love me sweet..."*) Her soul diving down inside him, Cygne'd discovered the acts he'd performed with a bayonet in an alley reeking of sesame oil, whispering; growling passages from Omar Khayyam in a country where women's genitals were mutilated by custom anyway.

And then their own baby brother, overdosed on heroin with eyes like fried marbles, mockingbird tracks etched on his forearms. But these were needle scars of a different sort for he'd never been a diabetic like Ruah. His lips were as shriveled as desiccated peaches when

Cygne kissed him and fell.

Had he only wished for this dreadful scene she found inside—or had he really done the deed? The vision stank of gasoline. Cygne saw baby brother jerking off as a school bus burned, as little shrieks popped like the dime firecrackers used to light up a May Cotton Carnival. Who knew? No one. Except now, for Cygne.

More she took from them, singing, "... *You have made my life complete and I love you so...*" Well, not 'love,' no. But they surely did fill her up and that was a sort of completion, wasn't it? Cancer casualties were raging lovers—as long as she kept her distance from the tumors bursting like alien seed pod aphrodisiacs. Coronaries were broken hearts to be savored.

"Surrender," Cygne demanded of the suicides who found that not quite all their troubles were over.

"Rare," she murmured to the burn victim, inside with spirit hands pressed to cooked walls, listening to the hiss of steam in the fissures.

"Child of death" gave way to whispers of "our local angel." Strange how no appellation was assigned to Ruah as they grew older. Even homely children could be cute if about the business of such lofty doings as showing up at a funeral where no one knew them. But an unattractive woman was another matter. No one noticed Ruah at all, as if she had indeed become only a shadow of Cygne. Who saw a non-person?

"Our local angel." Cygne didn't let her derision for that show as she left a trail of wreckage within that no one could see. The autopsies were over. If anyone saw the body twitch, they assumed it was gas or some other natural but disgusting process of decomposition. The evidence was soon gone at any rate.

Cygne obtained a job at Graceland as a tour guide. There was a co-worker who broke her neck falling down the long elegant staircase. The woman had been morbidly afraid of fire, although she evidently ought to have been more frightened of heights.

At the service Cygne descended, chattering to the ghost inside, "They're going to cremate you, you know."

Cygne knew damned well it was a boldfaced (shockspirited?) lie, that the hole was already waiting. The gravedigger had finished it, then leaned upon his shovel, humming an old Elvis hit called "Return to Sender."

The woman's bones had screamed, her marrow flinching in conscious cotton candy.

Then Cygne returned to Graceland, gripping the gates, staring at the mansion Elvis had lived in. People claimed to see him everywhere. But on this particular day, thunder booming dark clouds like Civil War cannons, she knew right where he was. At least where the pieces of him were which she'd stolen.

Love me tender, love me sweet, never let me go ...

"Oh, I won't," Cygne whispered, leering. "Never."

Sister Ruah followed Cygne, two years younger so she always had to follow. She frowned, watching Cygne kiss, then placed her own cool mouth to that of the dead, sensing fully the lexicons of torment and filigrees of shame.

Who hadn't at one time or another had a disgusting thought, harbored a sick tingling, sucked on a hidden jewel of vengeance? Ruah couldn't return what was stolen, only see it bleed in the sluice of contrition, and then shed tears for them.

Cygne read the daily obits, traipsing to funerals dressed all in white like the owl goddess of death who sees everything. She bent without compunction to the font of indiscretions, reckless in her adventures within embalmed scandals, rejuvenated by their lapses of conscience. Who was to know? *Angel of death!*

Ruah wore black as she followed, witness to the theft. She saw the fecal sweets craved by the devout, the horse phalluses nuns pressed their backsides to in deep R.E.M. sleep, the flayed skins of tormenters and cheats flapping in wet nightmare winds in otherwise gentle ordinary people. She even saw the angst of her own parents, dead together because of a gas leak behind the old stove in their kitchen. In unrealized visions invented during petty quarrels, glowing cigarette tips branded each other. There were the memories of sulking dreams: of acid to be poured in Mother's bath, rattlesnakes which might unfold under the front seat of Father's Oldsmobile (which he cherished because Elvis gave it to him). The hoarded confessions came out as Father had imagined aiming a pistol curiously resembling a blue-barreled penis, Mother thought about bringing a breast-shaped stone down to crack his skull, their cries, their rage and love.

The thick veil across Ruah's face concealed the horror at being privy to these internal shrieks of violation. Was nothing sacred? Was nothing left to bare to God alone?

One day the landlord found Ruah on the floor of her living room. Diabetes had suffocated the blood vessels in her legs. She'd toppled over like cattail marshes where flooding eroded the banks of the Loosahatchie.

She was rushed to the hospital. The doctors discovered that the gangrene wasn't Ruah's only ill. Her insides were so badly consumed by cancer cells that it was too late for radiation or chemotherapy.

How had this woman withstood the torture for so long, they wondered. Why didn't she come to see them before? Was she really so busy, wrapped up in whatever made up the industry of her life that she'd started to ignore completely the state of her health?

Ruah, dead at forty, looked old beyond her years, sorrow leaving marks on her face as clear as a serrated blade. Yet, Cygne, two years older, looked marvelous in her white dress with the organdy sleeves and collar of stiff feathers. She carried pale lilies in her hands and bent to the give the goodbye kiss that was part whispered prayer, part heat-seeking missile. She nursed a wicked smile as she pursed her rosebud mouth.

And prepared for the feasting. Hadn't some of the ancients literally devoured their dead in rites of remembrance? Hadn't fans eaten up everything they could get on dead Elvis till the bloated specter of him was eternally theirs?

"Hey, you feed your hunger; I'll feed mine," she whispered just prior to her kiss connecting.

Such a disappointment!

No secreted passions or carnal contortions percolated in the saintly relic of her sister. There was no jealousy of Cygne's beauty and vitality. She found no revelation that Ruah had all along been eating up the dead's vituperative scraps as she trolled after Cygne to every viewing, wetting her lips...

Cygne fell, searching the interior waste. Some juicy pettiness must be there for her to savor. Perhaps Ruah had an affair with a broken glass dildo strapped to a Satanist. Maybe she'd dug up the remains of Confederate soldiers to rattle into her bed. There must be something. Everyone had something.

There was nothing.

"Boring bitch," Cygne's spirit muttered, preparing to depart this linen-and-rosewater spinster. "No wonder I never liked you."

Cygne felt a tug, a stricture of basalt will. And it wasn't the delicate silver cord of psychic myth, but one of black chain forged from tubercles.

There *was* one arcanum wish Ruah had disguised. She would not let Cygne go until she'd told it.

Cygne was plummeted past the stiff blue leaves of lungs. She sailed down through the burst pomegranate of the heart, the tarry anise coils of intestine. She was thrown through the harlequin consciousness, belled with the beckoning beyond and all the undeciphered data in Ruah's cooling thoughts of unrequited vengeance.

Each scream in Cygne's wake which had pierced Ruah's psyche for more than three decades was shrieked afresh. Every bitter drop down her cheek as the dead wept across Ruah's lips flowed again. The defiled spirits who took up residence in Ruah's bone-domed anima after she helped them flee their own—after being degraded by Cygne—emerged to confront the ghoul.

The swirl of them from a thousand mortuary perversions was like a swarm of hornets in the ossa hive. Spiders scuttled on webs strung between corners of maya. Cygne saw hairless old-faced infants, hanged by pierced yet underdeveloped genitals, wailing along the windswept corridor of the Geist. They had been unable to be reborn because she'd extorted their unspoken sins.

"Ruah, I'm your sister... You can't do this to me!" Cygne's spirit traveler cried, the shout of it dulled within the flesh.

Ruah did not answer but let those inside her do it. Mouths opened for that hungry kiss which must return to them their private stigmas. It would reunite them with their untold terrors, returning to them their right to silence these purloined disgraces...

Cygne screamed, choking on fistfuls of transgression as she beheld the prison of the bleeding polemic walls, the rupture in dying electron spin which swallowed her in vortex gluttony. The dead had waited: family and total strangers, dirt farmers and stars playing guitars. They showed the handfuls of vermin which she must waltz with forever in the slow fizz-down to taffy.

Cygne saw how it had been a trap.

And how long had Ruah been planning this? Since that very first time when she felt how Cygne had defiled their Grandmother?

Probably. And each successive experience had only firmed her resolve. No wonder Ruah had followed Cygne to every single funeral. Death's shadow.

Ruah's body shrank and sagged in turns like a wormy greatcoat. The sepulcher flesh had nothing new to give her sister but the realization that this was Cygne's last funeral, her mausoleum of gangrenous slop. It was like drowning in a shit bucket with the bits of meat that wouldn't digest, bound and struggling to breathe between decaying nerve endings that twitched no more.

In the church in her casket, Ruah's corpse visibly bloated. It swelled until the boundaries on her burial garment burst at the crepe seams. The mortuary rouge ran, and gas fluted caries notes which drove the other mourners back. They watched Cygne convulse, unable to separate herself from the final kiss. They gasped as Cygne struck her dead sister in an effort to disengage the buss. Our local angel squealed in fear of the swollen mastic tongue and teeth unwashed before death. The residue of Ruah's last meal had transmogrified into a carrion trench mouth. The sewage tasting of the catalog of screams was a guilty backwash, gluing Cygne in shreds to the slick swill of Ruah's gums as every spiritual glob of her was sucked back unto retribution.

Cygne's body stopped shuddering. It slipped to the chapel floor upon a mandala of bubo thresholds. Screams issued from the distended bruise of Ruah's lips, puckered like the cross and round as a wreath of amaranthus. Screams puffed out, hosannas belching from this battered embouchement. A vast cemetery of voices rattled to the air, an exchange of hostages, as all but Cygne sighed to freedom.

Ruah's was the last soul to exit, in a pearl cloud like aura captured on a *fin de siecle* photograph. She followed everyone she'd given sanctuary to in the shroud of years. All of them knowing who was the local angel and who was death's shadow. There was no shriek from Ruah, only a musical sigh, a right golden archangel note. It was given once to her sister who clung inside amid caramel strands of putrefaction. Ruah spoke in it the only words to ever pass between the siblings, "Now you're the true connoisseur of maggots and beyond, bound to an uninterrupted journey. No visit this time; you own this palace."

Cygne floundered, at once in every part of the festering body, from balljoint mosques to sinewy gables.

"Let me out!" her spirit cried in fury.

Then she heard a sound not unlike ancient battle drums. From every corner, marching in soldier ant tides, came the carcinomatous Ton-Tons Macoutes. Figurative malignant lips pursed for an army's rapine welcome, neoplasmic with tumescent intent. Each raw recruit had the gullet of a felon cell, rampant with sins of conquest and murder, and the desire to destroy what they could not possess with grace. Up from Ruah's diabetic legs blackened to stink with gangrene came puffing grinning shadows, carnivorous and ready to french with a black slough smack. They took Cygne down into the square millimeters of tissue squalor, as greening as swarms of bottle flies.

Cygne couldn't sense the other mourners gathering around her body on the floor. Or the gentleman she would have recognized as coming round to Graceland once a week faithfully to take the tour. He took up her hand and tried to find a pulse. What defined her as Cygne was inside Ruah, assailed by crimes of the stubborn sore. They were delirious with darkness, horny within the sucking wound. Even disease had a life, holding an evil sentience which desired in millionfold particles.

Each leaned for Cygne's soul, voracious and multiplying the split of her into the millionfold shrieker, beckoning with legions of lesion orifices. They seemed to sing to her, mocking,

"Love me tender, love me sweet, never let me go ..."

Killing Softly
By Angela Wolfe

"Would you like another, ma'am?" The bartender asked, wiping off the ring of condensation from where he had just picked up the remains of her last drink. She shook her head, and he faded away, off to another soul seated along the long oak bar. Nancy stood up, straightened out her stiffened spine and put on her coat. She pushed her way out of the bar into the dreary, rainy night.

She was impressed that she could still walk reasonably well. Nancy had hit every bar on her way to Beale Street, and most of the ones along that tourist trail too. The gaudy bright neon signs hurt her eyes, and she eagerly sought darkness for her solace. An alley brought the opportunity and she seized it, not caring where it led.

Nancy's mind was still caught in the same eddy of thoughts that had sent her on this fool's errand. It had started the same way that most tragedies do; she went home early. Her boss had let her have the afternoon off as a well-earned reward for her excellent presentation that morning. Nancy had put more than two months of constant work into it, and was elated that it had gone over so smoothly. She had stopped on the way to pick up some champagne and a few items for a congratulatory dinner. She saw Bill's car in the driveway when she pulled up, so Nancy was not surprised to find the front door unlocked. They had only recently moved to Memphis, and she was nervous about crime in a district that was so close to downtown. Bill had a "devil-may-care" attitude and this impervious outlook seemed to repel harm. Bullets, she swore, would just bounce right off him. The smile of welcome fell from her face when she entered her home.

It was the noise. Nancy had only heard cries like that once before in her twenty-five years, and that was when she had walked in on her brother watching porn flicks when he thought that he'd be alone for the evening. The first thing that crossed her mind was not tremendously rational as she recalled. Nancy was hoping that the girl was faking because those cries sounded like she was in dire agony. Nancy walked to her bedroom like a somnambulist. She had to see, had to know, exactly what those cries belonged to.

Nancy pulled the collar of her leather coat higher around her neck. The sights and sounds of Beale Street were long behind her, and she had no idea where she was. Memphis was still a strange city to her, not at all like Fargo, where she had grown up. Bill had been from Bismarck, and they had met at the University of North Dakota at a frat party held by the river. At least, Memphis had that in common with Fargo, the river. But there were differences so vast that Nancy did not believe that she could make a go of it on her own here. She certainly was not going to run home to Daddy, and she was not going back with Bill. He did not even stop thrusting into the screaming banshee when he saw that Nancy was there, and he definitely didn't run after her when she tore out of the house.

She wandered from bar to bar in her quest to get blissfully drunk and slip into sweet forgetfulness. It was now 12:30 and she was still not able to decide where she was going to spend the night. To top it all off, the rain had increased its tempo, beating a staccato rhythm hard into Nancy's throbbing skull. Through the dark, shimmering curtain of falling water, Nancy was unable to recognize a single landmark. She had blindly followed the alley, not noticing when she had crossed streets, or even keeping track of how far she had gone. She stopped, defeated, noticing how the cold water had seeped through her leather shoes, and tried to wriggle her wrinkled toes.

Then a sound slunk through the rain to reach her. It came low over the puddles and piles of trash, wrapping itself around her. It was the sound of a band playing what seemed to be fairly gutsy blues. Nancy knew nothing of jazz and even less of the blues, but this called to her. She laughed as she splashed through an ankle-deep pool of water, thinking what she definitely needed on a day like this was a good dose of the blues, some decent soul food.

The music drew her straight to a small dark building that Nancy did not remember ever seeing before. There was a small red neon sign in the front window—CLUB DAMBALA. A couple of leather-shrouded customers walked in through the doors ahead of her, and the light strode out like a brazen beacon. Nancy was certainly not a bold person. She had a tendency to sit back and wait just to make sure that everything was absolutely secure before moving ahead. That Nancy would never have even entertained the notion of going into a strange bar alone, so far removed from anything safe and familiar. Tonight though, was all about being someone in total opposition to her usual self, and so she strode confidently across the street and pulled the doors open just as if she owned the place.

Despite the bright lights in the hall, the club was small and very dim. The bar took up the back wall where anonymous faces all stared down at the counter in the timeless manner of seasoned alcoholics. At the front was a small stage, barely raised up from the floor. A small band was bathed in the red and blue lights that beamed down on them from above, bathing their features in shadows of turbulent shades. The main part of the room was taken up by haphazardly placed wooden tables and chairs. Although there seemed to be a fair number of people present, the place had a smoky feeling of intrigue and intimacy. This is the way Nancy had pictured those first few blues bars, gutbuckets as the guide on Beale Street had called them all those long months ago.

There was only one table left that hadn't already been taken, and Nancy pulled a chair up to it in an almost defiant manner. She actually had to resist the urge to put her feet up on the wobbly table. One of the spotlights was misdirected and it shone its brilliant light upon Nancy, nearly blinding her. It didn't really bother her all that much, though. As a matter of fact, it seemed appropriate to Nancy, heightening her feelings of solitude and brashness. Besides, the light was most likely the reason that the spot was free in the first place.

A faceless server approached out of the smoky gloom. Nancy ordered a bourbon and had to bite her tongue to keep her from asking for a pack of Marlboros to chase it down with. Only the dimly recalled memory of her Grandmother dying of emphysema, hooked up to what seemed like a hundred pumping machines, with a cigarette hanging from the corner of her mouth, quelled the urge.

The drink came, and another followed soon after. The music throbbed in her brain. There were no lyrics, no tales of lost love, just the guitar, the harmonica and the saxophone. Nancy swayed to the beat, the alcohol numbing her senses, removing her sense of self, allowing her to flow into the riff. All she could see was the light, and all she could feel was what the music told her to.

The music stopped and Nancy looked up. Another bourbon appeared, unbidden, near her hand. A man climbed onto the stage. Nancy had to squint to see anything past his outline. He was extremely tall, bald and in the weird lighting, looked to be the color of night. She was instantly aroused by him, even though his features were lost in the void. Perhaps it was his physique that had piqued her interest, or more likely, it was Nancy's current blood alcohol level.

An expectant hush had fallen over the room. She could imagine the audience leaning forward in their seats, holding in their collective breath, waiting for the magic that this man had to be able to bring, to start. The atmosphere entranced her, captivated her. This was like nothing that she had ever experienced in her subdued life.

Then the drums started. They sounded deep and vast, like the boom of an ocean surf. Nancy could feel the reverberation in her chest as it tried weakly to echo the sound back to its source. She had not ever heard a beat like this in any of the blues songs that she had listened to before, but then again, she had never even heard the blues before she came to Memphis. She felt her blood pulse through her body in time to the heavy beat.

The guitar came in next, although it did not have the same sound that it had before either. The rhythm told Nancy's body of half-remembered voices that came from the deepest part of her genes. Untold grief at the wealth of this near remembrance of things long past brought tears to her eyes, burning salt springs of emotion that coursed down her cheeks, pooling on the dark, scarred surface of her table.

And then, the most amazing event of all occurred. The dark ebony god, who stood on the stage before her, opened his mouth and began to sing. Ecstasy like she had never even glimpsed before rode her body, as his low rolling tones slid down her back, awakening her senses. He sung in a language that she could not hope to understand, but the crowd knew it. They sang along with him, harmonizing with his vocals, adding in a background of unimaginable depth and color. It almost seemed to Nancy that it was a religious experience, that the crowd was chanting and he was their high priest. She downed her drink, almost oblivious to the fire that usually accompanied such an act. Nancy sat enraptured; nothing on earth could break this spell.

The longer she sat and listened to this strange language flowing past her, the more she believed she could comprehend. Of course, said the quiet voice deep within the recesses of her mind, Jack Daniels has a way of making sense out of nonsense all on its own. She thought that he sang of a far-off place, a place lost to the passage of time, a place that was rich in power. He sang of a way to reach that place, to connect with that power, to revel in the delight of the old ones who still lived in that special place. At least, that's what Nancy thought the song said.

She now felt eyes upon her. The gaze of a hundred people, hungry, famished for something that only she could give, burned into her. The dark man called to her—to her alone. He praised her and the crowd silently agreed. She could feel their approval of her, covering her like a warm blanket. He sang of her glorious long blonde hair, the color of desert sand, shimmering in the dry heat. She sat still, the music holding her fast, even as she felt her hair slide down her face and back. Nancy had to brush away the clumps that had gotten caught on her eyelashes. Her hand reached up automatically to her head. It was smooth, silky. It seemed very appropriate to her that it should be like this. Then he sang of her precious blue eyes, the color of the sky just after the fiery sun had set. It was a little more disconcerting to feel her eyeballs drop out of their sockets, especially when one of them slid down her top, leaving a slimy trail of goo that chilled her skin. Nancy thought vaguely that she really shouldn't have worn such a low-cut shirt.

It was at this point that the last sober part of her mind tried to get Nancy to run, to leave, at least to stand up and fight this madness somehow. But it was by then far too late.

Her beautiful pale white skin lay in a pool around her chair, like discarded clothing that had yet to be kicked off. The blood poured freely from all her tissues, as she happily sang along, as the dark man now asked for her heart.

Nifty, Tuff an' Bitchen
By Kiel Stuart

Nineteen sixty-eight was a year of many wonders, at least of the pop cultural variety: the Fillmore East opened, "Hey, Jude" charted, and the Nehru jacket flourished. But on the down side, the Vietnam war raged, racial tensions soared, political leaders were assassinated, and the Nehru jacket flourished.

And on a smaller scale, at Farley M. Wolverton Jr. High in Memphis, surprise ruler raids were the bane of many a girl's existence.

That October 18 was no exception. To Ellen Bergamott, in fourth-period gym class, the raid could not have come at a more inconvenient time.

"Step to it, girls, hut-hut!" The gym teacher's voice soared. Miss Joxstrapp was already taking out the ruler, and Ellen hurried to unroll the waistband of her skirt.

Rolling up her staid below-the-knee skirt was an action Ellen furtively performed each school day—once out of her mother's scrutiny. But today she was in trouble. The waistband wouldn't unroll. The plaid fabric seemed glued to itself.

"On your knees, ladies—you know the drill." As they scrambled to obey, the gym teacher strolled around, slapping one chunky palm with the ruler. Her real name was Miss Jogstedt, but young women of age 14 have a way of cutting to the chase.

Miss Joxstrapp's foursquare figure was not one that would have inspired Vermeer. For that matter, Goya would not have lost any sleep over her either. Blue eyes glinted from behind her wire-rimmed glasses, like an eagle's scanning for field mice. A pale squarish face made her hair seem like a last-minute hat she'd clapped onto her head.

Ellen wondered if either Goya or Vermeer would have taken a second look at her. Gulping, she eyed the girls around the fateful circle. It was pretty clear from the assemblage of knees and hemlines that there were two offenders destined for a trip to the principal's office: Ellen herself and one of the tough girls.

Ellen harbored a secret admiration for the tough girls, those who bouffed their hair to control-tower proportions, troweled on the black eye makeup, and deliberately, completely on purpose, wore skirts that ended at about the hip. Ronnie Velsmith, kneeling across from Ellen, came immediately to mind.

Of course Joxstrapp would tag Ronnie—she seemed to have it in for the Velsmith girl. Maybe that meant she'd overlook Ellen.

Ellen sighed and glanced at her own attire. What did other teenaged witches wear? She felt sure they didn't let their mothers outfit them in geekaholic plaid skirts with Kayopectate-yellow shirts. She would wager that they got to choose their own clothing. Ellen worshipped clothing, but most of this worship took place from afar.

Ronnie—who reminded Ellen of Tina Turner—obviously conducted her clothes- worship right out in the open. Today she wore a sleeveless black turtleneck and a knit skirt that could have passed for a belt. Her shining black hair was back-combed into a wicked bubble flip, and hazel-green eyes glowed eerily against her chestnut skin. Goya would have looked once, looked twice, thrown up his hands in despair, and come back with his paintbrush.

"All right, ladies!" bellowed the gym teacher. "Parade rest!"

Miss J was coming closer. Quick, what to do? Some of the girls would crunch down at the hips so their hemlines might brush the floor as proscribed. Desperate, Ellen tried this.

Whap! The ruler smacked across her rump.

"Straighten out, Bergamott," barked Miss J.

"Yes, Ma'am." She flushed.

Some of the other girls giggled, but Ronnie was not amused.

"Toady," whispered Ronnie. "You're in for it now."

Ellen bent her head to avoid the other girl's piercing glare.

"Bergamott! Velsmith!" A smile tightened Miss J's face. "Front and center!"

*　*　*

Outside the principal's office, Ellen tried to look down, up, anywhere but at Ronnie. No use. The other girl marched over, grabbed her Peter-Pan collar and sneered.

"You're deadasadoornail," growled Ronnie. "Dead-dead-dead."

She had a way of running her words together into one long, incomprehensible glob, but from the collar-grip, Ellen divined their meaning. "That's all there is to it," finished Ronnie.

Then she let go and sauntered to the opposite wall. Most of the other colored students would try to blend into the background, but not Ronnie—she courted trouble.

It wasn't fair. Ellen considered disappearing, but that was not yet in her witchy repertoire. How was she going to explain short-skirt detention to her fundamentalist mother, better known far and wide as

Hellfire Mom? Grounded for sure. That meant no Young Miss Fashion Show next week. No, it wasn't fair at all.

The door shuddered open. Both girls glanced at each other, then filed into the principal's office. Both sank into chairs facing the desk.

Mr. Dornacher had a red meaty face, which deepened its color as he regarded them. If he had been standing, he would barely come up to Ronnie's ear. Ellen figured that this sore spot was what made him such an obnoxious little pufferfish.

She sighed. Then the overwhelming, palate-clogging stench of his aftershave made her sneeze.

"Oh, you girls think this is funny?"

Ronnie snorted, rolling her eyes. Ellen opened her mouth to protest that a sneeze did not constitute a laugh, then thought better of it.

Mr. Dornacher pressed his palms to the desk and pursed his lips. "Disgraceful." He glared at Ellen, then Ronnie, and he his gaze lingered on Ronnie, his mouth changing in a way that made Ellen shudder. "Ronnie," he lectured, "I expected this from you, but Ellen? Shameless. How would you girls like it if I came to your houses and stripped down naked right in front of you?" The shine in his yellowish eyes reminded Ellen of a slug she'd once found in the garden. He pushed his face out another couple of inches. "I mean, right down naked?"

Was that a threat, thought Ellen, or a promise? Next to Ellen, Ronnie wrapped bare arms around herself.

The phone rang. Mr. Dornacher snatched it off the receiver.

"What?!" He listened for a while, then grunted, and slammed the receiver down. "You!" He pointed at the girls.

"Us?" They exchanged glances again.

"You," he barked, "Remain seated." Then he got up and scuttled from the office.

The instant the door closed, Ronnie leapt to her feet and levered open the window. She was halfway out of it when she turned her head to Ellen. "I ain't stickin' around to see what ol' Doorknocker's gonna do. You comin' or what?"

Oh, Diana have mercy! Piling on one offense after another.

Ronnie's eyes stabbed at her like green diamonds. One leg was out the window, the other foot still resting on the floor. "Ferget it," Ronnie said, "yer hopeless," and she scrambled out the window.

"Wait!" Ronnie was older; she was sixteen. Someone who had been left back so many times must know a trick or two, as surely as

Ellen knew her math. "I —I'm coming along." Ellen left her seat and wriggled out the window after Ronnie.

* * *

Ellen and Ronnie scurried past houses, churches and the library, nearer downtown Memphis. Then Ronnie stopped. "There," she pointed, and ducked down an alley between Piggly Wiggly and the Ford dealership. Ellen followed.

"Whoo!" Ronnie slid to the pavement, knees almost forming a chin rest. She dug into her bag and snatched out a pack of cigarettes, lit one for herself, and offered one to Ellen.

Tentatively, Ellen took it.

Ronnie was an efficient, dedicated smoker. She sucked in long drafts of her cigarette, spitting the smoke out in lazy overhead curls. Ellen watched, then imitated. A ten-minute spree of red-faced, lung-wrenching cough spasms was her reward.

"Face it," she gasped, when she could again speak, "I'm really in the soup now. I mean, I fully expect to be grounded until the end of this term, if not until the end of time itself.

"Short-skirted. Detention. Skipping out." She gave another lung-cleansing bark, then shot Ronnie a sideways glance. "And let's not forget associating with a shameless hussy."

Ronnie grunted. "Whadayamean?"

"I think that's how Hellfire Mom would describe you." Ellen didn't even want to get into what else her mother (who'd hated every moment since the schools were integrated) would say about Ronnie.

"Oh, yeah. Iseewhatchamean." Smoke dribbled from the corner of Ronnie's mouth, riding along with the words. "Your mama's that holy roller type."

Between coughs, Ellen tried to explain, then gave it up.

She gave up the cigarette as well. There was no advantage in telling Ronnie that her mother's vocabulary would not permit her to embrace terms like "slutty little whore," though she might be thinking it.

"Mind?"   Ronnie extended a hand for Ellen's stubbed-out cigarette. "Thanks." Resuming her artistic rendering of a chimney, Ronnie tapped out a rhythm on the pavement with one pointed toe.

"You must be cold." Ellen slid out of her cardigan and offered it to Ronnie.

"Thanks." Deftly forking the cigarette between her first two fingers, she next popped a pale-peach lipstick from her purse.

Ellen eyed the forbidden fruit with longing. When Ronnie was finished applying it she held out the lipstick.

"Wannatryit?"

"Uh, well, I don't…"

"S'matter? 'Fraid some black's gonna rub off onya?"

"Nothing of the sort!" Ellen burst out. "It's germs."

"Germs? Here." She rummaged and displayed another lipstick. "This one's brand-new. It's yours."

"Gosh," whispered Ellen, turning it over. Frosted Malt.

She swiveled it up and its untouched surface winked at her: the very symbol of glistening Babylon. Looking in Ronnie's borrowed mirror, she anointed herself with iridescent beige. Hey! Pretty neat. "But, Ronnie," she bubbled, "you really shouldn't have… I mean, a brand-new lipstick…"

"Oh, no big deal. I *stole* it."

Ellen sighed. "Well, that's it. My transformation is complete; I may as well march straight on down to Beale Street and sign on as a streetwalker. Or perhaps I'll forego that and simply take a parachute drop into Hades itself." Nevertheless, she secreted the precious icon in her purse.

"Yeah," mused Ronnie. "My fourth detention this month. What a drag! I mean, I'm gonna be a fashion designer." She shot Ellen a challenging glare. "Don't care what anyone says. I'm gonna. 'Sides, I was goin' to that Young Miss Fashion Show this weekend."

Ellen's ears perked up. "Hey! Me, too!"

Ronnie shot her a glance. "Yeah. You need it."

"Thanks. Now what?"

Ronnie shrugged. "We hang out." She jumped to her feet.

Ellen followed suit. "But we have to go back eventually. I mean, it's the law of physics."

"Naah. Sometimes they forget, ya know? Like that emergency that sent Doorknocker flyin'? Mighta drove us right outta his head."

They were strolling past Darlington's tobacco store now.

"But that still leaves Miss Joxstrapp."

"Yeah. Damn." Ronnie flung her cigarette away. "Lemme think a minute, wouldja?"

Ellen followed her down the street in silence, glancing nervously at the store windows, expecting the School Police to leap out and apprehend them at any second.

"Ronnie," she urged, tugging at the other's purse strap, "mayhap it is best if we just throw ourselves on the mercy of our persecutors. There will, in all likelihood, be other fashion shows—"

"Shut up," Ronnie hissed, her eyes focusing over the top of Ellen's head. "Shuddupanlissen. I got us a way outta this."

"What?"

"What wouldjasay if I told ya our Miss Joxstrapp is a... a..." She darted a glance around, then lowered her voice and pulled Ellen in close. "A lezzie, that's what," she whispered.

Then she sat back in triumph.

"I wouldn't say a thing. That's mere speculation on your part."

"Fine. I'll prove it." Snatching up Ellen's arm, Ronnie dragged her off once more.

* * *

"Shh," cautioned Ronnie, as they approached the school entrance just outside the gym. "Lookathere." She pointed.

Ellen followed the pointing finger. Inside the gym, Miss Joxstrapp was happily engaged in a corner. There, the light punching bag was set up, and Miss J was giving it a high-speed drubbing: *Pocketa-pocketa-pocketa.* Her face wore a beatific look that Ellen had only seen on portraits of the saints. *Pocketa-pocketa-pocketa.*

"Oh, really!" she said to Ronnie in exasperation. "That proves 0.0% of exactly nothing." She turned away from the gym.

"Doncha see? We lean on her, she leans on Doorknocker. We're outta trouble. I'm tellin' ya. For real!"

Ellen's lips tightened. "So what?"

"Whadaya mean, so what?" Ronnie plucked at her sleeve.

"Ithoughtyawanted to go Saturday. Me too."

Ellen kicked fiercely at a pebble. "I do want to go. Lots."

Ronnie threw her hands up. "So this is the way we do it. Maybe we could even get Miss J to chauffeur."

Ellen whirled. "It's not right to do things to people because of what they happen to be!"

"Whatcha mean by that?"

"Ronnie, you of all people should be more tolerant."

"Why? She's always hasslin' me. Why ya defendin' her so hard?"

"No reason."

"Oh?" Ronnie stopped dead. Her lips twitched. Her green diamond eyes shot sparks. "Hey, yer not sayin' that you're one, too?"

"No. Spelled En-Oh."

"Yeah. Thatmustbeit. You an' the gym teacher."

"Go away."

Ronnie cupped her hands. "Hey, everyone, Ellen's a lezzie!"

She whirled. "Shut the hell up!"

"Ooh, you said 'hell.'"

"You say worse before breakfast and twice on Sundays."

"Yeah." Ronnie's eyes snapped. "But you don't."

"So?"

"So ya got some secret, doncha? Doncha? Is ya or ain'cha?"

"Look, go and torture someone else with that extremely limited ability to see beyond your own nose!"

Ronnie yanked her arm. "Lezzie!"

Ellen pulled free. "I am not!"

"What, then?"

Flushed with anger, Ellen snapped, "I'm a..." She trailed off.

Ronnie leaned back, hands on hips. "Gotcha. Now gimme-gimme-gimme." Her hand went out, fluttering, snapping for information.

Here goes. "Well..." Ellen took a deep breath. "You know Angelique on 'Dark Shadows?'"

Ronnie's face lost all traces of expression for several beats. Then her eyes rounded, and her lips pulled back in a tight grin. "You're a witch? You sayin' you're a witch? For real?"

Ellen nodded, miserable. *You loudmouthed lily-livered idiot*, she berated herself. *Just because Ronnie gave you some stolen lipstick.*

"Whoa! Tuff, tuff, tuff! Awright!" Ronnie crowed. "Why didncha say so inna first place? A witch!"

Ellen blinked, unable to process what she had just heard.

Then relief flooded her. At last, her secret was out! She felt a hundred-pound weight float up and away from her chest. And Ronnie understood. Maybe even approved.

She sighed as they began walking again. "I never said so because it's not something you go around spewing at random."

"Nifty, tuff an' bitchen." Ronnie shook her head from side to side.

"And also," added Ellen, "I don't want to use my powers."

"Huh?" Ronnie's painted brows twitched into a peak. "Whythehell not?"

"Are you joking?" Ellen blinked. "Mom would ground me forever." She began to walk again, but Ronnie got in her way and pushed her down onto a nearby bench.

Next she sat patiently listening to Ronnie detail the many and various ways in which she was an asshole.

"Ronnie, perhaps I haven't fully explained my position..."

"Nevermind, nevermind. What can ya do? I mean, what are your powers? Can ya turn people into toads and stuff?"

Ellen slumped. So much for understanding. This was simply another way she could be used, another form of Ronnie looking over her shoulder during a spelling test. "Leave me alone! I just want to serve out my detention, go home, watch the Monkees and live to face another day of boredom and futility. It's for sure I'm not getting anywhere near that fashion show and I am not—repeat, *not*—risking anything else!"

She began to walk away, but Ronnie grabbed the sleeve of her shirt. "Not so fast. We gotta hatch a scheme."

* * *

Outside the church graveyard Ronnie paused. "Thisokaywith ya? I mean, can ya walk on hallowed ground and all?"

"Of course I can." Ellen strode forward, Ronnie following. "Don't be a simpleton."

They sat awhile in the chill damp earth. "So howdaya become a witch? Ya fill out an application or what?"

Ellen shrugged. "You study. Hard. I think perhaps I got the knack from my father, but he died when I was little, so..."

She trailed off, wondering if her miserable life with Hellfire Mom would carry any weight with Ronnie. She began to explain.

Ronnie listened, nodding absently. "Yeah-yeah," she shot, "My Mama works, it's just her and me and my two brothers. Ain'itashame." She stubbed out her spent cigarette, lit a new one. Then she spoke. "Well? Ya gonna turn Doorknocker into a frog?"

"I don't have to. He's already three-fourths of the way there."

"Come on. Doncha want power? Hey, maybe you could rule the world or somethin'."

"No! All I want to rule is my own destiny."

"Know somethin'? I ain't sure ya even are a witch. I mean, maybe you just said that to impress me."

"Oh, I am, never doubt it." She thought of the one spell she had studied, and perhaps mastered. "It's merely that I believe in doing things the right way." She gave Ronnie a stern glance. "As in not copying other persons' test papers and so forth."

Ronnie let this sail right over her head. "Still, we gotta come up with somethin' to get Doorknocker an' Joxstrapp off our tails."

"Anything as long as it doesn't involve the use of my powers."

Ronnie jumped to her knees. "But you have to use 'em! There ain't no other way."

Ellen shook her head.

"Awright, lissen. How many detentions ya got so far?"

Ellen made the goose-egg sign with her thumb and forefinger.

"There!" Ronnie stabbed a cigarette in her direction.

"Wanna keep that perfect record, doncha?"

"Yes. But this doesn't constitute an emergency, and I swore I would only use my abilities in case of one."

Ronnie scrambled to her feet. "Huh! And here I thought you were cool. Not like them others." Ronnie took the butt out of her mouth, looked at it, and blew a long wedge of smoke past Ellen. Then she turned and walked off.

Ellen blinked. She weighed. Clothes from the 1940's (and not the glamorous midnight-movie 40's either) versus—she looked at Ronnie's retreating form. *Call the shot.*

"Wait!" Ellen heard her own voice.

Ronnie stopped. She didn't walk back to Ellen. Ellen stood there, arms folded.

Yes. Ellen tried not to be like her mother, like Dornacher. For a moment she had a bright vision of wielding a witch-sword of righteousness against the unjust, so that... What? Everyone can be like you?

And that would make her precisely, exactly as her mother was.

Ronnie turned, head down, hands jammed into her skirt pockets, and hurried back. "All right. Whatcanyado?"

Sigh. "Well, there's only one spell I've mastered so far."

"Outasite. What's that?"

"It's known as the Spell of Irresistible Attraction. But I don't possibly see what it can have to do with the case at hand..."

"Nevermind." Ronnie grabbed her hand. "I gottanidea."

* * *

"This could very easily backfire," whispered Ellen. "You do realize that, don't you?"

"Shut up. Let's just waitansee."

Ellen grumbled. Both of them were now crouched inside the closet in Principal Dornacher's office. It was quite past regular school hours. They'd waited until the principal stepped out for a smoke, then sprung into action.

But, even before they'd reached the office, Ellen had completed her spell. Taking oil and water, shaking them to a smooth paste with a drop of lecithin and two small but powerful magnets, she had muttered incantations. When they'd reached the office she'd dropped some of the potion onto Dornacher's chair, and some on the threshold of the doorway. Then, disguising her voice, she'd phoned Miss Joxstrapp to come to the office.

But something had already gone wrong with their plan.

Dorrnacher had yet to return.

Now Ellen heard the door open and close. She grabbed Ronnie's arm. "'Kay," whispered Ronnie. "Joxstrapp's here. Now where's Doorknocker?"

Ellen maneuvered to peek out of the closet. The gym teacher sat in the chair, the magic chair, absently drumming out a tune on the desk: *Pocketa-pocketa-pocketa.* With each syncopated tap, Ellen's uneasiness grew. What was keeping Dornacher?

Flom! Someone flung the door open. Ellen held her breath waiting for the next moment: Dornacher would bound across the room, take Miss Joxstrapp into his arms and...

"All right! What kind of devil-worshiping operation are you running over here? Exactly where is my daughter?"

"Wha—?" Ronnie's fingers dug into her shoulder.

It wasn't Dornacher. Ellen's knees began to tremble. She shut her eyes, blocking out the sight. Then she forced them open again. Of course. Ellen had known it would all go wrong. Now it could not get worse.

The woman who stood transfixed in the office door had thin brown locks scraped back into a bun so that it looked more like paint than hair. The mouth, remarkably absent of generosity, would have caused Monet to mutter "Thanks, but no thanks." And the Salvation Army would have politely but firmly declined to accept the flour sack that passed as her suit. Hellfire Mom.

Ellen's mother stood open-mouthed, staring at Miss Joxstrapp, whose expression, in turn, would have done credit to a jack-lit rabbit's.

"Why..." stammered Miss Joxstrapp, "It's Mrs. B-Bergamott, isn't it?"

Ellen's mother blushed, then dipped her scraped-back head.

"Call me Gladys," she simpered.

Ellen held her breath while the two of them talked in hushed tones. Ronnie's fingers had already cut off circulation to her shoulder and were now working on her arm. What would happen if Dornacher blundered in now?

Ellen, watching them, stilled. Her brain ticked over feverishly. Finally the two women left the office. Dornacher still had not come.

"Ohmanohman, we are really screwed," said Ronnie, tumbling from the closet, zipping for the door. "I mean we are dead. Deaddeaddead, that's all there is to it."

"Not necessarily," mused Ellen, following her out of the office.

"Oh, whadaya talkin' about? Doorknocker's gonna be back any second now, we got twice the trouble on our hands as we started out with, an' I sure didn't like th' way he looked at me before."

But Ellen only smiled. "This time," she said, "I have an idea."

* * *

Thunderous applause greeted each new outfit at the Young Miss Fashion Show. Ellen's palms ached by now, and Ronnie stuck her cigarette back into her mouth so she could applaud, too. Her elbow dug into Ellen's ribs. "Wouldja lookitthat Mary Quant?"

Ellen looked. Oh, the colors, the lines, the drape and float of each new outfit! It was thrilling to have so many choices.

Mom was going to let Ellen go to a lot of fashion shows now.

She was going to let Ellen dress as she pleased. Ellen was very understanding about Mom's new relationship with Miss Joxstrapp, but Mom had to realize that even in cosmopolitan Memphis not everyone would be as broad-minded as her daughter, and it was best to be discreet.

And it hadn't been all that difficult to lure Dornacher to Ronnie's house. After all, it was the principal himself who'd practically begged to strip down naked in front of her. Ronnie's mother, who had been temporarily tied to a chair, would no doubt forgive them once she returned from her honeymoon as the new Mrs. Dornacher.

For Ellen was already fast at work on her Spell of Absolute Amnesia, and with the able help of witch-in-training Ronnie, she had no doubt that this time the spell would work perfectly.

Rendezvous With Fear
By Del Tinsley

For some reason the movie *Alien* came to mind. But a Sigourney Weaver I'm not. Still, I sat there by myself in the Peabody lobby watching the ducks. My husband Bob had already retired to our room.

When a good, well-behaved child came up, the ducks just swam around cute as a button. But when an ill-behaved child—all right, a *brat*—came up, the ducks lost all their feathers, sprouted horns on their heads and fangs from their beaks, and their webbed feet became cloven hoofs. No quacking, just hissing and growling.

I looked into my cappuccino. Had someone slipped something into my drink? Was this what a bad trip was like? I dared not ask anybody around me. They were all strangers and didn't seem to notice anything unusual. Perhaps I was hallucinating. Best that I simply leave. Get some fresh air.

It was very late. Something drove me to walk down the alley off Union Avenue between the Peabody and the Rendezvous.

Even at night, Memphis in the summer can be hot. Humidity equaling or surpassing the temperature. Conditions like this greatly intensified the odors coming from a nearby dumpster.

I heard a squeal and let out a muffled scream, afraid to make too much noise for fear of... for fear of what?

That question was answered, as a large rodent ran across my foot. Its long hairless tail looked like an antenna. An antenna to communicate with other rats? In the poor light, the rat seemed to have a pig snout instead of the usual long, tapered nose. What was in that cappuccino anyway?

The overloaded dumpster reeked. Bones. Piles of bones. And, blood? It looked like blood, plus slimy green stuff everywhere.

I attempted humor to ease my stress. Thinking of the situation as my having interrupted a bunch of rats at a dinner party didn't do a damn thing to ease my fears.

I was scared shitless. My heart was making a noise: *thumpa, thumpa, thump,* which kept pounding sound in my ears. Like someone bounding down a flight of stairs. If they missed a step, would my heart miss a beat? All the books I had read and stories I had heard hadn't been a pack of lies. It was physically possible to hear most of your own body noises.

Hey out there! This was more than I could handle. I was scared. Scared enough to wet my pants. Me, twenty-nine year old Melissa Montgomery, a newly hired nurse at St. Jude's Children's Research Hospital, with her drawers wet. That would really make some of my little patients laugh. God knows they had little enough to laugh about, but I really didn't want to be the brunt of anyone's joke. I had a habit of embarrassing myself, but this? This would take the cake. This would go on the top of my list of most embarrassing moments. I could all but hear the Depend jokes. At this stage of the game, I really didn't give two hoots and a holler if I were wet or dry.

I was too damn scared to care.

Get a grip! I couldn't. I was too terrified to even make a sound. I wasn't capable of squeezing out so much as a squeak. My throat was so constricted with fear, I couldn't even swallow.

And the bile. I think it was bile. In situations like this people didn't get heartburn, did they? Sweet Jesus, was I going to throw up? Could fear make a person throw up?

I inched my way along the building's wall. I came to a door. Thinking it might be a means of escape, I entered, only to find a flight of stairs. In my panic I took the stairs leading down into a nasty, dank, dark cellar. I heard something. More rats? I climbed up on top of a table that seemed to be suffering from St. Vitus' Dance... or was Memphis experiencing another earthquake? No. Just me. Shaking. In an effort to get as high as I could, I climbed up on some cobweb covered shelves. Now my mind held pictures of my body covered in spiders. (Too many Indiana Jones movies, Melissa.) I clawed my way up as far as I could go. My fingernails felt like they were in shreds. If I could only get just a little bit higher. Then, maybe, I could make a hole in the ceiling, gnaw my way through it, something, anything to get me on the floor above and to safety.

I had never given safety a second thought. Now I found myself praying for it with my whole heart and soul. My whole being. I'd do anything, give anything to be somewhere safe. But reality deprived me of that wish. There was no way on God's green earth I could leave this perch. I couldn't go any higher. Down? No way.

I was beginning to feel woozy. Was I going to faint? What would happen to me if I fainted? I had never fainted before. This was definitely not the time to start. I couldn't handle this, this absolute fear. I wasn't handling it. For the life of me, I couldn't think straight.

For the life of me? I started to cry.

But wait, what was that? I thought I heard something above the rat noises. There. There, I heard it again. A sound like someone sliding the grating that was sunk in the concrete cellar floor. Nah, it couldn't be ... could it? Gulping, stifled my sobs, I listened with all my might. There it was again. The grate *was* moving.

In the poor light I couldn't make out much but, what? What was that? It looked like slimy green stuff mixed with... my mind didn't want to register the word, but my eyes relayed a message to my brain that the red stuff was... BLOOD. Surely blood couldn't be oozing up out of the drain. Could it? And the smell, the horrible, awful smell. Like dead meat. Like someone who didn't use deodorant.

I gulped down a scream that struggled to erupt from my throat. Could this THING, whatever it was, hear? Could it hear my body noises, my swallowing, my heart thumping, my blood pumping through my veins?

What did it want? Me, obviously. I was doomed.

My ears seemed to be picking up voices, muffled, eerie-sounding voices. Voices that sounded like they were from the depths of hell. Dear God in heaven! I was losing it. The voices were calling me. The voices knew my name.

I felt shaking. Looking down, I saw the grate had been pushed aside. Now, whatever it was, was shaking the shelves I clung to. Gently at first, then stronger, more persistently. I put my hands over my ears. Over and over came: "Mel... Melissa ... Mel... is... saa ..."

I didn't know what to do, except I wasn't going to open my eyes. I squeezed them shut as tight as I could. I had no desire to see whatever it was, much less be fully aware of what horrible things it was going to do to me.

The shaking became more persistent, if that were possible, and the voice was saying something. I could barely make it out. Then the words finally registered.

The voice was Bob, saying, "Melissa, for God's sake wake up! You're having a NIGHTMARE! I told you not to make a pig of yourself. The Rendezvous is known for its barbecue, but damn, woman... your guzzling all that beer, eating all those pepperoncini with smoked sausage and cheddar cheese on crackers, then a bowl of gumbo, not to mention following up the Rendezvous barbecued ribs with a cappuccino chaser at the Peabody's Cafe Espresso... That combo would give even Elvis a bad dream!"

The Frequency of Violets
By Lou Kemp

The night turned white, and then more golden than a summer's day.

Like a rose unfolding, the first shell opened the hill from within, exploding the rocks and dirt, burying everything below. Under a barrage from Yankee guns, the cluster of houses at the top disintegrated and burning debris rained like confetti.

Finian felt more than heard the whine of the shells as soldiers cursed and screamed.

A bloody hand gripped his wrist. Finian turned, and a soldier without a face fell on him.

"Hell! Medic!"

"Move your ass Finian!"

The deafening roar of the battle faded to the south. The screams of the wounded billowed with the clouds of dirt that hung in the air. Finian stumbled on something that looked like a legless and bloodied sheep. He threw down his bag and knelt beside the first body.

As he turned the body over, a roll of cigarettes spilled into the mud. Finian stuck one in his mouth and pushed the corporal's guts back into his shirt, wiping the blood from his eyes before he moved to the next soldier a few feet away.

The night burned bright as the remaining trees on the hill caught fire. The stench of burning flesh wafted in a tangible cloud toward them, mingling with the sweet smell of ether. Finian didn't turn around; if it was a cow burning, or the body of a child, he didn't want to know.

Finian had bandaged five and bent over the sixth when he heard the Sgt. bark, "Over here, Finian! It's Carter." Finian pretended he didn't hear him, just like he tried not to see anything at all as he tried to help a soldier without a hand stand.

Sgt. Butler spun Finian around.

"I *said*, go help Carter." He pointed to a body lying under the glare of a burning pile of hay.

"Yessir."

"Don't fucking Sir me. Fix him up!" Sgt. Butler shoved Finian ahead of him. "You cold son of a bitch!"

Thunder opened the sky, the rains came, and the fires sizzled. Frank Carter breathed in short gasps, and his eyes had dilated to opaque disks. Finian glanced over his shoulder and knew the Sgt. still watched him as he bellowed orders and lifted a stretcher onto the back of a cart.

As Finian held Frank's hand and waited for him to die, the smell of violets pervaded the air, growing stronger. With a last shuddered breath, the soldier's soul lifted from his body.

Twenty-eight hundred men had arrived in LaGrange at dusk. Memphis lay east over the next hill, and it seemed the musty smell of the Wolf River traveled clearly to them. Amid the green-tiled roofs of the town, they'd set up the mess tent, the first aid station, and established headquarters in a barn that still held the faint odor of horses. As the sun set, the clouds cleared to the south and the sour smell of boiling beans rolled across the unplanted fields.

Finian cupped his coffee against his chest and waited for sundown. He sat just inside the perimeter, under the trees that bordered the town. To his left, gurgled the stream that fed the river, to the right stood a brick church.

Like almost every night, Finian dreaded what he'd see, denying the familiar tingle in his gut that impelled him to look. Whiskey, talking to God, and a blade across his wrist hadn't helped. The awareness felt alive, the impulse to look could not be ignored.

The scene appeared normal, men walking and talking, sitting and smoking. A few lay under makeshift tents, sleeping. When the darkness became complete, the faint smell of the violets would come, and then the first shimmering image. Maybe one, or maybe a dozen, but for every man who would soon die, Finian saw a mirrored pale shadow follow the living, shuffling close behind.

He remembered early in the spring, the first image had appeared outside the seediest bar in Richmond. They had gone drinking, then stumbled into the night as the nocturnal blasting by the Yankees started. The cook fell down the stairs by the river and into the water. When Finian reached to pull him up, the body seemed to turn white, and a pale shadow fled it. Finian screamed all the way back to camp.

Last night, Carter had walked the camp shadowed, as had more than 70 men. Finian huddled into himself, knowing his ability to see death intensified with each day. Maybe he'd always been able to see the shadows, maybe anyone could, or maybe it took too much death, the kind that saturated your nerves until you could *see*.

The frequency of death came faster after they crossed the Georgia border and began the long walk west. Men went to sleep and never got up again. The pale shadows followed the rest of the company, still dressed in gray, wandering as if they would wander forever.

"Fourteen villagers left. The rest are dead or in pieces hanging from the trees." Corp. Stenis pointed with his clipboard. "See the little girl, by the morgue tent? She's been sitting there all day, ever since the shelling stopped."

Morning had seeped from the watery clouds, and the cleanup begun from the night before. The remaining men of the company worked fatigue duty trying to establish order. Finian should have been sleeping, but it had been days since he could sleep. The fear of waking and finding his own image staring back felt real.

"Her mother got it last night. Father is the Deputy Mayor. He's the head civilian, since the Mayor was killed in the shelling. That's him over there, tall guy talking to the Sgt."

"What is her name?" Finian asked. She looked like a sparrow fallen from a nest and into cold water. He could understand.

"Suddenly you care about the civilians, Finian?" Corp. Stenis flipped pages on his clipboard. "Emily Gordon. Talk to her, Finian. You talk to yourself enough."

Finian walked across the square, around mounds of rubble and tired horses, to where the girl sat. The tent was open on three sides; the bodies lay in piles of legs, arms and red smears drying.

Tears dripped off her chin. He shoved a handkerchief into her hand. It fell into the mud. As he bent to retrieve it, he saw the anger behind the tears. She was looking at her father.

"I'm sorry about your mother, Emily." Finian said.

The girl shuddered. Eyes bluer than the river studied him with the inscrutable wariness he'd seen from Savannah to Memphis. She blinked several times. He recognized exhaustion.

"If you want to sleep. I'll be here."

Dusk fell, and Finian didn't move, just listened to Emily softly snoring as the camp settled in around the destruction. The moon rose. The poker games began and he heard the rattle of the dice as they rolled in the bedpans.

Finian lit his last cigarette. Emily shifted, curled into a tight ball and her breathing changed. She sat up as the mayor of La Grange walked toward them, talking animatedly with Sgt. Butler. He waved to Emily and walked by. She stiffened.

"Why do you hate your father?" Finian asked.

Her lips barely moved, and she wiped away the first tear.

"He killed my mother, Sir."

Two days more, and Intelligence had pinpointed the leading flank of the Union army. The advance shelling had been simple entertainment; stimulation for the officers in charge. As dusk bled like blood through water, Finian and the rest of the company peered from the trenches ringing the fields.

Like a morbid prelude to a play, the ground trembled from the tramping of thousands of feet, and the first wave of the Union soldiers poured out of the forest.

Minutes became years. Bandages, blood, and screams that didn't mean anything anymore. To Finian, the bodies lay in the trenches stacked like sausages in red gravy. Hours of grenades, explosions, and the staccato spit of the rifles intensified as the shadows multiplied. For the first time, he wondered if the company would survive.

Finian felt the hair on his neck prickle and then he was running, the smell of violets growing stronger. Pervasive.

"Emily!" He called her name and pried open the doors of the church, peering into the dark.

Beyond a mountain of rubble, in the farthest corner, the glow of a single candle wavered like life ebbing under water. Finian climbed over the last of the debris in time to see Emily's father lay her body before the altar.

Her throat dripped crimson. Beside the alter, drifted her pale image.

"Emily!"

The acting mayor of LaGrange backed away as Finian knelt beside the body and smoothed her brow. The words of her father came. "The Yanks'll kill you. They won't believe anything you say." The man spoke without remorse, but with the dedication and conviction of one who has succeeded in deluding himself.

"Emily couldn't forgive you." Finian said. The pale shadow seemed to intensify. "You informed on your friends, on the town. For money?"

The blast of the cannons vibrated the air and the first shell floodlit the night, staggering them where they stood.

"Does it matter, son?"

In those words, Finian saw it did matter. Life mattered, as much as death. Like a flood from a burst damn, he could taste every second, drink in each ray of the sun, weep over each drop of blood and every death. Finian remembered the wariness and futility in Emily's eyes as the bones in the mayor's neck snapped under his fingers, and the last breath hissed from his lips.

The battle raged and Finian stumbled outside to stand before the field of violets that shimmered in a thousand images over the dead and dying. Walking and never stopping, through the motherless cold, he carried a backpack of sorrows and a cane of bleached bone.

Peace Plan
By Billy Bob Patterson

Commander Brock Slater watched his aide, Chief Petty Officer Carl Register, "shoot the bird" at the car full of Lodi—humanoid lizards—that had almost run over them. They were Tutal, the red kind. Register's chocolate brown face contorted in rage, and Slater's anger nearly overrode his own reason as he watched the offenders laugh and drive off in their ancient, rusty Chevrolet Impala. What a terrific welcome to Memphis, named after the fabled ancient Egyptian city and its Tennessee counterpart destroyed in the race riots of 1999, the space mining colony beneath the surface of Jupiter's moon Europa!

Slater, the official peacekeeping delegate from the United Interplanetary Federation, had just stepped outside the Teleportation Terminal, when he and his aide were spattered by the hot-rodding vehicle with a plentiful mixture of rainwater and ronju—lizard feces—backed up from a clogged street drain.

"Damn lizards!" the Chief muttered. Fortunately, both men knew the mess would soon dry and could then be brushed off the special outer lining of their suits without a trace.

Slater looked up at the purple sky beyond the plexiglass domes which allowed sunlight to pass to the planetoid's subsurface and wondered, *How in the solar system could we ever allow such a crazy world to exist?*

He cautioned his aide: "Remember the mission, it's our duty to keep cool. So don't lose yours again, Mister. Understand?"

"Yes, Sir."

For as long as Register had served under him, Slater knew him to be dependable—more like a brother than an aide. But the Commander had to be in charge, the voice of reason and control who kept their mission on course. Even though both men were aware it was a mission of sheer lunacy.

A Lodi beggar in a worn wool trenchcoat bumped against Slater. The bum was a Tutal—judging from his squatty build and red-violet scales. He brandished a half-empty bottle of Thunderbird wine. "Hey, brother—howsabout lettin' me hold five space credits? I'll pay Saturday, if'n I see ya. Whajasay?" In his other hand he held a portable space credit transactor, the latest in interplanetary banking technology. Register, being the technological expert he was, must have noticed it right away. That beggar had quite an operation for someone supposedly indigent.

Slater avoided the beggar's gaze, remembering that some Lodi reputedly possessed the power to mesmerize.

Register snatched the transactor from the bum and smashed it against the wall of the nearest building, directly over an election poster of Juba Blan-Chard Tutal exhorting a vote for him. In an emotionless, sibilant voice, the mendicant lizard said, "You should not have done that."

With a turn that reminded Slater of a karate kick, the reptile popped his tail like a coiled whip. The C.P.O. ducked backwards, just in time to avoid having his face sliced open by three terminal tail spikes the size and sharpness of ice picks. Before the bum could lash out at him again, Register seized his attacker by the collar and slammed his face into the side of the building with a sickening thud. Blood and snot oozed from the lizard-man's nostrils as Register straightened him up and stared him down.

"Reg," Slater cautioned, momentarily forgetting military protocol, "don't look directly into his eyes."

Register replied without turning around, "Aye, aye, Sir." But he completely ignored the warning. Although the Chief's tone was calm as he began speaking, Slater saw the blazing hatred in Register's eyes and heard notes of menace rising as he said, "Now listen here, you fucking lizard, try anymore funny stuff and I'll make andouille sausage out of you, understand?"

"Yeah, Cap'n." From the blank look in the lizard's yellow eyes, he obviously didn't have hypnotic powers.

"We came here on business and that doesn't include being insulted by you or your four cousins who just spattered us with ronju. Who was in that car?"

Sniffling up his own blood and mucous, the beggar whimpered, "Don't know, Cap'n. I didn't see."

"And I guess you haven't made any ronju lately, either?"

"No, Cap'n. That's illegal."

"Bullshit! What's that goddamned wine bottle doin' in your hand? Why d'you think it's against the law for lizards to drink alcohol?"

Both Slater and Register were only too well aware of what was about to happen. If a Lodi swallowed alcohol, it would invariably, shortly thereafter, belch out a radiant bright blue-light air ball—a stefi. The beautiful illuminated globe would float around for a few moments—until it oxidized. Then stefi would turn into dark brown ronju, fall to the ground, and stink to high heaven as it further decomposed.

Register continued to reprimand the bum. "That ronju stuff smells so *awful.* Your breath, Godzilla's breath—hell, Godzilla's *shit* don't smell that bad. Who supplied you with that booze?"

The beggar shrugged. "Hey, bro, don't hassle me. I just found this."

Shaking his detainee, Register snarled, "I ain't your 'bro.' I'm 'Chief,' 'C.P.O.' or 'Mister.' Not 'Cap'n.' Not 'bro.' Got that, you miserable space reptile?"

"Yes, Chief."

No sooner had he finished answering, than the beggar belched. A magnificent globe of blue light erupted from his throat. The stefi ball floated dazzlingly upward—until Slater drew his laser pistol and blasted it into oblivion.

The screech of tires drew their attention to a vintage Cadillac Fleetwood that roared around the corner at a breakneck pace. Releasing the beggar, Register hurled himself into Slater, forcing him to the ground the same instant that a hail of machine-gun fire from the approaching car full of Zutal—blue lizards—felled the beggar.

Register was about to fire his laser pistol when Slater stopped him. "No use," the Commander said. "Our job is to implement the Peace Plan. Killing anyone, even killers, will weaken our effectiveness. I took the number on the license plates. Maybe the local authorities can trace them."

2

The two of them—just the two of them—comprised the peace-keeping force that the U.I.F. had sent to oversee the "free elections" on Europa.

Few humans had a working knowledge of Lodi customs. Slater and Register were considered experts—thanks to Marie, the beautiful and amoral vixen who also happened to be Carl Register's sister. Marie, the temptress who had deceived Brock Slater into marrying her, only to betray his love within a month after their marriage—and with someone she had met during their honeymoon on Europa.

To Slater's shame and disgrace, his rival hadn't even been human. He was none other than the leader of the Lodi resistance, Juba Tutal.

Everyone but the lowest members of society on Earth had shunned Marie after the gross indiscretion of her second marriage. Her own family openly sympathized with Slater. The irony of it all was that, because he was Marie's ex-husband, he held an accepted place in the Tutal social hierarchy. As part of her extended family, he supposedly was guaranteed safe passage whenever he came to, stayed on, or left Memphis.

All a dubious honor, as far as Slater was concerned. He was convinced that if Europa hadn't possessed some of the richest iridium, uranium, plutonium, and cobalt deposits in the solar system, and if it also weren't one of the few places that could sustain life in an earth-like environment, the U.I.F. probably would have blown that miserable chunk of space rock to oblivion decades ago. Because of its unique status as a life-bearing planetoid rich in minerals, U.I.F. troops were forbidden to use weapons against the Europans, except in absolute self-defense.

On Twenty-fifth Century Earth, corporations had plundered the treasures of the solar system and endowed the Mother Planet with incredible opulence. Famine, pestilence, disease, hunger, and warfare had been successfully abolished. Everyone lived in comfort and security. Racism had been eliminated, for there were very few members of distinct races left after centuries of extensive intermarriage. Slater had been one of the few pure Caucasians, and Register and Marie had been two of the few pure blacks remaining. Religious tolerance, like racial tolerance, was not only practiced, but also was fiercely protected.

However, people and politicians on Earth, which dominated the U.I.F., became riddled with guilt over the plight of the have-nots in the space colonies. That was all well and good, Slater reasoned, except on Europa, where most of the have-nots weren't even *human*.

3

Slater and Register were painfully aware that, if dealing with semi-intelligent lizards weren't bad enough, there were *two* distinct subspecies. It had begun, as it always does, innocently enough. The first settlers had been human and a hardy breed at that, sent from the space station on Mars in 2205. They had found a sparse atmosphere and little to sustain life, until tunneling beneath the orange sand that covered the moon's surface, they happened to discover a vast underground ocean of fresh water from which arose an underground continent. The subterranean soil contained many rich veins of an unusual green rock, which, when burned, released oxygen. Once the underground atmospheric temperature was raised, with heat drawn from the planet's molten core, the climate underground stabilized at a temperature range between 65° and 80° Fahrenheit, which could easily support life as it was known on earth.

Using underground caves as their habitats, those first settlers were able to grow lichens and toadstools, primitive but nutritiously effective sources of food. Using irrigation, and extensive, repeated fertilizer applications, they were able to raise some of the same fruits and vegetables found on earth. Low-level radiation from subterranean isotope deposits caused their crops to grow beyond the settlers' wildest expectations.

One exception to their success in gardening, however, was that legumes and other high-protein generating green-leafed plants withered in the dim light and in Europa's orange soil. Also, for some unknown reason, most domestic animals, and all meat and dairy producing livestock sickened and died within days after arriving.

One of the original settlers, in direct violation of U.I.F. orders, had brought pets with him—a male and a female iguana. Unlike most other fauna, they apparently thrived on Europa. The lizards mated. Soon the female laid eggs in copious quantities. Most hatched. Exposed to the radiation, the offspring matured to be much larger and smarter than their parents.

Within eight generations the lizards, which were called Lodi, were almost the size of humans. Evolving at an incredible rate, they not only walked upright like people, but learned to mimic human sounds. Eventually they learned to talk and showed reasoning capabilities. Although technically reptiles, they were distinctly hot-blooded, like the last of the dinosaurs on earth and the predecessors of the birds.

Over the course of the next half-century, the reptiles developed into two distinct subspecies. The Tutal became widely predominant. Pot-bellied and no taller than five feet, they were colored with red-violet scales, except for yellow-green coloring around the eyes, mouth, fingertips, and pubic region.

The other breed was Zutal. Its members were colored blue-violet, except for the same yellow-green coloring around their peripheral body areas as the Tutal. Zutal were closer to six feet tall and were known for their aggressiveness and rebellious nature. After two armed Zutal uprisings, humans all but gave up on training them, preferring the more generally docile-natured Tutal.

Before they mastered language, the two breeds of lizards were both treated as beasts of burden by humans. But as they learned to speak, and demonstrated the ability to reason, most of their owners began to show sympathy and compassion, and allowed them to adopt human customs, including wearing clothes, and associating in family units. Both Tutal and Zutal could be sold as property and had no guaranteed rights. Except for anti-cruelty laws that applied to all animals, and the limited property rights that evolved by custom, the Lodi had no individual protection.

What the humans did not anticipate was that the Lodi would adopt tribal customs and traditions of their own, including clan rivalry.

Before long the liberals in the Colonial government were pressing the U.I.F to accept the mutated iguanas as equals to the human race. The conservatives, on the other hand, insisted on keeping the mutants as slave laborers to eliminate all drudgery for humans.

The conservatives won. They had their way until the uprising of 2470, when the lizards, under their charismatic new leader, Juba Blan-Chard Tutal, rebelled and nearly overthrew their human masters. Juba and other Lodi of his generation not only possessed intelligence comparable to that of humans, but it was also rumored they had developed the power to mesmerize. Many humans thought Juba used mass hypnosis upon his followers. Slater was convinced Juba had utilized it to seduce Marie.

With their sophisticated weaponry, the humans had the tactical advantage. But the Lodi greatly outnumbered them. Casualties on both sides were heavy. Everyone realized the planetoid's fragile ecosystem would soon be destroyed if the fighting did not stop. A truce was declared, with both sides agreeing to formulate a peace plan.

As the wife of their leader and liberator, who assumed the title Blan-Chard—Lodi for "Highest Leader"-- Marie was looked upon by most of her husband's followers with reverence. Still, because she was human, there were those among the Lodi who considered her an aberration. To them her loyalty would always remain suspect, in spite of her having undergone micro-surgery to synthetically alter her chromosome structure and convert her reproductive organs so she could bear offspring for her non-human second husband.

Brock fought back his own gorge at the thought. When she'd been his wife, she'd refused to bear children. He had always wanted offspring. He struggled even harder when he remembered Marie had reportedly laid two eggs in the past two years, and that one of them had hatched. Liberals had heralded the birth of their daughter as an interplanetary breakthrough—the ultimate symbol for making love, not war. Slater had dismissed all their acclamations as the usual cant from bleeding hearts.

4

A blue air car with its lights flashing was on the scene within seconds. Two Lodi police officers, both Tutal, stepped out. The one who had driven saluted Slater. "Commander, we were sent to meet you. I'm sorry your arrival had to be marred by this unfortunate incident."

His voice was sibilant, both soothing and aggravating to Slater because he could never tell from the unchanging expression on the faces of Lodi, or from their voices, if they were sincere. It was as though they were all programmed to be pleasant no matter what. According to his high school and Space Academy history courses, the Lodi reminded him of how the Japanese had conducted themselves, right before they bombed Pearl Harbor.

"But I'm glad to see that you and the Chief Petty Officer here are not injured."

Register pointed at the body of the fallen beggar. "Who'd want to waste him?"

The second constable answered, "Happens all the time. Just another drive-by shooting. That makes the fifth today."

"My God!" Slater said, appalled. "What are you doing about it?"

The first constable shrugged. "All we can. But we only have three patrol cars. Bad feelings are running high between the Tutal and the Zutal. Even though Juba Blan-Chard is supposed to be the leader of *all* Lodi, many will simply not put aside their tribal differences."

"The Blan-Chard is expecting us. Will you take us to him?" Slater wanted to add, *"Before I go crazier than the folks on this freaking moon."*

5

It wasn't hard to spot the Supreme Lodi Headquarters, also known as "The Peabody," the only building in Memphis four stories tall. It had been originally built as a luxury hotel, named after the landmark at the ruined earth city for which the colony capital had been named. It was where Slater and Marie had stayed on their honeymoon.

But it had failed as a commercial venture and had to taken over as a government building. The gilded exterior made it stand out like a spike on a lizard's tail. The two Lodi constables waved onlookers aside and promptly ushered the human officers into the Great Hall, which, with its high stone arches, reminded Slater of Westminster Abbey. An extremely squalid one. Scattered all around were the most disgusting forms of detritus, from brown rotting banana peels to foot-high piles of ronju. Instead of a proper site for the seat of government, it seemed more like a cosmic dump. As they made their way inside, Brock's first impression—of the lunatic element's being in control—was reinforced. On an arm chair, which closely resembled a throne, sat a large and very obese red-violet lizard wearing purple robes and the white wig of an English judge. He looked much older than he did on the posters.

Beside him on his left, in a smaller replica of his seat, sat Marie, wrapped in a hooded gossamer lavender robe that permitted only her face, every bit as beautiful as he'd remembered, to be exposed. As far as Slater could tell, besides Register and himself, she was the only other human present. Where was the transitional government? Slater felt the hair on his neck bristle in apprehension, even as his heart raced at the sight of Marie.

Juba Blan-Chard rose, took three steps forward, and extended his right hand. "Ah, Commander Slater. Welcome to Memphis." Another sibilant voice. Jesus, all these lizards sounded exactly alike! "I understand your arrival was marred by another senseless act of violence. Please accept our regrets."

Slater clasped the cold saurian hand and winced at the contact with its claws. Those could prove a formidable weapon. He carefully avoided direct eye contact. "Thank you, Mr. Blan-Chard. Fortunately, Chief Register here and I weren't harmed. But we're more aware of the problem, now that we've experienced it first hand."

Register gave the Blan-Chard an obligatory salute and maintained the silence expected from a non-commissioned officer. Juba swept back his left arm to point toward his wife. "And of course you remember Marie."

Marie stood, smiled alluringly at the two visitors, and let the top of the robe fall down below her shoulders. It was obvious she wore nothing underneath. At once her full, milk chocolate breasts with their dark brown nipples came into view, a sight that once could have lured Slater to do any reckless act she might suggest. But that had been before he understood her true nature.

She hadn't ever been in love with him, only with whatever excitement he could provide. When someone else came along who could give her bigger, better, and longer lasting thrills—in her case, Juba—the romance, and the marriage were over, almost before they had begun.

Slater took it hard, worse than even he could have anticipated, because he had truly loved that crazy girl in a way few others could understand. There weren't many people left who would do something on a dare, whether it meant running naked down the main street of their home town, or trying to drink you under the table, or drag racing space shuttles at breakneck pace through the asteroid belt in defiance of all flight safety regulations.

How could she have just abandoned him for Christ sakes—for a goddamned lizard, yet? The only answer he could surmise was that, as strong as her will was, Juba's had been stronger, and his powers more subtle. Had it been a serpent or a lizard that despoiled Eden?

Juba's voice rose, for the first time clearly carrying a distinct note of pride. "Is she not beautiful?"

Register bristled. "Marie, cover yourself. Have you no shame?" He started toward her, his face contorted with indignation. Two large Lodi guards stepped in front of his path.

Slater gripped his C.P.O. firmly by the shoulder. "Easy. Remember our mission—and *their* protocol." Clothing was always optional for Lodi. They never minded what anyone wore, or didn't, unless it was required as part of a ceremony.

Register stiffened and shook himself. "Aye, aye, Sir." He turned to face the leader of the Lodi, carefully avoiding his eyes. "Please excuse me, Mr. Blan-Chard, Sir. Understand the personal situation, since your wife is also my sister."

Juba's voice was sympathetic. "Of course, Mr. Register. We all still have so much to learn about our... relationships. Apology accepted."

Marie smiled condescendingly at her brother. "Carl, it's okay. This *is* acceptable—and I *like* dressing this way."

Register scowled. "Mamma wouldn't like seein' you that way. Come to think of it, Mamma wouldn't like seein' you here at all."

She bristled, but relaxed and her smile returned. "Well, dear brother, aren't you glad to see me?" She offered her cheek, which he kissed reluctantly.

She clapped her hands. A little lizard girl in a black Afro wig, wearing a pink cotton dress with pinafore sleeves and a white lace collar, entered the room and ran to hug Marie. Disengaging herself, Marie announced with pride, "This is our daughter, Gay. Gay, these are your Uncle Carl and Uncle Brock." Gay curtsied to them. To Slater's amazement, Gay appeared to be approximately six years old, although he knew she couldn't be more than two.

Register glanced angrily at Slater and whispered, "Uncle Carl? Uncle Brock? Fuck that Shit!"

"Keep cool," Slater ordered under his breath. "Observe Lodi customs and law. That's part of our mission." He forced himself to give the lizard girl a pat on the shoulder.

Juba Blan-Chard extended his hand to Register. "Welcome, my brothers. You are the first human family we have had. Our bond is a *good* one. May it lead to many more."

Looking at the extended appendage as though it were a weapon, Register hesitated several seconds before he unenthusiastically accepted it. Cheers went up among the Lodi. Their whoops went unabated until Juba raised his hand to silence them.

"My brothers and sisters," he began, "this is a good day. These envoys assure we shall hold free elections. Human and Lodi, for the first time will vote together." More cheers interrupted him. He raised his hands again to silence his exuberant followers.

"Tonight we host a banquet in their honor." He turned his expressionless face toward his two human guests. "Gentlemen, I am sure you must be tired and in need of a chance to refresh yourselves. Escorts will show you to your quarters. I trust they will prove sufficient. A light snack is waiting for you there. We shall see you at nineteen hundred hours for dinner."

He bowed; they reciprocated. Then they were led down a hallway.

6

In his private room, Slater showered, towelled dry, and lay down on his bed. The tasty mushroom and onion chips he found in a bowl by his bed would tide him over until supper. He had just enough time to catch a quick nap before having to dress for dinner. Within minutes he was fast asleep.

Dreams came. Dreams of Marie. Marie on Earth, back when she had only been the impetuous, irresistibly alluring sixteen year old supposedly virgin daughter of a drill instructor at the Space Academy, and he'd been a senior cadet officer. She'd flirted with him, trying to distract him when he was commanding his battalion of lower classmen. When he'd resisted her attempts, she'd passed him a note to meet her after curfew. He did not oblige at first, and that made her want him more, as he soon discovered.

As a cadet officer, he'd been exempt from curfew on weekends. He'd returned from a Saturday night of heavy drinking at the local pub. He was showering before going to bed, alone in the cadet officers' bath, when Marie appeared, totally naked and totally irresistible. Perhaps it had been the many beers, but it also must have been his own loneliness—which came from subordinating his lusts and libido in order to be an honor student. For Slater, having been orphaned before adolescence, the Academy had been his whole life.

Women had been something he would get around to when time permitted. Marie became that occasion, the moment for his loss of innocence. In his own naivete, he had thought they were in love. Too soon, yet too late, he'd learned they were, but not with the same thing. He truly loved her, but Marie was in love with power and the notion of being the woman of a Space Academy cadet about to become an officer. Her ticket out.

The sex. God, how wonderful it had been! They were two children literally finding out for the first time what their bodies could do. They had discovered all the adult functions of organs that had heretofore been a mystery, whose most pleasurable purposes had been kept secret. Soon each found ways to make use of every opening the other had, in a pleasurable and meaningful way.

To Slater's surprise, after his graduation and placement on Europa, Marie quickly tired of their sex, of being a junior officer's wife, and of being forced to live on his meager junior officer's salary when they could have received a liberal stipend from the trust fund his parents had left him. Maybe he had been stupid for not taking the extra money, but he had been concerned about what his fellow officers and the men under him would think if he lived higher and better than they.

He and Marie had lived poor in comparison to the wealthy civilian colonists. She also tired of the stolid moral code of the U.I.F. Although bored with him and his lifestyle, she apparently wasn't bored with living on Europa. She had divorced him in the Europan civil court, but he'd never dreamed it would be for a *lizard*.

He had to give her much more out of their divorce than she would have received had he been a mere civilian. It amounted to blackmail for her silence—silence about her own infidelity, since an indiscrete wife was a stain upon the reputation of her husband as well. What he and Marie had done together during courtship and marriage might be considered eccentric. What Marie did with Juba could only be considered bizarre and depraved. When Slater contended she had not acted of her own free will, she denied it, asserting that no one can be hypnotized to act against her own desires.

She wanted financial independence out of her settlement and didn't care whom she hurt or what she did to obtain it. Her choice of Juba and money over Slater had alienated her from her own family. That was how her brother Reg became Slater's aide, siding with him in a vow to protect and serve the man his sister had spurned and hurt.

In his dream Slater remembered his first sexual encounter, in the shower. He recalled thrusting into Marie, shattering her already tattered maidenhead, feeling the incredible heat and wetness between her legs, just before he ejaculated his own scalding cascade to mix with hers. He dreamed of how they had thrust their tongues into each other's mouths and swirled them around, savoring each other's unique taste. Had it made even more of a difference that he'd been a white boy and she a black girl? Maybe.

It seemed so realistic, Slater's dream. So vivid. He could actually feel his own heat, her wetness. Her kisses. He opened his eyes and saw her. It was no dream. She was naked and beautiful on top of him. Her eyes were closed, her face contorted in a mask of animal lust. He was thrusting inside her. And it was all wrong. Deadly wrong. She was not hot inside, but cold. Icy cold. And her vagina was no longer an incredibly tight sheath, but instead a loose wad of wetness.

His feelings alerted him that all was not as it appeared. He hadn't allowed them to hypnotize him, so what was happening?

Hallucinogens. Something had been in those snack chips. He shook off the mental cobwebs and stared at Marie.

It was she, but not as he'd remembered. When he directed his gaze down between her legs, he saw to his horror, how her lower torso had been altered. Instead of the familiar black thatch of pubic hair he so fondly remembered, their was an upside-down triangle of tiny yellow green scales. Her vagina had become a cloaca, a fitting receptacle for the twin penises of her saurian husband.

Where he clasped the cleft of her buttocks, he felt a reptilian tail that must have trailed four feet behind her—replete with the customary three spikes. Looking at her feet, he saw lizard paws with splayed toes and sharp talons instead of toenails.

She opened her eyes and smiled. At that same moment he opened his mouth and would have screamed had she not thrust a still human hand over it. "Brock, don't," she cautioned in a soothing but firm voice. "It will bring the guards."

Violent waves of nausea battered against his stomach and his sanity. *Oh, Jesus*, he prayed, *please help me hold on*. Somehow he managed to contain his rising gorge.

"What's happened to you?" he croaked.

"Am I not truly beautiful?" she beamed.

Reason took over again as he answered, "Uh—sure. It's just taking me a while to fully appreciate your new... and great beauty." His penis had gone totally limp. She looked down as it flopped free from her loins.

Her face wrinkled in rising anger. "You don't like me this way, do you?"

To him, now, Medusa couldn't have appeared more repulsive, or menacing. He'd better put on a convincing act to placate her. "That—that's not it. What if Juba caught us?"

Marie burst into long, soulless laughter. "He wants me here. He and I are one—united in spirit. We can have no more children. Years in a sunless prison caused his testicles to lose their potency. He still has his libido, but is no longer able to reproduce. Gay is his only biological child.

"However, it is the ultimate status of a Lodi to produce as many offspring as possible. As my former husband, you would be the only other male who could legitimately mate with me under tribal law. That same law would make any children of our coupling *his*. But he wouldn't want anyone to know you were the real father."

Another wave of nausea pounded within him. How could he continue to act interested in this now repulsive creature he had once loved so?

She apparently had the answer already. In a lightning fast move, she ducked her head between his legs and drew his flaccid penis between her lips. Swirling her tongue around, she restored his rigidity.

At that moment he realized this was only a maneuver to make him copulate another time. There was one way to avoid it. Summoning all his will power, he blocked out any concept of this hideously altered Marie and forced himself to envision, instead, the love of his youth.

He tried to tell himself he was reliving the first time she had performed oral sex upon him. His body took the suggestion like an ideal subject of the most experienced hypnotist. Within seconds he ejaculated, causing her almost to choke.

Coughing, she drew away and spat out a mouthful of his spend. "Damn you," she snarled. "You're still playing games."

He laughed bitterly in response. "As if you're not!"

She swooped up her gossamer robe from the floor and put it back on as she stormed out.

7

At the banquet, Slater and Register were seated at the head table, to the right of Marie. She gave Slater a chilling glance when he entered the room but refused to meet his stare afterward. Except for Marie, Slater still had not seen any humans. Certainly not any *true* humans.

As a waiter poured zythum, green lichen beer—a brand proven safe from causing any stefi-ronju side effects—into Slater's baked clay chalice, the Commander asked Juba, "Mr. Blan-Chard, where are the other humans? We haven't seen any except Marie."

Juba looked sideways at Slater. "Most have been placed in protective custody until after the voting. However, to prove our good intentions, you can see for yourself." He turned to an aide. "Bring out Levingstone."

Within minutes two Lodi guards escorted in a hook-nosed, balding, bespectacled, slightly built middle-aged man wearing a green jumpsuit and sneakers. He appeared well nourished and healthy.

"Commander Slater," Juba announced, "may I present Deputy Commissioner Levingstone."

Levingstone reached out and eagerly shook Slater's hand. "Oh, Commander," he fawned obsequiously, "it is such a pleasure. We're so close to completing the transition. If only those troublesome Zutal rebels would honor the cease-fire."

"Cease-fire? I thought there was an official truce in effect. Don't tell me there's been a flare-up between the Lodi factions again. Where's Commissioner Foster?"

Juba looked disapprovingly at Levingstone. The Deputy Commissioner's face took on the appearance of servile apology. It sickened Slater almost as much to watch a human grovel before a lizard as it did to know his ex-wife had married one and tried to become one.

"Well, Commander," Levingstone began, "we simply cannot be certain of the intentions of the Zutal."

Talking in diplomatic vagaries also irritated Slater. "Get to the point," he snapped. "And what about Foster?" As he awaited the response, he carefully studied the Deputy Commissioner's face.

Levingstone's smile looked as contrived as a carnival mask. "I'm trying to explain, Commander. Three days ago, Commissioner Foster was assassinated. Someone planted plastic explosives in his air car. Soon afterward, our constables discovered similar plastic explosives along with laser weapons hidden near the headquarters of Chaka, the Zutal leader. He was under house arrest pending your arrival, but escaped. Levingstone held up a photograph of a blue lizard dressed in combat fatigues.

Slater studied the picture, sensing there was more. "And?"

"Papers were found among the arms that link Chaka with Dobbins & Company, the biggest mercantile business on Memphis. Since humans run that business, it appears there may be a conspiracy between certain colonists and the Zutal to revolt if Juba wins the free elections."

"Why didn't you inform U.I.F. about Foster's death and this suspected conspiracy?"

Levingstone shook his head. "Sun spots interfered with our transmission. Apparently they don't affect anything sent away from the Sun, only toward it. Even if the broadcast would go through perfectly, we couldn't afford to delay your arrival. You represent authority. Without your presence to support the Blan-Chard and the transition government, we would be plunged into anarchy."

"Anarchy?" Slater couldn't believe the Deputy Commissioner's words. "What are you talking about? Look, I realize things are a bit loose out here, but this *is* part of the United Interplanetary Federation. Lodi and human alike are subject to the same laws."

Levingstone gave a nervous laugh. His voice dropped to a barely audible whisper. "Uh—you still don't get it, do you, Commander?"

Slater felt himself being set up, as though for a bad joke. Only he suspected what the Deputy Commissioner was about to say wasn't funny.

A look of extreme anxiety spread over Levingstone's face. He glanced around and, apologizing to the Lodi dignitaries, drew Slater aside. "Listen, Slater," he hissed indignantly, "Juba is already in charge. It's what the U.I.F wants. Your presence here and the free elections are only a trumped up formality. He's going to be the ruler of Memphis no matter what you do."

His voice took on a menacing tone. "You and your aide had better go along, if you know what's good for you."

"And if we don't?"

"Remember what happened to the bum you met when you first arrived? You might meet with the same sort of accident."

Slater shuddered at the unsettling warning. So much for diplomatic immunity, he thought.

After a dinner of mushroom filet and fried bananas, interspersed with liberal refills of lichen beer, Slater felt a mild buzz coming on. Toasts went round saluting the interim government. Then it came Slater's turn. He made sure the video camera was on him. Let them try and tamper with that if anything happened to him afterward.

He winked at Register and lifted his chalice. "Here's to peace between the Tutal and the Zutal. That's what makes democracy work, y'know. Only, where are the Zutal? And the other humans? There are supposed to be another thousand people here. All I've seen are Marie and Levingstone."

The Lodi camera operator quickly shifted his focus to Juba, who forced a smile, to the extent a lizard could. In a voice so soothing it couldn't have been genuine, Juba replied, "Commander Slater, your concerns are well intentioned, but totally unfounded. All human settlers are safe."

Somehow that assurance afforded Slater little comfort. He turned to glance at Marie. She fluffed up her hair and licked her lips nervously before forcing a smile. As she sat there nude from the waist up, her breasts stood out proudly, as though she was defying the delegates from Earth and all their customs. She reminded Slater of Kali, the Hindu goddess of Death, who may have found her own kingdom on Europa. Trying not to make his thoughts obvious, he lifted his chalice toward Marie, and Register followed in the gesture. With everyone else, they drained their cups.

Seconds later a thunderous explosion shook the dining hall and threw Slater to the floor. Staccato reports from automatic weapons filtered in from outside.

Juba rose and helped Marie to her feet. "Guards," he barked, "take counteroffensive action."

"C'mon, Reg," Slater ordered, "we're gonna boogie with the bad boys." He drew his laser pistol and headed for the door. No sooner were they outside than a tear gas grenade exploded.

8

The air turned to acid. Slater's eyes and lungs burned. He could barely see or breathe, and noticed Register suffering the same fate. Slater's chest heaved and coughed in spasms until he tasted blood. Then unfamiliar hands dragged the two officers from the street inside a nearby door.

He was too weak to resist when a reptilian hand clamped an oxygen mask over his face. A hissing voice urged, "Breathe slowly. Take deep breaths."

It took about ten minutes for the searing pain to leave his eyes and lungs. As he regained his senses, he realized he and Register were in the company of the blue lizards. "Zutal," he declared.

The Lodi closest to him loomed over Slater by at least four inches. It pressed a digit against scaly green lips. "Shhh. The guards will hear you. If they find us, you'll never learn the truth."

Slater recognized the face as the one Levingstone had shown him in the photo. In a subdued voice he said, "You're Chaka."

The giant lizard snorted and extended his paw, "Exactamondo, Commander. Sorry about the circumstances, but glad to meet you."

He motioned to Slater and the now-recovered Register to follow him and his companions into a tunnel. Register's eyed Slater, questioning the wisdom of complying. Slater answered him with a reassuring glance to show he thought the gamble was worth it.

9

After walking for almost half an hour through the darkness with only dim flashlight beams for illumination, they finally came to a ladder. Once they climbed out of the manhole, Slater and Register found themselves in a lush tropical garden, surrounded by happy, smiling humans and dancing blue Zutal.

"Welcome to our secret base, Commander," Chaka said. "I'm sorry about your ordeal." His voice seemed much less mechanical than Juba's, more rich in tone and emotion. There was almost a warmth in it. He continued, "Juba has most of the humans fooled. They think he has forgiven them for the bad way they treated him when he was young. He has neither forgiven nor forgotten."

Slater felt confused. "You're a Lodi, too. If Juba hates us, why should you feel otherwise?"

"Juba was forced to work in the lower mines when he was young. His human masters tortured him for fun. One day he turned on them and killed two. Because the killing was provoked, instead of executing him, the court had him flogged. He was sold to a new master, a retired college professor—a humane man. He taught Juba to read and write, then set him free.

"Juba was the first Lodi to attend the university and obtain a law degree. Because he wasn't human, he wasn't allowed to become a lawyer. But when Lodi received the right to have limited, non-voting representation in the Colonial Assembly, Juba went as the delegate from Europa.

"And he has been working ever since," Chaka added, "for the independence of Europa as a province ruled by the Lodi, primarily his Tutal, with himself as the supreme ruler."

Slater shook his head in disbelief. "Juba claims he wants to represent all citizens of Europa. What makes you doubt him?"

It was the first time he heard a Lodi laugh. Chaka threw back his oblong head and opened his large jaws, revealing rows of ivory spikes. In long blasts came the sound of "Heeeeeee-eeeee-eeeh, Heeeeeee-eeeee-eeeeh!" It reminded Slater more of the wail from a high pitched siren than laughter, but he knew that's what it was.

After a moment the convulsions stopped and Chaka regained control. "You envoys do not have a clue, do you?"

Slater swallowed and stiffened. He didn't like looking or feeling stupid, and feared being both this time. "Well, I know something is very odd here, and I mean more odd than usual."

"Did you notice many humans at the Supreme Lodi Headquarters?"

"Besides Marie and Levingstone, none."

"The others are prisoners. The secret is out on Europa, and Juba cannot afford to let it get back to U.I.F."

"What secret?"

"Rather than tell, I shall show you." Chaka snapped his fingers. A Zutal in a white waiter's jacket approached and bowed. "Bring food," the warrior leader ordered. He motioned for Slater and Register to join him at a large dining table.

A few minutes later, the waiter wheeled in three covered dishes on a cart. He lifted the lid of one. It contained mashed overripe bananas, the reputed favorite food of Lodi. The waiter removed the cover of the second dish, revealing roasted loin of meat. Lamb? That must be for Reg and me, Slater thought.

The waiter raised the cover to the third dish. Another bowl of mashed bananas. Had he made a mistake and reversed the orders? But the waiter seemed to know what he was doing as he set the bowls containing bananas in front of Slater and Register, then placed the meat before Chaka.

Slater felt the hair on his neck rise again as he watched the Zutal warrior seize the meat with both paws and rip it from the bone with his teeth. Bloody droplets from the underdone joint fell upon Chaka's chest and the table. He physically resembled a miniature Tyrannosaurus Rex, yet one endowed with reasoning capabilities. That made him all the more frightening to Slater. What moral faculties accompanied that reason?

As Chaka ate, his eyes studied Slater and Register. Their Zutal host swallowed and belched. No stefi balls came out. "You haven't touched your food. Is there something wrong?"

Really wrong, Slater thought. "I was under the impression the Lodi were vegetarians. When did you acquire a taste for meat? And where did it come from?" He pointed at the bare bone. Meat on Europa was as rare as sunlight on Pluto. Chaka was intentionally turning the tables on them to make some point.

Wiping his mouth with his scaly forearm, Chaka said, "The taste grew over generations along with our intellect. You see, we are more like humans than you thought. Why haven't you touched your mashed bananas? Could it be that you find them unappetizing?"

Register wrinkled his nose and pushed the bowl away. "Yeah, just a little."

Chaka snapped his fingers. The waiter brought in two more plates. Both contained roast meat, new potatoes, and fresh-baked rolls. Everything smelled wonderful.

"You haven't doctored this, have you?" Slater asked. "Juba served me some mushroom and onion chips that nearly ruined my head."

Chaka laughed. "Everything you have before you is as it appears. There are no surprises. I will switch plates with you to prove it, if you like."

Slater and Register devoured their meal. As they ate, Chaka spoke.

"Most of us want the same things as humans. Unfortunately, Juba and his followers want *more*. All rational creatures desire necessary amenities, security, and to reproduce their line. In addition, however, we also require a sense of self-esteem. Two centuries of servitude and abuse have left the Lodi emotionally scarred."

Register pointed his finger and interrupted, "Hey, man. Don't tell me about your heritage. I'm black, from one of the last black families on Earth. I'm proud of it. My people had to overcome that same shit. We made it. You can, too."

Chaka cocked his head. "How long ago were your people in servitude?"

"Depends on how you measure it. Slavery ended about six and a half centuries ago, but true equality didn't come for another hundred years."

The Zutal leader sighed. "So you can only relate through your own race's distant past. But it is *within my own memory* when Lodi were treated like mindless animals who could even be killed if their owner wished. There were even instances when Lodi were *eaten* by humans. Those are deep emotional wounds.

"But I, at least, have always been free. I am a chieftain and the son of a chieftain. Unlike the Tutal, the Zutal were always rebellious. We fought you humans in the First and Second Colonial Rebellions. That is why there are fewer of us now than the Tutal, who cast their lot with humans until recently, when Juba persuaded them to join in the Third Rebellion."

"What's your point?" Slater asked.

Chaka's eyes narrowed to slits. "I am a warrior. I show you the way things are. Everything Juba has shown you is deception. The biggest deception you have not yet comprehended."

"What do you mean?" Register asked.

"I shall show you. Follow me." He lit a torch and led them into another tunnel that brought them into a small chamber illuminated by several more torches. In the center on a raised slab of rock lay an open casket. Chaka held his torch above the coffin so his guests could view the contents.

Slater gasped. Inside was the body of Commissioner Foster, in full uniform, perfectly preserved with his hands folded on his chest, as though asleep. The gold ring that bore Foster's seal of office was missing. "Why is he here?" Slater asked. "Levingstone says you killed him. Did you steal his body, too, like someone obviously has stolen his ring?"

With an almost sinister laugh, Chaka replied, "I did not kill him. I know nothing about a ring. But I did bring his body here to show you the depths of treachery in which you have become snared."

The Zutal leader lowered his torch until the flame touched the corpse's hands. Almost instantly, they melted.

"Wax!" Register exclaimed. "That's only a dummy."

"Does this mean Foster's not dead?" Slater asked.

Chaka shook his head. He pointed to the face on the body in the casket. "That part *is* Foster. From the neck down is a mannequin."

"What happened to the rest of his body?" Slater asked.

He wasn't prepared for Chaka's answer.

10

Back at court again, Juba greeted Slater and Register. "I am glad the Chaka Chard Zutal saw fit to release you. If I win the elections tomorrow, I will see that he is also punished for your abduction."

"Let's see that the elections are properly set up, Mr. Blan-Chard, and then we'll work from there."

"Of course, Commander. Of course."

Marie sat by his side. She said nothing, but smiled as though she knew a secret she did not intend to share.

Light footsteps echoed from down the hall. Gay ran into the room, bawling, "Mommy, Mommy, I'm sick!" Before she could reach Marie, her yellow eyes rolled back in their sockets and she vomited, spewing up a hideous ocher geyser. Something in it hit the floor with a *clink.*

Forcing himself to look, Slater saw, in the center of the vile green pile of regurgitation, a human finger. It bore the gold ring with Commissioner Foster's seal of office.

Juba shook his head. "I'm so very sorry you saw that. It changes everything."

Powerful Lodi paws seized Slater and Register from behind, trapping them at the same time.

11

In their subterranean cell, Register asked, "What the hell do we do now?"

The ultimatum Juba had given was simple, rig the elections or die. If they refused to help, their deaths would be blamed on the rebels, like Foster's had been. But Slater realized that even if they helped, Juba would still have to fake their deaths, since he could not afford the risk of letting them return to U.I.F. headquarters where they could reveal the true situation on Europa.

Slater answered, "Without our weapons or transmitters, there's not much we can do. But they still need us for the elections. You to operate the voting booths on our ship and me to certify the elections as free from improper influence according to the Peace Plan."

He remembered Nazi minister Joseph Goebbels' sinister boast, "Propaganda is everything."

Register started chuckling, then broke into laugher. He'd found a solution. "Commander, we have a way out. Let them think we're going to play along. I may be able to get us out of this."

12

Voting was heavy. Cameras controlled by Juba showed cheering faces of humans and Tutal as the citizens of Europa flocked to the Teleportation Terminal, which transported them to the voting ship Slater and Register had flown from Mars. The Zutal had proclaimed a boycott, so none showed up for the election. In groups of two's and three's, the Tutal were teleported up to vote and returned. A digital counter recorded the vote as it came in, approaching a landslide in favor of an autonomous Europa with Juba as premier.

When the time for voting was almost half over, Juba and Marie appeared at the Teleportation Terminal. Waving triumphantly at their followers and Slater—who had a Tutal guard poking a laser pistol into his back—Juba, Marie, and Levingstone entered the transporter booth together and were molecularly disassembled within seconds.

Customarily it took about three minutes between the time voters left and when they returned. About two minutes after Juba's trio disappeared, the air was rocked with a series of violent explosions. "Guerrillas," a Tutal sergeant shouted, just before a burst of machine gun fire cut him down.

Slater brought his left elbow around as hard as he could and caught his captor with a paralyzing blow to the jaw. Turning, he seized the guard's laser pistol and blasted his head off. Zutal soldiers in full combat outfits and gear appeared around him, firing Uzis and hurling grenades at their reptilian rivals. Humans fled in all directions.

The transporter booth glowed with blue light. As it subsided, Register materialized, brandishing a laser pistol. A Tutal soldier fired at him. He ducked and downed his assailant, slicing him in half with a return shot.

"Where are Marie, Juba, and Levingstone?" Slater asked.

"Gone. They're space dust. While they were voting, I reset the return controls to scatter their molecules in the direction of Uranus."

Even after all she had done and all she had become, Slater still felt a twinge of grief and remorse over Marie's fate. Register grabbed his arm. "C'mon. We've got to get back to The Peabody."

Resistance seemed to be thinning as the basically cowardly Tutal fled the concerted Zutal onslaught. Wary of sniper fire, Slater and Register cautiously made their way to the nursery.

Inside they found Gay whining. "Mommy! I want my mommy!" Slater knelt to comfort her. She stared at him, transfixing him with her gaze. Her golden eyes sparkled. He suddenly found himself paralyzed, frozen, completely unable to move. She rushed forward, heading straight for him, her jaws agape, displaying two rows of razor-sharp teeth.

Before she could get to him, the air snapped with the discharge of Register's laser pistol. Her skull disappeared in a crackle of fire and smoke. The headless torso flopped around on the floor as life gushed out of it.

Before he could collect his wits again, Slater saw another spectacle that strained his sanity. In a corner lay a semitransparent white globe approximately two feet in diameter. Inside, immersed in yellow-green fluid, floated a tiny reptilian form with a human face—a face that bore an uncanny resemblance to him. Horror overcame him as he thought, *"A goddammed lizard egg and—oh shit—it has my son in it! No, that's not my son, only something made from genetic material stolen from me—something that doesn't deserve to live any more than its sister did."*

Register gave Slater a puzzled look. "Commander?"

"Do your duty, Chief."

Register blasted the egg, sending half-fried yolk in all directions.

13

From the head of a triumphant procession of humans and Lodi, Chaka waved to Slater and Register. He was approaching the Peabody as they were leaving. "The elections are over," he announced. "We now have a coalition government of human and Lodi. Europa can now begin a new age of peace and prosperity."

Register ran the vote tally and Slater reviewed it. The vote came in at seventy per cent in favor of the Zutal-human coalition, although ninety per cent of the vote before Juba was dispatched had been in favor of the Tutal faction. With the transmitters working again, Slater sent his certification to U.I.F.

14

Dressed for the victory banquet, Slater knocked on Register's door. When he heard a muffled response, he assumed Register must be temporarily indisposed. Slater called out, "Reg, I'm going on. Chaka says there'll be some foxy women who've come out of hiding to meet us, so I'm gonna check 'em out. Don't be too long. I'll see you there."

A Lodi band was playing an Earth tune from the 1950's, "Earth Angel," and there were indeed many attractive, scantily clad young women dancing or standing at the bar, where Slater noticed more than zythum was being served. Bottles of bourbon, scotch, and vodka filled the glass shelves behind the counter, which also contained several large bottles of vintage wine.

Chaka approached, carrying a crystal chalice brimming over with what appeared to be burgundy. He took a hearty swallow, tossing down half his glass. Two steps later, he halted and belched out a stefi ball a foot in diameter.

When he threw his head back and laughed, everybody else joined in—except Slater. *What the fuck is going on?* Slater wondered. *Have we gotten rid of one mad lizard only to replace it with another?*

The beautiful blue light of the stefi ball quickly transformed into dark, smelly, vile brown excremental ronju and fell to the marble floor with a disgusting splat. Chaka laughed again. All except Slater joined in. Where was Reg? What was keeping him?

Several other Lodi were openly drinking and subsequently belching out their stefi balls. Household staff, mostly humans in white coats, went around hastily cleaning up each mess of resultant ronju as it occurred.

A lithe blonde who couldn't have been more than eighteen, wearing a gossamer green gown with a plunging neckline and a hem that barely covered her shapely thighs, arrived at Slater's side as he met with Chaka. The Lodi leader introduced her. "Commander, this is Marti Herron. She's been eager to meet you."

Marti held two fresh cocktails. She handed one to Slater—Old Charter and water, his standard. "Will you sit with me tonight at dinner?" she asked.

He gazed into her deep blue eyes and felt as if he would drown in them. How odd it was that beauty could come in so many forms, from the sepia seductiveness of Marie to the ivory allure of Marti!

Setting his half-finished drink down, he responded, "How about a dance?"

Once they were on the ballroom floor, the band began another 1950's oldie, "In the Still of the Night." During the slow dance, Marti pressed her full breasts against Slater's chest. Her eyes sparkled as she said, "We're so grateful for what you did today. It wouldn't have happened without you." She stuck her tongue in his ear, then nibbled on his earlobe.

Maybe this world was mad, but if it could provide the pleasure that Slater imagined would come from a night of passion with this girl, he would tolerate such madness.

"Ouch," he yelled, surprised by the jolt of pain he felt at his right ear where Marti had been nibbling. She had suddenly bitten him, hard. He pushed her away and brought his hand up to his ear, where he felt warm dampness and a jagged tear on the lobe. He saw blood dripping from his fingers.

Concern came over her face. "I'm so sorry," she apologized. "I got carried away. I've done without for so long."

Slater tried to flash a forgiving smile. "Maybe I can help."

Strange girl. Strange customs. Extremely strange fucking place. Slater rationalized away his discomfort with the prospect of pumping Marti's brains out in a couple of hours and maybe paying her back in some other way for her kinky little trick. Then, tomorrow he and Reg would be off this Looney-Tunes world for good.

The band stopped playing upon the announcement that dinner was served. Still no Reg.

Slater took his seat, with Marti on his left and an empty chair on the right awaiting Register. Of all the chairs, only his had arms on it. His concern over the Chief was beginning to weigh on his appetite. He barely picked at his salad. "Does anyone know where C.P.O. Register is?" he asked.

Chaka set his chalice down. "Yes. I am certain he will be out in a minute. In fact, we couldn't begin the main course without him."

A Lodi waiter wheeled in a large cart with a huge domed cover over the serving platter. Whirring sounds simultaneously on his left and right distracted Slater. He looked down to see steel bands had sprung from the arms on his chair, trapping him in it.

The waiter lifted the dome to reveal Register's severed head, with a large red mushroom cap stuffed like an apple in his mouth, and the rest of his body dressed, quartered, and cooked like a roast pig. Consciousness threatened to leave Slater as he witnessed the other guests, human and Lodi alike, rush for the cart and rip away pieces of flesh to fill their plates as though they were at a barbecue.

Loading his own plate, Chaka said, "You see, Commander Slater, Juba didn't want us to have our way. He wanted to boss us around, wanted us to remain vegetarians. But hypnosis and drugs failed. So did interbreeding and genetic alteration. Our carnivorous tendency is caused by prolonged exposure to Europa's nitrogen-poor orange soil.

"Without adequate livestock, cannibalism—a precedent established by humans—became the only logical alternative. And we pride ourselves on our logic, Commander. But Juba wouldn't give up trying to dissuade us, even when experimentation failed with his own daughter Gay.

"He really was unpopular and deserved to lose. We can now implement the Peace Plan. But, unfortunately for you and your aide, we do not recognize the same family immunities as the Tutal."

Slater screamed as Marti sank her teeth into his left ear and ripped it off.

About the Authors—Meet the Memphis Monster-Makers

BRENT MONAHAN, a resident of Yardley, PA, has had several novels published, including *Deathbite, The Book of Common Dread,* and *The Blood of the Covenant.* His latest release is a tale of Southern horror set in middle Tennessee, *The Bell Witch.* He is acclaimed for writing horror for "the thinking man." When not creating new fiction to seriously scare his readers, he works as an executive for Peterson's. He is an active member of the Horror Writers Association. A feature interview with him is scheduled to appear in a forthcoming issue of *Horror* magazine.

TOM PICCIRILLI lives on Long Island, NY, and serves as associate editor of *Pirate Writings.* He has had several novels and short story collections published, including, respectively: *Shards* and *The Dead Past; Pentacle* and *The Hanging Man.* His "Self" stories have nearly acquired their own cult. He is an active member of HWA.

DON WEBB hails from Austin, TX. and belongs to both HWA and Science Fiction and Fantasy Writers Association (SFWA) as well as the American Academy of Poets. For the last nine years his short fiction has been cited in at least one list of each year's best—usually in two or three. His work has appeared in more than 200 magazines throughout the world, including *Asimov's Science Fiction Magazine, Fantasy & Science Fiction, Amazing, Galaxy,* and *Pulphouse.* He was recently featured in an interview in *Scavenger's Newsletter,* August, 1997).

BEECHER SMITH is a native Memphian and a lawyer by profession. Among his clients was the late Elvis Presley. After Smith's short story "Return of the King" debuted in *The King Is Dead: Tales of Elvis Postmortem* (Paul M. Sammons, ed., Delta Books, 1984), Stephen King calls him, "the only person who really knows that Elvis has left the building." He is a member of HWA. Over 100 of his poems and 30 of his short stories and articles have appeared in magazines such as *Renaissance, Crossroads, Freezer Burn, The Black Lily, Writer's Block, Bardic Runes, Strange Wonderland,* and *The Sixth Sense.* He received The Darrell Award (best H/SF/F short story) from the Mid-South Science Fiction Association for both 1995 and 1996.

SCOTT SIGLER lives in Ann Arbor, MI, but yearns for the sunny Southern clime of Memphis, where he follows with great interest the Memphis University Tigers and the Oilers. He has had several novellas and one novel — *Shadows of the City* (1994) — published by Iron Crown Enterprises. He is an active member of HWA.

RICHARD HANCOCK is another local Memphis writer, making his maiden voyage into national publication through this anthology. Being included, he says, has made him "happier than a 'possum in a persimmon orchard."

JAMES S. DORR has had over sixty poems and one hundred stories published, including appearances in *Alfred Hitchcock Magazine, Wicked Mystic, Terminal Fright, Aboriginal Science Fiction, Strange Wonderland,* and *Tomorrow,* as well as in numerous anthologies. He also performs Renaissance and Elizabethan music. He is an active member of both HWA and SFWA.

H. DAVID BLALOCK, another Memphian, has had numerous poems published, but few stories previously. He was managing editor and publisher of *Engage* magazine from 1991 to 1996.

STEVEN LEE CLIMER, presently of Wayne, MI, is originally from west Tennessee and knows Memphis well enough from personal experience to tell convincingly about some of its monsters. His story "By Any Name a Devil" was among the publisher's favorites. He is a new member of HWA.

TREY R. BARKER hangs out in the Denver area, where he is active in the Central Colorado Writers' Workshop. His work has appeared in *Terminal Fright, Palace Corbie,* and *A Horror a Day,* and sold to *Eldritch Tales* and *Cemetery Dance*, among others. He is Tom Piccirilli's Number One Fan and an active member of HWA. For his contribution the editorial staff voted him an "honorary Southerner."

WILLIAM R. EAKIN lives in Clarksville, AR, where he stays busy writing his "Redgunk" stories. His science fiction and fantasy poems have appeared in *Realms of Fantasy* and *Space and Time.* He has also been accepted by *Dark Regions* and *Fortress,* to name a few.

He has won First Place awards in the 1996 Best Soft SF, 1995 Andre Norton SF/Fantasy Award, and 1996 North Texas Professional Writers' Association's Fiction Contest. He is an active member of SFWA.

RICHARD PARKS lives outside Jackson, MS (pronounced "Miss-sippee"), in Clinton. The only active member of HWA in that state, he, has been published in *Asimov's Science Fiction, Realms of Fantasy, Science Fiction Age,* and *Tomorrow.* He has also appeared in several anthologies, including *100 Vicious Little Vampires* and *Robert Bloch's Psychos.* He also is an active member of SFWA.

COREY MESLER. manages Burke's Book Store in Memphis and lives in the Cooper- Young Neighborhood, which was the setting for "Swift Peter." He has appeared in print on numerous occasions as a reviewer of contemporary books for *The Commercial Appeal* (Scripps-Howard).

TIM WAGGONER resides in Columbus, OH. An active member of both HWA and SFWA, his fiction has appeared in *Aberrations, Figment, 2 AM,* and *Thin Ice,* as well as numerous anthologies, including *365 Scary Stories, 100 Wicked Little Witch Stories,* and *100 Vicious Little Vampire Stories.*

H. R. WILLIAMS is a Memphis resident new to the horror genre. He recently sold to Stygian Vortex Publications. "People Change" is his first appearance in an anthology.

WILL DRAYTON, is a reclusive misanthrope who practices law occasionally and hates most lawyers. He leaves Memphis whenever he can, to visit New Orleans , where he consumes inordinate quantities of Foster's lager and Guinness stout at O'Flaherty's Irish Channel Pub and sings along (off key) at the top of his lungs whenever Danny O'Flaherty or Julian Murray (one of the few lawyers Will does like) performs. The contributions included in this anthology are among his first published works.

LANCE CARNEY lives in Scotts Depot, West Virginia, with his wife and two small children. A pharmacist, his stories have appeared in *Into the Darkness, Cimmerian Journal, Outer Darkness, Plot,* and *Story Rules.* Whenever he visits Memphis, he tries to stay at The Peabody.

VASSAR SMITH, a native of Memphis, lives in Palo Alto, CA. A Stanford Ph.D., he has had hundreds of poems published, as well as numerous scholarly treatises on Russian authors Pushkin, Sologub, and Lermontov. His contribution to this anthology is his first published work in the genre of horror/fantasy/SF. He is Beecher Smith's identical twin (really!).

FRANCES BRINKLEY COWDEN resides in Memphis, where she worked as a teacher until she retired to operate Grandmother Earth Creations/Press. Active in the Poetry Society of Tennessee, she has won countless awards for her poetry and prose at regional writers Conferences.

CYNTHIA WARD lives in Woodinville, WA, where she writes the "Market Maven" column for *Speculations* writing magazine. She has sold stories to *Asimov's, Absolute Magnitude, Space and Time, Fortress,* and *Midnight Zoo.* Her contributions to anthologies have been included in *100 Vicious Little Vampires, 100 Wicked Little Witch Stories, 3 Scary Stories,* and several others. Her story "The Big Chill" appeared previously in *Galaxy* (1994). She is an active member of HWA.

MARK SUTTON is a resident of Columbia, SC. His fiction has appeared in *Plot,* and *The Landing Place* (an anthology for *Young Voices Magazine). Crossroads Magazine* also recently accepted a submission.

STANLEY T. EVANS lives in Memphis and is known as "Tom" to his friends. Scout leader and father of three sons active in the Boy Scouts, his campfire ghost story "The Camping Trip Incident" is appearing in print for the first time in this anthology.

CHARLEE JACOB is a Texan, residing in Garland. Her most recent work has appeared in *Deathrealm, Women Who Run With Werewolves, Vision Quest,* and *Bending the Landscape.* She is an active member of HWA.

ANGELA WOLFE hails from Winnipeg, Manitoba (that's CANADA), where she says she learned on the Internet everything she needed to know in order to write about Memphis. Her story "With Pebbles for Eyes" is due for release soon in *Minions from Beyond*, a young Canadian magazine of dark fiction. She recently joined HWA.

KIEL, STUART lives in Stony Brook, NY. She submitted three times before we connected, so she receives the Persistence Award. Her work has appeared in *Hotter Blood, The Definitive Best of the Horror Show, Women of Darkness,* and *After Hours*. She belongs to the Authors' Guild and SFWA.

DEL TINSLEY resides in Nashville, TN, where she has embarked on writing mysteries and recipes for cook hooks. She was fortunate to combine these talents in her contribution "Rendezvous..." She appears in the Pillsbury *Best of the Bake-Off Cookbook*, and her "Aunt Mary's Coffin Caper" will soon appear in *Murderous Intent*.

LOU KEMP (Christine L. Cook) claims Pleasanton, CA, as home. She received the 1994 Santa Barbara Writers' Conference SF/Fantasy/Horror Award and her career took off, Her publishing credits include contributions to *Crossroads, Heliocentric Net, Eldritch Tales, Cabal Asylum,* and *365 Scary Stories*.

BILLY BOB PATTERSON has a post office box in Memphis, but his whereabouts are unknown since his recent parole. He grew up in the Mississippi delta and worked as an extra on the sets of the movies *Baby Doll* and *Ode to Billy Joe*. He has studied William Faulkner and H. P. Lovecraft extensively. "Peace Plan" is his only published credit.